"Adam," she whispered in a breathy, angel's voice. "I want you so badly, that I'm . . . afraid."

Blast, she had the courage to be honest, to say aloud the emotions clamoring inside him. Juliet, his valiant crusader, his guardian angel, his *love*. She deserved every drop of courage in his soul. He turned to her, his voice a gravelly rumble as he made an admission no torture master could ever have wrung from him before.

"I'm afraid, too. I don't want to hurt you. Don't want to sicken you when you see the scars—I've led a hard life, angel. Spent most of it on the opposite side of an enemy sword."

She reached up, touching the scar on his face. "You're beautiful to me."

The words touched him, wrung his heart. She could never know how much. "I don't want you to awaken tomorrow and regret this," he told her. "If you have the slightest doubt about what we're doing, you have only to ask, and I'll"—the prospect bit like a savage vise about his chest—"I'll let you go, angel, without a word of reproach. Look into my eyes, Juliet. Do you promise me?"

She caught her lip between her teeth, her eyes wide and full of wonder, her cheeks stained the hue of the roses she tended with such devotion. Then she stunned Adam by not waiting for him to make the first foray with hands and mouth. She reached between them, her fingers unfastening the ties that held the front of his shirt together. . . .

Praise for the Triumphant Novels of
Kimberly Cates

STEALING HEAVEN

"Kimberly Cates has the talent to pull you into a story on the first page and keep you there. . . . *Stealing Heaven* is a finely crafted tale . . . a tale you won't soon forget. It can stand proud beside Ms. Cates' other excellent romances."

—*Rendezvous*

"Stunning in its emotional impact, glowing with the luminous beauty of the love between a man and a woman . . . *Stealing Heaven* is another dazzling masterpiece from a truly gifted author."

—Kathe Robin, *Romantic Times*

"[A] beautifully poignant tale. Kimberly Cates can always be counted on for a choice reading occasion, and this time is no exception."

—Harriet Klausner, *Affaire de Coeur*

"A love story never to be forgotten."

—Nellie Eggert, *Hi-Tech Home*

"A powerful and enduring tale filled with the magic and lore of Ireland. . . . This idyllic romance will capture readers' hearts."

—Elizabeth Hogue, *Gothic Journal*

THE RAIDER'S DAUGHTER

"A wonderful and neatly blended mixture of romance and suspense. . . . Kimberly Cates always provides her readers with a treasure; but in this work, she displays new profound literary depths."

—Harriet Klausner, *Affaire de Coeur*

"A special book for readers looking for an out-of-the-ordinary adventure. You will long remember the tenderness, passion, and excitement of this well-written sequel."

—*Rendezvous*

"Spunky Lucy and tormented, sexy Valcour's thrilling adventures, dangerous escapades, and sensual encounters engulf the reader in a riveting tale. . . . Another stunning achievement from a master of the genre."

—Kathe Robin, *Romantic Times*

THE RAIDER'S BRIDE

"Kimberly Cates takes the reader to new emotional heights. . . . *The Raider's Bride* is more than just an enthralling reading experience; it's a gateway to a world of mystery, intrigue, and historical insights."

—Harriet Klausner, *Affaire de Coeur*

"High adventure, suspense, and sensuality . . . a story you must read."

—*Romantic Times*

"Original . . . endearing characters. . . ."

—*Publishers Weekly*

Books by Kimberly Cates

Angel's Fall
Gather the Stars
Stealing Heaven
Crown of Dreams
The Raider's Bride
The Raider's Daughter
To Catch a Flame

Published by POCKET BOOKS

ANGEL'S FALL

KIMBERLY CATES

POCKET **STAR** BOOKS

New York   London   Toronto   Sydney   Tokyo   Singapore

This book is a work of fiction. Names, characters, places and incidents are products of the author's imagination or are used fictitiously. Any resemblance to actual events or locales or persons, living or dead is entirely coincidental.

An *Original* Publication of POCKET BOOKS

A Pocket Star Book published by
POCKET BOOKS, a division of Simon & Schuster Inc.
1230 Avenue of the Americas, New York, NY 10020

Copyright © 1996 by Kim Ostrom Bush

All rights reserved, including the right to reproduce this book or portions thereof in any form whatsoever. For information address Pocket Books, 1230 Avenue of the Americas, New York, NY 10020

ISBN: 1-4165-0312-9

This Pocket Books paperback printing May 2004

10 9 8 7 6 5 4 3 2 1

POCKET STAR BOOKS and colophon are registered trademarks of Simon & Schuster Inc.

Printed in the U.S.A.

To my husband, Dave,
who taught me that dragons
can turn into princes just when
you least expect it; and to
Linda Marrow, editor extraordinaire,
who took my darkness and let in
some light.

ANGEL'S
FALL

Prologue

Adam Slade had always told his half-brother Gavin that no good deed went unpunished, but he'd never had perfect proof of it until tonight.

Only a monster could have ignored the supplicating hands of the figure reaching out to him from the edge of the Irish country road. Unfortunately, Adam hadn't managed to become that cold-hearted yet, but it wasn't from lack of effort.

He swore, cursing himself for a fool as he reined his gelding to a halt and dismounted beside the rain-soaked form huddled beneath a scraggly tree. The Irish coast was crawling with smugglers, desperate men trying to claw out a living from beneath the crushing grip of English law. Men desperate enough to murder the unwary who stumbled across their path to insure the shield of their silence.

It would serve him right if a band of outlaws was waiting in the underbrush to attack him, the shadow-shrouded form nothing but bait to lure him into a trap.

The moon peeked from behind the last bruised clouds of the storm that had flooded the coast half an hour ago, spilling silvery rays across an old man's haggard features.

Thick white brows banked like snow on the intelligent expanse of his brow, his Roman nose all but overpowering

1

his thin face. His garments, though torn and travel-stained weren't the coarse clothes of a wanderer with only the open road for a home. They spoke of comfort if not luxury. Warm firesides and book-lined studies. What the blazes was this man doing here?

Adam knelt down beside him, wounds from a dozen battles aching in the damp chill, the wind lashing his wild ebony mane into his eyes. He knew he looked more night-demon than deliverer as he bent over the old man. "Don't fear. I won't hurt you."

"Do . . . angels hurt those they . . . stoop to comfort?" the old man asked in English accents, tears of gratitude tracking the worn lines of his face. "Prayed so . . . long . . . and no one would stop."

The God who sent Adam Slade to answer a dying man's prayer must have a warped sense of humor, Adam thought. He loosened the man's collar, felt the faint threading of a pulse beneath his fingers.

"Who are you, where are you from, and what the devil are you doing out here in the blasted rain?" he demanded, not certain who he was most irritated with—the old man or the deity Adam pictured as laughing uproariously from his perch on a cloud.

"Name is . . . Joshua Grafton-Moore. Vicar of . . . Northwillow."

"Vicar?" Adam shrank back. He would have preferred a band of smugglers eager to slit his throat. What the devil was an English vicar doing lost on this deserted Irish road? Waiting to torment Adam Slade, no doubt.

Adam grimaced. It would be just his bloody luck to stumble across a vicar in the middle of nowhere. From the time he was a grubby-faced boy, they'd never been anything but trouble. But now that Adam had stopped, he could hardly remount and say, *Just remembered a pressing engagement. Hope someone else comes along.*

He started, realizing he was glaring at the man with the ferocity that had made entire battalions of soldiers back down. Thunderation, at this rate he'd scare the man to death.

"You needn't fear," Adam said gruffly. "I won't hurt

2

you." He hoped it was a promise he could keep. He'd never been able to be in the company of a vicar for five minutes without wanting to throttle him. "Are you injured?"

"No. Fever. Stricken . . . two weeks ago . . ."

"You've been sick for weeks? What the devil are you doing wandering about in rain? In Ireland for God's sake?"

"Had to . . . keep searching. Promised . . . I wouldn't come back to England until I found . . ." The old man's voice shattered on a racking cough that shook his very bones.

"We have to get you to shelter."

"Doesn't . . . matter. I'm going to die."

"Don't be absurd. You're not going to die," Adam scoffed, dragging the man to his feet and struggling toward his restive gelding. "There was a church about three miles back. I'll take you there." *Dump you into the lap of another do-gooder and be on my way.*

The old man's knees buckled. Rain-slickened, he slipped from Adam's grasp and sagged to the ground.

"There isn't time to take me anywhere," the vicar insisted.

"Hell, yes there is!" Adam started to hook one heavily muscled arm beneath the man's legs, the other around his back, but the vicar struggled free.

"Look at me . . . really look. You'll see."

Adam stared down into his features, wanting to deny the man's claim. But he'd fought on too many battlefields, seen too much death not to know the signs.

"You know . . . it's too late as well as . . . I do. I see it . . . in your eyes."

Frustration and more than a little alarm ripped through Adam as he faced the truth. Another man would have offered the vicar platitudes, comfort, encouragement. Another man would have lied. Adam looked square into the old man's eyes. "You are going to die. But you might as well do it somewhere warm and dry."

"Can't waste strength. Have to tell you . . . ask you . . ." A spasm went through his thin frame. "What—what's your name?"

"Sabrehawk."

The man swallowed hard, his eyes old and wise as the ages. "Christian name."

"Adam. Adam Slade." It had been an eternity since anyone besides his family had called him by that name. An eternity of blood and battle, swords and death and the gritty taste of exhaustion in the back of his throat. In the eight years since he and Gavin had sailed away from Scotland, outlaws evading the King's justice, countless opponents had hungered for Adam's blood. Not for any purpose but to gain the glory of being the man who cut down the legendary Sabrehawk. Even the pardons eventually granted by the Crown hadn't stopped the string of fools with their weapons and their dreams of fame. Adam grimaced. It could be damned exhausting being a legend.

The vicar's mouth tipped up in a ghost of a smile. "You're an honest man . . . Adam Slade. God . . . sent you to me."

"God doesn't have much to do with me anymore, old man. He leaves me to the devil's care."

"Not true." Those anguished eyes clung to him with the desperate tenacity of a doomed man's last hope. "You're a good man. Can see it in your eyes."

Hot blood flooded Adam's cheeks despite the chill. It wasn't any wonder the vicar was delusional. It must be a hell of a fever if it could drape Adam Slade in the guise of a hero. "You've never even seen me before," he scoffed. "I'm not what you think I am."

"You are . . . my last hope."

Adam flinched at the stark certainty in the man's voice.

"Have to get word to . . . Juliet."

"Juliet?"

"My daughter. At vicarage, Northwillow. Tell her . . . sorry failed her. Tell her . . . love her."

"Blast it, tell her yourself. We can send whoever's in charge of that church here to fetch her from England— he'd be a damn sight better at comforting a grieving woman than me. I'm terrible at it. Hell, whenever my sisters turn on the waterworks I end up bellowing at the top of my lungs."

The vicar arched up with strength born of despair.

"You'll do this for me. Go to her, if you have any mercy in your soul."

Mercy? Adam was taken aback. When was the last time the dread swordsman, Sabrehawk, had felt such a gentle emotion? As a youth, standing over the first man he'd killed? On the bloody battlefields leading to Culloden Moor? He had lost it so long ago he couldn't even remember.

The man's hand clawed at Adam's shirt. "Don't understand. My daughter is alone in world . . . so fragile. Sheltered her . . . whole life. She was . . . sickly as a child. Thought heaven would take her . . . before me. Not afraid to . . . entrust her to Heavenly Father. But never imagined . . . I would have to leave her behind on earth."

Adam saw hellfire reflected in the old man's eyes. Fury and denial welled up inside him. He prayed like blazes that they'd drown out the tiny ache somewhere in the heart he claimed he didn't have.

"She doesn't . . . know the . . . horror waits in the world. Didn't teach her . . . to survive. You know how. See it in your . . . face. Know how . . . cruel . . . the world can be. Oh, God. I was a fool."

Adam groped for words of comfort that were foreign to him. "Parents make mistakes all the time. Just ask any grubby brat, and they'll tally up a list of transgressions. You did what you thought best. She was damned lucky that she had you."

"Love . . . only thing can take with . . . you to heaven. Always knew that. But my love can't . . . protect her anymore. Didn't know . . . how much would hurt . . . not to know she is . . . safe."

The death rattle sounded in his throat as he groped for something in his waistcoat pocket.

"Damn old fool! We could be halfway to the church by now—"

"You will . . . take this . . . necklace to my Juliet, Adam Slade. It was her . . . mother's." Grafton-Moore held out a delicate chain of golden lilies, the heart of each fragile blossom a glistening diamond.

5

Perfect, Adam thought. He'd probably crumble the thing to dust in his pocket. He was forever breaking things. He could only hope to get it into the hands of a messenger in one piece.

"I'll see that she gets it," Adam said gruffly. "I'll post it to her—"

"No. Take it yourself. Promise me you'll make sure she is . . . safe. Taken care of. Swear it."

Thunderation! He didn't even know the father, and he was supposed to cart this gewgaw back to a grief-stricken daughter and tell her, what? That her father had died in the muck on a deserted Irish road, half out of his mind with fear for her?

"You don't want me anywhere near your daughter!" Adam attempted to dissuade him. "I've got a dozen scars from irate fathers who were trying to drive me away at the point of their sword."

"Swear it," Grafton-Moore demanded. "Word of . . . honor."

Adam's jaw clenched. His word of honor. The last vestige of the reckless youth who rode out to be a hero and discovered that only death could be won by the tip of his sword. A boy who had wanted to win eternal fame, but had walked away from Culloden Moor wanting only to forget. Forgive. Especially himself.

Damn, he couldn't make the promise this old man needed. It was insane. Impossible . . .

"I have urgent business. I can't go chasing back to England searching for a girl I don't even know—"

"If ever . . . loved anyone, help me. Help me!" The plea was like a sword thrust, boring into Adam's chest. In a heartbeat he was back in a Scottish dungeon, the half-brother he loved more than anyone on this benighted earth mere hours away from facing a traitor's death. Adam could still taste the terror, the horror, feel the desperation pounding inside his chest as he fought to save Gavin.

It was the reflection of those same raging emotions that contorted the Vicar of Northwillow's face now.

Adam had two choices.

He could let the old man die in agony and have those old

eyes join countless others that still haunted him in night-mares. Or he could give Joshua Grafton-Moore his word and let himself in for a cartload of trouble.

"Damn it to hell . . ." Adam grimaced, neatly trapped by the dregs of his own conscience. "I swear it, old man."

A smile, almost angelically beautiful, transformed Joshua Grafton-Moore's face. His trembling hand pressed the necklace into Adam's palm, his transparent lids fluttering shut. "May God . . . grant you peace for what you've done. . . ."

Peace? Not bloody likely, Adam thought grimly. What was that philosophy rubbish Gavin was always prattling about? That at the gates of heaven you're given universal knowledge? One thing was certain. If that were true, the instant Joshua Grafton-Moore glanced at Adam Slade's tally of sins in St. Peter's book, the old vicar would be rising from his grave.

The clipper ship *Geana Fiadhaine,* stole through the billows of mist like a phantom, leaving the harbor of Derrynane behind. Her hold, emptied of contraband French silks and brandies, tobacco and gilt mirrors, had been refilled with Irish wool for the return trip to France—and the captain of the smugglers had hardly objected to taking the notorious adventurer Sabrehawk on board. Especially when Sabrehawk's purse was stuffed with gold.

Adam leaned against the aft rail, watching the wild-spirited island as it seemed to sink into the sea. He should be feeling a keen sense of satisfaction. He'd cheated the fates again. Instead he was edgy as bedamned.

Why the blazes should he feel so guilty? No one in their right mind could have expected him to drop everything and race back to some obscure village in England. The very notion was absurd. He'd gone to a hell of a lot more trouble than most men would have.

He'd dispatched the vicar's body to his landlord in England, instructing the man to see it delivered to Miss Juliet Grafton-Moore in the village of Northwillow. He'd dashed off a note to the woman and stuffed it into a box along with the necklace.

Doubtless he'd made a muck of the note. He'd always avoided women like Joshua Grafton-Moore's daughter as if they would give him some strange pox. No wonder, since they'd always looked at him as if they were Andromeda lashed to the rocks, and he was the monstrous Kraken ready to gnaw their flesh from their bones.

Still, he'd done what he could to fulfill his promise to the old man, and he'd told Grafton-Moore from the beginning he had urgent business demanding his attention.

He'd still keep his blasted oath, check on the woman as soon as possible. But he had more pressing matters to tend to first.

What difference would it make if he were a few months late?

Adam closed his eyes, imagining the vicar's daughter—thick brows, prominent nose, her mouth pinched from showering disapproval down on the village sinners. The old dragons of the parish were probably clawing each other to ribbons, fighting over who got the privilege of tending Juliet Grafton-Moore in her grief.

Better she get her wailing done before Adam made his appearance, anyway. He scowled, irritated as the vicar's voice echoed in his memory, desperate, imploring.

Make certain she is safe . . .

Juliet Grafton-Moore would still be there when he returned to England. What trouble could a vicar's daughter possibly get into anyway?

Chapter

1

Someone had shattered the window again. Juliet Grafton-Moore's hands trembled as she stared at the jagged shards of glass scattered across her desk, the plane of wood gouged by the chunk of brick in its center.

She sucked in a steadying breath, trying to still the erratic thud of her heart. But it plunged to her toes as she glimpsed the grimy bit of paper tied to the missile. Another warning. There had been so many, they blurred in her mind.

Wary, she reached out and tore the note from its mooring. She opened it with fingers that trembled.

This time the window, a crude hand scrawled. *Next time your face.*

She dropped the missive as if it were a snake, rocked to the core by the violence in the threat. God in heaven, who would write such a hateful thing? But the instant she conjured the question, she crushed it. How could she even begin to count the legions of enemies she'd made? Half of London would cheer at any attack on one of the most notorious and hated women in the vast city.

"You should be used to such nonsense by now, Juliet," she chided herself sternly. "Last week they shattered all the windows on this side of the house."

But never, in the year since she'd left the village of

Northwillow, had she been able to become inured to such loathing. Never had she stopped being afraid.

"Papa always said it was all right to be afraid as long as you still did what was right," she murmured. And she was trying. Trying desperately hard.

But she was failing. Miserably. And her gentle father could not help her anymore. A blade of grief imbedded in her heart, twisted, pain rippling out afresh.

He was dead, his compassionate eyes closed forever, his gentle hands stilled, the glow of faith and hope and love he'd worn like a mantle snuffed out.

And she could never return to the rose-draped vicarage in sleepy little Northwillow. Never run to him with her troubles, kneel down at the foot of his chair, and be told everything would be all right.

"Papa, I'm sorry," she whispered through the raw void that was her throat. "I'm so sorry."

Sorry for so many things she could never make right.

That they'd parted in anger. And that the gentle man who had guided so many souls to the gates of heaven had died forsaken by the side of an Irish road, with only a stranger at his side.

Juliet sank down on the worn chair and opened a tiny door in the desk's center. Pooled upon the golden lilies of her mother's necklace lay a note from a man she had never met. She drew it out, her talisman, to shore up her father's belief that most men were good, that dignity of spirited triumphed, and that guardian angels watched over all.

> It was unfortunate there was no one to hand but a gruff old soldier like myself to help, but I did the best I could by him. Your father asked me to send you this necklace. I did my utmost not to break the thing. I gave your father my word of honor that I would come to you. I will do so as soon as I am able. Yr. most obedient servant . . .
>
> Adam Slade

Adam Slade. She'd pictured him so clearly in the months that followed. Grizzled and gallant, with dozens of scars upon his jowly face and gnarled hands. One of those military men who would rather face a firing squad than anyone in petticoats. A man who turned brick red and blustered with excruciating shyness around females. She'd imagined him bent over his desk, blotting up a letter to a girl he'd never met, trying so valiantly to get the words right.

She'd had a hundred questions she'd wanted so desperately to ask about her father's final hours. And she'd wanted with all her heart to thank this generous stranger for caring for her father when he could so easily have turned away. But Adam Slade had never marched up the winding road to the vicarage.

She'd waited for him while she packed her few belongings. She'd watched for him as she tidied up the only home she'd ever known for the sour-faced new vicar and his prim spindle of a wife. And the instant she'd unpacked her inkwell in the little house she'd bought with her modest inheritance, she'd written a letter to old Widow Widdlemarch telling her where the old soldier could find her should he still come seeking.

But he had never come.

Juliet smoothed out the deep creases her fingers had worn into the parchment, an unexpected ache in her chest. Perhaps the old gentleman had grown ill. Maybe he'd even died. She hoped that there had been someone there for him, that he hadn't died alone. But, most assuredly, she was certain that her papa had been waiting to welcome him into heaven.

Every night, she'd offered up prayers for his soul. But considering the crusty old man's kindness and tender heart, she was certain he didn't need them. He'd doubtless spent his life doing just such good works. And he'd not have allowed anyone to frighten him into behaving otherwise.

She stiffened her shoulders, her spirits shored up just a little. She'd clean up the glass as she always did, summon a glazier to mend the window.

Her enemies would never drive her out with shattered glass or crude threats. She'd go on just as she had from the beginning. Marching off about her business, smiling in their faces, and wishing them good day as she passed.

Nothing like dignity of spirit to put such cowardly foes in a murderous temper. But it was getting harder to keep her chin up every day.

A timid knock at the door made Juliet straighten her shoulders, her chin bumping up a notch as she smoothed the last ripples of trouble from her lake-blue eyes.

"Come in."

The door creaked open, the woman revealed in the opening hovering there like a wary fawn. Huge dark eyes bruised by secret sorrow peered out from a fragile face that looked far younger than her twenty-two years, the soft pink of her lower lip caught between her teeth. A tumble of dark gold hair flowed in a nimbus of curls around cheeks pale as porcelain.

Juliet felt the familiar urge to hasten over to Elise St. Aubin and shelter her from whatever was draining the light out of her eyes.

"They—they broke the window again," Elise quavered, eyeing the mess, her lips trembling.

Juliet hastily scooped the scrawled threat up, crumpling it into the depths of the pocket tied round her waist. "I'm beginning to think that the glazier sends his apprentices around to do it so they can be assured of work. I vow, they must be eating beefsteak seven days a week on what I pay them." She flashed the girl a smile, but it died upon her lips. "Elise, what is it? What's wrong?"

"Th-they're coming again," the young woman's eyes glistened with tears. "A whole m-mob of them."

Juliet didn't even have to ask who Elise meant. She raced to the window on the east side of the room, and gazed down into the street below. The distinguished homes of bankers and merchants were closed up tight with disapproval where they faced the brick front of Juliet's Angel's Fall, their stuffy facades seeming puffed up with the righteous indignation of a row of crabbed spinsters.

It was as if the buildings were drawing their skirts of stone out of the way, so they wouldn't brush the crowd of people jostling its way toward Juliet's red brick house. Torches ripped orange holes of flame in the twilight, raucous voices slurred with gin battered against the prudish rows of houses. Juliet could imagine the uproar the crowd was causing behind each of her neighbor's shuttered windows.

"Oh, bother!" Juliet said, bolting to her feet. "The last time these fools charged down here, Solicitor Barnes summoned the charley to accuse *me* of disturbing the public peace!"

"What are you going to do?"

"Go out there and chase them off, of course."

"No, Juliet! You cannot! It's too dangerous!"

"If I don't chase them off, the constable might be inclined to take me on a visit to Newgate!"

She winced, cursing herself for her carelessness as she heard Elise's tiny cry. The girl's face turned ashen with panic—the legacy of a childhood spent with her debtor father behind the prison's cold walls. "I'm sorry, Elise," Juliet said, laying a hand on the girl's cheek. "I was only jesting. Nothing is going to happen to me."

"You can't be certain of that. They're in an ugly temper, Juliet. Even uglier than last week. I—I heard them."

Juliet battled the urge to dive under the covers and drag pillows over her head, blotting out the sounds until the mob tired of tormenting her and wandered off to find other prey. She shoved down the lump of dread in her throat and forced a game smile. "Listen to me, sweeting. These people are cowards. Cowards only fling words and nasty threats. But if they're confronted face to face, they flee."

"You don't know these men like I do. You don't know how—how cruel they can be."

Yes I do, a voice echoed in Juliet's head. *I see it every time I look into your eyes, into the eyes of all the other angels of Angel's Fall. And I vow, they'll never be able to hurt you again.*

"Stay up here, Elise. Lock yourself in your room. I'll come for you when it's over and we'll go down to the kitchen for a bit of tea."

"N-no. I . . . oh, please, Juliet. Please don't do this!" Two huge tears welled up, flowing down Elise's cheeks.

But Juliet was already hastening down the stairs. She heard the hesitant patter of Elise following her, saw a half-dozen other ladies peering at her from doorways or behind corners.

She reached out to open the door when a hand caught her elbow. She turned, to find Elise thrusting something into her hand. A frilly parasol.

"I don't think I'll have to worry about my complexion out there," Juliet said gently.

"I thought . . . if you needed to—to drive them away . . ."

Juliet couldn't help the wry smile that tugged at the corners of her mouth as she imagined this surly mob confronted with such a fearsome weapon.

But she'd never hurt the fragile girl's feelings. "Lock the door behind me," she said gently.

Elise nodded.

Sucking in a steadying breath, Juliet opened the portal and stepped out into the twilight. Hostility hit her in a blistering wave, a roar erupting from the mob as they saw her.

She battled not to flinch, show her fear. But the crowd was larger than before, and angrier. Twenty-five, maybe thirty people. Mostly men, from half-pay officers eagerly flinging away their fortunes to rough-hewn sailors red-faced from gin.

But all of them had traits in common as well. Their eyes were heavy-lidded from debauchery, their mouths curled in ugly sneers. At their head sailed a woman decked out in puce satin, her eyes hard as agates, her hands thick and strong as a man's.

Juliet could imagine just how hard those hands could be, cuffing frightened girls as she forced them into the elegant rooms she kept for her wealthy patrons.

Mother Cavendish. Of all the wicked people she'd met in her year in London, there was no one Juliet loathed more. Notorious for her nursery for courtesans, Mother traveled the London stews, paying coin to starving families to sell their most beautiful daughters—promising they'd never be hungry again. And they hadn't been. They'd traded the crude gnawing in their stomachs for a more exquisite kind of hell.

The merest glimpse of that woman poured steel down Juliet's spine.

"There she is, lads!" Mother Cavendish cried. "There's the woman who's stolen what's ours!"

"We've come for our women!" a half-pay officer of about thirty called out, brandishing his walking stick in the air. "Violet!" he bellowed at the window. "Come out here at once! You know I've got just what you need tucked beneath the flap o' my breeches!"

"Violet has made it quite clear she doesn't want anything to do with you or your breeches," Juliet said steadily. "You've no right to continue harassing her this way."

"No right? I've spent a bloody fortune on that greedy little piece—sapphire bracelets, silks, and satins. Her bill at the dressmaker's is twice as large as my wife's!"

A roar of laughter erupted from the crowd. "At that price you should own the girl, body an' soul, Percival!" a portly man with missing teeth blustered. "By damn, this bonneted thief stole three of my favorite wenches! I'm not leaving till I get 'em back."

"You'd best get used to sleeping on the cobblestones then. I'll not surrender one of them back to you."

"Then maybe we'll have to take them!" A brutish little man shouldered his way to the front. "I vow, we could tear this place down brick by brick with you inside it, and no one would lift a finger to stop us!"

It was all too true. The danger was, her neighbors would come out with their garden wheelbarrows to help.

"We don't want any trouble," Juliet said.

"Then ye shouldn't o' stole from us!" Missing Teeth blustered. "Damnation, I'll not be turned away without Millicent! No bloody interfering thief in petticoats will stop me from taking her!"

Juliet glimpsed Mother Cavendish's sly eyes, her carmined lips twisted in a triumphant grin. "They're mine," the old woman murmured. "Body and soul. And they always will be." The bawd wheeled to the mob. "Fling 'er out of our way, Percival, and let's get what we came for!"

Dread thrummed through Juliet's veins, and it was as if she could feel Elise's terror, as she cowered behind the door. She'd promised she'd keep her safe. . . .

The man called Percival took a threatening step toward Juliet.

She thrust the parasol toward him. "Come one step nearer, and I'll—I'll stab you!"

"Be careful, or she'll skewer your man-parts so you won't be shaggin' anyone, Percival!" Mother Cavendish jeered.

"I'm bone-deep terrified, so I am! Take a hell of a lot more t' drive me off than a parasol!" The man laughed, a nasty sound. It erupted into a howl of pain as the parasol smacked dead-on into his nose. Blood spurted out, a roar of fury echoing from the rest of the crowd.

Juliet stumbled back a step, her back colliding with the door to Angel's Fall. She didn't dare ask Elise to open it. If she did, these animals would pour into the corridors and chambers.

In a heartbeat, Juliet heard a swish of steel as a sword-stick was unsheathed, Percival's features twisting into a brutish snarl. "You'll pay for that, woman! I swear—"

"You're absolutely right, Percival," a rich baritone rang out. The crowd split in the wake of a man's massive shoulders. "Someone should definitely take the woman in hand."

Juliet gaped at the daunting figure that jostled toward her. A giant who seemed carved of stone cliffs and midnight. He towered above the other men. His ebony hair was drawn back from a face that was hard as granite, all stark planes and angles. Eyes black as the devil's soul seemed to pierce past the rigid shoulders and determined set of her chin to where her knees were wobbly with terror.

Which one of the poor ladies of Angel's Fall had been at this monster's mercy? Juliet wondered faintly. His mere presence was so overwhelming she could scarce draw breath.

Percival shot him a fulminating glare. "Who the devil are you? And what's your business here?"

"I've come to fetch a lady, just like you. She's led me the devil of a chase." White teeth flashed in a dangerous smile. "As for my name—they call me Sabrehawk. Perhaps you've heard of me?"

"Sabrehawk? The Prince of Sin!" a carrot-topped sailor crowed. "Stand back, boys! He'll pluck this pigeon right enough!"

Juliet stumbled backward, feeling as if this crowd had summoned up the very devil to pit against her. She brandished the parasol, doubting she could move this mountain of a man if she fired a cannon square into that impossibly broad chest. "Don't make me hurt you!" The words were absurd, and she knew it.

Twin devil's danced in the man's eyes, the sensual fullness of his mouth curving in an arrogant grin. One that told her exactly what he thought of her—that she was about as threatening as a half-drowned kitten, and someone should grab her by the scruff of the neck and deliver her back to her mama.

The insufferable cur glanced about, feigning knee-knocking terror. "Oh, Avenging Angel, I humbly beg your mercy."

A rare flash of temper surged in a crimson haze. Juliet swung the parasol at him with all her might. She didn't even see his hand flash out, but in a heartbeat, the parasol splintered, a cascade of broken sticks and crumpled lace, caught midswing in one bearlike hand.

"Ah, you see, a perfect example of the problem," the barbarian said, tugging the carved ivory handle from her fingers and flinging the ruined parasol to the ground. "Your parries are competent enough, but your thrusts leave a great deal to be desired." He shot a broad wink at the men behind him. "If you would allow me to demonstrate?"

"His thrusts! Aye, man! Show 'er yer thrusts, Sabrehawk!" Someone in the crowd chortled with glee.

He swung around, and Juliet gasped as a sword appeared as if by sorcery, the naked blade a slash of silver against the night. The crowd gasped, scrambling back until only Percival stood there, slack-jawed, his sword-stick in his hand.

"What the devil?"

"I thought we agreed that someone needed to take her in hand," the barbarian said with silky menace. "I'm afraid yours are so filthy they'd soil that lovely white skin." Those black eyes angled a wry glance at Juliet. "Now, my sweet, nobody should be allowed to swing a weapon so poorly. Even when that weapon is a parasol. When an enemy attacks, you want to defend yourself, yes. But it's far better to put him on the defensive. Like so." Quicksilver, the sword lashed out, catching the tip of Percival's blade, knocking it aside.

A yelp of anger came from the officer's throat, and he leapt back, sword at the ready, teeth bared. "What are you doing, you bloody idiot?"

"Giving the lady a lesson in swordsmanship," he said. "And making a fool out of you, Percival. Though I must admit, it's hardly a challenge."

"I'll ram your words down your throat for that!" Percival charged, sword slashing, a cruel gleam in his eye. The man fought with far more fury than finesse, blinded by rage at his humiliation. But he might as well have attempted to hack down a mighty oak with a wisp of straw.

The barbarian met his attack with a bored elegance designed to make him furious. "Observe," he said. "Drive your opponent back. *Quinte pointe, pointe tierce.* Or perhaps *quatre,* thus."

The blade darted, taunted, tormented Percival, the man's jowly face turning red, sweat beading his brow. The knot of his neckcloth was ripped away by a quick thrust, leaving a tiny gash in its wake, the top button of his breeches tore beneath the blade's sting, a lock of hair was snipped by the gleaming metal edge, leaving Percival looking like a strangely shorn dog.

Juliet's mouth gaped open as this Sabrehawk engaged in this most deadly dance, his movements holding the wild fascination of watching storm waves crash against cliffs.

She could see the instant the realization struck the

officer's drink-numbed brain—he had trifled with a master swordsman. One who could kill him at will. The face that had been so hungry for revenge upon Juliet now contorted in very real fear.

"Of course, you may prolong the battle as long as you enjoy it," the barbarian continued. "Nothing quite so entertaining as a good sword match. But one of the most revered rules of swordsmanship is that you must choose an opponent worthy of you. And, alas, Percival wouldn't be worthy of challenging the most unskilled boy in my salon."

"Bastard! Why are you doing this? This witch stole your woman as well! For God's sake, you should be helping us batter down that infernal door!"

Sabrehawk's weapon flashed, quicksilver, and Percival's sword-stick flew from his hand. The barbarian smiled—the most devastatingly wicked smile of satisfaction Juliet had ever seen. "I never take part in mob actions. Men who run in packs have the most distressing tendency to look like cowards." There was a rumble in the crowd, but not one dared to challenge the flashing brilliance of that sword.

"But your woman—"

Sabrehawk's smile faded into a line of grim intent. "Oh, I damned well intend to reclaim the wench. But I don't intend to do it before an audience, so unless the rest of you have a desire to become likewise acquainted with the sharp edge of my sword, you can go back to your gin and your gambling and find yourself another lady's charms to enjoy."

Juliet quaked, uncertain as to whether she'd rather face the entire mob or this one terrifying man.

"We'll be back for you, we will," Mother Cavendish snarled. "And next time, Juliet Grafton-Moore, we won't be turned away."

"What the devil?" The dark barbarian slashed Juliet a glare of disbelief.

"When you come, I'll still be here," Juliet flung back, trying to still the horrendous trembling of her knees as the mob melted back into the shadows, leaving her alone with the ebony-eyed stranger.

He turned on her with the menacing grace of a panther,

dark and deadly, something dangerous in his eyes. "And now, to deal with you," he snarled, slamming his sword back in its scabbard.

"I'm not afraid of you," Juliet lied, chin high. "And I don't care who you've come after. You'll never get your filthy hands on her again!"

"Is that so?" Black eyes speared through her, his fingers flashing out to manacle her arms. "The woman I've come for is *you.*"

Chapter

2

During his years as an adventurer, Adam believed he'd seen everything. Nothing from the goings-on in a sultan's harem to an officer's bedchamber could shock him. But as he glared down into Juliet Grafton-Moore's defiant face, he knew he'd been wrong.

He felt as if the woman had just leveled him with a cannonball to the chest. That nice old man's daughter a harlot? And damned proud of it from the fierce expression on those celestially lovely features.

Hell, what had she done? Danced a jig on her poor besotted papa's grave and tripped merrily off to London to fling herself into a life of sin? No wonder the old vicar had been so bloody desperate for someone to play guardian to her!

And who had been fool enough to be coerced into taking up the damnable position? Adam The Bloody Idiot Slade. The minute the old man had demanded his word of honor, Adam should have dumped him in the mud and ridden like hell in the opposite direction!

A whole blasted year he'd fought off waves of guilt emanating from a conscience he didn't even believe he had, the vicar's haunting, pleading eyes begging him to take care of his fragile little darling.

21

Fragile darling? Hellfire! Juliet Grafton-Moore was misery on two legs!

"You're a vicar's daughter! How the devil can you be one of the ladies in this place?"

"I'm not." She lifted her chin, those celestial-blue eyes shimmering with passion. "I'm the one who owns it."

Adam reeled. "You can't—I mean, own this place! I can't believe it. What are you saying? That you gathered up your inheritance and trundled yourself off to London to buy this establishment?"

"That's exactly what I did, not that it's any of your business. The money was mine to do with as I wished."

"And you wished to—to do *this?*" Adam waved a hand at the building.

"I'm good at it. You might say it's—it's a gift."

Adam almost strangled on his own neckcloth. What the devil—had she been "practicing" up in the choir loft while her papa was scribbling down his sermons? "You're gifted at . . . this?" Why the hell couldn't he just blurt it out— you're good at flipping up your skirts? Bloody hell, even the thought made his cheeks burn like fire, and the dread Sabrehawk hadn't blushed since he was ten years old.

"I am a very sensible woman, and it's up to me to teach them everything I know. I'm proud to be able to help the girls here."

Adam gaped. What the blazes could a vicar's daughter teach these women? Was this some sort of establishment catering to particular tastes? Hell, he'd heard of men who preferred women young and innocent-looking—every lovemaking seeming as if a man were seducing his first virgin. Life in the vicarage must be a damn sight different than he'd imagined.

"They're fast learners," Juliet insisted. "All of them. They amaze me with their energy. I delight in their progress."

"You—you oversee their . . . progress?" Adam choked out, flabbergasted by the vision of Miss Fragile Angel Grafton-Moore tutoring her little flock on how to bring a man pleasure.

"It's my most abiding passion. Everyone must earn their keep at Angel's Fall."

"Wh-what about you?"

She flashed him a fierce smile. "I work hardest of all. Papa always said that people learn best from example."

But Adam was damned sure when "Papa" was tutoring his daughter in that maxim, the old vicar hadn't figured his precious darling would employ it in a bedroom full of lightskirts!

"And this mob who was ready to toss you on a pike? Why the blazes were they charging down on you?"

"Because I took my ladies away from them."

Whoring *and* thievery—from some damned ugly customers at that? No wonder the vicar had been wandering around Ireland—he'd been looking for a cliff to jump off!

Adam's jaw clenched, grim. "Well, madam, you're going to have to find another grand passion—like needlework or—or boiling calvesfoot jelly—because I'm packing you up and hauling you out of here by your bloody petticoats if I have to!"

"I've never even seen you before! Who do you think you are, ordering me about?"

"I'm the damned fool who swore a blood oath to see that you are safe."

"I don't understand—"

"Of course you don't! You've never even seen me before! I should be off in Italy drowning in a cask of wine, or in France, sampling the . . . delicacies. Or, hell, I could be enjoying myself mightily, with an enemy's sword-blade slashing at my heart. But no. I had to ruin everything. I had to play the bloody hero!"

The girl stumbled back, those blue eyes capturing his. "Who are you?"

"The biggest fool in England! The moment I get back in the blasted country, I race off to find you in that infernal little village. But are you there? No! Widow Birds in Her Belfry tells me you didn't have the brains to stay put! You've struck out for London! I chase all over the blasted country searching for a grieving vicar's daughter, and what do I find? Miss Prim and Proper has carted herself off to London to become the madam in a blasted brothel!"

"A brothel?" Those soft cheeks went ashen, then flooded with hot color. "You think I . . . that this . . . Angel's Fall is a . . . house where ladies—"

"I don't have to elaborate for you, I'm sure," Adam snapped. "After all, you're the one who's taught them everything they know!"

That soft pink mouth dropped open, hot blood spilling into her cheeks. Hell, with all the adventures she'd indulged in since her papa's death, he was stunned he could shock her.

"There's been a terrible mistake!" she stammered.

"Damned right, there was, and I made it!"

"Angel's Fall isn't a brothel. It's a place where . . . where ladies come for shelter so that horrible people like Mother Cavendish and the rest of that mob can't exploit them."

"I see. You bring them here and expect them to perform—what? Only once a night with men you choose?"

"There are no men allowed at Angel's Fall!"

"But you said everyone had to earn their keep! You said it was your grand passion!"

"To turn them into ladies' maids and seamstresses. Give them something good to do with their lives."

What the devil? This was a place for wayward lightskirts? She had a houseful of demimondaines trading what? Diamond bracelets and satin fripperies for years of growing blind and stoop-shouldered from bending over a needle all day? Or running themselves ragged to answer some demanding rich witch's every command?

Hellfire! He should have known better, after meeting the father! Of course the stupid little fool had charged off on some idiotic quest! Just like that Quixote lunatic Gavin was always reading about!

"Who are you?" The woman demanded, her eyes sparking fire. "I demand to know who sent you!"

"Your father!" Adam blazed back.

She seemed to crumple in on herself, that fierce belligerence, her blistering determination wilting like the fragile curl of an ash. Eyes that had faced down that ugly mob with such tenacity grew large and soft and wounded, her lips trembling. Somehow, her reaction only made Adam more furious—at himself, and at her.

"You knew my father?" she asked.

"No. I didn't know him. I just—" Adam rammed his fingers back through the tangled mane of his hair. "Just stopped by the side of a blasted road."

"You're the one. The kindly old soldier who—" Stinging disappointment washed across her face. Crushing disillusionment. It shouldn't have mattered a damn to him.

"No! You can't be Adam Slade!"

"At the moment, I wish to hell I wasn't! I gave your father my word of honor that I'd see you were safe. I don't think dangling your little nose out as a target for angry mobs was what your papa had in mind for your future. Now, you go inside, gather up whatever female nonsense you need, and I'm hauling you back to—to—whatever relative of yours has a spare dungeon still hanging around to lock you up in."

The words poured steel into the girl's spine. It stiffened beneath the soft blue of her gown. "I'm not going anywhere."

"I gave your father my word of honor," Adam enunciated, as if speaking to a particularly dull child.

"I release you from it."

"Oh, no. It's not that simple. The only one who can release me from that vow is your father. And he's probably sitting up in heaven laughing his bloody head off! Now that mob I just sent packing was as ugly as they come. And the next time they pay you a visit, I might not be around to reason with them."

"I never asked for your interference! I had things well under control myself."

"Hell, yes! One parasol against thirty furious men! I must have imagined that they had you flattened against that door like a bug under the sole of a boot! Now, damn it, woman, I'm tired. I'm hungry. And I'm trying bloody hard to keep my temper and not throttle you. If you have any sense of survival instinct—which I doubt—you'll bustle your little petticoats into this—this Angel's Hell, and *do as you're bloody told!*"

"Does bellowing usually get you your way, Mr. Slade? It's a reprehensible habit. Along with swearing. Papa always said it was the sign of a weak vocabulary. *I* attribute it to laziness."

Adam's cheeks burned, his jaw clenching into an aching knot. No hardened officer in his right mind would defy Sabrehawk in one of his notorious tempers. But this—this slip of a woman was flying in his face with such infuriating dignity, he was tempted to bellow at her until her ears turned numb.

"Damnation, woman, I—"

The sound of a horse charging toward them at breakneck pace made Adam wheel around, half expecting another attack from the woman's legions of enemies. He would have welcomed about a dozen of them, swords slashing, murder in their eyes. A nice bloody battle with opponents he could actually fight. What he saw instead made him let out a long-suffering groan. As if this whole fiasco wasn't bad enough!

A youth of about nineteen thundered toward them, his carroty hair whipping over his face, his sword waving in his hand. Adam wondered how many innocent passersby who'd been in the idiot's path were lighter by the weight of a head.

"Blast it, boy! I told you to stay in your room!" Adam raged as Fletcher Raeburn reined in his frenzied gelding and flung himself from the saddle.

"I'm hearing there . . . was a . . . fight. Knew was . . . needed to watch . . . your back."

"How many times have I told you I've been watching my own back for thirty-seven years, and it's still in one piece."

"Sure an' you couldn't have expected me to stay in that room with trouble brewin'!" Eyes like a Kerry lake glinted with raw delight. "The . . . innkeep said there was a . . . mob bent on murder."

"I'm beginning to understand the temptation," Adam said, slashing a glare at the woman. "But as for a fight? Hah! Behold Sir Bonnet Brave-Heart. She drove them off with her parasol."

"You mean 'tis over?" The boy looked crestfallen.

"But . . . well, 'tis possible they'll come back!" He brightened a little. "Thievin' scoundrels often do!"

Adam ground his fingers against the throbbing pain in his temples. "It won't matter if they come back, because we won't be here. We're escorting Miss Grafton-Moore . . . well, I don't know exactly where, but I'll find somewhere to put her!"

Fletcher flashed her an ornery grin. "Be careful he doesn't nail you in a barrel! 'Twas that he did to me!"

Startled blue eyes flashed to his. "What kind of a monster would do such a thing?"

"I drilled airholes in it!" Adam snapped, furious at himself for the searing of embarrassment that flooded up his neck. "And I left food and water."

"Good thing, too," Fletcher observed. "Spent the night in it, I did. Beginnin' to wonder if I'd ever get out."

"You'd already jumped ship three times, and I was getting damned tired of swimming to shore after—oh, bloody hell!" Adam swore darkly. What the blazes was he doing? He didn't owe Juliet Grafton-Moore any explanation of his behavior. He didn't give a damn what the woman thought of him, did he?

"Fletcher," he began again, "put your damned sword away before you slice Miss Grafton-Moore's petticoats, and . . ."

Adam stammered to a halt. He wanted nothing more than to drive the boy away from this place pell-mell, like some pesky gosling. But sending Fletcher Raeburn careening back through London alone was like flicking burning brands at a powder keg. Like most of his infernal Irish breed, Fletcher was spoiling for a fight. Doubtless the boy would find one.

There was nothing more dangerous than a brainless youth packed chin-deep in fury with a desperate need to prove himself a man. An uncomfortable throb of kinship pinched at Adam as he remembered another youth—dark-haired and defiant as bedamned—charging out to carve his fortune with the blade of his sword.

"*This* lady is Miss Grafton-Moore?" Fletcher's eyes widened in astonishment as he settled his grandfather's smallsword back in its scabbard.

"If it wasn't, I'd hardly be standing here making an idiot out of myself, now would I? Miss Grafton-Moore, meet Fletcher Raeburn. It's my job to keep his hide in one piece."

Delicate brows arched in surprise. "You're taking care of him, too?"

"I'm getting paid to do it!" he snapped.

"Paid?"

"Don't mind him, mademoiselle," Fletcher said. "He's crusty as a barnacle-infested keel, but 'tis all in show. Has a tender spot in his heart for me, he does. Like a mammy for its babe."

Adam growled something vile under his breath.

"As for meeting you, miss, 'tis enchanted I am!" The boy swept her an elegant bow and caught her hand, raising it to his lips. "I've been half out of my mind fearing that some calamity had befallen you! When they told us at Northwillow you'd fled to London, I feared I would go mad."

"Don't be overly concerned, Miss Grafton-Moore. It's a recurring condition with young Racburn."

But damn the woman, if she didn't turn to the boy and smile at him, the kind of smile ladies-fair had been bestowing on their knot-headed heroes since the beginning of time. "It was very kind of you to worry, but as you can see, I am quite happy here."

Adam swore darkly. "Blast it—"

"But you're in danger, milady!" Fletcher protested, alarmed. "I pledge my sword to protect you."

"Oh no you don't, Fletcher. Keep your sword in your scabbard for God's sake. Miss Grafton-Moore is my curse to bear. Now, we've matters to discuss, madam. You must have *some* unsuspecting relation out there. All I have to do is dump you on their doorstep."

"There is no one," she said.

"Bloody hell, what the devil am I supposed to do with you?" Adam muttered, then glanced hopefully at Juliet. "I don't suppose you have a spare barrel lying around?"

Pink cheeks whitened in affront. "I most certainly do not! We have nothing further to discuss, Mr. Sabrehawk."

Adam grappled with the frayed ends of his temper. Sabrehawk hadn't triumphed in so many battles by allowing himself to be blinded with rage—no, keep your head, he'd told his students in swordsmanship time and again. Your wits are far mightier than the blade of your sword. And from the moment he'd ridden up to this Angel's Hell, he'd been fighting from pure gut-level fury. What had he gotten for his trouble besides a splitting headache? Fletcher barely sketched the woman one bow, and she beamed at him as if he was Galahad returned with the Holy Grail.

Adam forced his lips into a smile, fearing his jaw would shatter at the effort. "Miss Grafton-Moore, it's obvious I began wrong. You must excuse a crusty old soldier. I have been searching for you for several months, haunted by my vow to your father."

She drew herself up with icy dignity. "It couldn't have been haunting you terribly bad, Mr. Sabrehawk, since you took nearly a year to keep your promise."

Adam ground his teeth. Damn, he wouldn't be accountable to a snippy little Miss Perfect like her—he'd not give her the satisfaction. "Perhaps you're right. After all, it's meaningless that your father begged me with his dying breath to find you. And it's obvious that you have no interest in his final hours. Poor old man. How could he have guessed what reception you'd give his emissaries?" Adam started to walk away. "Come along, Fletcher. We'll go toast the poor old vicar's memory at the Hart's Crossing Inn."

"B-but, Sabrehawk!" Fletcher stammered. "We can't be leaving her here! 'Twas your word of honor you gave the man!"

"I know. But my word of honor and the old vicar's last words are of no importance to Miss Grafton-Moore. She's moved on with her life."

Adam could almost hear the wheels whirring beneath the infernal woman's curls. He could only hope a healthy dose of guilt would kick in before he reached the end of the street. He'd hate to have to turn around and ruin his boots breaking down her blasted door.

At the last possible instant, he heard a soft cry. "Wait. I— I do want to hear about . . . about—what Papa said before he . . ."

Adam fought to squelch a surge of triumph—there'd be

hell to pay if the chit caught a glimpse of that in his eyes. But as he turned, the emotion fizzled and died. An unaccustomed jab of guilt jolted him as he saw the expression on Juliet Grafton-Moore's face. Grief and regret and self-blame bruised the tender skin beneath her eyes. Emotions he'd learned to understand far too well in the wild highlands of Scotland during the hellish year after Culloden Moor.

He crushed the sensation of empathy. This woman had been nothing but trouble from the minute he'd heard her name. He was going to storm her defenses, use any means in his power to get her delivered somewhere safe, and then he was going to wash his hands of her once and for all.

"I am most grateful for the chance to talk with you," he said with as much gallantry as he could muster.

She folded her arms across her breasts as if trying to shield something from him—perhaps too tender a heart? "This changes nothing, Mr. Sabrehawk," she said, meeting his gaze. "Nothing will induce me to leave Angel's Fall."

Adam's eyes narrowed. He'd been present at half a dozen sieges in his time in the ranks. Learned military strategy from the masters. No one knew how to storm walls better than Sabrehawk—be they carved of stone or stitched in billowing petticoats. A smug smile tugged at the corners of his mouth. A sheltered vicar's daughter was no match for him. Let the battle of wills begin.

Chapter

3

A battery of females peered at Adam as Juliet Grafton-Moore led him into her inner sanctum, Fletcher following like a puppy in their wake. Eyes of every shade from cornflower to violet to chocolate to amber—some long-lashed and darkened with soot—peeked from behind doors; others, tip-tilted and exotic, observed him from the bars of the stair rail.

These were the women she had gone out to defend? The whole lot of them had been hiding in here, allowing her to charge out alone into the street to beard the lion. The vicar's daughter might not have had any idea what the people she was confronting were capable of, but Adam was dead sure Juliet Grafton-Moore's fallen angels knew.

A wave of disgust washed over him, combined with an unexpected jab of protectiveness toward the woman who had gone out to batter back the dragons with nothing but a parasol and the white-hot fierceness of her own convictions.

He looked away, damned uncomfortable, his gaze colliding with those of the other women. The instant their gazes locked on Adam, he saw their eyes widening in wariness, mistrust, and an almost reluctant appreciation as they glanced from the crown of his dark head to the scuffed toes of his travel-dusty boots.

KIMBERLY CATES

There was one woman in particular who captured Adam's attention—the woman who had unlocked the door to let them in. He was certain she'd once been lovely—hair the color of molasses and honey around a face that could have been carved into a cameo. Great dark eyes peered up at the two male intruders, reminding Adam of a wounded doe he'd once stumbled across, too delicate for the world beyond the doors of Angel's Fall.

"Miss." Fletcher's voice was low, gentle. "Now what would a lovely lady like yourself be doin' with that?"

"With what?" Adam's gaze flicked to her hands. Clutched in trembling fingers was a pistol. Hellfire, it was dumb luck she hadn't already shot herself in the foot!

"Elise!" Juliet gasped, her gaze snagging on the shining barrel at the same time. "Wherever did you get that? You know how I feel about violence!"

The cameo-woman seemed to fold in upon herself beneath Juliet Grafton-Moore's disapproval. Adam could only thank God there'd been one woman behind that locked door who wouldn't have allowed the vicar's daughter to be rended limb from limb.

"It's obvious Sir Bonnet Brave-Heart, here, prefers whacking people with parasols instead of mounting a truly effective defense," Adam muttered wryly, hoping to startle a smile out of the dark-eyed young woman. But she only turned her face to Juliet's, lines of suffering carved deep about her lips.

"You want to know why I bought this thing? I found those threatening notes when I was mending your torn apron. Juliet, they frightened me."

"Threatening notes?" Adam cast a glare at Juliet. "What the devil?"

Juliet waved one hand in dismissal. "I could pave the road to Norfolk with them, I've received so many. They mean nothing. Elise, I've told you a dozen times that they're only a coward's attempt to scare me. Those who write such vile notes seldom have the courage to follow through on their threats."

"Are you insane?" Adam demanded. "Some might hope to scare you off with words, but I'm bloody certain there

32

were plenty among that mob more than willing to escalate this battle further, take steps you couldn't even begin to imagine."

"The scope of my imagination has grown a great deal since I've moved here, Mr. Sabrehawk."

Adam wanted to snap at her, argue with her, bellow at her, but there was no point in doing so in front of all these people.

Instead, he turned back to the woman she'd called Elise.

"You needn't fear me, madam. I mean no harm," he said softly.

"I saw what you did for Juliet. I cannot thank you enough, sir. I don't know if I would have been strong enough to—to . . ." She glanced down at the silvery gun as if it were a snake in her hand.

Ever so gently, Adam disengaged the weapon from her fingers. He smiled. "It doesn't take strength to pull the trigger, Miss Elise. Only deep enough fear."

Gratitude flickered in those dark eyes, and Adam knew in that instant this girl had known deeper fear than any soldier he could name. He would have said more to soothe her, but she was nudged aside.

Adam was overrun by the mingling of a dozen expensive scents—rose water and lavender, gillyflower and violet, as he was enclosed by a wall of multicolored petticoats. Doubtless the other women descended because they no longer feared little Elise would accidentally bury a pistol-ball in their corsets.

A fine-looking woman with red-gold hair drew close to him. "I'd wager you've never been afraid in your life, sir. I was watching through the window! Saw how you sent that bunch of cowards running!"

"Just like one of the Titans!" a golden-haired miss piped up. "Or Zeus hurling thunderbolts!"

"Don't forget Zeus was usually bent on seducing some poor lass in a shower of gold," a woman whose large breasts overshadowed the rather understated beauty of her face said in quelling accents. "Perhaps instead of praising him we should be asking *why* he stooped to help us."

"It's a disagreeable habit of mine, stepping between brainless women and angry mobs," Adam muttered. "But believe me, it's a habit I intend to break!"

"Mr. Sabrehawk and I have things to discuss," Juliet snapped. "So if you'll excuse us?"

"Sabrehawk? Not *the* Sabrehawk?" Gillyflower exclaimed.

"I'm aware of only one," Adam said, oddly nettled by Juliet's curtness.

"I was mistress to General Haviland. I heard the most marvelous tales of your exploits! Is it true that you once fought off twenty Italian assassins with nothing but a rusted dagger?"

"Actually, it was closer to twenty-three, but the other opponents didn't put up enough of a fight to count."

"I was told you got the most dashing scar in the battle. Right across your left shoulder! I would pure perish to see it!"

"Marguerite! Absolutely not!" Juliet squawked, so emphatically that it was all Adam could do to keep from starting to unfasten his buttons. Lord knew, there was nothing he enjoyed more than tormenting prudish women with attitudes. But the last thing he needed was to get Miss Grafton-Moore's back up.

He did the next best thing. "Perhaps when Miss Grafton-Moore and I are done with our meeting, I can entertain you with tales of my adventures." He'd need something to do while the woman was packing, wouldn't he?

But he was met by the most implacable feminine disapproval he'd ever confronted.

"When our conference is over, I will escort you to the door at once. There are no gentlemen allowed in Angel's Fall, Mr. Sabrehawk. The reputations of my ladies must be protected at all costs."

"Their—their reputations?" Adam echoed, thunderstruck. "Isn't that a little like attempting to bar the stable door after the mare's had a wild gallop across the meadow?"

He caught a glimpse of the vicar's daughter. He'd seen warmer eyes across a dueling field.

"Elise, please show Mr. Raeburn to the library, where he can await Mr. Sabrehawk, and see that he has anything he might need."

She grabbed Adam by the arm, all but dragging him up the stairs.

"One more comment like that, Mr. Sabrehawk, and I shall expel you from Angel's Fall myself. I'll not have past mistakes flung up to anyone here. Aren't there things in your past you wish you could change? Decisions you could make again?"

Adam laughed. "My life's been one long adventure. I've won a fortune with my sword, seen the world. What man in his right mind could have regrets for living a life like that?"

Yet even as those words tripped off his tongue, memories spilled in a burning wave into Adam's chest. The suffocating darkness of his father's bedchamber, the reeking stench of sickness searing the insides of his nostrils, the earl's once-powerful body wasted away, pale as a corpse, upon his bed. And Adam's half-brother, Gavin, his golden head bent over his father instead of his beloved books, enduring the old earl's constant scorn.

Join Adam, the earl's brittle voice echoed in Adam's mind, the crabbed hand clasping that of his only true-born son. *For once in your life, Gavin, fight so you won't shame me! Be a man.*

Then, most unforgivable of all, Adam's own voice . . . *Ride with me, Gav—*

He crushed the memory—the horror that had followed. He'd lured his gentle brother into hell, and learned from Gavin the meaning of true courage. Gavin had forgiven him, but if he lived for eternity, Adam would never forgive himself.

Resentment welled up in him at the woman who had loosed those demons on him yet again, demons he'd battled for years to bludgeon back into the dark recesses of his soul where they couldn't tear at his sleep with their vicious teeth. Damnation, if she'd unleashed the nightmares again . . .

But she knew nothing of nightmares—not this woman, with her petticoats flowing about her waist, her straight back, the delicate hollow of her neck exposed where she'd tried to catch her curls up in pins. Her hands were so slender and pretty, so pristine white—clean in a way Adam's hands could never be again.

She ushered him down the corridor, past the open doors of rooms bursting with feminine fripperies, rainbows of petticoats and bodices cast across beds, ridiculous bonnets draped across every surface. Even the narrow tables that flanked the side of the hallway groaned beneath the weight of abandoned fans and parasols and pearl-buttoned gloves.

Juliet fumbled with a door at the end of the corridor and opened it. Adam followed her inside. The room was as tidy as its owner—every book in its place, a cluster of tiny portraits on the mantel. Tucked into an alcove at the rear he could glimpse a narrow bed. No danger of the vicar's daughter entertaining any gentleman here, Adam thought. Unless that gentleman was the size of a pug dog, he'd never fit upon that mattress.

But it could be a lot of fun trying . . . a voice in Adam's head whispered. His mind filled with images of big blue eyes peering up at him, the dove's-breast softness of skin no other man had ever touched.

Adam brought himself up short. Where the blazes had those thoughts come from? The vicar's daughter and a man like him? She wasn't even his type! He liked them eager and laughing, well-schooled in the arts of pleasing a man. Not trembling and awed and looking for a hero.

At that instant, she turned to face him. His cheeks burned as if she could peer into his eyes and see the lewd thoughts that plagued him. "Mr. Sabrehawk," she said, knitting her fingers together in a white-knuckled knot. "About my father. I want to know everything you can tell me."

No, angel. You don't want to know how desperate he was, how he cried out your name. You don't want to know the terror that stalked him. Damn. Gavin had always been the brother best at dealing with tragedy, understanding the tenderest reaches of the human heart. Adam had always raced off on horseback until the weeping was done.

But Gavin wasn't here. And Joshua Grafton-Moore's daughter was staring up at Adam, dread in her eyes.

"How did my father die?"

"Your father had a fever. When I found him it was too late. He'd had it for two weeks, he said. But there he was, wandering around the country road in the middle of nowhere. It had been raining but he . . . he said he couldn't stop searching."

The words were like hot knives in Juliet's chest. He could see the pain in her as they twisted deep, and there was nothing he could do to stop it.

"I don't know what he was searching for," Adam said, "but he asked me to tell you that he was sorry he didn't find it."

She turned away, her spine rigid beneath the softness of her gown, her shoulders almost painfully square. He knew how much the effort cost her.

"Strange, Papa traveled all over Ireland—ran himself to death searching, and I came to London and stumbled by accident across the truth. . . ." Her voice cracked. "How could I have been so wrong?"

"Wrong?" Adam battled a sting of reluctant curiosity. "What was it you sought?"

"Someone dear to me. Someone I failed miserably."

A lover? Surely not. Adam recoiled from the possibility with an unaccustomed twinge. Then who? Blast it, only an idiot would ask. He didn't need to know. That was always the best course—don't listen to heart-rending tales, don't learn people's secret sorrows, don't allow yourself to be vulnerable to pain—anyone's pain—because if you do you might stumble across your own.

"What's done is done," Adam said gruffly. "Raking yourself with guilt will change nothing. What matters is where you go from here."

His sister, Christianne would have rounded on him in a tearful tirade, while the youngest, Maria, would have clasped his reprieve to her bosom with fierce delight, then skipped off on her way with a careless toss of her head. Juliet raised her gaze to his with such indescribable sorrow it caught like tenterhooks deep in his chest.

"You're right, of course. I'm glad to know that you understand why I have to stay here."

Lines of frustration and anger furrowed Adam's brow. "Why—hell's bells—the point is you *can't* stay here. Your father would go mad with worry if he knew you were in such danger." Sweat beaded his brow from the effort it took him to gentle his voice. *Remember—charm her . . . disarm her . . .* but the rest of the bawdy soldier's rhyme spun out in his head . . . *bed her, but flee before you are made to wed her . . .*

Adam felt hot blood surge to his cheeks. "Juliet . . ." Using her Christian name was supposed to whisper of intimacy, of kindred spirits, one more weapon against the naive. The name wasn't supposed to ripple from his tongue with the sweet taste of music.

He reached out, clasped her hand in his two strong ones. Her fingers were so small and pale, the tiny calluses so oddly endearing he didn't have to orchestrate the hesitation in his voice. "May I call you *Juliet?* After listening to your father speak about you, and worrying about you for so many months myself, I feel as if . . ." He chafed his scarred thumb over her knuckles. "As if I know you well. But if you think me too forward—" Damn, that was troweling it on a bit too thick.

Most women he knew would have dealt him a stinging set-down for his obvious insincerity. Juliet's slender throat constricted, as if she were swallowing what? Tears? Her voice quavered. "You were a friend to my papa when he was alone, Mr. Sabrehawk. You may call me anything you like."

That was a damn dangerous prospect. Adam wondered how many shades of pink the woman would turn if he launched into a litany of the sobriquets he'd laid on her during the past hellish months. He'd bet they'd sizzle her soft little ears right off.

"Juliet, you must allow me to—to fulfill my vow to your father. Whatever went awry between you—I'm certain all is forgiven. The man loved you to distraction."

"He loved me to his death." Droplets clung to her lashes, Adam was in abject terror that they'd fall free. It was acceptable to pretend there was something in a lady's eye, a stray lash, a speck of dust, as long as tears didn't go drizzling down her cheek.

"You are in danger here. Terrible danger. You are not so blind you don't see it."

"I accept the risk." That damnably sweet chin was tipping up again. He'd better stop it before she straightened her spine or all was lost.

"Juliet, your father is dead. His final wish was that you be safe, protected. Don't you owe him that much at least? Peace of mind? It seems little enough to ask. Especially if some misunderstanding between you had some part in sending him to his grave?"

"His death must count for something."

"And your death? What will it count for?"

Juliet's lips wobbled into a smile that tightened a fist in Adam's throat. "I'm not going to die. I intend to minister over Angel's Fall until I'm as old and toothless as Mother Cavendish."

"That harpy was born to this life, this world. While you— blast it, you cannot even fathom what horrors await you."

"Can't I? These women you think are so coarse, so hardened to their fate—I've heard them at night, weeping like desolate children into their pillows, but they would die before they let me comfort them. I've heard them cry out in nightmares, caught glimpses of happenings so horrible they make me sick to my stomach, and so very angry that I wish—wish I could take my parasol to the breech-flap of every man who ever breathed."

"Then I suppose I should be grateful your aim was so bad." The corner of Adam's mouth tipped up. "Juliet, I am a rough old soldier—weaned on battle-cries, and rocked to sleep to the lullaby of cannonfire. I wish to God I knew the right way to express how I feel, to make you understand. If I roar at you, it's because I fear for you. If I'm obstinate and bullheaded and sharp-tongued, it's because I know those 'cowards' who stormed your door tonight far better than an innocent like you ever could." It was damned uncomfortable to realize that in his attempt to charm the woman into acquiescence, he'd cut so close to the truth.

He battered back the jab of panic, his jaw clenching. This

could be damned dangerous—the only saving grace the certainty that within a few days, a week at most, he would put a bloody ocean of distance between himself and those melting summer-sky eyes.

"They will hurt you, Juliet, if they get the chance."

"Then I shall have to lay up a great supply of parasols and consider boarding up the windows on the east side. Glass is so abominably expensive."

"Damn, lady, listen to me! There are things beasts such as those can do to a woman, things worse than death."

He cursed himself for resorting to such a dark weapon against her when he saw the darting of raw terror in the depths of her eyes.

"I think I am quite safe from their attentions. I'm not the type to stir men to passion."

"Some men would call you beautiful." What the blazes roughened the words in Adam's throat? Why was he suddenly staring into the creamy oval of her face, aware of the rose-silk gloss of that prayerful mouth, the lush curl of her lashes, the shadowy hollow of her throat, where he knew the most feminine of scents clung to tantalize a man.

For a heartbeat, just a heartbeat, he saw a question as old as Eve shimmering in her gaze. One it seemed even a vicar's daughter couldn't resist asking.

Do you think I am . . . beautiful?

Did he?

The query echoed back. He'd skewer his own hide before he explored that minefield. It was all he could do not to shove her away and scrub the feel of her off his hands. But he'd been schooled from the time he'd been a raw recruit to press his advantage. And at the moment, he definitely had the advantage. One little nudge, and the vicar's daughter would tumble into his hands.

But what could he do to push her over that edge? How could he entice her to fall?

Her tongue darted out to moisten her lips, and Adam's gaze fixed on the curves of her mouth, tempting as if it were spangled with sugar. He sensed her pulse quickening, her breath catching.

This was a language he understood. In that instant, he knew what card he needed to play to gain her surrender.

A rush surged through him, the sensation that gripped him in the heartbeat before he plunged into battle. As if gripped by a sudden impulse he couldn't control, Adam drove his fingers into her curls and lowered his mouth to hers.

It was all part of the battle between them. That was the only reason he felt this fierce urge. He wanted to kiss the bejesus out of her, drive the starch from her spine, the stiffness from her knees, until she melted against him, unable to fight his will. He wanted to play her with the exquisite skill of a master violinist with a familiar instrument, leaving her throbbing and humming and trembling with the chords he'd strummed in the very heart of her woman's core. And he knew how. Hell's bells, Sabrehawk was an able swordsman upon the dueling field and in the bedchamber as well.

Yet never, in scores of years of carnal delight had he ever tasted anything so sweet.

Warm, so warm, her mouth yielded under his, and he captured her stunned gasp in his mouth. Of its own volition, his tongue stole into the honeyed cavern beyond, tasting her with practiced fervor.

Her hands flattened against his chest, then curled into the fabric of his midnight-blue frockcoat like kitten paws as he sent her equilibrium winging off its axis just as he'd expected. What he hadn't expected was that his own thick-muscled legs, hardened from hours of bracing themselves against the onslaught of sword and dagger, would suddenly feel unsteady.

Blast and damn! This wasn't in the battle plan! Adam grasped Juliet by her upper arms, and broke the kiss, his breath rasping in his chest, his gaze burning, hot with accusation on her face.

She staggered back a step. Her fingers pressed against her lips, her eyes so wide he was dead certain he'd just given the vicar's daughter one hell of a first kiss. "Wh—why did you . . . do that?" she demanded, breathless.

Because I was insane. Because it seemed like the thing to

*do at the time. Because I made the first mistake I warn my
students against when tutoring them in swordsmanship—I
vastly underestimated my opponent.*

But there was no way he would admit such a thing to this
terminal do-gooder with her trembling lips and such incredibly sweet confusion clinging to her lashes.

"Now do you see how much danger you're in?" Adam
growled in self-defense. "If I was moved to kiss you, who
knows what the men in that mob might be plotting. How
many times have they watched you, swooping out into the
night like some guardian angel? Untouchable. Innocent.
Defying them. Villains cut of that cloth don't tolerate a
woman's defiance. They'll use any weapon at their disposal
to teach her her place."

He was suddenly aware of Juliet's intent gaze on his face,
something disturbing washing over those celestial features.
The kiss-blush had been driven back by an intellect surprisingly keen in such an angelic face. Her expression left Adam
feeling as exposed as the time a rival officer had ordered his
aide de camp to purloin Sabrehawk's breeches the morning
of a duel. Adam had stalked to the rendezvous point with
nothing but a bedsheet knotted about his waist.

"Is that what you were doing when you kissed me?" she
charged, her fingertips touching her lips. "Teaching me a
lesson?"

Adam sputtered a denial, but heat stole into his cheeks.
Might as well have flown scarlet banners of guilt and chagrin
and outright anger at being bested by such a slip of a girl.

She drew herself up with icy dignity. "Mr. Sabrehawk,
there is nothing more loathsome than a man who preys on
those more innocent than he is."

"It was a kiss! Just a kiss! I hardly stole your virtue!"

"No. But you stole something precious to me. My good
opinion of the man who aided my father in his last hours.
You see, I'd colored you quite a hero. Not the kind you
would favor—racing about battlefields blazing in glory. But
one who stopped at the side of the road, seeking no glory for
himself, seeking only to ease a stranger's suffering."

"Well, that's what I did, didn't I?" Adam blustered. "I
stopped. I sure as hell didn't get any glory. And I chased

halfway across the world after you because of a promise that infernal old man wrenched out of me. I—" Nothing like flinging away one's advantage by losing one's temper. Adam brought himself up grimly, folding his arms across his massive chest. "Listen to me, lady. I'm no hero. But right now I'm all you've got."

"You're wrong. I have Angel's Fall, and Elise and Millicent and a dozen other ladies here safe tonight instead of in the clutches of men who would use their power against them. I have my faith that something good will come of my work here. I know that I am doing the right thing, even though it's not the easiest course. Despite what you think, I don't need your help. I have angels fighting on my side."

"I didn't notice any of them swooping down to bang Percival in the head with their harps when that mob was about to tear your hair ribbons off!"

"Go back to wherever you came from, Mr. Sabrehawk. I promise you, if my father had had any idea what sort of man you were, he never would have sent you to find me."

"Next time he coerces blood vows out of unsuspecting strangers, perhaps he should demand references. Unfortunately, this time there's not a damn thing either one of us can do about it. I gave him my word I'd see you safe, and I will, even if it kills me."

She stalked to the door, flinging it open. A half-dozen eavesdropping women scattered, rubbing reddening bumps on their curious little noses. Adam stormed after her, the tramp of masculine boot heels echoing down the hall.

"You're not getting rid of me, lady."

"We'll see about that," she said, charging down the stairs, hurtling through a sitting room where Fletcher Raeburn was ensconced on a wing-chair, ladies clustered in the far corner of the room, whispering as if the Minotaur had been dumped into their midst.

"Sabrehawk?" Fletcher piped up, red as a brick from his neck to his hairline as he struggled to his feet.

But Juliet didn't even flicker so much as an eyelash. She merely stormed into the cozy kitchen.

"I hope you enjoy sleeping on the cobblestones, Mr. Sabrehawk."

"The—what the devil?"

She flung open the door at the rear of the kitchen. "You insist you're staying put here. I've told you, no men sleep in Angel's Fall. I'd hardly make an exception for a man bearing the shameful label of Prince of Sin, now would I?" She leveled him the quelling glare governesses had been terrorizing schoolboys with for a hundred years.

Adam gaped at her, aghast. The woman was flinging him out of her house? If he hadn't been so furious he would have roared with laughter at the absurdity. Juliet Grafton-Moore, every Angel in her house, and the dray horses in every barn on the street couldn't budge Adam Slade unless he damn well wanted to be budged.

But the woman's back was up enough after the disaster of that kiss. One more blunder of that sort and he would have to nail her in a barrel to get her away from here. Considering how that tactic had backfired with young Fletcher, he dared not take the risk. The thought of Juliet Grafton-Moore emerging from the barrel professing undying devotion was enough to traumatize Sabrehawk for life. No, there had to be another way.

At that instant Fletcher stumbled through the door, the youth looking glaze-eyed as a schoolboy who'd got himself sick on a surfeit of bonbons amidst so many women.

"What about Fletcher?" Adam demanded, taking one last shot at female soft-heartedness. "You've seen how devoted he is. You know he won't leave me. Are you going to make him sleep on the stones as well?"

"Of course. But I'm certain he'll be much more comfortable."

"Why is that?" Adam demanded, aware of every old wound, every dull ache in a body that had once been tough as oak.

She smiled at him with grim satisfaction. "I'm going to give *him* a blanket."

Adam gave a gruff bark of laughter and stepped out into the night, Fletcher following in his wake.

"If you think you're going to drive me off this way, you're sadly mistaken. I've slept like a babe in far worse places than a lady's garden," Sabrehawk taunted. Then his brow furrowed as he noticed Juliet's lashes drift to half-mast, those lips he'd kissed murmuring something unintelligible.

He hoped like hell she was swearing under her breath.

"What are you doing?" he growled, scowling.

"Praying," she said, flashing him a heavenly smile.

"For the redemption of my sin-scarred soul?" Adam sneered.

"No. For a lovely cold rain."

Adam sputtered an answer, but it was too late. Juliet Grafton-Moore shut the door in his face just as the first fat raindrops began to fall.

Chapter

4

From the time she was a babe, Juliet had been taught to eschew violence. But as she watched Adam Slade tramp about the confines of her garden, she could barely resist the impulse to knock his head against the stone wall. She threw the bolt across the back door, releasing a general outcry from the assembled ladies.

"Juliet, how can you treat him so shabbily?" Millicent Hampton asked. "I know he's a man, but he saved you from disaster! Heaven knows what would have become of all of us if he hadn't come to your rescue."

"And God alone knows what will happen the next time that mob comes calling," Violet St. Amour warned. "I know Mother Cavendish. She's venomous as an asp when she's crossed. And that hero of yours made her turn tail and run."

"He's not my *anything,*" Juliet bristled, the thought of any part of Adam Slade belonging to her hideously daunting. "Certainly no champion! He's an overbearing, pigheaded, interfering barbarian!"

"You'd best pray he is!" Isabelle du Ville tossed her dark curls, casting a vaguely scornful look down her catlike nose. "He made Mother Cavendish lose face before that hellish coven of villains she led against you. It's a slight that vindictive old hag will never forget, I assure you."

In the three weeks since Isabelle arrived at Angel's Fall, Juliet had often felt that the fading beauty was mocking her behind her back. It had stung more than a little. But as those worldly-wise eyes met hers, Juliet couldn't quell the icy chill that ran down her spine. Mother Cavendish's thirst for vengeance was legend on the streets of London, and she had an army of minions awaiting her command. Kindred spirits who delighted in cruelty, and other, more reluctant allies, men and women she could twist to her will with the most horrible kind of blackmail.

Papa's sermons had been full of gentle warnings not to let hate take root in your heart, because it would spread, like vile weeds, crowding out forgiveness and compassion and love. The most villainous sinner had once been an innocent babe, the only difference that fate had shaped them with harsh hands. *"The most evil of all creatures grow afraid when darkness comes,"* he had said. *"If one should ever reach out in their fear, my hand will be there to hold."*

The sentiment had seemed so beautiful, glowing in her father's ageless eyes. Never had she suspected the effort it must have cost him to cling to that belief. Until now.

Hate was a hard kernel in her heart. She could feel it chafing there, and it wore Mother Cavendish's face.

"I think it was wondrous kind that Sabrehawk came to Juliet's rescue," Millicent insisted. "He could have merely walked away."

"I wish he had!" Juliet burst out. "He is exactly the kind of man I detest. One who tyrannizes over women, as if they'd no will of their own." *One with kisses so hot and fiery they'd made her very knees melt.*

"It's only right that we should be grateful for what he's done," Elise said. What he'd done? Juliet thought. They couldn't begin to guess.

"Enough!" Heat spilled into Juliet's cheeks, and she raised a hand to her lips, feeling as if Adam Slade had branded whisker burns into the soft skin for everyone to see.

"All this blather is for nothing," she said, trying to ignore the keen-eyed stare of Isabelle du Ville. "Mother Cavendish will not budge me. And Adam Slade might stomp around Angel's Fall for a few days, attempting to drag me away, but when he sees how resolved I am, he'll grow tired of the game and storm back to wherever he came from. Men are notoriously short of patience."

"What do you know of men?" the Frenchwoman asked with a smirk. "You are innocent as a little nun. You know nothing! Nothing of a man the likes of this one. He is . . . *magnifique*. It would be as impossible for a *real* woman to resist him as it is for the sea to stop crashing against the shore."

"I had no trouble resisting him," Juliet blustered, then realized she had exposed more than she intended. Isabelle's feline lips quirked in the smile that had enslaved two dukes and a prince.

"Of course, my sweet. But you have not a woman's blood in your veins, only milk and honey and prayers. *Oui*, the only burning inside you is the desire to reform your fallen sisters. But how can you ask others to avoid the nectar of wine unless you have tasted it? How can you appreciate the suffering it takes to sacrifice a man's touch forever?"

"Isabelle, after what the gentlemen of your acquaintance have put you through, how can you have any regrets—"

"My dear little innocent, there may be pain in affairs with the gentlemen, but I assure you, there can also be pleasure, no matter how much dour-faced preachers would like to tell you otherwise."

It took all Juliet's stubborn will not to turn away from Isabelle, but the Frenchwoman's greatest joy since the duke had cast her out was shocking the vicar's daughter, and Juliet had resolved early not to give her the pleasure of seeing her discomfited.

God forbid that Isabelle ever get wind of the kiss that had transpired up in Juliet's chamber. What delight Isabelle would take in the kiss that had introduced Juliet to just how intoxicating a man's mouth could be, and how dangerous.

Juliet's spine stiffened at the image of Isabelle bending close as Adam Slade whispered of the incident into her shell-like ear, the two of them laughing at the saintly little nun's fall from grace.

"Juliet, you look positively wretched." It was Elise, her trembling hand curving over Juliet's arm. "And Isabelle is teasing you terribly. But I know you're afraid of Mother Cavendish. It may be true that no one before has escaped her wrath, once she pointed that finger of doom. But now that Sabrehawk has become your champion—"

"For pity's sake! All of you are driving me mad!" Juliet's temper snapped. "I intend to go up to bed, and I'd advise the rest of you do the same! And just so there is no question, Sabrehawk is not to be allowed inside this house on pain of death, do you understand me?"

Isabelle let out the trilling laugh that had made a duke her slave. "You think a man like that will spend the night standing about in the rain like some green lad, *ma petite innocent?*"

"He's probably halfway to The Fighting Cock already." Millicent sighed.

"Juliet, he just rescued us from that mob—" Violet insisted, tossing her curls. "How can we abandon him in the rain?"

Juliet cast a glare about, saw mutinous glimmers in a dozen sets of eyes.

"That door remains locked even if the house is afire," Juliet snapped, praying she'd put down the rebellion as she turned and stalked up the stairs. But in the little time since Adam Slade had charged into her life, she'd begun to feel hopelessly outnumbered. Like other brilliant strategists, he was building his forces from inside the fortress he had under siege, buying the ladies loyalties with his *heroic deeds*. With her luck he'd be storming the ramparts before breakfast.

No. She was being absurd. Doubtless Isabelle was right. Slade had stomped off, consigning her to the devil. There was a good chance he might return. If he did, she would merely send him packing as she had tonight. She would put an end to this nonsense, and then things could get back to normal.

Normal. A strained laugh escaped her lips. Rows of

shattered windows, ugly mobs, anonymous threats that turned every shadow darker, every creak in the night more sinister. She gritted her teeth, shoving back that subtle cloud of dread, focusing instead on the nefarious Adam Slade. *He* was a foe she could battle face to face. One not woven of mists and possibilities.

Inside her own room, Juliet slammed the door with a thud loud enough to rattle the prisms on the crystal candlestick in the hallway below.

She expected to leave the madness behind, bar her door against it, and find the haven, the sanctuary that had always awaited her in this quiet chamber. But the room had been changed forever. The pale rose-colored walls seemed to have shrunk. The furnishings, dwarfed by Adam Slade's presence, suddenly appeared to be fragile as a doll's.

It seemed as if he'd burned himself into the room's memory—the worn rose-flowered carpet was shadowed where he had stood, as if he'd branded his image in the fibers. The scent of him clung to the dust motes illuminated by candlelight—foreign, masculine, musky, not the metallic tang of ink-smears or the musty odor of books, but rather, horses and sweat and leather, along with the wild tang of Slade's very own, gathered on his numerous adventures. Spices from the far east, dark scents from Italy, a subtle layering of lavish elegance from France, all sharpened by the man himself, like the weapon he had wielded against the mob.

Every crag and line in his arresting features, each scar and honed muscle whispered of violence, a terrible grace that could deal death with a flick of his wrist.

He was a man who had challenged the fates countless times, against appalling odds, and emerged triumphant. A man who had decided with that same implacable will that he was taking her away from Angel's Fall.

She'd seen the hard light in those Stygian eyes when she'd evicted him from her house. He'd gazed at her with the menacing indulgence of a jungle cat letting its prey squirm free for just a heartbeat, just long enough for the shivering quarry to feel a surge of hope that they might escape, while the cat—the cat always knew escape was impossible. The prey was there for the taking whenever he tired of the game.

He had nailed Fletcher Raeburn in a barrel when the poor boy defied him. A tyrant, bending him to his will. But Slade would not batter her into submission. He might have more brute strength than she, but she had far more determination. She would outlast the barbarian, and then, word of honor or no word of honor, he'd tire eventually and go off, seeking adventure. And she would still be here, the doors to Angel's Fall wide open to any woman needing sanctuary.

She would outlast him, and pray that she could keep the ladies at Angel's Fall from taking up his cause in the meantime.

She unfastened her gown with so much energy that stitches popped, then, casting a cascade of petticoats and bodice onto the chair, she jerked on her prim nightgown and crossed to the window.

A thin cold veil of rain glistened beyond the jagged points of glass that still clung to the wooden windowframe, the dampness turning everything muddy and miserable. She felt a sinful surge of pleasure, knowing Adam Slade was out in it. She flopped down on her bed and pictured water drops running down beneath his collar as he stomped down London's streets, but her stomach heated at the knowledge that the path the drops took was traced by the corded muscles of his neck, the shaggy thickness of hair dark as midnight.

She imagined him swearing as rain trickled into his mouth, but that was more dangerous still as his tongue swept out to swipe away the cluster of drops on his lips.

There was something wickedly delightful in knowing he was furious. Anger, never acceptable in the vicarage at Northwillow, was oddly pleasurable in the dark of her own bedchamber. But not half so pleasurable, Juliet realized with a shiver, as Adam Slade's mouth, hot on her own.

Rain. It drenched Adam—cold and miserable as he stalked down the London Street, Fletcher all but running to keep up.

Blast that woman anyway! He'd fought off assassins and rival armies, battled enemies so dangerous they'd make an avenging angel tremble.

But never, in all his years as a warrior, had Adam contended with a foe who fought with a vindictive little prayer—one that was answered so swiftly he'd barely been a step from the door before the rain began to fall.

Hell, he supposed he should be grateful the spiteful little witch hadn't called the Four Horsemen of the Apocalypse down on his head. He'd already come face to face with War. Doubtless, she'd have sicced Pestilence on him. Aye, that was what she might have prayed for. A cluster of lovely boils blossoming on his body. He grimaced. Considering what a man-hater she was, he knew exactly where she'd have instructed God to put them.

"Sabrehawk! Sabrehawk, wait!" Fletcher's strident voice grated across Adam's nerves, and Adam caught a glimpse of the youth, elbows and knees pumping, red-faced and breathless, with all the desperate determination of a little brother trying to keep up with a pack of older boys.

But a single glance at the Irish youth's eyes made Adam lengthen his stride in a vain effort to escape. Censure. Disapproval. Confusion clouded Fletcher's features.

Adam gritted his teeth. Damned if he'd be raked over the coals of guilt by an empty-headed stripling like Raeburn.

But before he could dodge around a copse of roving sailors, Fletcher launched himself, catching Adam's arm with surprising strength. "Confound it, you can't just leave Miss Grafton-Moore like this!"

Adam rounded on him, rain streaming down the rigid muscles of his face. "In case you didn't notice she threw me out of her house and slammed the door in my face. I've already had my nose broken three times, boy, and I like the angle it's bent at now. I have no intention of letting Miss Prim and Proper smash it flat."

"You gave her father your word of honor you'd protect her," the boy asserted stubbornly.

"Blast it, I chased all over England after that infernal wench. And I *did* pluck the vicar's daughter out of that mob when they looked ready to dangle her by her corset-strings from Tower Bridge. In case you didn't hear, she wasn't overwhelmed with gratitude. She swears she's not leaving that Angel's Hell of hers. I considered nailing her in a barrel the way I did you, but I'd have to let her out sometime. And the instant I pried up the first nail, she'd be charging back into this mess, parasol waving. So I might as well save myself a hell of a headache and just leave her be."

"She's in danger. Desperate danger. And she's helpless against it, despite her courage."

"*Courage* is another word for *idiocy*. My brother, Gavin, taught me never to stand in the way of someone anxious to get their head blown off for a righteous cause. They'll just keep sticking it out there until you get yours blown off, too. God forbid that I stand between Miss Grafton-Moore and her chosen martyrdom."

"You don't mean that." Fletcher went ashen in the light of a coach lamp passing by. Disillusionment haunted the youth's features. Adam should have rejoiced in it. He'd been waiting to see it for almost a year. God knew, he'd never wanted to be anyone's hero. Why was it that Fletcher's expression jabbed at him, making him squirm inwardly?

"Fletcher, she flung me out of her house and prayed for rain. What do you expect me to do? Stand guard all night out in her garden like a bloody fool?"

"I expect you to honor your promise to a dying man. Not turn your back on a helpless woman who needs your protection."

Protection, hell. After what had happened in Juliet Grafton-Moore's bedchamber, it was *Adam* the woman needed protection from!

Adam's memory flashed—his own reflection captured in wide blue eyes, sweet lips he'd wager no man had ever tasted parting in a shocked gasp just as his mouth closed over them. A jolt of raw heat searing through his shameless attempt at manipulation, leaving him stunned and needing and, yes, damn it, scared as hell.

He jerked away from Fletcher as shame darkened his cheekbones, half afraid that the boy would suspect something in Sabrehawk's protestations wasn't ringing true.

Blast, if Fletcher had an inkling of the depths Adam had sunk to, the hotheaded fool would be challenging *Adam* to a duel!

"I don't care if you scowl until you blister me!" Fletcher insisted. "You pledged your sword to Miss Grafton-Moore."

"She won't be needing it this evening. Even that surly mob of hers wouldn't be roaming about on such a miserable night, I promise you. Now, you can stand here in the rain all night if you want. I'm going into a warm tavern, dry out by the fire, and drink myself blind."

"I'll go back to guard the lady myself," Fletcher insisted, jaw jutting at that pugnacious angle that had tempted half of Christendom to take a swing at it.

Adam resisted the urge to grab him by the scruff of the neck and drag him inside the tavern. "Fine. Go sit in the rain like a half-wit. Just leave me in bloody peace!"

Adam turned his back on the youth and tramped the last few steps to a tumbledown tavern tucked beside a pawnshop that marked the edge of a seedier part of town. The dens Mother Cavendish's mob had sprung from.

It made him more than a little uncomfortable that he was stalking into the same tavern where some of those animals had doubtless drunk their pint of courage before they marched on a house full of women. But Fletcher had riled up his stubborn streak, and he'd be damned if he'd turn back now, like a green lad shamed into behaving himself.

He flung open the door, heard the sullen roar of those within. Instincts honed in years of battle had given him the ability to gauge the mood of any room he entered. This tavern was a cave filled with spitefulness and anger, edged with just enough cruelty to make Adam's fingers check the hilt of the sabre strapped to his lean waist.

He'd been in worse places. More dangerous ones. He preferred them. One step into a hell-hole, and a man knew where he stood—a heartbeat away from an honest dagger in the back. Here, violence and ugliness would be cloaked behind benign smiles and drooping lashes, in a place where nothing might be what it seemed.

Adam made his way to a scarred table and sat down, his

back to the wall, his eyes scanning the room. He could tell the instant the rest of the occupants noticed him. A choked-off sentence. A forced cough. Elbows poking ribs, stubbly chins jerking in his direction.

More than one of the patrons looked vaguely familiar. And after a moment, Adam could feel the press of two dozen furtive gazes. He glared back, a cold warning that he was aware of the attention and alert to any movement. Sabrehawk's warning. One he had perfected in countless years of trying to discourage the foolish from seeking death at the point of his sword.

His ebony gaze clashed with that of a portly man who had been among the mob at Angel's Fall, and the coward all but dove beneath a serving wench's skirts.

But there were plenty of other culprits that weren't so wary. The half-pay officer who'd led the attack nursed his wounds in the corner with a half-dozen cronies. Percival's eyes shimmered with hate, and Adam was dead certain that the man was imagining his pistol-ball splitting the flesh of Adam's chest.

Ah, well. If the fool attempted to strike, it would be the last mistake he ever made. Sabrehawk's enemies claimed that he could hear the whisper of a dagger being pulled from a boot top on the other side of the city. It was the greatest gift any soldier could have—that fierce instinct as much a part of him as his dark hair, his sinewy hand. Never, in the years since Adam first took up the sword, had it failed him.

With arrogance born of that certainty, Adam surveyed the rest of the establishment, a motley collection of men and women who hovered beneath the gloss of respectability. Black sheep from merchant families, sailors doing their best to live up to their vile reputations. People smart enough to know they were scorned by decent society and mean-tempered enough to make someone pay.

It would be easy enough to raise a mob out of such rabble. Easy enough to goad them into a frenzy, Adam realized with a chill, recalling the cozy house just down the street, its tidy garden and doors not half thick enough to ward off the crack of one sturdy boot-kick.

He frowned, his gaze snagging on a caricature of a man

across the room. More cadaver than human he was, bone-thin, yet wiry, his face carved with ivory hollows beneath eyes so pale they seemed milky as a witch's charm. An austere nose and thin lips slashed across that face, a smattering of thin black hair revealing glimpses of his scalp. But it was the fact that he sat, like Adam, alone in the crowd that was strangest, as if contempt had drawn an invisible circle around him.

A thin walking stick was leaned against the table at the man's side. Adam was dead certain it concealed something lethal—a sword-stick, probably so rusted it would shatter at the first blow, and so dull-edged it couldn't cut warm butter. Not that the man would be able to wield the weapon, anyway. Juliet could doubtless defeat him with a single wave of her parasol.

But, incompetent as the man seemed, his glare was obviously in working order. He leveled it at Adam with burning intensity.

What the blazes had he done to offend the scrawny cur? Adam wondered idly. The man hadn't been in the mob, of that Adam was certain. He would have noticed someone like that, wouldn't he? Adam grimaced. He'd have been lucky if he'd recognized his own brother in that mess. His whole awareness had been stolen by the golden-curled angel with her parasol.

A buxom serving-maid sidled up to him, her eyes huge beneath an off-kilter mobcap. "Eh, there, me fine sir, do ye be thirstin'?" she quavered, casting a nervous glance over her shoulder.

"Whiskey. A big glass of it."

"Aye, sir," the girl replied. But instead of bustling off in a swirl of threadbare petticoats, she lingered, hovering beside Adam like a jittery butterfly.

Adam cast an impatient glare at her. "What is it? Did I forget to say 'please'?"

The girl's cheeks went pale, and she twisted her fingers together. "They're whisperin' that you were at the Angel Lady's house today. That you sent Mother Cavendish an' her crew scramblin'. Be you that same gennelman?"

Perfect. Adam frowned. Doubtless Percival had sent the girl over to check out his identity before he blasted him to eternity. Surprisingly civil of the bastard. "I was at Angel's Fall. But I'm certain if you asked the *Angel Lady,* she'd tell you I'm no gentleman. Tell Sergeant Percival, over there, to blast away."

"P-Percival?" The girl's lips curled as if she'd just seen a dead rat floating in her bath water. "I'll not be tellin' him anything, the slimy, no-good cur! I just . . . just wanted to say thank you, sir, fer helpin'," she whispered in a tiny earnest voice. "The lady, she be so all alone. And kind. When my baby sister was sick, she . . . well, doesn't matter. Jest, thank you. When next ye see her, will ye tell her that little Janey's back at her mama's knee?"

"Pegeen!" the tavern keeper's bellow made the girl whirl around. "Ye'll not make me any coin standin' there yammerin'! Fetch out some drinks or go home!"

"Aye, Traupman! I'm comin'," the woman called, but she turned to flash Adam one last grateful smile before she bobbed a curtsey and dashed away. Adam stared after her, bemused. It seemed as if Miss Grafton-Moore had *one* champion in this mess. Something hard lodged in Adam's chest at the memory of the gratitude in the serving girl's eyes, and his mind crowded with images of his own younger sisters, headstrong termagants, every one, yet, the notion of them far from home, sick . . . frightened, alone. The mere thought scuttled a chill through Adam's veins.

He drove his fingers through the thick waves of his hair, as if he could scatter such thoughts to the wind. His sisters were daughters of an earl—illegitimate, though they might be. Their lives were worlds away from the hardscrabble existence of Pegeen and little Janey. Yet if circumstances had flung them into the snake pit that was London, wouldn't he have been grateful if there were someone like Juliet Grafton-Moore waiting to take their hands?

The thought was damned disturbing—bloody inconvenient. Far better to hold on to the opinion that the woman was a rattlepated fool. One who had tossed him onto the prongs of a dashed irritating dilemma. Keep his word to a dead man and drive himself insane, or walk away, leaving not only one wide-eyed angel behind, but the last tattered remnants of his honor.

Pegeen slid a glass of whiskey onto the table, and he flipped her a coin with a smile, then downed the fiery liquor in one gulp. When he opened his eyes over the rim of the glass, he caught the thin black-garbed stranger staring at him with a hostility hotter than the whiskey's burn.

The stranger got to his feet, rumpled frockcoat tumbling around lanky legs, one hand closing around the silver-headed walking stick leaning beside him. Those pale eyes fixed on Adam as he crossed the room.

Loathing, pure and cold, shone out of odd lashless eyes. "Is it true?" his voice rasped. "You are the man who was at Angel's Fall today?"

Adam's eyes narrowed. "And if I was?"

"I should kill you for what you did there."

Thunderation. That was all he needed. An offended starveling cur trying to sink its teeth in his ankle. Adam wanted nothing more than to shake free of the fool.

He slashed a scathing glance from the man's thinning crown to his shabby boots, letting contempt glimmer about a hard-edged smile. "Kill me? You are welcome to try it. Don't tell me you are one of the poor sots whose doxy has run away from home? Save your shillings, buy a decent wig, and I'm certain you can find another ladybird."

Hot color surged into those wasted cheeks. "How dare you even imply that I would soil myself fornicating with—with some sin-spawned slut! It is Miss Grafton-Moore who concerns me."

Why was it that the very sound of Juliet's name on the man's tongue made Adam's fists clench? "Miss Grafton-Moore is your concern, is she?" Adam repeated. "Just exactly who are you? And what have you to do with the lady?"

"My name is Barnabas Rutledge. Proprietor of the shop across the street from her establishment."

Adam searched his memory, recalling the painfully tidy shopfront beyond the wall of Juliet's garden. "The pawnshop?" Adam grimaced in distaste, abhorring vultures of this sort who preyed on the desperate. "What's the problem, Rutledge? Afraid Miss Grafton-Moore's ladies will move away, and find somewhere else to pawn the jewels and trinkets their protectors gave them? You must be doing a lucrative business with Angel's Fall so near."

Rutledge bristled until Adam half expected that thin chest to explode. "I am only a neighbor. A friend to Miss Juliet. I wish only to save her from this madness!"

Adam had stayed alive by reading people's emotions. The flicker of an eyelash, the infinitesimal twitch of a lip could reveal much to one attuned to it. Barnabas Rutledge's pale eyes were almost feverish, his hands fitful on the head of his cane. Devotion. That was what it was. It seemed Pegeen was not the only one loyal to the lady of Angel's Fall.

Adam should have been amused by the absurdity of it all—this spindly crow of a man tripping all over himself because of a woman, flinging himself into the fray against a man who was five times his size. It should have been funny as bedamned. But it seemed as if Adam had lost his irreverent sense of humor somewhere in the rain.

Impatience surged through Adam, mingled with an odd twinge of possessiveness that made him mad as hell. Possessiveness where Juliet Grafton-Moore was concerned? Blood and thunder, he couldn't wait to be rid of her!

"If you have business with me, Rutledge, conduct it before I lose my patience. My affairs with the lady in question are none of your concern."

"Affair?" Rutledge's cheeks went waxen. "You stay away from her! After all the damage you've done—"

"Damage? From what I could see the least I saved her was a dozen more broken windows. And when that mob descended, matters could have been a lot worse."

"It couldn't possibly be any worse than you've made it, you fool! Miss Juliet is—is misguided. In terrible danger. And now, after what you've done—"

"You must have heard a mangled version of the tale, sir. I am the one who drove the mob *away* from her door. I didn't invite them in."

"It would have been more merciful if you had!" Rutledge raged, his whole body trembling in indignation. "You made Mother Cavendish a laughingstock. Aye, and all those with her. Simply flinging Miss Grafton-Moore out of the city will never be enough for those animals now. They'll make her pay for every lash of humiliation you dealt them—make her pay in ways you cannot even imagine."

"The devil they will!"

"I've heard them, blast you! Planning, plotting for two hours now! Heard the ugly things they are promising to do to her! If you had left things alone, Miss Grafton-Moore would have been frightened, would have fled. Then she would have been safe."

Adam snorted in derision. "That woman wouldn't turn tail and run if the devil's own army was charging her, cannonballs firing."

"What would you know of a woman like Miss Juliet? You—an animal of the flesh, a libertine! Yes, *Sabrehawk,* I heard all about you! Morals so debauched that your very name is linked to sin. A bastard, conceived by a nobleman's whore!" Rutledge's eyes burned with the savage satisfaction of a man who'd just delivered a death blow.

Red haze simmered before Adam's eyes, but the smile on his face never wavered. He'd been barely six years old when he'd learned that only a fool would give an enemy such a powerful weapon.

He arched one dark brow, staring into Rutledge's wildly expectant features. "Waiting for the explosion, man? Sorry to have to disappoint you, but when you've been called *bastard* as many times as I have, the word loses its sting."

His mother's face, laughing and lovely, danced in his mind, and he wondered why the vile label *whore* never did.

"You find it amusing, do you? What an abomination you are?" Rutledge poked his bony nose inches from Adam's face. "You should be sickened by the tainted blood that runs through your veins! Animals like you destroy everything they touch, and now you've spilled your poison on an angel. Because of your interference, Mother Cavendish will make certain a special kind of hell awaits Miss Juliet. Even now, her beasts might be stalking Juliet, prowling in her garden, testing the locks on her windows."

The image speared icy slivers beneath Adam's skin, twisted his stomach into a hard knot of denial. But the image Rutledge painted was so clear—all the more nightmarish because it was anchored in a very real possibility.

Adam fought back the only way he knew how. His face contorted with raw scorn, mockery, the desire to lash back in him so thick and suffocating he couldn't resist it. "And I suppose *you* will prevent this disaster from befalling Miss Grafton-Moore?"

"I will do whatever I have to do to pluck Miss Juliet from the jaws of those demons. And as for you, you stay away from her, or else any horror that befalls her will be on your head!" The man whirled around in a sweep of crumpled frockcoat and a black haze of hatred.

And Adam cursed himself for his gift of reading emotions. Barnabas Rutledge might be a pompous fool, an enemy. But his warning about the dark fate that would befall Juliet Grafton-Moore had been the absolute truth.

Adam hadn't protected Juliet Grafton-Moore from danger when he'd driven Mother Cavendish's horde away. He'd brought Armageddon down on Juliet's head. He gave a savage tug at his neckcloth, feeling well and truly trapped. He'd had no choice but to interfere when the mob had descended on one lone woman. Blast, but he'd do the same thing again in a heartbeat. But there was no question he'd stirred the fires of violence hotter through his actions. Considering the damage he'd done, how the devil could he turn and walk away?

He levered himself to his feet, suddenly unable to bear the clamor of voices, the stench of unwashed bodies, the swirling thickness of smoke. He edged away from the table, his mind filled with images of an angel-face and a zealot's eyes, a flailing parasol and shining courage and the stark danger that awaited the woman who had owned them all. Danger deeper and darker and more chilling because of him.

One thing was certain. Juliet Grafton-Moore's enemies

wouldn't wait long to close in for the kill. But when they struck, Adam resolved, he would be there, waiting. He had to get back to Angel's Fall before the unthinkable happened.

Growling an oath, he stalked toward the door. Adam didn't see the shadowy form steal up behind him, hear the barmaid's cry of warning. He only felt the skull-cracking pain as something heavy and hard shattered over his head.

Chapter

5

Juliet should have slept like a babe—she'd been exhausted for hours. And the confrontation with the mob had drained what little energy she'd had left after her busy day. But she lay for an eternity, hearing the tiny brass clock on the mantel tick, the spatter of rain beating on the roof tiles

She could still feel Adam Slade's presence, despite the vast city that doubtless now stretched between them. Despite walls of brick and the thick bolted doors that were supposed to block him out.

At last, she muttered the nearest thing to a curse she could muster, flung back the coverlets, and stalked to the windows beside her desk.

She should have enjoyed the rain immensely since there was a good possibility Slade was out in it. After all, she couldn't sleep, but at least she had the satisfaction of knowing that he was probably worse off, traipsing through muck and misery. But as she peered out into the night, she caught a glimpse of a little scullery maid running down the street under the meager shelter of a ragged petticoat.

Poor moppet, Juliet mourned, the child tugging at her heart. She must be chilled to her bones. More than one lady had come to Angel's Fall in such weather, led to the promise of a warm fire and a dry bed by the beacon that always glowed on the iron hook by the back gate. She hoped this child knew of the basket always sitting on the bench just inside the garden of Angel's Fall so she could tuck a warm bun into her pocket. Millicent had burned her finger baking a rather lopsided batch of them this afternoon.

Blast! Juliet flattened her palm against her aching brow, remorse a dull throb in her temples. For the first time in nine months she hadn't left a light burning, nor the basket of food tucked beneath a stone overhang for those who were hungry. And it was all because of that insufferable Adam Slade. He'd made her so angry, it was a wonder she could recall her own name.

She ground her teeth in irritation. Oh, well. It was too late now. She'd locked the back door, leaving strict orders it was not to be opened.

If, by some chance Slade had lingered, spent hours sleeping on marble benches or pebbled paths amid a miserable rain, he might storm his way into Angel's Fall and refuse to budge. Not to mention the fact that there might be other, more dangerous things lurking in the night, things promised in the scrawled notes that had haunted her nightmares.

She was tempted to crawl back between the covers and drag the pillow over her head. Far better to pretend she'd never thought about the basket than risk confronting Sabrehawk or some other enemy. But duty and guilt had been schooled into her at too young an age, and the little maid had looked so small and cold and hungry.

Merciful heavens, Slade was probably clear across the city by now, a flagon of ale in his hand, some lovely tavern-wench cooing and simpering over him like a ninny. And she doubted even Mother Cavendish could induce anyone to go stalking on such a dismal night.

Grumbling, Juliet gathered up a soft gray wool shawl that had been Elise's first effort at needlework and wrapped its folds about her shoulders. Propriety demanded that she should drag on her dress, but the thought of tangling with a mass of laces when her nerves were already so frazzled drove her to madness. She'd merely gather what she needed, slip out into the garden. She'd hang the lantern, leave the basket, and scoot back inside. She was being absurd. Between Slade and Mother Cavendish and the threatening notes, she'd soon be seeing maniacs behind every copse of shrubs. There was far greater danger of Isabelle catching her and giving her no peace for breaking her own edict.

Smiling ruefully at her own silliness, Juliet crept down the corridor, carefully avoiding boards that creaked, slipping past doorways where the rest of the ladies slept.

The stairs were trickier. At one deafening squeak, Juliet nearly jumped out of her skin, glancing over her shoulder as if she were indeed stealing out for a forbidden tryst. To meet with a lover . . .

She swallowed hard, a wistful sting of remembrance twisting inside her. There had been a time she had been like a sea of other girls, dreaming of just such romantic folly, pulses tingling at wondrous possibilities. Before she'd stepped out into the world beyond the vicarage at Northwillow. Before she'd realized that dreams could turn into disasters, that lives could be shattered, and that innocents could pay a price beyond imagining.

Jenny had run away, certain she was in love. But she'd given her heart to a man not worthy to touch the sole of her slipper. A man who had promised to wed her, but left her pregnant and alone, penniless and too ashamed even to seek shelter again at the vicarage.

After all, if Jenny's own parents vowed never to forgive her for the shame of kissing her dancing master, she couldn't have known Juliet and her father would welcome her back to Northwillow, swelling with a bastard child.

She couldn't know how desperate they'd been to find her, or how hard the vicar had searched.

It had been months after Juliet's father died that she got word of Jenny from a chimney sweep she'd helped. Jenny had died in childbirth in a rat hole like the one Mother Cavendish ran. And it had haunted Juliet's dreams, knowing that Jenny had suffered, afraid and alone, swallowed up by the city of London.

She'd seen a dozen Jennys since she'd arrived at Angel's Fall, and what she'd discovered since that time had made her certain of one thing. She never wanted to tangle her fate with that of a man. No grand adventure, no wild, romantic folly was worth the aftermath that could follow.

Besides, she told herself, she had not the slightest interest in Adam Slade *that* way. There was no reason to get all fluttery in her chest, no reason to dread one of the ladies discovering her on this late-night foray. After all, they knew the ritual with the lantern as well as she did.

She slipped into the kitchen, saw the banked coals glowing on the hearth. She drank in the scent of scorched bread that accompanied cooking lessons. Bending down, she lit a bit of straw upon a glowing coal and touched the tiny flame to the candle wick in the pierced-iron lantern. Dropping the straw onto the hearth, she shut the tiny tin door of the lantern to guard the flame, a pattern of dancing lights from the pierced pattern of holes darting like a bevy of fairies across the room.

Scooping up the basket she'd packed with buns and gingerbread, cheese and apples, earlier, and tucking a bit of canvas atop it to keep it dry, she slid back the bolt on the door.

Her fingers hesitated on the door latch for a moment before she steadied them in annoyance, and opened it. She'd planted every flower or herb that blossomed along the meandering paths. She'd fashioned nooks of bushes into quiet refuges where her ladies could go for self-reflection. She'd nurtured the most woebegone buds to show how they could blossom if given a little light. And, most cherished of all, she'd planted a knot-garden filled with herbs said to cure everything from heart palpitations to headaches to broken hearts.

The garden was as familiar to her as her features in the cracked surface of her mirror when she scrubbed her face each morning. But tonight, just the slightest possibility that Adam Slade might be prowling in any pool of shadow made it stranger, wilder. It took more effort than she could have imagined to step out of the warm dry kitchen onto the crushed-pebble path.

The storm was drifting away, back over the distant ribbon of the Thames river, the sky above sullen and bruised, growling distant thunder. A last smattering of rain dampened her face and chased a chill beneath her skin, a puddle splashing muddy water between her bared toes. She wanted to behave like a child, bracing herself to race to her papa's room after a nightmare, tucking the skirts of her nightgown up and pelting toward the back gate as swiftly and silently as if there were an entire battalion of dragons laying siege to the pathway.

But she steeled herself to walk with rigid dignity—no small feat considering she was already drooping and damp, spattered with raindrops the wind shook down from the trees, her feet clammy with mud. She was grateful it was no longer pouring, but it was just wet enough to make her miserable—a fitting punishment, no doubt, since she'd called the rain down on Adam Slade's head.

She grimaced. How ironic that would be, if Slade were warm and dry and drowning his frustrations in a flagon of ale, and a brace of Mother Cavendish's cohorts were skulking about.

"Fool," she muttered to herself, trying to hush the crunch of her footsteps against the pebbles. "Stop this nonsense at once. There is no reason to be imagining brigands behind every clump of gillyflowers."

Yet as she wound her way deeper into the shadows, she couldn't help wondering what lay beyond the wavering circle of light. Her pulse thundered by the time she reached the black iron gate, slick with moisture. Someone had locked it. Strange. Her brow furrowed. The gate had never been locked before. It had always been open to let people in. There could be two reasons to lock it—to lock enemies out or . . . to keep anyone inside from escaping.

A chill scuttled through her. No, she was being ridiculous. One of the women in the house had stolen out to bar the gate, nervous after the house had been stormed by the mob. Maybe Elise? Even if it were, it was impossible to scold Elise, what with the reflection of so much nameless terror in her doelike eyes.

Juliet tucked the basket into its sheltered nook and hung the lantern. With rain-slick fingers she wrestled the iron bolt, gritting her teeth at the squeal the hinges issued in protest as she swung the gate wide.

She heaved a sigh of relief until she turned to retrace her steps. Darkness. Thick. Impenetrable without the lantern. She curled her fingers so tight the nails cut into her palms. So what if it was dark? She knew the way back. She needed only to reach out her hand, search for familiar landmarks by touch. Casting one last glance back at the street, she began her trek, fingertips gliding over wet tree bark and trimmed hedges, the sides of stone benches and rather risqué statues the house's former owner had left behind. Statues she'd draped modestly in togas of bedsheets.

She turned a corner, catching a glimpse of watery golden glow against the darkness, the subtle light from a hearth fire. It should have made her feel better, but it didn't. Alarm trickled down her spine. Was someone watching her?

Sabrehawk? Or one of Mother Cavendish's vile henchmen? No one in the house knew she had stolen outside. If anything should happen . . .

She hastened her step, bit her lip to keep from crying out when her bare toe smacked into a stone. Her hand sought the familiar roughness of a hedge row, then groped for the next landmark, a stone bench. Sensitive fingertips skimmed the surface, then collided with a beard-stubbled jaw. A scream froze in her throat as something sprang from the darkness, driving her off her feet.

She flew backward, struggling to scream, to escape, but an iron-hard claw clamped about her throat. She crashed to the ground, the beast landing atop her, something hard and pointed driving square in her chest, hammering the breath from her lungs in a desperate croak.

She couldn't breathe, couldn't move, her entire body crushed beneath a mighty weight. Terror slashed through her, cut deeper still as lightning flashed, illuminating the blue-silver kiss of death in a dagger's blade. A hand knotted in the hair at the crown of her head, yanking it backward to expose the vulnerable curve of her throat. Dear God, she was going to die.

"Help! Please, help!" she choked out, knowing it was futile.

She closed her eyes as the weapon slashed down.

Juliet barely felt a sting of cold metal against that skin, when the monster erupted in a horrendous oath.

"What the devil?" In a heartbeat, he was off her, but she barely had time to suck in a tortured breath past her half-cracked ribs when a hand closed about her arm, and she was yanked upright with a force that would have launched her to the moon, if it had been visible through the clouds.

She found herself inches away from the formidable countenance of Adam Slade.

"Wh-what are you doing here?" she stammered. "You're supposed to be getting inebriated."

"It's a damn good thing I'm not! If my reflexes had been even a whisper off, you'd be dead. Blast it, you little imbecile! I could have killed you," he snarled. "Never—by God, *never*—sneak up on a soldier when he's sleeping! We have a damn uncivil way of burying our daggers first, and asking questions later."

"Y-you go about . . . s-stabbing perfectly innocent . . . b-bystanders?"

She could sense the horror pulsing through him, feel his hand tremble where it grasped her arm. But his voice was harsh with the sarcasm she'd begun to loathe. "There are a score of trained assassins who would love to see me dead, Miss Grafton-Moore. I've awakened to find more than one of them bending over me, and I assure you, they're not checking to see if the coverlets are tucked up beneath my chin."

"But—but what about Fletcher? Doesn't he help you—"

A harsh bark of laughter breached Adam's lips. "Ah, yes. Fletcher, the ever vigilant. My bold compatriot who charges off to be protector of maidens in distress. The rock that will guard my back to the death. I returned here to find him curled up under that tree, sleeping like a bloody corpse. I'm damned certain he could doze away in the middle of a battlefield as long as a warhorse didn't trample over him. He's of no blasted use to me."

"But h-he's so devoted to you. Worships you. Anyone can see the bond between you."

"There is no bond except his uncle's full purse, so don't

be twisting it into any female sentimental nonsense. I'd guard the devil himself if the price was right."

"But where is Fletcher now?"

"I sent him to the inn to gather up our belongings. He should be back sometime after breakfast. At least, if he manages the task without getting into trouble." Slade's brows crashed together in a scowl. "Now, my question is this. What are you doing out here, wandering around in the rain? Hell, that's how I found your father, as well. What is it with you people?"

"It's not raining. At least, not anymore." Juliet drew herself up as primly as possible with her feet half buried in mud. "As for what I was doing, well, I had to go out to unlock the gate."

Sabrehawk's jaw went slack. *"Unlock* it? Are you insane?" He released her so abruptly she almost landed smack on her rump. His mud-spattered boots ate up the distance to the open gate.

Juliet stumbled after him, sputtering a protest. But before she could reach him, he slammed the iron portal shut with a crash so loud it should have shaken the shingles from the roof.

"Stop that!" Juliet cried, grappling for the iron bars. "No one can get inside if you close it." She might as well have battled with Achilles for possession of his heel.

Slade flattened one palm against the gate and threw the bolt with the other.

"Let go of this at once!" Juliet blustered. "You have no right—"

"You're damned right, I don't! But, fortunately, I don't give a damn! Now, you take your behind back inside that house before I carry you in and lock you in the pantry."

"Lock me—you—you—how dare you even—"

"What the blazes—" he snarled as lightning drizzled blue glow over her, those tempestuous eyes sweeping a scathing path down her body. "You're wearing an infernal *night-gown!"*

Juliet choked out a horrified cry, as the realization she'd lost her shawl in her struggle with Slade swept over her. She might as well be stripped bare for all the damp, mud-spattered garment did to conceal her body. If it weren't for the sheltering darkness . . . She crossed her arms over her breasts, stumbling back away from those piercing dark eyes.

"Oh, no, madam. You're not going to catch your death of lung fever out here! No more blood-vows or rain-soaked feverish tyrants ordering me about."

Swear words, so blue they should have blistered her ears rang out. But she didn't even have time to draw a shocked breath before sword-toughened hands closed around her waist. He launched her up and smacked her, belly down, across one broad shoulder.

She squawked, kicked, hammered with her fists against his back with all her might, but he only clamped an arm immovable as an iron manacle across her thighs to hold her. Then he strode through the night-shrouded garden like Hades dragging Persephone down into his dark kingdom.

When he reached the house, he gave the door to the kitchen a kick with his boot, and it swung open. In a heartbeat, he kneed it closed, then dumped her into the chair tucked in the nearest corner.

She scuttled across the wide seat to make her escape, but his hands clamped down on her shoulders, pinning her in a cage formed of chair-spindles and brawny masculine arms. His breath rasped, hot against her cheeks. His jaw knotted with fury.

Fury that spawned an answering rage deep down in Juliet's core. She tried to kick at him, but her bare feet only skidded harmlessly off his thigh. He planted his knee across her legs, holding her helpless.

"Let me go, or I'll scream," she vowed, outrage banishing all thought of her questionable attire. "Scream loud enough to bring every woman in this house down here."

"Do it! By God, I'll summon 'em myself. They probably know the safest place for me to lock you up in this accursed place. Hold still, damn you, and listen!" he growled. "The game is over, Angel Lady."

"G-Game? It's not a game!"

"You bet your infernal prayer book it's not! I spent some time at a place you might know of—a tavern called The Fighting Cock."

Juliet couldn't stifle the shudder that ran through her at the mention of that establishment. "I couldn't care less where you spend your time, as long as it's far away from here."

"Their main form of entertainment tonight has been planning what kind of hellish things they're going to do to you. How do you feel about this house being burned down about your head? Or how about a more fitting vengeance still? Giving you a taste of what these ladies have endured?"

What little blood remained in Juliet's cheeks drained away. Her stomach lurched. "I'm not afraid," she lied. "Threats . . . they're none of your . . . concern."

"That's right. You've heard all this before, haven't you? In those notes—those meaningless notes you consigned to the fire."

Juliet's heart was hammering its way out of her chest, her whole essence seemingly dwarfed, crushed by the pulsing power of Adam Slade's. "Why should you care what happens?"

"I shouldn't, damn it! You want to play Christian and feed yourself to the lions, I should just stand out of the way and ring the dinner bell."

His eyes flashed black fire. "Well, I can't, blast you to hell, no matter how much I might want to. You say you won't leave this rat trap? Fine. Then until Mother Cavendish and her horde are driven back into the hell they came from you'd better just get accustomed to having me shadow your every step. You aren't going to pick a flower, bake a biscuit or go to the privy without me being a sword's length away from you."

"There is absolutely no way I will tolerate that!" Yet despite those brash words, Juliet couldn't help the tremor of unease that racked her. The notion that this giant of a man—Adam Slade, Sabrehawk, who feared no man— should be frightened for her was more sobering than anything that had befallen her since she'd walked through the door to Angel's Fall.

It was easy enough to close her eyes against the danger when she was alone. But Slade was forcing her to examine things that made her quake inside. Possibilities so horrible she didn't know if she were strong enough to endure them, no matter how much she wished that she was. "Why can't you just go away? Pretend you never found me?"

"Because they are going to hurt you, woman. Badly. The instant they get the chance. And there's nothing you can do to stop them."

"But you can?"

"I already have," he said grimly. "At least for tonight."

He released her and turned away. Juliet tried to straighten her nightgown, her cheeks stinging as the wet cloth clung to her breast.

Adam stalked over to stir up the fire. It flared to life, tongues of flame dancing, shoots of light writhing up to tangle in the ebony waves of his damp hair, gild the sun-bronzed planes of his face, the hard curve of his mouth.

His mouth . . .

The outrage that had been sputtering in Juliet's chest died as her gaze locked on his lower lip. That blatantly sensual curve was just a little swollen, a fine red line splitting it near the left corner, a smear of fresh blood just beneath. Fire-shine danced over his brow, revealing a darkening bruise around his right eye, and a nasty scrape near his temple.

"You—you're hurt! What in heaven's name happened?"

"Percival broke a chair over my skull. Fortunately, I have the hardest head in Christendom."

"You were fighting?"

"Like the foul fiends of hell, lady, the odds seven to one."

"Those—those reprehensible, villainous . . . *curs!*" She scrambled up from her chair, flitting toward him like a wary, yet determined dove. "It's a miracle you escaped!"

"Escaped? Bah! They were the ones who turned tail and ran." Despite the injury, those lips pulled into a wolfish grin. "I'd wager the good sergeant will never make the mistake of underestimating me again."

A shiver of something foreign tingled deep in a secret part of Juliet's soul—the dark part, the unruly part that had been shuttered away by her father's saintly patience and gentle remonstrances.

Pleasure, heady and sweet and intoxicating that this man had battled those craven curs, faced them down and scattered them to the winds. Heaven forgive her, but Juliet would have given a year of her life to witness those scurrilous knaves, frightened themselves instead of terrorizing someone helpless. No wonder legends were filled with feminine glee at heroes riding back from doing battle.

She fought against the primitive surge of triumph no gently bred woman should entertain, praying that Adam Slade hadn't seen the flash of sinful delight in her eyes. Heaven forfend—he wasn't her champion. The only way she wanted to see Adam Slade was riding away from Angel's Fall, leaving her in peace. Wasn't it?

She avoided that too-keen gaze, dashing away her emotions by bustling about. "Let me tend your injuries at once! I won't have your wounds becoming putrid on my account."

"I've had worse splinters, Miss Grafton . . ." He started to scoff, then stopped, watching her for a moment out of heavy-lidded eyes. Awareness sizzled along her nerves. This man had fought for her. Interposed that hard-muscled body between her and her enemies. Been injured . . . and might have been killed. Tears stung her eyes.

Adam stared down at the gleaming droplets that clung to her lashes, seeing the gratitude in her eyes—reluctant yet undeniable. Only a son of a bitch would use that to his advantage. A knot of self-loathing tightened in his belly, but he stepped toward her, his legs wobbling, just a whisper unsteady, his hand groping out to brace himself against the table.

Juliet cried out, rushing toward him to steady him. "You can barely stand! Look at you! Sit down before you fall!"

"I'm not . . . going to fall." Adam acted as if he were mustering his strength of will, his brow furrowing with concentration, his teeth clenching until his jaw ached, but not half enough to drive away the sensation of self-disgust that stirred inside him. But hell—he had to find a way to get inside the blasted house, didn't he? To protect her for her own good? He might be play-acting now, but the savage hate in the faces at The Fighting Cock were no illusion. They were real. All too chillingly real.

"This is nothing," Adam insisted, brushing his cut lip with the tips of his fingers. "It's the tiniest scratch. And God knows, I'm such a scarred-up beast of a man, it wouldn't matter a damn if Percival carved his initials all over my body. But you . . ." He leaned heavily against the table. "I don't want to see this to happen to you, Juliet."

He could see the fear flicker in those celestial blue eyes. Knew in that instant that she understood more of what she faced than he'd imagined. He didn't want to respect her courage, her strength of will. But he did.

She crossed to a bench, gathering a bowl of water and a clean cloth. When she returned to him and placed her supplies on the table, her gaze was so earnest it wrenched at something buried deep, all but forgotten, in his heart. "If something bad befell me, it would be because of the path I've chosen. Freely, Adam Slade. Willingly."

"As I choose to protect you." He caught her hands in his, held them, tight. Blast, what a beast he was to prey on her this way. "Let me guard you, Juliet. You and your ladies."

He could see it in her face—a moment of sweet temptation before she withdrew her hands and shook her head in denial. "But you cannot say you have had a change of heart. You made it clear what you think of my quest here. That it is foolhardy and futile and—"

Her fingers fluttered to her throat, drawing Adam's gaze. Awareness shot through him, the muscles in his chest clenched as his eyes locked on Juliet's garb, his gaze heating so fiercely it should have sizzled the lace from her wrists and bodice. Light poured silver-blue down into the hollow of her throat, exposed by the open collar of the most angelic nightgown Adam had ever seen. One that would have tempted a guardian angel to sin.

It was all he could do to drag his eyes away from the delicate gown before he terrified her in her innocence. He swallowed hard, struggling to focus on her words, fashion a reply that made some vague sense.

"That will be our bargain if I stay. You can attempt to teach me how wrong I am. While I . . ."

"Can nail me in a barrel and ship me off somewhere?" she asked with a light laugh, retrieving the cloth and dunking it in the water.

He could think of a hell of a lot more appealing things to

do with her than lock her away in a keg. Holding her prisoner in a silk-lined bed, with the softest of chains wrought of his kisses. Where the devil had that thought come from? Adam's cheek burned in alarm.

"No barrels," he croaked out as she dabbed at the cut on his brow. "I give you my word as a former officer." She curved one soft hand beneath his jaw, tipping his face up to the firelight. Her fingers were feather light, stirring as brands, as they drifted across his swollen lip, delicately swabbing away the dried blood.

He flinched, and she gave a soft cry of regret, as if she'd hurt him. But she'd done worse than that. Adam's loins knotted, and he knew he needed only to turn his head a little bit to bury his lips in the soft dark cup of her palm. The image appalled him.

Blood and thunder, he had to make an end to this before he botched it beyond repair.

He groped for a plan, desperate. Then he hesitated, weighing a tactic in his mind, measuring the risk. A lieutenant colonel had once taught him that one of the best strategies for gaining someone's trust was sharing a vulnerability of one's own. It could be the most dangerous, or the most successful, of gambits. But he had little choice. Adam sucked in a steadying breath and cast out the dice.

"There is another reason I'm asking to stay here. Juliet, your ladies are not the only ones who are fugitives from their past."

"You are . . . running from something?"

Not nearly fast enough, he thought as her sweet brows arched in astonishment, concern. She was woman enough to adore some wild tale about his adventures, Adam thought. But for once, the truth would serve his purposes better.

"Not me. The boy."

She dropped the cloth back into the bowl of water. "Fletcher? He's like a great gallumphing puppy. What could he possibly be running from?"

Adam leaned forward, his hands framing her cheeks, his gaze burning into hers with the fierce fervor he knew no woman could resist. "Can I trust you, Juliet Grafton-Moore? Do I dare?"

Her pulse quickened under his thumb, and Adam felt his own mouth go dry, the need to press soft circles into the ivory satin of her skin astonishing him. He forced his fingers to stay still, concentrating on what he needed to accomplish.

"Fletcher's real name is Kieran O'Hara. There is a price on his head and a hangman's rope waiting for him in Ireland and a firing squad in France."

Horror drew an ash-hued veil over her face. "But he—he's only a boy! He . . . what could he possibly have done?"

"Attempted murder of a peer of the realm. Assaulting an officer."

"Stuff and nonsense! He'd have to be a monster! There's nothing of that kind of evil in his face!"

"You want evil, my lady, look into the eyes of his accusers. But it won't matter. If they get their claws in him, they'll hang him. Do you wish me to tell you the boy's story? All of it?"

"It doesn't matter. He's innocent. Anyone who looks in his eyes can see it is so." Adam felt a bitter stab of envy, wondered if he'd ever been so certain of the goodness in a stranger.

Still, telling Juliet the whole ugly tale could only help convince her to let them stay under her roof. He drew in a deep breath. "Kieran, or Fletcher, as the case may be, blew a sizable hole in the shoulder of a nobleman who had seduced his sister."

He saw Juliet's eyes flash with admiration and grimaced. "And here, I thought you abhorred violence," he muttered. It seemed Miss Grafton-Moore and Fletcher were two of a kind.

"Fletcher was most put out when the blackguard didn't die, and was damned determined to go back and finish the cur, but his uncle hired me to snatch him out of harm's way. The boy was eager to fight, so old O'Hara hoped Fletcher could make his way as so many other Irish exiles have done before him. Fighting another country's wars, spilling his blood for another man's cause."

"But then how did you end up in England?"

"My young charge is a trifle like a powder keg. I had delivered him to his regiment, and was downing a celebratory bottle of whiskey when I heard he'd pinked some colonel's son in a duel. The officer intended to fling the boy to the wolves. There are a hundred ways a commander can rid himself of a soldier if he chooses."

She shuddered. After so many years in the military, Adam knew he could tell her tales that would make her hair turn white. "But Fletcher is only a boy," she said.

"Boys are an expendable commodity in the army, my dear. It would have been one thing for the young fool to get his head blown off because of his own stupidity. Another thing entirely to be sent on a suicide mission because some spoilt military brat has gone whining to his papa. If I hadn't intervened, Fletcher would have been dead within the first week."

"So you *are* risking your life to protect him."

"I won't let you entertain any romantic notions about it. It only stands to reason that if his uncle had been willing to pay to keep Fletcher alive once, he'd be happy to do so again. I much prefer the boy stay alive so I can collect the fee.'

He was stunned to find himself wincing at the disappointment that clouded those incredible eyes at his words. "I expect to receive a second payment once we're settled somewhere. The problem is where to settle with him. He's guilty of attempted murder in Ireland and desertion in France. I had to come to England because of my vow to your father. There was nothing to do but bring the boy with me and try to keep him alive until his uncle decides what to do with him next. Miss Grafton-Moore, the Irish nobleman Fletcher shot has offered a sizable reward for his capture, and there are plenty of men greedy enough to take it. Angel's Fall would be the last place they would search for him. But if we continue battling our way through your enemies, and camp in your garden there is a good chance someone will recognize him. That is, if any of those employed in hunting him down should manage to trace our path to London."

She was pale, suddenly very still. "You're pressing an unfair advantage. Using Fletcher's plight to get your way."

"Maybe I am. That doesn't change the fact that I've told you the truth."

She paced away in an agony of indecision, gnawing at the full curve of her lower lip. Adam remembered all too well what it felt like to taste it.

In the end, her gaze flicked to the bruise beneath his eye, the cut on his lip. Blood and thunder, if he'd known they would get this much reaction from her, he'd have been tempted to break a chair over his own head.

"All right," she said, drawing in a shuddery breath. "You can stay."

It was all Adam could do to stifle a war-whoop of triumph.

"But there are conditions you must meet."

"I understand," he managed solemnly.

"I'm certain that Fletcher will respect the fragile state of my ladies if I explain it to him. I know he'd do nothing that might harm them."

"Without a doubt." But the boy would be in absolute agony in the meantime. Adam grimaced. Obviously the naive Miss Grafton-Moore had no idea of the volatile relationship between a sweet-faced youth and the demon he kept tucked beneath the flap of his breeches.

"You, however, pose a—a dilemma of sorts." Rose bloomed in her cheeks, her fingers plucking nervously at the wilted ribbon-tie that streamed in a blue river between the swells of her breasts.

"A dilemma?" Adam echoed hoarsely.

"You must understand that I cannot put the ladies at risk. They have worked so hard to put their pasts behind them, and your reputation is most disturbing."

"Would it be enough if I pledge you my word that I'll not be the fox that raids your hen house?"

"No." She frowned in concentration. "There is only one way to be certain nothing can happen."

Adam would bloody well like to hear it.

"You will take the bedchamber that adjoins mine."

"Yours?" Adam choked out.

"You recall my suite of chambers?"

He did. And it was no grand suite. More like a linen box tacked onto a child's room.

"I can sleep out in the room where my desk is, and you can have the smaller chamber. That way, there is no way out or in except by passing me."

Adam remembered all too clearly the cozy nook where her virginal bed had been tucked. But the idea of sleeping in there, with the scent of her all around him would be pushing the bounds of temptation too far. He'd been without a woman for—hell, who knew how long. And heroic self-denial had been more his honorable half-brother's trait.

"I don't think—I mean, I . . ." His blood was heating at the mere memory of what had occurred in that room hours before, the yielding of her breasts against his chest, the hot gasp of her breath captured in his mouth as he kissed her—and the instinctive reaction in that most masculine part of him, a hardening of need, a hungering for more.

"I assure you, I am a very light sleeper," she said. "I awaken at the tiniest sound."

"Juliet, I—after what happened between us . . ." He started to protest, knew he was on dangerous ground. He'd been angling for hours to be allowed into Juliet Grafton-Moore's inner sanctum. The woman had agreed to let him into the house. What was he doing? Trying to get her to boot him out the door?

"You only kissed me as a ploy. It's not as if you were attracted to me *that* way." She said, and he knew in that instant how reprehensible he'd been when he'd done it. That he'd bruised a tender corner of the woman she kept hidden behind the guise of angel. The problem was, he had been so attracted to her his whole body burned.

She crossed to the fire, and Adam groaned inwardly as fireshine shone through the delicate fabric of her damp nightgown, outlining the delicate shape of her body with its glow. A tiny waist, hips full enough, womanly enough to cradle a man, slender legs that seemed to go on forever, and breasts with rosy tips pressing kisses of temptation against silvery embroidery.

"What about your reputation?" he asked quietly.

"Everyone knows that I have no interest in—well, in carnal relations. I mean, I'm certain they are lovely in the bonds of marriage. Papa always said so. But—" She stumbled to a halt, her cheeks flooding with an especially kissable shade of pink. "I have my mission here, and it is the most important thing in my life. I would never allow anything to endanger it."

She gestured toward the corridor beyond. "I'll get you settled for the night. I'm certain you are anxious to get out of your clothes. I certainly want to get out of mine."

Color flooded her cheeks yet again.

"I mean—because they're wet," she choked out. "It's only natural to want to be rid of them." Then she glared at him, a stern line between her finely drawn brows, a dimple peeking from one cheek as a smile darted about the corners of her mouth. "Don't you dare laugh at me."

Adam was charmed by her humor.

"You needn't fear, Mr. Slade. I'm certain we'll rub along well enough. After all, it will only be for a little while. Do you think you can manage to get up to my bedchamber in the dark?"

"The dark?" he echoed, edgy with unexpected shame at the memory of how many times he'd slipped into other women's rooms—past fathers and zealous brothers and jealous lovers pure frothing for the chance to plant a sword-thrust through his heart—one more part of the sensual games they played.

He'd always taken almost boyish delight in scandalizing prim-nosed ladies with vague allusions to his adventures. Why was it the thought of Juliet knowing his notorious past made him feel old and jaded and somehow soiled.

"I'd light a candle, but there's no sense creating an uproar among the ladies tonight," she explained, sweeping a tendril of angel-gold hair from her cheek. "There is plenty of time for them to be astounded by the arrangement in the morning."

"Oh. I—I think I can manage to travel the stairs without breaking my neck," Adam allowed. "Lead the way."

She doused the candle he'd lit and locked the door,

casting one more glance at the rear gate. From the sudden determined angle of her chin, Adam realized that battle was far from over. For a second, he half expected her to argue with him again. But she left that for another time.

Then she turned and made her way out of the kitchen into the hallway, a slender wraith leading him up the stairs. An odd tightness bit at Adam's chest as shadow dipped its fingers into her curls, reminding him of their clinging silkiness. Ripples of angel-white floated against the darkness ahead. Once, Adam banged his boot against some object in the hall, and Juliet gasped, both of them freezing as a tinkle of prisms knocking together sounded like pistol shots in the stillness of the sleeping house.

Juliet turned, groping along his damp sleeve, until she found his large hand. She slipped hers into the cup of his fingers, like a trusting child, or a battlefield angel come to lead a war-weary soldier to a place where there was no more blood or death or terrified men battling for their souls.

Damn, what was he thinking such rubbish for? Adam brought himself up short with a throb of panic.

They would only be together a little while, just as Juliet said. Then why was it that any time in her presence suddenly seemed an eternity?

Bah! He'd just have to convince her to leave this place as soon as possible. And he'd have all day, every day to chip away at her resistance. It couldn't take that long to make her see reason, could it?

He cursed the sudden jolt of memory regarding the last time he'd tangled his fate with a determined good Samaritan—recalling his idealistic brother, a cave in Scotland, and the highlands crawling with troops hungering for Gavin Carstares's blood. In the end, Gavin had left that embattled land only because it was the one way he could save a dozen orphans and the woman he loved.

Hell, Adam realized grimly, he could be stuck at Angel's Fall forever! Eternally condemned to earnest blue eyes and ripe lips any man with the least vestige of honor would be a churl to kiss.

Adam closed his eyes, remembering that long-ago night

he'd stopped on the storm-swept Irish road. And he wondered if he could hear the faint sound of the vicar laughing.

Vicar? Maybe the old man hadn't been mortal at all. Maybe he had been an avenging angel come down to get Adam to atone for his sins. And the tiny chamber in Juliet Grafton-Moore's bedroom? That would be the perfect place for Sabrehawk's own especial hell.

Chapter
6

There was no door.

How could she have forgotten there was no door? Juliet lay stiff as a victim on the rack despite the feather tick Adam had carried in to make her bed. Eyes, gritty from lack of sleep, locked on the gaping archway that served as entrance to the tiny antechamber where he had disappeared hours ago.

To sleep—God knew, he'd probably been slumbering like Zeus enthroned upon his cloud-bed for hours now. While she had lain awake, her nerves a dreadful tangle, every fiber of her being aware that beyond that shadowy arch lay a mountain of muscle and sinew and arrogance with eyes like chips of midnight and a smile that could turn even the most staunch female heart wobbly as blancmange.

What in heaven's name had she been thinking of, blithely inviting this man to her bedchamber? In the months since she'd come to Angel's Fall, she'd heard the ladies refer to men as beasts of various kinds—but in a world of scurrilous curs and thieving jackals and ravening wolves, Adam Slade was a mesmerizing tiger, a fierce predator, as dangerous as he was beautiful. A hunter who made no attempt to hide the latent power that was twined, not only in his corded muscles, but in the shrewd labyrinth of his mind as well.

She shivered and clutched the coverlets tighter under her chin. Don't be absurd, Juliet, she muttered under her breath. He might be in her room, but there were conditions he'd agreed to abide by. He'd promised to remain what? An obedient tiger? Claws tucked cozily in his massive paws, fangs sheathed beneath that roguish smile? No small feat, especially when she knew for certain that *she* was the prey he was hunting, and that he'd journeyed halfway across England to find her.

Lord above, she'd never even been able to keep a pet when she was a child—the tiny puppy she'd smuggled into the vicarage had charged through its serene confines like a pirate raiding a treasure ship. It had chewed up three of her papa's favorite books, tugged his vestments from their hook and made a puddle on them, and crept into the church and made afternoon tea out of the gillyflowers Lady Shifferby had put upon the altar in honor of her dead mama.

As if those inquities weren't bad enough, the pup had made Juliet sneeze until the doctor and her papa had been alarmed for her health, and the mischievous bundle of fur had been banished to some other lucky little girl's arms.

If she couldn't handle one small puppy, how could she, for a moment, hope to control a potent male animal like Adam Slade?

She heard a rustling sound, the baritone rumble of a curse from the other room, then a guttural sigh.

Night time had always been solitary for her—no nursery full of siblings wrestling and jabbering before they drifted off to slumber. But these two rooms were so tightly packed together she had heard the buttons of his rain-dampened breeches hit the floor when he'd stripped them away. The images that had played in her mind at the noise were so scandalous her poor papa would have been much aggrieved.

And she had been brought to a swift, paralyzing realization of exactly what a calamity her rash impulse had plunged her into.

Merciful heavens, there was a mountain of naked man in the next room. And that was the least of her problems. What was it going to be like with Adam Slade underfoot every hour of the day and night? His oversize boots tramping about her bedchamber, his massive shoulders crowding at the dining table, his mocking laughter and granite-tough stubborness laying in wait for her in the drawing room and the garden, with no place she could go to escape his daunting presence.

And why had she consented to this disastrous arrangement? Because the man—who was a master of strategy—had spun out some heart-wrenching tale about Fletcher being in danger? Since the moment she'd arrived in London, there had been nothing but trouble. And lately it seemed every time she turned around another challenge was brewing, making things even more complicated than they already were. But this time she had a sinking sensation that she'd plunged into a raging river far over her head.

It wasn't as if she could bear-lead Adam Slade around like a governess with a particularly unruly charge. She had work to do, obligations she intended to keep. Like the one at the pleasure garden of Ranelagh tomorrow night.

Juliet ground her teeth. Of all the irritations and inconveniences that sprang from the threats and harassment she'd had to deal with, the most frustrating thing of all was the fact that the uproar they created had distracted her from the real work she needed to be attending to. Confronting the men who had victimized these ladies. Healing the wounds and opening the door to a new chance, a new future.

And now, with Adam Slade racketing about like a bellicose cannon, wouldn't everything be even more difficult? Six feet five inches of male bumbling around would hardly create an atmosphere that would inspire sharing confidences.

No. Her brows lowered in determination. She wouldn't let him interfere. Especially tomorrow night. It was far too important a mission. A delicate face drifted in the darkness above her, a wraith with haunted eyes reflecting so much pain, pain too intense to be shared.

Lord Foster Darlington and his cohorts had chosen the wrong lady to harass three days ago. It wouldn't be easy, but

Juliet would make certain they were reluctant to make the same mistake again.

Slade grumbled in his sleep, something thudding against the wall as he rolled over. Picturing the massive warrior, Juliet couldn't help a momentary twinge of pleasure in imagining the reprehensible peer's reaction if she were to approach with Adam Slade at her side.

She was human enough to know the dark part of her would enjoy seeing fear flicker into those exalted eyes. To see Darlington and his cronies stumble over each other to extricate themselves from the situation without seeming to be what they were: Bullies and cowards with no will to fight with someone who might be a match for them in a battle of swords or of wits.

Juliet shook her head, blotting out the appealing image, knowing how dangerous and seductive it was.

Her independence had been far too hard-won. And Slade wouldn't be at Angel's Fall forever. The most important lesson she wanted to teach these women was that they could handle any situation themselves, that they didn't need to rely on a man's intervention or protection. But she couldn't help smile at the image of her own guardian tiger, one who would charge out to do battle, right the wrongs that had been done to those more helpless than he.

A hero.

Even she was not naive enough to believe cynical Adam Slade could fill such a role. The mere notion of it would probably send him into gales of laughter. That or make him demand to know how much she'd pay him for his services.

She kicked at her coverlet in frustration, the restlessness that possessed her all but driving her mad. Throwing the bedclothes aside, she clambered up to her feet and jammed her fingers back through the tangled masses of her hair.

"Oh, Papa. What have I done now?" she murmured. "Worst of all, I lied to him, and to myself. I'm no light sleeper to stand guard over him. I doubt I'd awaken if he and Isabelle tipped over my dressing table on their way to an assignation. And I have to be awake to deal with that monster, Darlington, tomorrow night."

When it came right down to brass nails, how could she even be certain Slade wouldn't do what he had to Fletcher, nail her in a keg or roll her up in a rug and carry her out of Angel's Fall over one broad shoulder?

She jumped as a low growl came from the adjoining room, one that made her think of a tiger anticipating his next meal.

Saints alive, she had to think of some way to get through the rest of this eternal night. A method that would hopefully cleanse away the redness from her eyes, the grogginess from her brain.

What should one do with a tiger, once you got it in your room? she mused. Feed it. The thought sprang to her mind. But she didn't even want to think what Slade might be hungry for.

No, the most important thing with a tiger, she supposed, was to make certain it remained in its cage. They were prone to such nasty surprises if allowed to run wild. But how could she achieve that?

A sliver of moonlight streamed through the opening between her damask draperies, snagging on the array of articles arranged with such precision atop her dressing table. A veritable feast of metal and glass, objects that could make noise enough to wake the dead.

Grabbing up a heavy blue sash, she crossed to the table, slipping the thick length of ribbon through the handles of her sewing scissors, knotting the sash around her letter opener and a porcelain bell painted with violets, attaching the top of her ink bottle and the silver handle of her brush, all so close that stirring them would make a deafening racket. Then, she set the crowning jewel into her makeshift alarm. She tied the handle of the small iron Japanware tray on which Elise had brought up her tea that afternoon.

Juliet surveyed her work with some sense of satisfaction. Now the question was how to string it across the door. She grabbed two spindle chairs and arranged them against the wall, one on either side of the arched opening of Adam Slade's quarters. Then, with the greatest care, she strung her alarm between them, tying each end of the sash to one of the spindles. For a heartbeat, she was afraid the weight of the tray would overset the chairs, but after a moment, she heaved a sigh of relief.

"There. That should keep the tiger in its lair," she said, satisfaction stirring in the exhausted reaches of Juliet's mind. "Or at least, alert me when it comes stalking.

She crossed to her pallet, rejoicing in the fact that she'd somehow regained control of the situation. It seemed even Sabrehawk was no match for her after all. Sinking down into the feathertick, she was smiling just a little as she drifted off to sleep.

Light. It pried through the crack in the blue damask curtains. It wedged brilliant splinters under her eyelids and pricked at her with a dozen needles, alarm spilling in their wake. She was late. What was it she was supposed to do today? Prune back the roses? Mulch the healing herbs in the garden? No—it was her turn to stir up breakfast. If she were late, she'd never get the other ladies to do so on time.

She scrambled to her feet, rubbing her eyes with her knuckles, vaguely aware of her desk, the hearth. What had she done? Fallen asleep over some accounts? It wouldn't have been the first night she'd done so.

But she hadn't the least bit of energy to figure out the puzzle now. She had to pull on some clothes, race to the kitchen, and pray she could stir up something vaguely edible in half an hour or Isabelle would delight in an entire week of teasing her about it.

She stumbled toward the antechamber where her gowns were, nearly tripping over the hem of her nightdress. Bother! She had no time for this! She fumbled open the bodice, wrestling one sleeve from her arm as she hurtled toward the doorway. But at the last instant, a spark of metal glinting in a sun ray snagged her gaze, the events of the night before flooding back to her. She tried to slam to a halt, failed.

Bare feet skidded out from under her and she collided with the length of sash. It twisted around her waist. One chair smashed down on her as she struggled to keep the alarm from sounding, but she'd done her work all too well. She careened to the ground in a crashing, clanging mass of noise that would have awakened even the deafest old widow in Northwillow.

She barely heard a masculine roar of rage through the clatter, caught a glimpse of gleaming swordblade and a blur of sleek bronze as Adam Slade sprang from the antechamber, visions of her enemies doubtless dancing in his head. He curled his body around her, rolling her to one side, to protect her from an imaginary foe. But he only succeeded in tangling her ever deeper in the trap's coils.

"Picking on women again, you son of a bitch?" he snarled. "Fight me, man to man!"

"Adam! Wait! There's nobody here!" she choked out. Curses erupted near her ear, wood splintering, iron clanging in a wild racket all around her, a sword clattering to the floor. She heard the racing sound of feet, running toward the chamber, knew that in an instant there would be a plethora of people there. Merciful heavens, the ladies—they were charging toward the room!

The realization slammed into her as if the ceiling had disintegrated over her head. "Quick! Get us out of this! You have to get us out of this," she begged Slade, all too aware of hard sinews and silky-hot skin pressed against her own. Lord, it was bad enough that *he* should witness how idiotic she'd been! But for Isabelle and Elise and the others to see . . .

Humiliation exploded inside her as the bedchamber door flew open, every lady in Angel's Fall charging into her chamber.

Armed with a motley array of homemade weapons to rival her parasol from the day before, they spilled into the room—Elise and Millicent, Violet and Isabelle in front.

In the months since she'd arrived at Angel's Fall, Juliet had tried and failed to fight through the masks the ladies had learned to wear, to guard their emotions. But in that instant, they were stripped away.

Huge eyes stared down at Juliet and Adam tangled on the floor, mouths gaped open in disbelief. Elise's pistol clattered to the floor from shock-numbed fingers.

"Juliet?" the girl choked out amidst a chorus of gasps and cries of alarm.

"Bloody hell," Adam growled, grabbing Juliet and dragging her in front of him. She made a meager shield at best for such a mountain of a man. "This is not what it looks like."

"Is that so?" Isabelle demanded.

Juliet angled her gaze around until they fell on something far more disturbing than the faces in the doorway. A swath of bronze skin pulled taut over the corded muscles and shadowy valleys of a man's naked shoulder. Skin—hot, naked—burned like liquid satin against the place where her nightgown drooped off one bare arm, while a sinewy thigh prickly with fine dark hair imprinted itself in the soft column of her leg.

"You're—you're naked! Lord above!" Juliet gave a cry of alarm, tried to struggle away from him, but the trap of heavy satin sash was too tangled around them both.

"You're not particularly well covered yourself," Slade muttered, one arm curving beneath her breasts, crushing her against him like an iron band, the other fumbling to draw her nightgown bodice back up over a generous slice of bare breast. But the gown was pinned beneath her, and it was a futile effort.

"Let go of me!" she demanded, wriggling in an effort to get free.

"I can't," he growled. "Unless you decide to leave your nightgown behind. I'm bare as the day I was born."

Awareness jolted through her like a lightning-strike. The only thing between his nude body and her own was an infinitesimal web of fabric. If that was so, then the firm bulge pressing into her buttocks was . . .

She gave a horrified squeak, the notion of getting away from him was almost worth risking the horrific chance of catching a glimpse of naked male flesh. But she didn't dare expose Elise and the other women to such a thing.

She steeled herself to hold perfectly still. Fire spilled into her cheeks as she peered up at the gaggle of ladies. "Please, listen. I can explain."

"Sabrehawk, the Prince of Sin, naked in your bedchamber. Your nightgown hanging half off. I'd like to see you try to explain, *ma petite.*" Isabelle crossed her arms over what had once been called the most luscious breasts in France.

Juliet would have expected the Frenchwoman to pounce on this situation as if it were a tray full of her favorite French bonbons, reveling in a delicious bout of teasing. But not so much as a glimmer brightened those eyes that could dance with such unholy glee, no hint of bell-like laughter clinging about Isabelle's mouth.

Juliet gave another futile tug at the lace-edge of her shift, and met the older woman's gaze. "I came upon Mr. Slade in the garden last night when I was taking the basket of food out to the back gate. He had an altercation with some of the wretches who have been tormenting us. After discussion, we decided it would be best if Mr. Slade stayed at Angel's Fall for the time being."

"That doesn't explain why he's naked as the day he was born." Isabelle's eyes narrowed.

"My breeches were damp from the rain," Adam growled, "and though I probably should have spent the night wet and itchy and miserable in them, I took them off. That's all there is to it."

"Isabelle, fie on you!" Violet objected. "You cannot be hinting that our Juliet has been seducing Sabrehawk!"

"Look at her, for Christ's sake," Adam blustered. "Does she look like the kind of woman I'd fling myself at in a fit of passion? I prefer my women a trifle older and more worldly-wise."

Juliet had no idea why a swift surge of hurt should rise in her breast at his dismissal.

"Perhaps in the future you should confine yourself to the bedchambers of women who know what to do with that magnificent weapon of yours?" Isabelle snapped.

"Stop it, Isabelle! This isn't the time for such games," Elise quavered. "Let Juliet explain." Great chocolate-brown eyes turned to her with the desperate hope of a child who wants her mama to reassure her that the tooth-drawer won't hurt her or that a lost kitten will come home. Juliet's greatest terror had always been that she would somehow fail Elise.

"Juliet, why is he here?"

"Because, you see, he—" Juliet started to explain, stopped, suddenly helpless. Her gaze darted over her shoulder to clash with Adam's dark eyes. Eyes clouded with warning, caution. Saints above, what could she say? She could hardly tell them the truth, that Fletcher was being hunted, a fugitive. No one knew better than she did how unguarded her ladies' tongues could be. It would be unexcusable to put the boy in more danger. Especially for so weak a cause as to quell their gossip.

"Explain it to us, Juliet." Isabelle's winged brow arched over one lovely eye, its jewellike brilliance suddenly glittering, hard. "No men are allowed here. 'Tis the first rule. I remember you drumming it into my head most insistently the first night I arrived on your doorstep. And last night you reiterated it quite clearly."

"I know," Juliet said, groping for something to sweep away the brittle challenge in the older woman's face. "But you don't have to worry about Mr. Slade, I promise you. He will lodge here, in my chambers. He won't be a threat to your reputations."

"Eh, bien. But what about yours? There is to be a different set of rules for you, is that how it will be? The angel so far above us sinners can entertain a dozen men in her chambers if she wishes. Isn't that a trifle hypocritical?"

"Stop!" Elise pleaded. "You cannot say such things about Juliet." But Juliet couldn't help knowing what Isabelle said was true. From the beginning, these women had teetered with one foot in each world. The world of carnal pleasuring they had inhabited for so long—terrible, yet familiar—and the other, a chance at the fresh beginning Juliet offered. Juliet had always realized it would take only the tiniest push to shove them either way. That most of the women still hung in the balance, undecided . . . afraid . . . Could Juliet be making a fatal mistake?

"He kept the mob from overrunning this place yesterday," Millicent said. "I think we should let him stay."

Juliet could feel Slade's muscles tense against her back and buttocks. "I'm staying here to protect Miss Grafton-Moore, protect all of you from the slime who want to hurt her. That is my sole purpose for lodging at Angel's Fall."

"But our Juliet has made it clear we're to protect ourselves," Isabelle insisted with a wave of one beringed hand. "You may gather up your things, *monsieur*. We have no need of your services."

"It is my decision to make, Isabelle," Juliet said firmly. Though why in heaven's name she wasn't using the Frenchwoman's reaction as an excuse to oust Adam from Angel's Fall she had no idea.

"Both Mr. Slade and Mr. Raeburn will be residing here for the time being, and that is final." She saw the women exchanging uneasy glances, while Isabelle's eyes grew strangely flinty.

"Now," Juliet continued, "if you would all leave so that Mr. Slade and I can . . . can get dressed, we can finish this discussion at the breakfast table."

"We might as well spend breakfast jabbering, since we'll certainly not be eating anything," Isabelle sniped. " 'Tis your turn to make the meal, Juliet, and I doubt you have it steaming on the back of the stove. Of course, Violet and Millicent and I, we must—"

"Enough!" Millicent grasped Isabelle's arm. "Get out, now as Juliet asks."

One by one, the women drifted away, but Juliet knew she'd remember forever the expressions on their faces— disbelief, disillusionment, and confusion. The only thing that was certain was that suddenly the rules had changed, and that had unsettled them all.

Elise paused at the doorway, two hot spots of color on her wan cheeks. "Juliet, do you—do you wish me to remain? To help untangle you."

The prospect was horrific. Elise flinched when she faced a fully clothed man on the street. Juliet knew the depth of loyalty in the girl, offering to confront a naked Adam Slade.

Juliet swallowed hard. "No. I'm certain we'll be able to manage just fine."

The girl exited, casting back one worried look before she shut the door. The instant she disappeared, Juliet started wrestling against the bindings.

"Ouch!" He grabbed at his lean middle. "Bloody hell, something *bit* me!"

"The scissors," Juliet explained, pulling their gleaming silver points away from his flesh.

"Blast and damn, what are your scissors doing strung across my doorway?" he demanded incredulously. "For that matter, what's the rest of this junk clattering about for? It almost looks as if someone set it up on purpose."

"I did."

"Why?" Adam growled, plucking at the blue ribbon. "What the devil is this contraption?"

"A trap," she admitted, abashed. "I made it out of my sash to catch you if you should decide to roam about."

"A *trap*," he enunciated slowly, starting to untangle it with one hand. "What a relief. For a moment, there, I thought it was some odd fashion you females had cooked up. This snare was damned resourceful, angel. Except that you caught yourself. In a beastly compromising position, I might add. Thank God I'm not some noble gentleman, or the two of us would be on our way to the altar right now."

The prospect would have been enough to chill Juliet to her marrow, if it hadn't been for an unexpected, hot prickle of excitement in some hidden part of her. But Slade had already brushed the subject aside and was groping for the bedclothes dangling off her feathertick.

"Can you reach a hank of that sheet?" he asked.

She scooted over a bit, Adam following, his other hand still clamped on the bit of nightgown. And Juliet was struck again by what a meager shield she made for such a large helping of masculinity.

"Blast, we're never going to get out this way," Slade groused. "The devil with modesty. Just close your eyes."

Juliet screwed her eyelids tight. She heard the sound of fabric ripping, felt that hard hot body disengaging from hers one heavily muscled limb at a time. The japanned iron tray gave a ringing bong as it wobbled down onto the floor, the remains of a porcelain bell giving an off-key tinkle. There was a whisking sound as he grabbed up something, doubtless to cover himself.

"You can open your eyes now," he said.

Under any other circumstances she might have found it outrageously amusing, the mighty Sabrehawk, legendary swordsman, standing there with his hips swaddled in one of her cast-off petticoats, his face thunderous with aggravation and chagrin. But it only made him look all the more masculine, potent and powerful and dangerous.

Despite her burning humiliation, Juliet was mesmerized by sleek sinew and bulging muscle, a warrior's body—hard-used in battle, honed into a weapon of human flesh, still bearing the pale white tracks of scars carved by other men's swords. Men, Juliet knew instinctively, who had not lived to wield their weapons against any other foe.

"They would have had to find out about this arrangement somehow," he said, tightening his grip around the cascade of beribboned fabric.

"I suppose so." Juliet climbed to her feet. "But I would have preferred to discuss it when we were both fully clothed."

"They'll get used to the situation in no time. As for their doubts, they'll dismiss them soon enough. Only a lunatic could believe anything could arise between the two of us— the angel and the sinner."

Surely he was right. Why did that certainty make her a trifle sad? And why did she keep chafing over the censure in Isabelle's eyes?

She chewed at her lower lip, tired and troubled, uneasy at the memory of the expression on Isabelle's face. Was it possible that by allowing Adam Slade to remain at Angel's Fall she'd shaken the foundation of everything she'd built here? Broken faith. Trampled trust.

Juliet has made it clear we're to protect ourselves— Isabelle's words echoed in her mind. She'd worked so hard to instill that sense of self-reliance in these women, women imprisoned by society's idiotic views and their own crippling self-doubt of confidence in their own strength.

It had been a grueling battle. A never-ending one— defying the dictates of society. And from the moment Isabelle had arrived at Angel's Fall, she'd been the most resistant to the new philosophies. The first to dismiss such preachings with a jest and a mocking laugh. She had seemed almost eager, anticipating the crumbling of Juliet's convictions when they crashed headlong against the doctrine of the real world.

Then why had Juliet seen such a sense of betrayal buried in the courtesan's eyes moments ago? Just a flicker of disillusionment from a woman so cynical Juliet was certain she believed in nothing, in no one. Not even herself.

It would be all right, Juliet assured herself uneasily. She'd calm Isabelle's misgivings through her actions. Make certain Adam Slade did not interfere in the workings of Angel's Fall. She would remain in control, not abdicate her authority, her responsibilities, or even surrender the threats made against her to this hulking warrior of a man. Beginning with her confrontation with Lord Darlington tonight.

She paced to her desk, opening the tiny drawer, her fingertips running over the golden petals of her mother's necklace as though it were a talisman.

She couldn't fail. She'd done so before, and her father had suffered. Papa and Jenny. She closed her eyes, remembering flyaway copper curls and a smile so bright it could light up the world.

Remembering a desperate search mounted after it was too late.

No. She'd never fail that way again. Especially tonight.

Because if she did, innocent Elise would pay the price.

Chapter

7

If Adam had to listen to women's chatter for one more minute, his head would explode. He pressed his fingertips against his temples, Millicent's tinkling laughter making him grind his teeth. Fletcher sat before the lady, a study in youthful captivation, his eyes glistening with fervor, his cheeks blushing every time Millicent spoke to him—an all too frequent occurrence during the endless hours of the day.

It seemed they were to be flooded with women, drowned in them, overrun by them—except for the one woman he needed to see.

If Adam had hoped to plead his case with Juliet, pressure her into leaving Angel's Fall, he'd been thwarted at every turn. For after a breakfast so tense even the mouse under the table couldn't eat, she'd bustled off in a flurry of activity, brushing him aside as if he were a bothersome fly.

"I have work to attend to, Mr. Slade," she'd said with crushing determination, then she'd disappeared into a whirlwind of lessons—cooking lessons and lessons in reading, mending, and stitchery. She'd presided over the household like a militant mother hen, barely sparing a glance to the two men underfoot, while most of her ladies squabbled over everything from who was to do the dishes to what was supposed to be baked for tea.

He should have been relieved things were so calm. After all, there was a small chance Juliet could be attacked inside the house. But instead he'd felt tension coiling tighter in the back of his neck as the day wore on, a dull throbbing in the old wound in his left thigh—sure signs that trouble was brewing.

He levered himself to his feet, pacing the drawing room, feeling suffocated with lace and ribbons and women's furbelows. But maybe his problem was that he remembered all too clearly the feel of a female body without the mountains of padding and petticoats, whalebones and lacings, that were supposed to come between a man and a proper lady.

Somehow, despite all the amorous liaisons Sabrehawk had experienced, the most bone-melting, soul-searing contact he'd ever had with a woman had been when he'd found himself trussed up like a roasted partridge with a vicar's daughter. He just hadn't realized it until he spent the entire day recalling the lush curve of her half-bared breast, the delicious weight of her against his chest, the heaviness she'd caused to gather in his groin.

The windows were catching fire with sunset. Blast, where was the woman? He could hardly begin his campaign to extricate her from the city if she wouldn't even speak to him.

"Where is Miss Grafton-Moore?" the demand sprang, unbidden, and more than a little gruff from his lips.

"I believe she had some sort of engagement tonight," Violet stammered. "It's impossible to keep track of where she buzzes off to."

"Yes," Millicent added. "But she was putting her fighting bonnet on."

"Her fighting bonnet?" Fletcher echoed.

"The black one she wears whenever she's off to beard the lion in its den. It doesn't suit her at all, and it's monstrous severe," Violet offered.

"Perhaps I should find out exactly what mischief she's getting into," Adam snapped.

"She won't thank you for it, that I promise you," Millicent said, nibbling at her bottom lip. "She doesn't like interference."

He muttered a questionable suggestion of what she could do with her objections and stalked out of the chamber. But when he reached Juliet's room, the woman and her objectionable bonnet were nowhere to be found. What he did find, however, sent a chill scuttling down his spine.

Elise was curled up at Juliet's desk, trembling like a doe with a wolf's jaws about its throat.

"Where is Juliet?" Adam demanded, the tension in his neck knotting tighter.

"She went out . . . I begged her not to. She said they wouldn't dare hurt her with so many other people around, but I think they'd all be glad if something bad happened to her. All of them."

Hellfire, the woman was already gone! He wanted to bellow at Elise, but feared that one roar from him would shatter the girl. "You're not making any sense. Where did she go? What mischief is she up to?"

"Ranelagh Gardens. He's got a box there for tonight. He and the duchess. She—I don't know why she has to face him, to—to . . ." Elise's throat clenched in a wrenching spasm. "It's my fault. I should have kept her from finding out. Maybe if I'd given Millicent my bit of lace she wouldn't have told."

"Told what? Blast it, what happened?"

"L-Lord Darlington and his friends. They—they came upon me while I was at the market a few days ago and—" The silence was dark and damning.

Adam's gut clenched with raw fury. "What did they do?"

"Nothing, really. Just . . . just forced a kiss on me, and pinched my bodice—" She gave a sick shudder. "Told me what I already know. That I'm not pretty. Not anymore."

Adam's blood thickened with fire, muscles tensing with the need to smash something—preferably Darlington's face. "And Juliet?"

"She intends to take him to task before the duchess and everyone in his party. Intends to shame him."

Thunder and fire! The whole time he'd been downstairs

grinding his teeth in frustration, Juliet had been plotting mutiny. No wonder half of London was ready to dangle her from Tower Bridge. Damn little fool. Damn brave-hearted little fool.

"How long ago did she leave?"

"An hour. She rode off by herself on her mare."

"She's ranging through London at night by herself? Hell, if Darlington doesn't murder her, God knows who will. Half the city would give its right hand to catch her alone!" Adam raged, stalking into his part of the room, scooping up his sword and scabbard, belting them around his waist. "You know how much danger she is in! Why the blazes didn't you tell me?"

Tears welled up in chocolate-brown eyes. "She made me swear I wouldn't."

In that moment, Adam was certain that if Elise had been placed on the rack, she'd never betray her lady. What kind of woman was Juliet Grafton-Moore, to inspire such fierce love and devotion and loyalty, such scorn and outright hatred?

And what was happening to her now? Alone somewhere in the vast London night?

He started to stalk to the door, heard the softest whimper behind him. He turned back to see Elise's face buried in her hands, her molasses-colored tresses tumbling around her shoulders.

He'd always been damned bad at comforting weeping women. But he crossed to Elise, laying one scarred hand upon her curls.

"Don't worry. I'll find her."

"You will, won't you? You won't let anything happen to her. She doesn't know how—how awful it can be. She's never learned to—to be afraid."

Fletcher was waiting in the entryway as Adam charged down the stairs.

"What is amiss?"

"The infernal woman has gone on some brainless quest. I have to stop her. Saddle up my horse."

"As soon as I get my sword. I'm going with you."

That was all he needed—Fletcher charging about, sword

flailing. Hell, his nerves were so taut at the moment Adam was afraid *he'd* bludgeon the youth in frustration.

"No. You have to stay here. Juliet's enemies won't know she's left the house. And there's no way to know when those cowardly curs might strike, or where. You have to guard the house and the ladies inside it." He saw the boy getting balky as a farmyard mule.

"You just want to be rid of me—brush me out o' harm's way as if I were a raw lad. I won't be shunted aside—"

"Fletcher, you'll damn well stay put! I need to know you're here to watch over things. I trust you."

At the word *trust*, the boy seemed to grow a full two inches in height. "That's it, is it? You're not lyin' to me?" His Irish lilt slipped through, making him sound even more boyish and so oddly vulnerable it tugged at a raw place in Adam's chest.

"Why the devil would I bother to lie?" *I'd have to care about the boy to lie.* A frisson of unease spread across Adam's shoulders.

"But who'll be watchin' your back? You're not as young as you once were."

Adam grimaced, embracing the familiar prickling of irritation with something akin to relief. "I'll just have to manage on my own, won't I? Now, go get that infernal horse!"

The boy raced off, leaving Adam with his own chaotic thoughts.

Blast and damnation, how was he ever going to find Juliet in the mayhem of Ranelagh Gardens? Throngs of people, insanity everywhere. And in the darkness to make matters worse.

But he knew exactly where to find her. At the box Lord Darlington had reserved, getting into an abundance of trouble. He knew enough about the ways of the aristocracy to know they did not suffer public humiliation calmly. Especially from what they considered social inferiors. Even an innocent like Juliet had to realize that.

Yet, did she have any idea what lengths such men might go to in order to silence a slandering tongue? No one knew better than Adam that wealth could buy anything—a sword-blade in the night, a silent death while sleeping in one's own bed. Or punishments far worse—tortures so slow and diabolical an angel like Juliet could never begin to imagine them. And when wealth was mingled with power . . .

Adam grabbed up his cloak, swirling it around his shoulders with a grim scowl.

What was it Elise had said? Juliet Grafton-Moore hadn't learned to be afraid.

It didn't matter. Adam suddenly realized he was afraid enough for them both.

Ranelagh Gardens glittered like a duchess's jewel box. Ladies in elegant confections of satin and lace flirted above the delicate scallops of painted fans, their hair teased and powdered into impossible masses of curls piled so high it seemed their necks must snap.

London's most notorious beaux meandered down lantern-lit pathways, their handsome figures draped in their finest garb as they minced along on shoes with dazzling buckles, black velvet patches affixed to their cheekbones, debauchery on their minds.

Juliet shivered beneath the folds of her simple cloak, feeling like a drab gray moth among an explosion of gay butterflies. Quite invisible among the crowd.

She'd never seen the famed Pleasure Gardens before, but she'd dreamed about them during the long winter nights at the vicarage. She'd seen the beauty of that famed site reflected in Jenny's sparkling gray-green eyes as tales were spun out over the drawing-room hearth. Glorious, breathtaking tales of dashing men and their glittering lady-loves that had danced into the corners of Juliet's mind that had previously been occupied by her father's serious sermons and gentle attempts at guidance.

Jenny.

The distant cousin who had come to the vicarage to escape the whispering of scandal, and to be "improved" by serving as Juliet's companion. Yet instead she had opened doors inside Juliet she'd never realized were closed, revealing worlds Juliet had never even begun to imagine.

Jenny had glowed as she rhapsodized over all the wonders

she'd seen. And in the months she'd come to live at the vicarage, she'd dragged all such marvels into the staid little house in her wake, like a trailing cloak of the most magnificent hues ever woven.

In those delicious months Juliet had been desperate, eager to gather up every drop of sunshine Jenny had brought, as if it were some mystic elixir from another world. A world as fantastic as the fairy tales she'd read. And as far beyond Juliet's reach.

But now she saw past the glitter and the laughter and the music, and understood far too well how they could lure the unsuspecting, like a moth to a flame. Beauty—there was that in abundance. But also, destruction.

A pair of macaronis, dressed with impossibly ludicrous elegance, teetered past, the absurd dandies all but tripping over her as they ogled the ample bosom of an opera dancer strolling by.

"Dull little bird," one of them dismissed Juliet, pulling a sour face.

She shouldn't have minded. Heaven knew, the last thing she wanted was admiration from two such ridiculous figures. The last thing she wanted was admiration from any man, wasn't it? Yet it was Adam Slade's scoffing dismissal that sprang to her mind, bringing with it an echo of unexpected hurt.

And a thick lump of dread that lodged beneath her ribs.

Lord, instead of indulging in this preposterous melancholy over his reaction to her charms, her frazzled emotions would be far better employed in wondering what kind of fury he'd kick up if he ever learned of her trip to these gardens.

No, Juliet brought herself up short, her heels clicking with renewed militancy on the pathway. She shouldn't be thinking of Adam Slade at all. She should be thinking of Elise, the shame that had enveloped her like an unholy aura, the fear that had clouded her eyes, and the terrible burden she'd suffered, trying to keep it secret.

She should be concentrating on finding Lord Darlington, and confronting him. A number of inquiries led her to a row of boxes in the grand rotunda, the most festive of all led by a handsome man of about thirty-eight, dripping jewels and arrogance. His powdered wig was curled to perfection, tied with a silver ribbon, his white frockcoat and breeches trimmed with silver *galon* that glinted like ice in the sun. But the effect of deep-set eyes and a patrician nose were spoiled by just a hint of cruelty playing about the weak curves of his mouth.

Juliet watched the man, all but certain she'd found her quarry.

"Pardon me," she said, stopping a spritely servant. "Can you tell me who that gentleman is? The one in the ice-white frockcoat?"

"That be Lord Darlington. And the lady, there is the Duchess of Glynne and her daughter. Darlington's just gotten himself betrothed to the girl and is celebrating right proper tonight." The servant looked at Juliet, taking in her simple garb, then gave a conspiratorial wink. "Can't blame him. Earned a bleedin' fortune in the bargain."

Juliet felt a twinge of discomfort as her gaze skimmed over the features of the young woman at his lordship's side—a conservatory-bred rose of a girl, pruned and tended, fussed over and spoiled, yet unmistakably beautiful, and innocent in this disaster. The thought that she might merely be a means to settle gaming debts was repugnant. Juliet genuinely regretted the hurt a public scene might cause her. And yet, wouldn't it be better for Darlington's betrothed to discover the truth about her intended husband before the wedding ring was on her finger and it was too late to escape him?

The servant nudged her and pulled a sour face. "'Course, no doubt the entire affair will be paid for with the duchess's coin." His voice dropped to a conspiratorial whisper. "Darlington gets a nice enough income, but he's ever squandering it away on prime horseflesh, absurdly expensive garments to rig 'im out, and lights o' love for entertainment."

Juliet's lips compressed in a thin white line at the memory of how he and his friends had entertained themselves at Elise's expense. She slipped the servant a shilling, then sucked in a steadying breath, heart hammering, stomach churning. Her fingers knitted together, clutching tight to still the trembling of anger and outrage that beset them every time she sought out this sort of confrontation.

She glimpsed the duchess patting one of her daughter's curls into place—not with the brisk efficiency of one who disliked any imperfection, but rather, it was the tender touch of a mother, eager for any excuse to surreptitiously caress a child who was grown.

Juliet couldn't fight a twinge of longing, remembering the last touch of her own mother's hand, frail and wasted yet indescribably gentle before death had scooped her into it's ghostly-white arms. *Do not be afraid, little one. Every time you feel the wind upon your face, it will be my spirit, kissing your cheek.*

Had Elise ever known a mother's worship-filled touch? Was her mother weeping, even now in heaven over her daughter's plight? Or was her mother one of the hideous beasts she'd stumbled across all too often in the London streets, eager to trade a daughter's budding beauty for a half pint of Blue Ruin. That secret was locked with the rest of Elise's past behind gates of pain reflected in her dark eyes. But it didn't matter now, Juliet resolved. Elise had her to come to her defense.

Lifting the veil that concealed her face, Juliet draped the delicate webbing back over her bonnet and straightened her shoulders as she approached Darlington's box.

"Lord Darlington?" Her voice, clear and insistent, cut through the babble of the throng; all eyes, from the duchess's to Lord Darlington's lovely fiancée's turned toward her, regarding her with the mild astonishment of pedigreed dogs who had just discovered a raggedy cur in their midst.

"I am Lord Darlington," the gentleman allowed, a faint sneer in the curl of his lip. "Though that can be none of your concern."

"I fear you are wrong. There is a matter of the utmost importance we must discuss."

"And what, pray tell, is that?" he asked.

Juliet's chin jutted up. "A debt you owe."

"A debt?" Darlington blustered. "God's teeth! Cannot a peer of the realm even enjoy a night of diversion without being plagued by tradesmen! You should be grateful I even patronize your paltry shop! For your impudence, you may wait until hell freezes over for payment."

"I have no shop. And the debt you owe cannot be paid by something as simple as coin."

Darlington took a pinch from his emerald-encrusted snuffbox, and lifted it delicately to one chiseled nostril. "You have grown quite tiresome. Perhaps I should summon a servant to eject you from the premises. I have no intention of allowing you to upset the duchess and her daughter."

"You are the picture of chivalry, I am sure." Disgust laced Juliet's voice. "I am sorry for any distress I might cause them. But in my opinion it would be far worse for them to be upset later, when nothing could be done to mend it. Their regret would be far greater."

The duchess arose in all her splendor, her proud daughter at her side. "I dislike veiled accusations! Do the lower classes have no respect for their betters anymore?"

Juliet looked at the older woman, prying beneath the veneer of cold hauteur that years of preparing to take her place in society had glossed over her handsome features. Juliet fixed her hopes on the fact that the hand that had rested ever so briefly on the daughter's head was that of a loving mother.

"Your Grace, Lord Darlington is not a man to warrant esteem or respect. No man who treats a woman as he has should be given such accord."

"Treats a woman—God's Feet! What did I do, madam?" Darlington straightened the lace of his neckcloth with a laugh. "Tramp on your toes in my haste to get to my beloved's side? Splash your cloak with mud from my carriage wheel?"

Juliet turned her gaze to Darlington's face. "You and three of your associates pinned a helpless girl in an alley and used her most unforgivably."

The outraged chatter of the other guests shifted into coughs and gasps and murmured denials. The duchess's face went white. But it was her daughter's tiny cry that made Juliet wince.

"See here, young woman!" A portly papa blustered, all

but diving to clap his hands over his gap-toothed daughter's ears. "Enough of this insolence!"

"Don't be absurd!" Darlington scoffed in a brittle laugh, but his powdered pale face whitened another shade. "Why would a gentleman of my caliber lower myself to such depths? Especially when my betrothed is the most lovely woman in London?"

"I cannot begin to guess," Juliet said. "Perhaps you should tell me."

"You will leave these premises at once," the duchess ordered imperiously, "before I have you flung out for these ridiculous accusations!"

"No, Mama." Miss Stonebridge sprang from her seat, capturing Darlington's sleeve, turning hazel eyes incredibly young and surprisingly sweet toward Juliet. "Please, miss, I am very sorry for this poor girl who was hurt, but there must be a mistake. I assure you, Foster is the very soul of gallantry." A brave smile curved her lips. "Isn't it possible there was a mistake?"

In that instant, Juliet wished that there were. "No. I am sorry, but the lady in question identified Lord Darlington in absolute certainty."

"Posh!" Darlington scoffed. "In the dark? How could she recognize——"

"She was once your mistress."

Juliet hated herself for the ashen hue of the girl's cheeks, the wounded light in her eyes. She strained to remember that she had not been the one to put it there, that Darlington was the betrayer. She turned her gaze back up to the nobleman, hating him with a virulence that would have saddened her papa's heart. "And if you want to guess which of us is lying, Lord Darlington, may I point out that I never mentioned that the incident occurred in the dark. Strange that you should know it did."

The nobleman's eyes bulged, his cheeks a sickly pink beneath their layer of powder. "How dare you accuse me of lying! The woman was a whore! She accosted me on the streets! By God, if she was bruised in the process it was because I was trying to yank her skirts back down over her——"

"You and three of your friends pinned her against the wall by Tarleton's Fishery. You ripped her bodice open and jeered at her because she is no longer beautiful. A shrunken cat, you called her, because she is skin and bones and can barely eat because of the pain you caused her."

"What the devil? Is that what that bitch told you?"

"One of my other ladies came upon Elise afterward, found her cowering in that corner, holding her bodice together, sobbing."

"Isn't it possible she tempted some sailor and he got too rough?" Darlington sneered. "She is a whore. Once a whore, forever a whore."

"I beg to differ." Juliet turned back to the duchess. "Your Grace, I am Juliet Grafton-Moore, the mistress of a place called Angel's Fall. It is a home for prostitutes and courtesans who have lost their way. Women who are attempting to rebuild their lives. I've been having some success. I desperately hope to have more."

"I have heard of you!" the duchess said. "The house is on Crompton Street."

"It might as well be on Jester's Row," one of Darlington's compatriots interrupted. "She is a laughingstock neck deep in harlots! By glory, the article in the *Spectator* regarding her absurdities had every man at White's in gales of laughter."

But Darlington was definitely not laughing now. "I must insist that you leave our party in peace, Miss Grafton-Moore—"

"Your Grace," Juliet appealed to the duchess. "The girl in question is a gentle soul, trying to rebuild her life. Never have I met one more determined to put her past behind her, or more horrified by the mistakes she'd made in the past. She is suffering terribly. And is so afraid of all men, any men that I assure you she would never attempt to entice—"

"This is not for my daughter's ears! Have you not the slightest scrap of decency? Exposing her to such a creature?"

"Elise was once very much like your daughter. Innocent. Trusting. The one difference between them is the fact that your daughter is fortunate enough to have you to protect her from men who would take advantage of her helplessness."

"Of all the impudence!" The duchess quivered with outrage, but Juliet saw the sick cast to her features.

"You are a woman, Your Grace. For all your power and exalted station, you know how defenseless a lone woman can be."

Darlington gave a snort of derision. "For God's sakes! The streets are full of such women. I had the ill luck to stumble across Elise. I took what she offered, and paid generously for the folly. Not an admirable act, perhaps, but one almost any gentleman you might name has indulged in upon occasion. It happened long before Miss Stonebridge and I met. The rest of these accusations are just some Banbury tale the girl brewed up to make mischief."

He leveled a scornful glare at Juliet. "Frankly, madam, if I were you, I'd not get so distressed over the tales Elise tells you. After all, she might be confusing me with one of countless gentlemen she's serviced."

It was the curl of contempt in his lip that did it, dismissing Elise so callously that Juliet's fiercely held control snapped. She grabbed up a pitcher of wine from a tray and dashed it onto the snowy white of Darlington's exquisite frockcoat, the pewter pitcher banging down onto the floor.

A roar emanated from those inside the box, shrieks and cries that sent servants bolting toward Juliet as red wine ran down Darlington's body like blood.

Rough hands clamped on Juliet's arms, two of Darlington's burly footmen bruising her with their grip.

The glare Darlington turned on Juliet left no illusions as to the depth of cruelty he was capable of. "Barnes, this woman accosted me. You will remove her at once and teach her the proper way to behave toward her betters."

A look of complete understanding flashed between servant and master, chilling Juliet's blood.

"Unhand me at once," she demanded in her most imperious voice, struggling against the servant's viselike grip.

"You all saw her," Darlington raged. "She assaulted a peer of the realm! I vow, she should face the magistrate."

"Please, Foster." The duchess's daughter intervened. "Let her go. Misguided as she might be, I . . . I do not wish her harmed."

He gazed furiously at his intended bride. "After what she's accused me of? After what she's done you would have me let her go?" He waved one beringed hand at the ruin of his frockcoat and scowled. "This does not speak well of your loyalty toward me, my love."

"It's obvious there has been a terrible mistake." The girl flushed, and the one thing Juliet regretted was the sting of hurt and disillusionment she'd put in Miss Stonebridge's eyes. "This is my betrothal party. I couldn't bear to recall it as the night someone was cast into gaol."

"After what this woman said to hurt you? You think I would let her free?" Impatience flashed across Darlington's handsome features, the expression of a man who loathed being thwarted. Juliet felt a swift surge of pity for the girl who would be his wife.

"Foster, I beg you. If you care for me, you will let her go."

Darlington hesitated a long stormy moment, then muttered an oath under his breath. "Fine, then," he snapped. "You have the gift of your freedom, given by my betrothed's hand. But if you ever harass me again, or anyone connected with me, I promise you, I will prosecute you to the fullest extent of the law." His eyes glittered, slits in his face, full of threats he couldn't voice with his betrothed and her mother beside him. Threats Juliet understood perfectly well.

They only served to make her square her shoulders. "I will do everything in my power to protect Elise. I'm not afraid of you."

"You should be." His pug-faced compatriot chortled. "He has a demned ugly temper, he does. And the thing I adore most about Britannia is that nearly everything's a hanging offense. Have to entertain the masses, don't you know?"

"The one thing we could be certain of is that Miss Grafton-Moore's hanging would be particularly well attended," Lord Darlington said with a nasty laugh.

"Personally, I much prefer a nice bloody duel to a hanging." A deep voice, cold and hard as an ice-sheathed saber, cut through the din of the crowd. Darlington looked up, fury and challenge twisting his mouth at the brazenness of this new intruder. Juliet wheeled around, her stomach plunging to her toes.

"A-Adam."

He walked toward them, magnificent as a knight's destrier amidst a stable full of overblown peacocks, his unpowdered hair flowing loose about his shoulders in a wild mane. The rippling muscles of his powerful thighs were sheathed in midnight-blue breeches, his frockcoat straining over the bunched muscles that capped his broad shoulders. He towered over the other men, turned the heads of every woman within the rotunda.

Juliet could scarcely breathe. How had he discovered her? Oh, Lord, Elise had sworn she wouldn't betray her!

"Wh-what are you doing here?" she stammered.

"Discussing hangings with Darlington." Adam crossed his muscular arms over the daunting breadth of his chest. "Damned cowardly business, if you ask me, watching while someone else slips a noose on a person who's bound hand and foot. As if there were any sport in that! Entertainment for those without enough nerve to drive a sword thrust to the hilt and feel the blood spatter on their own lily-white hands. But I suppose hanging would be a fitting diversion for a man so craven he would threaten a woman, Darlington."

"How dare you!" The aristocrat's long fingers groped for the hilt of the dress sword at his side. For a heartbeat, some bloodthirsty corner of Juliet's heart fluttered with anticipation at the prospect of swords unsheathed, Adam Slade driving fear into Darlington's eyes with the point of his blade—the same emotion Darlington had saddled Elise with. Yet she brought herself up short. Lord, the last thing needed here was bloodshed!

"Adam, I am finished here. Perhaps we should leave."

"Not before his lordship decides what to do about his hand on his sword hilt. Are you using that for a prop for tired fingers, or do you intend to draw your blade?"

"His sword hilt? Foster, no!" Miss Stonebridge pleaded, her voice breaking. "You mustn't fight. Oh, Mama! Stop him! This is just too awful!"

"Darlington, enough of this nonsense!" the duchess commanded, gathering her daughter into her arms. "Can't you see that you're upsetting the poor dear? I forbid any swordplay. I absolutely forbid it!"

She sounded like a nursemaid attempting to separate two brawling boys.

"What's it to be, Darlington?" Adam demanded with silky menace. "Blood to join that wine stain? I will be happy to oblige you."

Juliet could almost hear the instinct for self-preservation whirling madly in the nobleman's head as he eyed Adam—legs thick as tree trunks, arms solid as ships' masts, the scar on his jaw hinting at another challenge, another rival who might be long dead.

"Who the devil are you?" Lord Darlington demanded, glaring. "I feel like I've seen you before."

Slade's sensual lips curved in a smile dripping with derision. "I doubt we move in the same circles. But it's possible we've met, I suppose. Have you locked horns with my philanthropic half-brother, the Earl of Glenlyon? I recall dropping in to watch him battle the rest of the House of Lords on one or two occasions."

"Glenlyon?" Darlington echoed. "The traitor?"

"Not *the* Glenlyon." Miss Stonebridge asked, a fervent glow in her cheeks. "The gentleman who saved so many poor children in Scotland? He was pardoned for his courage."

"In case you've forgotten, Annemarie," the duchess said, "the Scots were in rebellion at the time. They brought Armageddon down on their own heads. Why, your own cousin was injured in the fighting."

"I know, Mama. But I hardly think the children had any choice in the matter."

Juliet found herself liking the duchess's daughter immensely as the girl braved her mother's displeasure.

"I was so glad to hear that some of them had been spared," Miss Stonebridge said with tender ardor.

"Annemarie!" Darlington snapped. "I will not have you conversing with this interfering scoundrel. Now, sir." He turned a scathing glare on Adam. "I asked you a question!"

"You might be careful of the tone you ask it in, *sir.* Since the most likely place you might have seen me is at a salon of swordsmanship. My name is Adam Slade. Otherwise known as Sabrehawk." Adam bowed with an elegant flourish and flashed his most diabolical grin.

What an unholy pleasure he took in seeing the reaction that name garnered, not just among a low-born mob, but here, as well, amidst the most powerful in the land. And, God forgive her, elation flooded her as well as Darlington's lips tightened, the other guests in his box gasping and murmuring recognition.

She had seen Adam Slade do battle before, but this time was different. The hard glaze on his eyes was fiercer, his mouth the feral slash of a warrior defending something precious. Or *someone* precious. The notion thrilled her, stunned her, terrified her.

"Adam, please!" she said, grasping the iron-honed muscles of his arm. "There is no need to pursue this further! I wish to leave! I—I want to see the fireworks."

"Astonishing." He slanted her a glance beneath lashes as thick and curled as a child's, made all the more dauntingly masculine on that rough-hewn face. "You create so many wherever you go, I'd think the fascination would have palled. However, I am at your service. But before we go, I wish to make something clear to His Lordship, here."

Dark eyes pierced Darlington's arrogant mask, searing him with a warning so intense it made Juliet's knees quake. "I am a particular friend of Miss Grafton-Moore's. And of Miss Elise as well. I will consider any further harassment on your part a personal affront. And I can assure you, I have no aversion to wetting my hands with an enemy's blood, should the need arise."

"I would not lower myself to shed my blood over a harlot and a whorekeeper." Darlington sneered. "But it's no wonder you're neck deep in them." A cruel spark lit the backs of the nobleman's eyes. "Ah, yes, Slade. I remember you now, the stories about you and your sordid origins. A harlot's blood flows in your veins."

Adam didn't flinch, didn't move, but Juliet felt a jolt of

emotion shooting through his body, savage, tearing, fierce—anger, and yet something more.

Pain?

The possibility slayed her, left her bleeding for him.

Lord, was it possible that proud, fierce Adam was the son of such a woman? If so, it was a gaping chink in Adam Slade's emotional armor, one Darlington had pierced with a poison-tipped lance.

She wanted nothing more than to get Adam away from this place, to shield him—of all the ridiculous, impossible urges, that she might be able to protect this strapping mountain of a man from biting words.

"Adam, please," Juliet said, her voice trembling at the force of emotion she sensed in him. "Please."

His eyes cleared just a whisper, those dark depths glancing down at her. And she perceived in that instant that he wanted to fight his lordship. Fight to obliterate whatever dark emotion had engulfed him in that moment. Fight forever to keep it at bay.

She reached up, laying her fingertips upon that stubborn jut of jaw, her thumb skimming the faint scar that marred his face. A scar that hinted at one she sensed cut far deeper.

He jerked a little in surprise, then stilled, like a wild thing experiencing its first fleeting communion with another creature. And in that instant, she sensed him wrestling his demons under control, and knew somehow that she had won.

He sucked in a steadying breath, his voice a low growl as he turned back to the nobleman. "It seems the lady wishes to escape your company. Don't forget my warning, Darlington."

"I'll try to remember, Slade." Darlington scowled at Adam, then Juliet felt the nobleman's gaze fix on her, cold, arrogant.

"Miss Grafton-Moore, don't forget my promise."

Juliet shivered, all but hauling Adam to the door. But even as she stepped into the night, she could still feel the hot press of Darlington's eyes upon her back.

Chapter

8

Night air struck Adam's face, cool and scented of wind and dusk-shadowed blossoms from the gardens just visible by the light of colored lanterns. He sucked in a deep breath, but it did nothing to soothe the raw places the encounter with Darlington had raked open somewhere beneath the crusty layer of warrior he fought so hard to hide behind.

He held Juliet's hand tighter, so tight he almost feared he'd bruise her. But he couldn't will himself to let go. He had to cling to something, someone, had to clutch tight to safer forms of anger so that the true reason for his rage could stay where it belonged. Buried in the deep hole a boy had dug inside his heart years ago.

"Adam, please. I can't keep up," Juliet cried, stumbling. "I know you're angry, but——"

"Angry? I'd like to wring your meddling little neck! How the devil am I supposed to guard you when you go racing off in the middle of the night like some accursed crusader? Attacking someone like Darlington, for God's sake. And you didn't even bring your parasol to spear him."

"I agreed you could stay at Angel's Fall. I didn't agree to allow you to interfere in my work."

"And what I just witnessed was your *work?* It's a miracle you've survived a year! Blast, do you have any idea how far-reaching Darlington's power is? Someone like Mother Cavendish and her surly mob might be swept up by the authorities and tossed in prison for harming you, but Darlington—he could have you destroyed with a snap of his fingers and no one—*no one*—would dare bring him to trial—that is, if they could even catch him."

"He's nothing but bluster. Preying on the weak. Something I believe I showed him that I am not."

"No, you just raked up all that muck in front of his betrothed—his very *rich* betrothed. Made things dashed uncomfortable."

"I hope Miss Stonebridge refuses to wed him! The girl would have made a grand escape."

"Don't hold your breath. Marriages in the aristocracy are planned out like the siege of a fortress, down to the tiniest detail. Properties, dowries, and matching the appropriate bloodlines are far more important than such trifling matters as being a cruel, stinking, cowardly son of a bitch who preys on women. The duchess will have her daughter hustling up the aisle with Darlington before the year is out. It's just that the poor girl will know earlier than most what a villain her husband is."

A gasp from a gaggle of passersby made Adam glance over to see that they were once again the center of attention. Growling an oath, he hauled Juliet across the grassy lawn to where a towering oak spread a canopy of green, a brace of colored lanterns bobbing from low-hanging branches.

"You were every bit as outraged as I was on Elise's behalf, Adam Slade. I could hear it in your voice, see it, sense it. You wanted to fight—"

"Of course I wanted to fight. I adore fighting. Have since I was a grubby-faced boy. Nothing more fun than bashing and thrashing. And God knows, no one's better at it than I am. Made me a bloody fortune."

"The question is, what are you fighting for?" She peered up at him, eyes huge and earnest in the lantern light.

"I just told you. Money. Perhaps a little fame."

"Or perhaps there is another reason."

Adam squirmed inwardly, pinned by the solemnity in

that soft oval face. "Bloody hell! Don't you dare start trying to unscrew the top of my head and peer inside, madam. I'm not one of your fallen angels."

"But your mother could have been."

Adam felt the blood drain from his face, forced himself to release her hands. "Blast, my secret is out." He struck his brow with bitter sarcasm. "It's true. I'm a bastard—by birth as well as by temperament. Conceived in sin, born on the wrong side of the blanket. Are you shocked, Juliet?"

He'd wanted to disgust her, to knock the compassion from her eyes, but her gaze only darkened with understanding.

"I don't mean to judge, Adam. I'm just saying you bear no fault in your birth. It was your mother's choice—"

"My mother is doing just fine, thank you very much. She's the mistress of a large estate with so much wealth she couldn't spend it in three lifetimes. I hardly expect she'll be showing up on your doorstep anytime soon."

No, the possibility was as remote as Adam himself, arriving at the manor house at Strawberry Grove.

"You're right to be annoyed with me. It's none of my affair. It's just—I hurt for you when Darlington was so cruel."

"I don't give a damn what that fop says." Adam gave a harsh laugh. "Juliet, when you're born a bastard, you have two choices. Go into a towering rage every time you hear the word, or laugh in people's faces when they fling it at you."

"But you weren't laughing inside, Adam."

He should have roared with laughter, should have cast out some witty, biting words to distract her. But her perception lanced through the hard shell of mockery, cynicism, years of denial, leaving him stunned. Only one other person in his life had realized that truth, slipped past his guard to discover the raw place, the vulnerable place he'd struggled so hard to conceal.

Gavin—his half-brother, the boy who had been his nemesis, the youth who had been his conscience, the man who was the person Adam loved most in this infernal world.

Gavin, who had seen but never spoken about the pain, the hurt, the isolation of bastardy, any more than Adam had spoken of Gavin's secret pain—the fact that their father had quietly despised his true-born son.

"Adam?" Juliet's hand, angel-soft, warm, curved over his jaw, her thumb tracing ever so delicately the ridge of the faded scar. His jaw knotted beneath her touch, a touch so searingly tender his chest ached. "I don't mean to poke about in something painful. It's just . . . I want you to know that it doesn't matter to me that you were born out of wedlock. It can never change the man you are."

"What's this? The bright angel granting me absolution?" He should have laughed at the absurdity. Might have, if it weren't for the strange tightness in his throat.

"Juliet, Juliet, don't bleed for me. My life was far better than most. My father loved my mother, and they raised a batch of children together. There was always plenty of coin—a stable full of horses, presents and trinkets, the best to be had—to make up for the fact that we didn't carry his name. And I was the luckiest of all."

"How?"

"I was the earl's favorite."

The knowledge should have given him some sense of satisfaction. Why was it then that the thought of his father made his stomach burn? Burn with frustration and anger and a hundred issues that could never be resolved between them.

"You must have loved your father very much."

"Too much." Adam closed his eyes against a hundred memories. How many times had he all but broken his fool neck in an attempt to impress the earl? Sometimes, when a sword flashed toward him and death glinted on its tip, he wondered if he was still trying to reach his father beyond the grave.

"It isn't a sin to love."

"The love between my parents was. But why did God plant such a raging seed of loving in their hearts if it was such a vile sin? For the entertainment of watching them suffer an eternity, not able to touch each other, possess each other the way their souls burned to?"

Juliet's cheeks flooded with color, and Adam wondered if this bright angel with her loving heart and generous spirit had any idea of the kind of passion that could exist between a man and a woman—hot, raw desire flaying to the very bone. Obsession so deep every breath drawn echoed in their beloved's heart. No, her one taste of physical passion had been the kiss he had forced upon her. But, God, the temptation to teach her . . .

"I don't pretend to understand the reasons why God gives us the challenges he does. But my papa—"

Adam shoved back the unexpected haze of need that tightened his loins, grasped bitterness and cynicism and safety. "Yes, your papa, the vicar. I'd wager he had all the answers. Our vicar certainly did. I remember the old curmudgeon letting loose a particularly nasty sermon on sins of the flesh one Sunday when my father wasn't at Strawberry Grove. My mother and all the rest of us children sitting there in the pew, while he rained fire and brimstone down on our heads."

He should have stopped, withdrawn, brushed her aside with a laugh. God alone knew what power goaded him to go on sharing things he'd never shared, speaking of things he'd never voiced even to his own brother. "The villagers looked down their noses. The only time they dared was when Father was away. They knew my mother would say nothing to him. She always did her damnedest to hide that kind of ugliness from him. That Sunday, she didn't turn so much as an eyelash. And after the service, she bid the vicar farewell the same way she always did, with a radiant smile."

"The vicar's cruelty must have hurt you very much."

"Hurt me? Bah! I've never believed in wasting time being miserable. No, I spent the whole service plotting vengeance—a much more productive business." A faraway smile nudged the corner of his mouth.

"Adam, you didn't . . ." She hesitated. "Surely you didn't fight the vicar with a sword?"

"It occurred to me, but no. I was barely ten, but I already knew a challenge like that would have revealed more than I cared to. I crept into that sanctimonious dog's bedchamber while he was sleeping. I filled his hand with ink and then took a feather and tickled his nose."

"Oh, my!" She pressed one hand to her lips, but her eyes filled with admiration.

"The result was quite spectacular. In fact, the whole affair would have been altogether perfect except for one small problem. When my father returned, he somehow got wind of the affront to my mother. In a belated effort to silence the man's denouncements, the earl offered him a bribe of sorts. He hired the vicar in the one capacity he might serve at Strawberry Grove."

"What was that?"

"My tutor."

"Oh, Adam." He'd never heard such gentleness, such soft empathy.

"You can imagine the kind of scholar I made. Nothing brought out the demons in me more than being locked up in a schoolroom reading a bunch of moldering old texts until I was half blind. Played havoc with my aim when I got to the important part of my day—my lessons at swordsmanship with Monsieur le Trec. It was a battle of gargantuan proportions between old Vicar Tinworthy and me. The only question was who loathed the other one more. He spent the next year trying to beat the devil out of me, and I spent it showing him I didn't care a jot."

"But your father—how could he have let that beast abuse you?"

"I went to the greatest lengths to hide it, so he didn't know. No one did until . . ." Adam stopped, staring down into that creamy oval face, bathed in the rainbow colors from the lantern light. "You know, I never breathed a word of this to anyone before. How strange. Is that how you lure your fallen angels into your toils, Juliet Grafton-Moore? With those heavenly eyes that seem to hold all the light in a dark, dark world?"

She nibbled at her lower lip, looking for all the world like a guilty angel caught pilfering the secrets from a mortal's soul. "You don't have to say anything more if you don't want to." It was the tiniest catch in her voice that yanked something tender in his heart.

"God, you remind me of him." Adam grimaced. "I should have run when I had the chance."

"Who do I remind you of? Your father? The vicar?"

"My brother. Half-brother, really. Gavin Carstares, Earl of Glenlyon."

"The one Miss Stonebridge was talking about? Who saved the Scottish children?"

"It might sound bloody heroic and romantic to the ladies, but it's still a wonder to me that we weren't both hanged in the bargain. It surely wasn't for lack of effort on Gavin's part." Adam couldn't stop the smile that played at the corners of his mouth any more than he could stifle the surge of loneliness at the thought of his brother.

How long had it been since he'd seen Gavin, his wife Rachel and their brood of children? Too long. Ever since he noticed that when he gathered his newest little niece or nephew in his arms he felt raw, knowing that such familial bliss was forbidden to him—a bastard who could only leave his children a heritage of shame.

Never had he felt that rawness more acutely than he did now, with Juliet Grafton-Moore so close he could feel her breath against his jaw, see the pulsebeat in the delicate hollow of her throat. So close, yet far beyond his touch.

"Gavin came to live at our house ten months after the vicar was put in charge of my education. I hated him. The true-born son, the heir. It was easy to pretend that he didn't exist when he lived with his mother across the county. It might as well have been on the moon. But after his mother died, father brought him to Strawberry Grove."

Adam raked back a lock of hair tumbling over his brow. "Gavin was the one who stopped the vicar from beating me. The old devil was lashing away at my hands until they bled, and I was staring him in the face, daring him to hit harder . . . harder. Gavin grabbed the switch, stepped between us and said . . . said that if Tinworthy ever dared strike me again, Gavin would make certain he was driven away from Strawberry Grove forever."

"But what could a mere boy do?"

"Gavin would be the earl someday. He told Tinworthy that the instant he was, he'd use every bit of his power to make certain the man never stood on a pulpit again as long as he lived. Ten years old, scrawny as a drowned rat, Gavin was, but I'd never seen anyone so infernally brave."

"You must have loved him then."

"Loved him?" A bark of laughter erupted from Adam's chest. "Lord, I almost killed him for interfering. The instant we got outside, I flew at him like a fury. Didn't need his damned charity. We fought like tigers, both of us full of grief and anger, resentment and rage. I outweighed him by twenty pounds and he barely reached my shoulder. But he landed one hell of a punch, and I crashed into the stable door. Split my jaw wide open." Sword-toughened fingers caressed the old scar.

"Gavin stood there, silent, while the doctor stitched me up. And afterward, when father summoned us to his study, demanding an explanation, Gavin didn't tell father I'd flown at him. Made up some wild story. I think it was the only time I ever heard him lie."

Adam was astonished to feel delicate feminine hands enclosing his massive paws, smoothing over them with such a gentle touch they could melt away the rough-hewn edges, the calluses worn in by battle. She turned over his palm and laid one cheek in its cup. He knew the instant she felt the raised ridges the vicar had left in his flesh. She dampened it with tears.

"Poor hands," she whispered. She shifted her face against his palm until her lips, soft and moist and healing, pressed feather-light kisses upon the faded ridges of the scars Tinworthy had lashed into his skin.

Adam remembered the countless times he'd rammed his clenched fists into his frockcoat pockets, shoved his swollen hands into riding gloves in an effort to hide the bloody slashes. Determined that no one would ever know. How could that gruff, stubborn, fiercely proud boy ever have guessed the healing power of feminine tears and soft mournful kisses? Yet her sweet sorrow tightened a knot in his throat.

"It was all a long time ago, sweetheart," he said, capturing her chin between his fingers, tipping her face up into the lantern light. What he saw stole his breath away. Bright droplets of tears clinging to thick lashes, streaking rose-petal cheeks, lips trembling with an innocence he'd never known, and a compassion that had terrified him forever. A willingness to take another human being's pain into her own heart, to ache for them, bleed for them in a way that selfish Adam Slade never would dare.

He'd been subjected to bouts of hysterical feminine tears, performances created to bend a man to a lady's will. They'd been easy enough to dismiss. But this . . . this quiet anguish of the soul, this desperate wanting in her face, wanting, nothing for herself, but rather, wanting to wipe away his pain—it cinched about his chest, tightened his throat, drove him to take mad risks like threading his rough fingers through the golden silk of her hair.

Need pounded like battle drums in his belly, fear made his fingers tremble. But nothing could stop him from lowering his mouth to the quivering sweetness of Juliet's own.

She gasped at the contact, her eyes widening, and he would have drawn away except that at that moment, she gave a tiny whimper and melted against his chest.

Adam shuddered at the unbearably precious weight of her as he gathered her in his arms, drinking in the honeyed sweetness of her mouth. He could feel the dampness of her tears against the beard-roughened surface of his cheek, the inner light in this valiant woman warming places chafed by his soldier's uniform, washed with other men's blood—men whose only crime had been that they stood beneath another man's command on the opposite side of a battle-field.

Like a man lost in a frozen wasteland, he sought that warmth, fastening his mouth tighter over the swells of her lips, tracing the delicate bow with his tongue. Her fingers swept up to clasp his waist, and he probed the crease between her lips, seeking entry.

Trusting, ever so trusting, she opened her mouth to him with the same generosity she opened her heart. And Adam delved deep into the hot, moist cavern beyond, tasting all of her, sweeping the delicate inner flesh, rubbing his tongue against hers, savoring the tentative seeking of her, the fragile questing of fingertips upon the rigid muscles of his back, the trembling weight of breasts quivering with her breathless little gasps against the hard wall of his chest.

She felt so damned fragile, like one of the porcelain figurines his mother had polished upon the mantel of her bedchamber. Fairy-queens and woodsprites whose wafer-thin wings had disintegrated at the merest brush of a callused hand.

Every fiber of his being was excruciatingly aware that the slightest roughness would bruise her, not only the pale satin of her skin, but a heart far too tender for the brutal reality of this world.

An honorable man would have pulled away from her, knowing it was wrong to steal even this little taste of the goodness inside her. But Adam Slade was no hero. And never, in the multitude of years since he'd lost his virginity to a pretty dairymaid, had he felt such sweet madness consume him as at her yielding—this thirst nothing could quench, this hunger, deep in his vitals.

"Juliet," he murmured into her mouth. "So damned sweet. Tastes like . . . redemption."

Her fingers traced the muscles of his arm, caressed the caps of his shoulders, found the sensitive cords of his neck. Her hand burrowed beneath his hair, settling into the hollow at his nape, drawing his mouth tighter against hers.

Fire—she painted it onto his lips with tiny forays of her tongue, pooled it in the corners of his mouth as she tasted them, her face shining with a child's wonderment at discovering something beautiful.

Yet Juliet had no idea that she brought all the beauty to this forbidden kiss. Or that she was wasting it upon a man who could never give her what she deserved. The kind of love Gavin had given to his lady—a hero's heart, passion and light and sensitivity.

Tenderness instead of the raging lust, gentleness in place of the fierce desire of a warrior, a bastard without even an honorable name to give her. Even now, Adam would have ransomed his soul to the devil to be able to sweep his scarred palm up between their bodies, fill it with the liquid heat of her breast, feel the nudge of her nipple as it pearled, her body's sweet invitation to taste that place where she was dark and rosy and aching.

Adam deepened the kiss, a low growl of frustration in his throat, his imagination tortured with images of Juliet last night in her nightshift, firelight turning the gown into gossamer petals so sheer he could see the dusky centers of her aureoles, tempting, untouched, so sensitive he could imagine with agonizing clarity how her untried body would react the instant his mouth fixed upon that delicate crest.

He felt his sex go rigid behind his breech-flap, his hands gliding down her tiny waist, the subtle flare of her hips beneath their layers of petticoats and panniers. His imagination plunged deeper, bunching up those yards of fabric, parting her thighs and—

Sweet Judas, he thought with utter self-disgust. He was such a blasted monster of a man he'd cleave her in two if he were ever so insane as to—to what? Seduce the innocent young woman he'd vowed to protect?

"No!" he growled the denial, his fingers clenching on her ribs, pushing her away. He knew he'd always remember the gasp of disappointment as those soft lips pulled away from his. "Juliet, no. This is . . . we have no business . . . bloody hell, angel, do you really want to fall?"

She blinked up at him, awed and a little frightened and so beautiful his breath was a jagged thing in his chest. "Fall?" she echoed faintly.

"Because I'm more than ready to shove you off the cliff, sweetheart, and I'm not much of a man for heroic fits of self-denial. I want you, Juliet. Like a man wants a woman. Like the men who despoiled your ladies wanted them— lying in my arms, my mouth drinking pleasure from yours, my—"

He had wanted, needed to drive that dream dust from her eyes, banish fairy tales and dash the salt of reality across the tumultuous emotions playing like quicksilver across her exquisite features. But he'd had no idea how deeply it would cut him to see her fold in upon herself like a tender blossom burned by too-fierce sun, closing herself off from him in a dozen subtle ways.

"Oh, my . . . my goodness," she stammered, pressing her shaking fingers to her lips, skittering back a step, her eyes wide with chagrin. Someone passing by on a nearby path tinkled out a laugh, and Juliet's cheeks went pale as parchment as she turned to look around her.

Adam lashed himself with self-revulsion. Yes, he'd drawn her into the shadow of the tree, but even that couldn't totally conceal them from the other pleasure-seekers wandering the paths of the gardens. There were plenty of Londoners just burning for Juliet Grafton-Moore to slip, to make a mistake, so they could brush her aside. And he'd almost created a spectacle with her more damaging than any Mother Cavendish might have orchestrated.

"Juliet, forgive me," Adam said, feeling like the scurviest cur who ever breathed. "I just—when you cried over my hand, I—"

Felt my heart shatter? Wanted to turn and run like the veriest coward? Forgot who I was, who you are . . .

She glanced at her surroundings, horror spreading over her kiss-blushed features. "This was . . . I cannot think what possessed me to . . . to allow . . . no." Her voice fell. "I cannot cast the blame on you, when I was kissing you back."

"Juliet, don't." Her self-blame raked at Adam. "This meant nothing," he said, relieved he'd learned to be such a good liar. "We were both still unnerved by the scene with Darlington, and all that happened last night. God knows, neither of us had much sleep."

"Is that what you do when you have a restless night, Adam? Run about kissing people until their hair ribbons melt?"

Not like I kissed you, angel, Adam thought. *Never like I kissed you.*

"Juliet, I'm sorry. I had no right."

"Perhaps God meant it to be a lesson. A warning. To show me how weak the flesh can be."

If it was such a demonstration of weakness, then why did the surging beneath the flap of Adam's breeches feel stronger, more undeniable than ever before? Why did he want to throw caution to the wind and drag Juliet deeper into the shadows, lay her down upon a coverlet of grass and kiss her until she was drowning in the taste of him, the feel of him, hungering for things she couldn't begin to imagine, things he could show her with his hands and his mouth.

Bloody hell, he'd never been the least attracted to big-eyed virgins. Truth to tell, they'd always scared the bejesus out of him. One slip of a man's tongue using a perfectly good Anglo-Saxon swear word and they'd go off in a fit of vapors, all that whining and waterworks. Then why was it he couldn't tear his gaze away from Juliet, with her quiet dignity that transcended mere innocence, her courage that outshone her naiveté? Why couldn't he stop tasting the sweet blossoming of a woman's passion on her guileless lips, feeling the exquisite yielding of her soft curves against his hard planes?

"It's late," Adam growled. "Past time to get back to Angel's Fall. We'd best both forget this ever happened and take ourselves off to bed—I mean, sleep." His cheeks burned, and he groaned inwardly, aware this interlude would turn the sleeping arrangements at Angel's Fall into holy hell, yet he continued stubbornly. "But we have to reach an understanding here, lady."

"Obviously we cannot let anything like . . . like this happen again." Her fingertips fluttered to kiss-stung lips, her gaze fluttering away from his, fixing on the crumpled fall of his neckcloth.

"You're damned right. Not just this kissing insanity but this whole disastrous night. No more of this running off alone, stirring up catastrophes. You were completely vulnerable tonight." Yet wasn't she even more vulnerable when he was within arm's reach of her? A voice inside Adam whispered. The taste of her kisses still on his lips, the memory—no, blast it. He was a soldier, well schooled in enduring necessary hardships. He'd look at this relationship with Juliet as just one more battle.

"Promise me, Juliet, that you won't go running off without me anymore."

"But I . . . the ladies . . . I have to be a good example for them. Show them that a woman can be independent, strong. Fight her own battles."

"I've fought a hundred battles, angel. And no one—not even the strongest warrior ever fights alone. He carries with him the skill of every one of his teachers, the prayers of his mother and sisters and lovers. The one thing I couldn't bear is to have you on my conscience. If you were hurt, or lost, or—"

"Why, Adam? Because you gave my father your word you'd protect me?"

"Maybe at first. But now—" He turned away from her, feeling like a knight of old, stripped of his armor. Uncertain. Oddly defenseless.

"I won't lie to you, Juliet. My life has been hard-edged— swords and battles, death and blood for as long as I can remember. But through it, I've learned one thing. The world is a dark place. It would be a hopeless one except for a few people fashioned of light. My brother, Gavin, was the first person I ever knew that was all goodness and honor and nobility of spirit. You are the second."

"Oh, Adam." Her voice quavered and she shook her head in denial.

"Maybe I can never touch that light, Juliet. God knows I'm not worthy to. But I can use my strength and skill to protect it, guard it, shelter it."

A soft sob tore from her throat. "You're wrong about me, Adam. So wrong. I—I'm ever so wicked inside sometimes. I grow so impatient and angry with Isabelle, no matter how hard I try. And, though I know I should be forgiving, turn the other cheek like Papa taught, there are times I just want to bash men like Darlington with something far heavier than a parasol."

"That's only being human, sweetheart." Adam crooked a half-smile. "It keeps you from being a saint so the rest of us sinners can quell our impulses to string you up on Catherine Wheels and skin you alive and shoot you full of arrows and such like."

"But there's so much more. It was my wickedness that drove Papa out onto that Irish road to die. And Jenny . . . my poor Jenny. I failed her as well."

"Thunder and nonsense."

"Adam, you don't know me—the truth—"

"I knew you from the moment I looked into your eyes, Juliet, even though I tried to deny it." Adam touched her face, the warmth of that creamy satin melting into his rough fingertips. He'd spent a lifetime selling his sword to the highest bidder, fighting battles he didn't give a damn about—other men's battles, other men's wars. But never had a vow cut so deeply to the heart of him as the one he made now.

"I'll take care of you," Adam pledged, losing himself in those angel's eyes. "Let me take care of you."

She gazed up at him, a trembling goddess, her golden hair shimmering about her face like a holy aura. She slipped her hand into his. "I trust you, Adam." Such simple words. Such an impossible mass of feelings tearing at his chest.

He'd guard her with every breath he drew, every sinew and bone of his body. From the wolves that snarled outside her door, and, most valiantly of all, from the beast inside his own soul. The one that, even now, was raging, hurling itself against the bars of his own self-control, demanding that he take her into his arms and cover her with the shadows in his own soul.

Taking her hand, he led her back through the winding paths to where his horse was waiting. He lifted her into his arms and rode for Angel's Fall.

Back to the throng of women waiting there, the virginal bed where she slept alone, and the tiny antechamber where Adam knew he'd spend night after night wanting her.

Damnation, what was he going to do? Find some way to carry her away from all this madness? He'd tried to do so once before on a wild Scottish moor, scooping his brother out of harm's way. There was only one problem about people woven of light. They wouldn't stay safe in their ivory towers. God curse them all, they had to go forth to face the darkness.

Chapter

9

It was a wonder that Mother Cavendish hadn't just huffed and puffed and blown Angel's Fall down, Adam thought with a wolfish snarl as he put a new lock upon the front door. In the two days since the fiasco at Ranelagh Gardens, he'd flung himself like a fury into securing the premises—doubtless an instinct held over from the days in which he had to entrench his men in the most advantageous position for a battle.

Fletcher had pitched in with puppy-dog enthusiasm, gallumphing about fixing iron bars across the first-floor windows while Millicent and Violet handed him his tools.

The whole scenario might have been endurable if Adam had managed to get an hour or two of sleep at night. But no. He'd lain on his pallet in the tiny antechamber hour after hour, as wide awake as if every clang and crash of Juliet's ridiculous alarm were still battering his eardrums.

But she was tormenting him with something far more subtle now. The restless noises of her supple limbs shifting against the coverlets, the soft moans of defeat as she, too, struggled to sleep. The scent of her—meadow flowers and rain water and honey—teasing his nostrils until it took every ounce of will he possessed not to charge into her bedchamber and bury his face in the fragrant cascade of her golden hair.

Blast it, he was slowly going insane, Adam thought, tightening the heavy iron latch with ferocity. There were times when he was almost tempted to surrender, to acknowledge that London needed Angel's Fall, and that women like Isabelle and Millicent and—yes, damn it—his own mother needed a gentle spirit like Juliet to gather them into the warmth and safety of her arms.

But monsters like Darlington would never stand for it. Greedy animals like Mother Cavendish would do their best to destroy anything decent and good Juliet could build here. Perhaps she could survive if she had someone to guard her, a voice inside Adam reasoned. A strong man, a good man willing to place his sword between her tender heart and those who would shatter it if they could.

But Adam Slade could never be that man. He was no selfless noble idiot ready to sacrifice himself on the altar of philanthropy. Especially when he spent every hour of the day reliving the moments he'd crushed her in his arms, kissed her as if her mouth held all the secrets of salvation. Tasted just enough of her astonished passion to drive him wild with the need to delve deeper, drink in more—devour all of her, from the tips of her rosy toes to the crown of curls at the top of her head, and everything between, branding it as his.

"Sabrehawk?" Fletcher's voice startled Adam so much he jammed the point of the awl into his thumb. Adam spat a rain of curses, sticking the gashed digit into his mouth.

"Hellfire, boy, don't you have anything better to do than torment me? I told you how to put those bars on the windows once, for God's sake. A child could do it."

"I know." The smug smile more than one man had tried to wipe off Fletcher's face with the point of a sword tickled the corners of the youth's mouth. "Unfortunately, a child could get past that lock you're putting on the door as well."

"The devil you say! The smith vowed to me this was the sturdiest lock he'd ever forged."

"That may be true, but you've put it on so the latch is on

the outside panel of the door. Of course, it would work perfect if you wished to keep Miss Juliet and her ladies locked inside. Is that your goal?"

"You flaming idiot! I can damn well put a latch on a door—" Adam glared down at his handiwork, sputtering a denial. But his tirade died the instant he saw that the boy was right. He wanted to throttle Fletcher as a chorus of giggles erupted behind him.

"I wish every woman in creation was at the bottom of the infernal ocean," Adam growled with abject sincerity. "But the well out in the garden is deep enough to serve my purpose. If the lot of you don't leave me in peace, I vow, I'll stuff you all down the shaft—and Fletcher, you'll go first!"

"That would be most unchivalrous," Fletcher observed with a chuckle. "Ladies should always precede gentlemen."

The glare he shot them should have sent his tormenters careening away in a panic. Fletcher knew him well enough to beat a hasty retreat. But the ladies merely flounced their petticoats and sashayed away, their laughter filling the entryway.

Grinding his teeth to dust, Adam began the insufferable chore of removing the latch, thinking it would be far more satisfactory to take an axe to the door and turn it into kindling. These women would be the death of him.

Adam had been around plenty of women, and had experienced his share of sexual escapades. He'd been chased out of more bedchambers by jealous husbands than any officer in the king's army. But what of *love?* Turn all pale and miserable chasing after one woman?

He'd only been fool enough to dip his toes into that quicksand once, and the spritely Miss Adina Neville had driven some sense into his thick skull straightaway, bless her. She had informed him that it would be far too humiliating to marry a bastard. No, she would marry a baronet, thank you very much, but she and Adam could still be lovers.

Adam squirmed under the memory, thanking God he'd been able to shrug off her rejection with a laugh. *Hell's bells, woman, you didn't think I was serious? Me, tie a female millstone about my neck when there are hundreds of sweetmeats to sample? It was a jest. Only a jest.*

A green lad's first heartache? Some would say so. But he couldn't even recall the woman's face. There hadn't been months of anguish, only the resounding certainty that she'd told the truth. *Bastard* was an ugly word. No man should willingly saddle a wife and children with such a legacy of shame. For while Adam could shrug off the label, lash it into nothingness matched against his prowess with a sword, it had been far more difficult for his mother and his sisters to escape the repercussions of their birth.

Hellfire, what was he doing, standing in the doorway like a dolt, dredging up such ancient memories? So, he desired Juliet Grafton-Moore. He was a man, wasn't he? And despite all the wounds he'd sustained over the years, that particular part of his anatomy was all in one piece and fully functional.

Juliet was a beautiful woman, with the added allure of being far different from his usual fare. To make matters worse, she was sleeping barely five steps away from his bed every night, doubtless wearing that nightshift he'd seen her in the first night they'd clashed in the garden.

Even now he could recall with absolute clarity the lush promise of breasts straining against the nearly transparent cloth, the shadowy triangle of curls at the cleft between her thighs just visible enough to tease a man's senses to madness.

He ground his fingertips against eyes gritty from lack of sleep. Blast, he'd always known he was a blackguard, but he'd never expected to sink to such depths, entertaining the most carnal of fantasies about a woman like Juliet.

Did she have the slightest idea of the kind of roiling need she stirred up in the most primitive part of him? Or that she increased the potency of her spell a hundredfold when her cheeks stung pink with remembrance every time their gazes locked across the dining table, across the drawing room, or, worse still, across the tiny bedchamber before they both made the futile attempt to sleep?

Adam shook the thought away, appalled to feel himself

harden at the misty images that danced across his imagination. Perfect. A wreath of golden curls and pansy-blue eyes had reduced the notorious Sabrehawk to having all the finesse of a blundering seventeen-year-old about to shed his virginity.

There was only one thing to do. Make dead certain nothing could happen between them again. He'd not so much as brush Juliet's fingertips with his while passing the biscuits at tea. And then, he'd think of some way to resolve this tangle without making a complete ass out of himself before it was too late.

His mouth twisted into a sneer. Blood and thunder, he'd willingly trade a year of his life for one good set-to with swords to rid himself of his frustrations. But there hadn't been any sign of Mother Cavendish or any of her crew since Adam and Juliet had returned from Ranelagh. Adam sighed. Typical. When a man wanted a little peace, the bushes were fairly bristling with assassins. But if he wanted to fight, there was not a decently wielded sword in five counties.

Grabbing up the pieces of the latch, he eyed one of the iron spikes that had anchored it to the wood. Frustration burned in him, so hot the metal should have glowed red. The infernal thing had cracked off in the middle. He could only pray there was another one left in the mess of accoutrements he and Fletcher had spread out on the bench in the garden house.

He stalked through the interior of the house to the rear door. Sunshine struck his face as he stepped out into the garden, the musty scent of herbs and the rich odor of flowers and freshly turned earth mingling in his nose.

He wanted nothing more than to retrieve another nail and return to his hellish task—without running into anyone who giggled or flirted or dithered about. But he'd barely taken three steps when he saw her.

Garbed in coral pink, a sheer white linen apron about her waist, Juliet knelt beside a clump of green stuff, the cloth at one shoulder drooping to expose a pure curve of pale skin. The sunshine of her curls played hide-and-seek with the edge of a delicate white lace cap just visible beneath the broad brim of a straw hat with cherry-colored ribbons holding it in place. A beatific smile curved her lips, and her eyes purely shone as she tilted her face up like a blossom to the sun.

It would have been hard enough on Adam's pulses to see her thus, but the fact that she was casting that smile up at another man yanked at the most primitive part of Adam—the secret corner where knights still made war on those who dared so much as touch the hems of their ladies' gowns.

At that instant, Juliet tucked a sheaf of flowers into the crook of one arm, brushed the dirt off her fingers, and offered her hand to the figure, rising to her feet. Blast her innocence! The gate was wide open again. And the man who had entered by it could have a slaughtering knife tucked up his sleeve! Not that it would matter. She'd probably still be offering him tea and biscuits!

Adam bolted toward her, his fingers tightening on the pieces of the lock he held as the vaguely familiar-looking gentleman swept a low bow and raised Juliet's dirt-smudged hand to his lips.

Shifting the pieces of iron into the crook of his left arm, Adam snatched Juliet's hand out of the man's grasp so suddenly she gave a startled cry.

"Adam, what—"

The man turned, and Adam felt a jolt of recognition. Barnabas Rutledge. The idiot from the tavern come to irritate him again. That was what came of not slitting an imbecile's gullet the first time one had the chance.

Rutledge looked as stunned as if Adam had just cleaved him down the middle. "What is this—this person doing here? Miss Grafton-Moore—"

"What the blazes is *he* doing holding your hand?" Adam countered, scowling at the crow of a man. "I was informed that such attentions from a man are not allowed at Angel's Fall."

"Mr. Rutledge is not a man!" She flung out the questionable defense hotly. "I mean, he's not that kind of . . . of threat!" she stammered, drawing a pointed chuckle from Adam as he cast a scathing glance the length of Rutledge's form. Color flooded her cheeks, outrage sparking in her eyes. "He is our dearest neighbor, and great friend—and you will apologize to him this instant!"

Adam felt hackles of something damnably like jealousy rise at the back of his neck. Her dearest neighbor? Great friend? Pink-cheeked grandmotherly ladies who should fill that role must be in short supply.

He glared at Rutledge—the man looked as if he had gruel for blood and there was something about the way those beady eyes regarded Juliet that made Adam want to clobber him with the pieces of that infernal lock.

All things considered, Adam would sooner swallow a ball of fire than say he was sorry to the wretch. "What the devil is your neighbor doing wandering around in this garden? It's forbidden, isn't it? The blasted gate should be locked tighter than the portal to the Garden of Eden. We agreed—"

"We didn't agree on anything," Juliet insisted. *"You* started bellowing orders. I was merely gathering up some fairyfingers for Mr. Rutledge's tea."

Adam slanted the man a mocking grimace. "Haven't you ever heard of cream and sugar, Rutledge? There's nothing so unsightly as a fairy flitting around with little bloody stumps."

"That's disgusting!" Juliet shuddered. "It's a plant, for heaven's sake." She gestured to the stalks bearing clusters of cornucopia-shaped blossoms she held cradled in her arm. "Foxglove. Sometimes called fairyfingers. Mr. Rutledge has palpitations of the heart and the tea brewed from these plants eases it."

Adam should have felt chagrined at the mention of the man's supposed illness. Or at the very least chastened by the blatant disapproval in Juliet's features. But he fought back the tide of red threatening his cheeks by taking refuge in his most favored mode of defense—a biting wit. "I'm certain the fairies will be most relieved."

"Miss Grafton-Moore, forgive me, but what is this *person* doing on the grounds of your establishment?" Rutledge demanded, stiffening his meager shoulders beneath their sheath of oversize frockcoat. "He's most dangerous, I can assure you!"

Adam took unholy pleasure in piercing that waxy skin with a glare. "I *live* here."

"L-Live . . . no! That's impossible!" The last drops of blood seemed to evaporate from under the scrawny man's skin.

"Adam!" Juliet wheeled on him, looking as if he'd just described in detail their bedchamber arrangements—adding a few embellishments to the kiss they'd shared. The temptation to follow through with it was almost more than Adam could withstand, but he managed to leash his tongue with great effort.

"I'm here as a guardian angel of sorts until these threats die down," he said with a mild arch of one dark brow.

"You? Serving as guardian?" Rutledge challenged, incredulous. "Isn't that like having the king of thieves guarding the crown jewels? Miss Juliet, I must insist you listen to me! This man is a reprobate! The worst sort of scoundrel! I encountered him in the worst sort of tavern in London. A veritable den of iniquity."

"The two of you have already met?" Juliet asked, dazed.

"The night your friend Percival broke a chair over my head," Adam said. "Of course, I had no way of knowing I'd entered such a degenerate tavern. I was a stranger in town, merely quenching a hellish thirst in the first establishment I ran across after my encounter with that mob." Adam turned to flash a glare at his outraged rival. "Perhaps a more interesting question is what were *you* doing there, Rutledge?"

The pawnbroker fairly swelled with indignation. "I—how dare you question me! Miss Grafton-Moore knows the mettle of my soul, sir. But you are nothing but a stranger preying upon her innocence!"

Adam felt a dashed uncomfortable twinge of conscience.

Rutledge raged on, imploring Juliet. "You cannot tell me you've allowed him into your home! It is that—that insatiable baggage Millicent who has preyed upon your generous heart to gain entry for him! Or Violet or any of the others! You cannot let them corrupt you! How many times have I pleaded with you to be on guard against their licentious influences?"

Frost crystallized Juliet's smile, turning it brittle as a rose petal glazed in ice. "I have warned you before that I will not have you speaking of the ladies in that tone, Mr. Rutledge. As it happens, you accuse them unjustly. I am the one who asked for Mr. Sabrehawk's help."

Rutledge staggered back as if she'd booted him in the solar plexus. "You? I don't believe it!"

"Mr. Slade was a friend of my father's. And——"

"Your father? The Vicar of Northwillow befriend a scoundrel like this man? Impossible! No man of God would lower himself to consort with such sin-begotten filth! How could you believe such a thing for a heartbeat?"

Adam started to rap out a sharp-edged jibe, but stopped himself, as he saw Juliet bristle. "Mr. Slade helped my father when he was dying of fever. He aided a complete stranger lost by the side of the road, gave him comfort, when heaven only knows how many people had passed by, terrified for their own skins."

A swift stab of pleasure jolted through Adam at her defense.

"By whose words were you told such a thing?" Rutledge argued. "Your father's? Or this lying scheming woman-izer's?"

The truth flashed across Juliet's face. "I received letters from Mr. Slade and he returned mother's necklace," she insisted, flustered. "Mr. Slade sent Papa home to North-willow."

"You cannot know for certain how that all came about! For all we know, Slade might have trampled the vicar with his own horse and attempted to hide it with lies. The one thing I know for certain is that your father would be rolling in his grave if he suspected this depraved cur was anywhere near you! Think, Miss Juliet! You already walk a dangerous path and Slade's presence can only make it more perilous. There are those just waiting for you to make a misstep."

"There are a hell of a lot more ready to shove her off a blasted cliff if they get the chance," Adam snarled, but the man ignored him.

"With a man like Slade in your household, people will believe this is no more than another brothel."

Every ridge in Juliet's spine seemed to straighten, the fetching straw hat taking on the militant angle of a colonel's plumes. "Mr. Rutledge, you're overwrought," she said in precise accents. "I don't care what such people think. I know the truth, and so do the ladies. It's vital that I protect them."

Rutledge blustered. "You know exactly how I feel about your work, my dear. It's admirable, no matter how ill-advised. A gesture made because of a misguided passion for these women's redemption. But you might as well sweep the corners of hell itself, trying to reclaim souls shattered beyond repair. Consorting with such sinners will only put you in danger, soil your very soul."

"We sinners take special care to wipe our boots before we trample on her angel's wings," Adam muttered.

"Make a mockery of this, you spawn of Satan! She'll be the one to pay for your stubbornness. Is that what you want?"

"What I want is for you to take your fairyfingers and go before I boil *you* into tea, Rutledge." Adam threw the pieces of latch onto the ground, damned well ready to fling the insufferable vulture out of the gate bodily.

"That is enough, both of you!" Juliet cried, brandishing the stalks of pink and gold foxglove.

But Adam closed the space between himself and the toes of Rutledge's scuffed shoes. "Let me just say one last thing, Rutledge," he warned. "I am here to guard Juliet. Nothing—not these ravening masses you threaten her with, no, nor Satan and all his fallen angels—will harm her while I am at her side. You profess such devotion toward her, such fear at what she faces, that I have one question. When those cowardly sons of bitches were shattering her windows and that ugly mob was battering at her door, where the blazes were you? Hiding under your bed?"

"Adam! Adam, please!" The flowers fell in a cascade from Juliet's grasp, and she caught the rigid muscles of his forearm in a pleading grip.

"Arrogant fool!" Rutledge flung out. "Do you believe something so crude as one sword can stand between Miss Juliet and disaster? Her enemies will go to any lengths to drive her from this place. Aye, and so would anyone who truly cared about her!"

"I haven't noticed you mounting any campaigns to get her to leave."

"I did not offer her a sword. I offered her my name." Rutledge's lips twisted cruelly. "But then, for all your arrogance, that is one thing you could never give any woman."

Something dark and deadly hurled itself against the bars of Adam's soul—rage that this man would dare to even think of Juliet as a wife, and more infuriating still, a swift jab of self-loathing that he—Adam Slade—was jealous for just one instant, coveting anything belonging to a witling like Rutledge. Coveting the one thing Adam could never have—an honorable name.

But Adam would sooner have plunged his own sword in his chest than allow the man to see how well his blow struck its mark.

Adam looked down at Juliet, saw her face go scarlet, her eyes wide with distress. And he wondered if—even just for an instant with the mob swelling in the street and fear rising in the back of her throat—she'd considered becoming Rutledge's wife. The possibility sawed at some raw place inside him like a dull blade.

"It's hard to imagine any woman rejecting a fine specimen of a man like you," Adam sneered silkily. "But then, I'm forgetting. Like Juliet says, you're not a man."

"I never said any such thing!" Juliet sputtered. "This is abominable! Both of you should be ashamed!"

Veins bulged against Rutledge's white-marble skin, his eyes pits of loathing. "Laugh, you insolent bastard. Laugh. You have no idea what you are unleashing upon her head!"

Adam crossed his arms over his chest. "I fought off a hundred of England's finest soldiers at Prestonpans. Surely I can thwart a half-dozen London street ruffians."

"Whatever happens, the two of you will stop this bickering. Mr. Slade is residing at Angel's Fall for the time being. And Mr. Rutledge has been one of my few friends since arriving in London. I'll not tolerate this nonsensical masculine butting of heads between you. Is that understood?"

"You are making a terrible mistake," Rutledge said. "Send this beast away, for God's sake, before he brings out the lascivious streak in one of the women beneath your roof. Females are tragically weak!"

"Rutledge, I've fought on a score of battlefields, and witnessed the aftermath as well. This much I can tell you— if the men who fought beside me had half the courage of the women who come to bury them, I would never have had to sound retreat."

Rutledge turned to Juliet. "Do you wish to stumble across Slade and one of these lightskirts in your charge, groping in some corner? I guarantee you, he'll not be able to keep his hands off of them!"

Anger and a healthy dose of guilt seared Adam at the memory of just how full his hands had been—full of Juliet's kisses and precious tears, his arms filled with her softness as he gathered her against his chest, his mouth bursting with the taste of her as his tongue filled her mouth.

"There is not one of the women under Juliet's protection that tempts me," Adam said. It was the truth. There was only one woman he wanted—and that was Juliet herself.

His gaze snagged Juliet's for a heartbeat, and he knew the same certainty was flooding through her. She all but dove down to gather up the foxglove. When she rose again, it was with the dignity of an embattled queen.

"Good day, Mr. Rutledge," she said, putting the blossoms into the man's white hands. "I do hope you'll still come for tea as usual next Tuesday."

She invited the vulture to tea? Hell yes, and probably dosed the concoction with barrels full of sugar in an attempt to sweeten the dour idiot's disposition.

Rutledge drew himself up to his full height. "I'll not set foot in Angel's Fall as long as this man is on the premises! To do so would be to grant my tacit approval. And I withhold it, adamantly."

Did it matter to her? This caricature of a man's approval? The thought nettled Adam beyond bearing. But there was something fragile in Juliet's features as she smoothed one of her curls back inside the ruffle of lace cap that caressed her cheek. And Adam saw, with an unexpected flash of insight, a little girl with golden curls and a vicar father, wishing desperately for approval—the same way Adam had when he'd been a grubby-faced boy. Lord, what a secret poison that desire could be!

What had it cost her to defy all of London? To walk down the streets, feeling the press of loathing-filled eyes upon her? The scorn of everyone from coachmen to ballad sellers. The pointed swish of catty women sweeping their skirts away from her as they passed, so as not to be tainted by so much as brushing against her?

Something twisted deep in Adam's gut as he remembered another woman enduring just such slights, her head tilted up with pride, a smile of determined cheerfulness upon her face. His own mother . . .

"Whether you come to Angel's Fall or not is your choice, of course," Juliet shattered his musings, addressing Rutledge with gentle dignity. "Your place at the table will always be open. Do let me know when you need more fairyfingers for your tea. I'll be happy to gather some or you're welcome to pick them yourself." With that, she turned and walked away.

Adam stood, arms crossed over his chest, masking the astonishing twinge of pain he felt with a rascally grin of triumph. "It seems the lady doesn't give a damn about your approval, adamant or otherwise," he said, wishing to hell it was true. "Considering all the other mischief she's been up to, who would have guessed she was a woman of such good sense?"

Rutledge was trembling with wrath. "Play out whatever game you're dabbling in, Slade!" He jabbed a finger at Adam's chest. "I know what you are! A man who cares for nothing, no one but his own selfish pleasures. The time will come when you tire of this amusement. And then, you'll leave Miss Grafton-Moore alone. When that happens, I'll be waiting."

"With that wedding ring she's already rejected?" Adam was stunned by the rush of fury and futility that jolted through him. "Perhaps Miss Grafton-Moore and I will surprise you, Rutledge, and settle down with her ladies in a house in the country."

Who would have suspected that such simple, impossible words could make a man trip over an unexpected chasm in his own soul?

"Mock me, Slade! Mock me!" Rutledge raged. "There is only one thing I wonder—will you be still be laughing when Angel's Fall lies in ashes around Juliet's feet?"

Adam watched Rutledge storm away, Juliet's fairyfingers crushed heedlessly in his hands. A trickle of foreboding dripped down his spine, pooling in the place in his gut where his instincts lay.

Blast, he had no fear that he'd protect her from Rutledge's throngs of torch-wielding cutthroats or even from Lord Darlington's minions. He'd defeated legions of such foes in the past.

There was far greater danger of leaving something else in ashes when he walked away from Angel's Fall forever—the fragile dreams he'd glimpsed in Juliet's eyes when he'd kissed her.

A shudder worked through him, so deep it shook the very marrow of his bones—a fierce, primal need Juliet had released from its cage with her soft angel's kisses and tears that had dampened the scars upon his palms and others that lashed far deeper. . . .

Adam's jaw clenched, and he slammed the garden gate shut, locking it tight. But it didn't matter.

His most dangerous enemy was still inside—a knight's hunger for his lady fair trapped in a forgotten corner of the warrior's heart Adam had thought buried long ago.

Chapter

10

Juliet stormed into the tiny garden house and sagged down onto a cushion-strewn bench, burying her face in one dirt-smudged hand. Adam Slade was insufferable! Charging up to poor Barnabas Rutledge like one of the Horsemen of the Apocalypse, fire fairly shooting from his eyes, just burning to start a fight.

What in the name of heaven had she gotten herself into? she wondered for the hundredth time in the days since the confrontation in Ranelagh Gardens. Iron bars on the windows, new locks on the door. A growling bear of a man prowling around snarling out orders, and following her about as if she were a particularly troublesome meal he wasn't about to let escape him.

A wild twinge of hysteria bubbled in her chest. What was she? Someone who *craved* punishment? There had been enough mayhem to satisfy the most dedicated of disaster-mongers at Angel's Fall with threats flying and enraged mobs charging about. But no. That hadn't been miserable enough for Juliet Grafton-Moore. She'd had to invite Adam Slade right in the front door.

The whole situation would have been enough to drive any sane woman mad. But it seemed she'd already lost her mind, because despite all the snapping and snarling and surliness inherent in Adam Slade's residence at Angel's Fall, there was some traitorous corner of Juliet's heart that actually *liked* having him here.

She'd done her best to deny it, avoiding him like a skittish doe, all but diving out of his way whenever possible. But she hadn't been able to escape the gruff rasp of his voice emanating from some other part of the house as he snapped orders at Fletcher or growled something at the ladies.

She hadn't been able to keep her eyes from his rugged features, his warrior's body, seated across from her at the long mahogany dining table. And late at night, in the darkness, she felt the soft pulsings of pain radiating from every scar that marked those powerful hands, and heard again how gentle his voice could be.

Most perilous of all, she'd relived their kiss beneath the lanterns of Ranelagh Gardens so many times that the feel of his mouth seemed branded upon hers, the places where his hands had touched her tingling and burning and aching for the return of that caress.

He'd infused lightning into her veins, an intoxicating mixture of wantonness and fear, desperate curiosity to learn more—what lay beneath that pirate's smile and those ebony eyes, to plumb the depths of the pain he'd brushed aside in his tale about his brother. And to discover the secrets of her own flesh he'd promised to unlock with his hands and his mouth, and the gruff moan of surrender that had shaken his stalwart form at the searing intimacy of his tongue sweeping against her own.

Juliet hugged her arms tight against her ribs, trembling, horrified at the impact the mere thought of the man could have upon her senses. An impact that increased a hundred-fold whenever he was in the vicinity.

Most distressing, most miraculously wonderful of all was the knowledge that he had changed her forever, as certainly as the fairytale prince who had kissed a sleeping beauty awake. How many times in the months after Jenny had dashed away from Northwillow had Juliet regarded her with pity, certain that with just a little determination, Jenny could have resisted the charms of the dashing squire's son who had convinced her to run away with him?

Juliet had mourned her dearest friend and cousin, worried about her constantly. Prayed that the fairytale ending Jenny so desperately dreamed of would indeed come true. Yet now, within the shadowy musty confines of the garden house, with only discarded pots and spades and rakes standing sentinel in the corner, Juliet could admit that her compassion had been tinged with a poisonous drop of arrogance.

Juliet had been absolutely certain that she would never drift into the same treacherous waters Jenny had sailed, that no man would ever tempt her onto the rocky shoals of her own destruction.

How could she have guessed what mesmerizing power a pair of ebony eyes could hold? How velvety hot a man's mouth could feel upon her own, initiating her into a world of thunderous pleasure and primal need? How could she suspect that he could sweep away all her rigidly held ideals with one touch of his strong hands and sprinkle stardust in her eyes?

A tremor shook Juliet to the soles of her slippers and she caught her lip between her teeth. She wanted Adam Slade. Wanted to feel the virile planes and hollows of his body against her own in the tumbled coverlets upon her bed, wanted him to reveal even more of the potent secrets of pleasure that lay behind his insufferable smile. Wanted to see fires of adoration flicker like living flame beneath his thick lashes.

Her eyes slid closed, her nipples tight against the fabric of her shift, all her secret places tingling with need. Merciful heavens, was it possible that she was . . . *falling in love with him?* A jolt of raw panic pierced her like a well-shot arrow, its impact quivering in every nerve in her body.

What insane folly that would be—to surrender her heart to a man, any man. Especially Adam Slade. Her work was far too important to jeopardize.

But every sardonic sneer that had curved that sensual mouth flashed in her memory, the hard shell of cynicism encasing him like the armor that shielded knights of old.

Yet where such knights had been willing to sacrifice their very souls to the fires of hell for love, Adam Slade wanted nothing but to ride away, unfettered by such emotions, free of any sort of commitment, to Juliet or to the gangly youth, Fletcher, who idolized him.

There would come a time when Adam would break the boy's heart, Juliet knew instinctively, severing the bonds of his adoration with a ruthlessness he perceived as mercy. And if Adam ever suspected the emotions he'd loosed in her, he would do the same. He was the embodiment of every heartache Juliet had seen reflected in the eyes of the ladies of the street she'd gathered in Angel's Fall, every impossible passion, every glittering future that could never be.

He was the tempting apple in her very own Garden of Eden, and if she ever took a bite of what he offered, it would mean the end of everything she'd tried to build here.

She knew it in her head. If only she could convince her heart.

The sound of the garden-house door slamming open tore a cry from her throat, and she wheeled around to find Adam towering in the doorway.

For an instant, she thought he'd followed her to the garden house, and her heart gave a wild flutter, but then she saw the dismay in his features, the pieces of an iron latch in his hand.

He recovered in a heartbeat, flashing her a devilishly handsome sneer. "Come in here to dab a little essence of garden dirt on your pulse points to captivate your ardent suitor?"

The words were cold, a little cruel, but beneath his cynical facade, Juliet saw something in his face that would send him running out of the shed like the basest of cowards if he suspected it was there—the tiniest glimmer of dread. Dread of what? The power the kiss had unleashed between them? Or that she might entertain some affection for poor Barnabas Rutledge?

She stood up, trying to keep her knees from trembling as she smoothed the folds of her embroidered apron. "I told you from the beginning, I have no desire to *captivate* any man," she said briskly.

Adam gave an ugly snort. "You seem to be collecting a fair share of admirers. Rutledge, bumbling at your back gate like the fool he is. Fletcher—hell, the boy would cut out his heart if you asked him."

The need to jab at him cast any sense of caution to the wind. "Well, neither of them has kissed me."

Was relief the emotion that almost overcame his surliness? It took him but a moment to shutter it away. "That kiss was a mistake," he ground out. "One you can be damned certain I won't be making again."

That was what she wanted to hear, wasn't it? Reassurance that it would never happen again. Why was it, then, that his words hurt her more than she dreamed possible? What had happened to the man who had gazed into her eyes in the garden at Ranelagh, his warrior-king features so haunted and filled with yearning, his voice roughened with feeling as she wept over his hands? The man who had bared secret places in his soul to her?

She stopped, suddenly. He'd been rampaging around the house like a wounded bear because he was—what? Ashamed to have shown her the slightest vulnerability? This man who had spent a lifetime burying his tender feelings, hiding them from a world that would use them as a weapon against him.

Juliet's heart wrenched. Where had he learned that skill? Echoes of Adam's gruff voice echoed through her, images he'd painted with his words of his mother smiling at the condemning vicar, never letting anyone see her pain, nor acknowledging that it ever existed, even to her own son.

Did that lady realize how much pain Adam had hidden away? Or had she ignored it the way she had ignored her lover's wife and legitimate son, pretending, forever pretending that they didn't exist, or that they didn't matter at all?

Perhaps it was time to stop giving Adam places to hide. "You behaved like a witling out there! Bellowing at poor Mr. Rutledge. What on earth possessed you?"

Adam glared at her for a moment. "He was making

calves' eyes at you like some besotted fool, acting so supercilious, I wanted to . . . thought he . . ."

"Surely you didn't think he could be any danger to me?"

"Are you mad?" Adam scoffed. "He couldn't hold his own in a fight with a three-day-old kitten!"

"Then why did you get so angry?"

"Because I—didn't want him looking at you that way!" Adam flung out. "Don't want any man to . . . blast! I've been around Fletcher too damned long. Next thing you know, I'll be blotting up reams of execrable poetry comparing your eyes to polliwogs or somesuch. I need to get the devil away from here before I lose my mind!"

"Maybe you'd be happier without it," Juliet suggested with acid cheerfulness.

"Juliet, don't tell me you have feelings for Rutledge, that—that scrawny yapping dog of a fool!"

"I do have feelings toward him. Sympathy. Gratitude. He is terribly alone in that little pawnshop, and so very unhappy. And he *was* kind to me."

"Exactly how did this kindness manifest itself? He's the only one in the neighborhood who hasn't heaved a brick through your window? That's not kindness, madam, it's poor aim."

His scorn rankled, driving her to a rash confession she'd sworn never to tell another soul. "I had to pawn two links of my mother's necklace to keep Angel's Fall running smoothly." Juliet couldn't totally hide the twinge of pain the memory caused her, the pulling apart of the precious necklace had been like tearing out bits of her own heart.

"That bauble I sent all the way from Ireland?" Adam stared at her, stunned. "You turned it over to that penny-grubbing fool. I'd have thought you were the sentimental sort."

"He gave me a most generous price. And he tucked the bits into the corner of one of his shelves, half hidden by other trinkets so his customers wouldn't see them. I hope that someday I'll be able to buy the pieces back."

Black eyes glittered beneath the sharp slash of Adam's brows, but he was silent, too silent—a giant jungle cat watching its prey. "I wonder, is that possible?" he demanded a little hoarsely.

"Is what possible?"

"To buy back the pieces that you've stolen from me?" But he didn't explain his cryptic comment, only turned and stalked from the garden house.

Chapter

11

It was quiet. Too quiet, Adam thought grimly as he paced through the night-darkened house. There hadn't been so much as a ripple in the still waters that enveloped Angel's Fall, no threats or angry clusters of Mother Cavendish's throng. Any normal man would have been relieved at the relative peacefulness outside the haven for fallen women—especially since the inside of the infernal place was buzzing like a hollow tree stuffed with honey, the women continually flitting about, stinging each other with their biting words.

But in his years as a warrior Adam had learned to mistrust the most peaceful of glades—the more serene the setting, the more potentially deadly it could be.

He paused at the doorway, and checked the latch, making certain it was still bolted. God knows, two days ago, he'd found it wide open, and Millicent in the garden with the butcher's young apprentice. He'd hauled the woman inside with all the finesse of an outraged papa, sending the fledgling butcher fleeing with a cuff to the shoulder.

He should've turned the girl over to Juliet for a rare fine scolding, but he found he couldn't—especially with Millicent pleading, very real tears streaking her face.

"Please, I beg of you, don't tell Juliet!"

"Do you fear she'll fling you out of the house?" Adam had asked.

"Never! She never would unless I did something to harm one of the other ladies. It's just . . . I know you'll never be able to understand. But she'll look at me, so sad, like the madonna in St. Columcille's church where I went as a child. She'll clasp my hand and stroke my hair and tell me to try to do better next time. I know it sounds mad, but I'd rather she get out the horsewhip like my father did, and just beat the devil out of me instead of staring at me, so forgiving."

It was a sentiment Adam understood only too well. There were times he'd have preferred facing a firing squad rather than confront the disappointment in his brother's face.

"I know it's hard to understand, but since I was scarce thirteen, I'd spent every night in a man's arms. I know he cared nothing about me, but still, I could pretend I wasn't alone."

Wistfulness clung to the dulcet tones of her voice, a hollow, aching emptiness that spoke volumes. *"Please Mr. Sabrehawk,"* she'd said.

He'd stroked Millicent's pretty hair the way he would have petted one of his little sisters' curls, and sent her up to bed.

But he'd been shaken by how alike he and the courtesan were—for he'd dreamed night after night of arms holding him, shielding him from his own night-dragons. Arms pale and innocent as the light of the new moon. He'd buried himself in countless romantic liaisons. He'd garnered the admiration of even his most dreaded enemies. He had a family who adored him, who clamored in every letter that they missed him, and a half-brother he knew was hurt by the fact that Adam couldn't bear to face him. But Adam had never realized why he'd withdrawn from his family until now.

He'd been alone forever, until Juliet Grafton-Moore had wept over his scarred hands.

He gave a final tug on the lock, then froze as he heard a noise out of synch with the night.

It was coming from the direction of the pantry. Stealthily,

he crossed to its half-open door, then, every nerve humming with readiness, slammed it open. A startled cry reverberated from within. Light from the kitchen lamps spilled into the space, and he caught a glimpse of golden curls and wide blue eyes that appeared guilty as bedamned.

Juliet. She whipped around, facing the worktable and the pantry wall, thrusting something beneath a linen towel. Adam scowled at the back of her neck.

"What the devil are you doing running about?" Adam demanded, oddly irritated.

"Eating gingerbread. If you must know, I have a secret passion for the stuff." A kind of light fog seemed to obscure the words, her voice the tiniest bit indistinct. Blast if she didn't sound a little tipsy.

She was so obvious in her efforts to conceal something, Adam couldn't resist tormenting her. "I'm rather fond of the stuff myself. Perhaps I'll try a piece."

"No!" she exclaimed far too emphatically, rushing to dump the whole pan into the rubbish pail. Adam knew he'd never seen her waste so much as a thimbleful of food, always gathering every scrap to put out for the poor.

"This batch is absolutely dreadful," she rushed to explain, never even turning to glance at him. "I'll make another tomorrow. Now shouldn't you be off changing the guard or whatever you and Fletcher do all night?"

Suspicion stirred in Adam's chest. His angel was the sort who liked looking straight into the eyes of whomever she was speaking to. What the devil was the matter with her? What was she hiding?

Adam closed the space between them. "What are you up to, lady? Dipping into the medicinal wine?" He grasped her arm, to turn her toward him. He was stunned as she resisted, grabbing up the linen towel, pressing it to her mouth, as if dabbing away the crumbs.

"I'm gorging myself on sweets. I do it when I'm nervous. Now are you satisfied?"

"So you're human after all, I—" Adam started to tease, then his gaze locked on the bright crimson stain spreading upon the towel. "What the hell! You're bleeding!" he accused.

"It's nothing! The tiniest cut."

He ripped the towel away from her face. A wound as long as Adam's smallest fingernail marred the ripe perfection of her bottom lip, a droplet of blood marking the injury. "How the devil did that happen?"

"There was something in the gingerbread. A piece of glass." She gave a brisk laugh. "That's one of the hazards in teaching cooking to reluctant students. I should have made it clear they were supposed to crack the *eggs* into the *bowl,* not the *bowl* into the *eggs.*"

Adam looked down at the worktable, saw the crumbling piece of gingerbread she'd attempted to hide. A shard of blue bottle glass nestled in the spicy cake, a wicked point at its end. He shuddered as he pried the triangle of glass free. "Who the devil did this! It was damned careless! Hell, you could have been badly hurt."

"I—I don't remember who baked today. I—I'm sure it was my own fault the bowl broke."

Something about her protests made Adam scowl. His gaze locked on the shelf above the worktable, crockery bowls lined up in careful precision. He held the piece of glass to the light. "Just a damned minute, lady. How stupid do you think I am? There's no way in hell you'd have a glass bowl here. Too damned expensive. How the blazes . . ."

She turned away, but not before he saw hot color flood her cheeks. A sick sensation gripped his stomach. "If this glass couldn't have broken into the batter by accident then someone did it on purpose."

"Adam, please. Don't jump to conclusions! There's no harm done."

"No harm done!" he roared. "You're bleeding, damn it. Whoever planted this in Angel's Fall meant for someone to cut themselves. And badly."

"That's one blessing. No one else was in danger."

"How can you say that? How could even the most devious of minds know that you would be the one to take that particular piece of gingerbread? They'd have to be some sort of conjurer, able to predict the future."

"I'm the only person at Angel's Fall who likes gingerbread. It's a particular weakness of mine. Papa's cure for all ills—a nice hot plate of it with some milk. I know it's silly, but the taste of it has always made me feel safe, somehow. As if I were sipping a bit of my own childhood." Trembling fingers touched the cut, and Adam saw the dart of sorrow in her eyes, knew instinctively what she was thinking. Now, instead of remembering warmth and safety and her father's love, whenever his angel smelled the spicy cake, she'd remember this—something lethal buried inside it by someone who hated her, wanted to hurt her. The knowledge made him wild with impotent rage.

He fought it down, and tipped her face up into a puddle of lamplight, then grabbed up a bit of clean cloth. "Open your mouth, sweetheart," he ordered. "Let me see . . ."

"It's nothing. I told you—"

"Open your mouth or I'll pry it open with a spoon," he threatened.

She grimaced, wincing in pain, then surrendered. Those ripe lips that had been the most kissable he'd ever tasted parted, and he saw another small gash on her tongue and one on the inside of her cheek.

"You didn't swallow any of the glass? You're sure of that?"

"I'm sure."

"Thank God." A streak of relief shot through him that the injury wasn't far worse. Adam dabbed at the cut on her lip, certain he could have cheerfully used the bit of glass to carve into ribbons whichever sick son of a bitch was responsible for hurting her. But first he'd have to find out exactly who it was. He raked through his mind, trying to grasp infinite possibilities.

"Whoever planned this would have to have been inside this house," Adam mused, a sick knot tightening in the pit of his stomach. "And they'd have to know your ways. Hell, what are the chances that you'd be the only person in this whole place who liked gingerbread? I didn't even know it, and I've been living in your infernal bedroom for days."

Horror beyond imagining dawned inside him, his voice

grating like the hinges on a long-sealed tomb. "The only people who could know such a thing are living here," he said slowly. "Isabelle, Millicent, all your angels."

Juliet struggled to pull away from him, but Adam held her still with one mighty hand. Hot indignation flooded her eyes, turning her features militant. "None of my ladies would do such a cruel thing to anyone! I'll not tolerate you accusing them of something so despicable!"

"Who else could have arranged this little present for you? No one else has been inside this benighted place since the day I first arrived. The doors are latched, the windows barred. The gingerbread has been in the kitchen the whole time—"

"No it hasn't. I put it out in the garden to cool. Anyone could have gotten to it there."

"But the gate was locked, wasn't it?" Adam almost bellowed, but no one knew better than he did how fragile such measures of security could be. He'd picked more locks, broken more bolts, and wedged open more windows than a house-breaker in his years earning his bread at the point of his sword.

"I don't know if everything was locked. I think so, but—but the butcher's lad has to be able to bring the chickens I ordered for pie tonight into the kitchen, and the ladies are constantly having things delivered to the house—fans and bits of ribbon."

Fear throbbed through Adam's veins, an unfamiliar elixir that made him feel helpless and weak for the first time in his life. The notorious Sabrehawk who had made a fortune guarding black-hearted villains and greedy tyrants with his sword hadn't been able to protect this compassionate angel of a woman, not even here in her own house.

Was it likely that someone had managed to break into the garden? Adam puzzled in desperation. That the perpetrator of this vile deed had merely slipped into Angel's Fall like a shadow, left their horrendous warning, and then melted into the night?

There was always the possibility that it was so. But there was another possibility so bitter Adam could barely form it in his mind—the chance that more delicate, more trusted hands had slipped the glass into the gingerbread. That someone inside Angel's Fall was responsible for Juliet's injuries. Adam had spent a lifetime witnessing the starkest of betrayals—his father's betrayal of his wife, officers' betrayals of the men they led into battle, but never had the prospect of such dishonor stricken him more deeply.

Adam gathered her into his arms. "What in heaven's name are you doing?"

"Carrying you upstairs where you belong."

"I can walk by myself, you know. I didn't cut my feet."

What would she say if he admitted the truth? That he was holding her for himself, to assure himself she was safe. That he felt as if he would keep her there forever if by doing so he could keep every danger that stalked her at bay.

After a moment, she stopped her struggles and nestled against his chest, burying her face in the lee of his shoulder with a sigh. He carried her up the stairs, heedless of the noise he made, his boots sounding like cannonfire against the risers. Doors popped open along the faintly lit corridor, mob-caps of every size and style poking out into the hallway as women thrust out their sleepy heads.

"What is amiss?" Millicent cried, rubbing at her sleep-crusted eyes with one fist.

"Nothing," Juliet said, struggling against his arms. Adam held her pinioned against his chest as if she were a fluttering hummingbird.

"Which one of you is missing a piece of blue glass?" Adam demanded, sweeping a scathing glance at the women. They were white-faced, more than a little frightened—except for Isabelle who stood, as ever, an ice queen, untouchable. Suspicion tugged at Adam's chest. But it was not the Frenchwoman who cried out in dismay.

"Blue glass?" Elise echoed, her wan face the color of old wax. "Oh, no! Don't tell me I didn't sweep up all the bits of my scent-bottle!"

Adam gaped at the trembling woman, so fragile, so devoted to Juliet. Surely it was impossible that Elise was responsible for something so horrendous.

"I thought I got all the pieces wrapped up in paper and

put them into the rubbish, but I must have dropped some. Why do I always have to be so clumsy?" Savage guilt racked Elise's delicate features. "Did you cut your foot?"

"No, Elise," Juliet soothed. "Don't concern yourself. Adam, there's no reason to upset everyone. Now stop—"

"Juliet cut her mouth on a piece of glass someone wedged into her gingerbread," Adam said ruthlessly. "It's a miracle she didn't swallow it!"

The consequences of that calamity rended Adam in the deepest part of his vitals, conjuring up pictures of what might have befallen this angel of a woman with her madonna eyes and her tender hands. Death of the most horrific, torturous kind imaginable.

Silence crashed down on the women, an utter sick silence as they grappled with his words. Elise cried out, racing to Juliet's side, catching up her hand. "Are you all right? Oh, sweet heaven!"

At her words, the others spilled forward on a wave of disbelief, concern, only Isabelle standing back, regal as an empress. "Stop your blathering, all of you! Of course she is all right. Open your eyes! Angelina, go make her some tea. Elise, quit your wretched caterwauling. She's not dead. See if we have a little sticking plaster, though I've no idea how it will work on her lip."

"No," Juliet interrupted, like a general mustering her troops. "Elise, get herbs for a poultice. You know which ones to pick. And Millicent, put the gingerbread into the fire. We don't want any children or animals to dig it out of the rubbish by mistake."

The women nodded and raced off.

Adam reached the door to Juliet's bedchamber and booted it open. By instinct alone, he carried her into the alcove, laid her down on his own tumbled bed. God in heaven, he thought, half profanity, half prayer, what the hell was he going to do with her? How was he going to keep her safe? Especially if the animal stalking her was so crafty it could strike with such demonic cunning within the confines of her own home?

"There is no reason for everyone to—to make such a fuss

over this," Juliet insisted, levering herself to a sitting position. "After all, as Shakespeare said, all's well that ends well."

But you could be lying in my arms right now bleeding to death from wounds I could never reach, a voice inside Adam tormented him. *The light could be draining from your eyes one star at a time, the life ebbing from your hands. I could be helpless . . .*

Adam reached up, stroking back a lock of her hair, reassuring himself with the faint throb of a pulsebeat at her temple. Despite her brave words, he saw the echoes of his own horror in her eyes, curling deep into hidden places she would never let anyone else see.

"I don't know who did this," she said. "But they must hate me, Adam. Hate me terribly."

She gave a shaky laugh, and Adam saw her hands knot in the fabric of her apron in an effort to still their trembling. "Do you know that all the years I was in Northwillow no one ever did? Hate me, I mean. It's one more novel experience."

"Nothing makes people angrier than having someone else point out what hypocrites they are," Adam said.

"Maybe. But I think it's a good thing that they're attacking me this way."

"A good thing?" Adam echoed, incredulous. "Hell, you really have lost your mind."

"No, really. Think. When I first arrived, they only jeered at me, laughed at me, took wagers on how long it would take me to pack up my trunks and flee back to Northwillow. But lately, everything has gotten so much uglier, the threats, the—the things they do to warn me. I can't help thinking that they must not see me as quite the same laughingstock they did before. That they perceive me as an enemy now, a real threat."

"That seems a reasonable assumption since most people don't saunter around flinging bricks through their friends' windows."

"I keep thinking that maybe, just maybe, they're angry because I'm starting to win."

"Oui, and maybe they're sick of you making a fool of yourself." Juliet recoiled as if Isabelle had slapped her. The Frenchwoman loomed over her, features haughty as an ice queen's carved in the most scathing of scorn.

"Enough of this nonsense!" Isabelle exclaimed. "You playing the savior, as if you are so much better than the rest of us! I believe it is time to gather up your toys, my sweet, and run away home."

Adam maneuvered himself between Juliet and Isabelle, his face grim. "This is no time to be battering at her! Can't you see she's hurt."

"Oui, I can see that. And *I* say it is no surprise. She will be bleeding from far worse wounds if she does not give up this so foolish quest of hers." Isabelle faced Adam, another soldier of life, one whose features held the same world-weariness, the same cynicism, carved in the lines a hard life had etched into her face. "Adam Slade, do not even try to deny that you feel the same way I do about her ridiculous attachment to this house and the women inside it!"

There, beneath the flinty beauty of eyes hard and clear as gemstones, Adam saw a silent plea, suspected he'd won an unlikely ally, albeit maybe an untrustworthy one.

"You're wrong, Isabelle," Juliet said with absolute certainty. "Adam doesn't feel I should leave Angel's Fall. Not any longer. He knows that my work here is important." Those angel-blue eyes flashed to his in total certainty, confidence and trust shimmering with untold beauty in her face. "Tell her, Adam."

Adam gazed at her a moment, his heart giving a painful throb. And in that instant he knew he'd never feared anything as much as failing this woman of light and love and soul-deep goodness. There was only one thing he feared more. That she would be caught in the jaws of something more horrible than she could comprehend. She could be hurt, hideously, irrevocably, or worse still, she could be killed. His whole being recoiled at the thought. In that instant, he knew what he had to do.

"Isabelle is right. It's time to go home, Juliet."

His words struck her a far more brutal blow than whoever had put the glass into the gingerbread.

Her eyes darkened with hurt, her fingers trembling as she pressed them against the oozing wound in her lip. "No."

"Damn it to hell, Juliet, you could have died in that accursed pantry tonight. If you'd swallowed that glass—"

"But I didn't! A few tiny cuts are nothing to get in a fuss about!"

"What if Elise had taken that piece of gingerbread? Or Millicent? Or Fletcher? Hell, you say you're the only person here who likes gingerbread. I doubt you could manage to shovel down the whole pan of it before it went stale. Then what do you do with it?" He'd always had a knack for finding an opponent's vulnerability. He'd taught himself to be ruthless enough to press the advantage when he found it. And he knew, in his gut, he'd just discovered Juliet's.

"You've always put the remains of the cake into that beggar's basket you set outside the garden gate every night, haven't you?" Adam demanded. "What if some climbing boy or pauper's waif had tucked it underneath their rags to fill their pitiful stomachs? What if they'd wolfed the thing down like the ravening little savages they are?"

Every drop of color was sucked from her face until only her eyes remained, a hot tortured blue more cutting than the edge of any blade ever forged.

"No, sweet heaven!" She pressed quivering fingers to her lips, looking as if she were about to be sick.

"Damn it, Juliet, how long are you going to keep careening along this insane course? Are you going to wait until someone gets injured beyond repair? Or worse still, until someone is killed? I know all about terminal do-gooders like you. You always think you're willing to sacrifice yourself in some grand gesture. But what happens if your enemy's plans misfire and it's Elise laying in your arms, bleeding to death because a bullet or a brick or a piece of glass meant for you ends up striking her instead?"

"You don't understand! I can't . . . they'd be in far worse danger out on the street."

"The only thing I was in danger of was straining a muscle in my arm from the weight of the jewels the duke showered upon me," Isabelle declared with a toss of her regal head.

"As for your philanthropic zeal, I'd sooner feed my finest gown into the fire as thank you for all you've done for me. This is a mere way station, one every courtesan and lightskirt in London knows about. On the street, they laugh about it—Angel's Fall, the perfect place to mount a campaign to find a new protector, one richer or handsomer or more generous than the one you had before."

Juliet stiffened. "Maybe some of them think so. Others might say they believe as you do. But I know that there are some I can help, some lives I can touch if I only reach out . . ."

Isabelle laughed, the sound like crystal bells shattering. "From the time we first hoisted our skirts for the pleasures of a man we've been schooled to grasp whatever advantages come our way, coin or jewels, pretty gowns, a warm bed or food to fill our stomachs. It just so happens that the price you demand in return is different."

"Price?" Juliet echoed, indignant. "I don't demand anything in return!"

"Don't you?" Isabelle's eyes narrowed, shrewd despite their beauty, and Adam wondered how many hurts her duke had dealt her to leave such a grim legacy in those eyes. "You make us play house like a convent full of little nuns—stitching perfect seams, baking little cakes, reading improving tomes. One thing I've learned in life is that everything can be bought. But some bargains are better than others. If I happen to prefer mine with broad shoulders and powerful thighs and a family treasure chest full of jewels, then who can blame me?"

Juliet's gaze flashed from one feminine face to another, her eyes searching, questioning. "Do the rest of you feel this way? Millicent? Angelina? Violet, say something for pity's sake! I can't believe you are just using Angel's Fall as a place to launch a search for another man."

Millicent pinkened. "That's not such a terrible thing as it sounds, Miss Juliet. You've given me time so's I don't have to take the first Reginald or Philip to saunter down St. James. I can take my time, real slow, like. Look them over careful and pick the best of the lot."

"It's considerable work, slaving over stitches all day," Angelina admitted, scuffing her toe against an uneven floorboard like a child caught in some mischief.

"At least she's not training you up to be a governess!" Violet said.

"But you're wonderful with children! I've seen you slipping the little ones *nonpareils* at the confectioners!"

"That doesn't mean I want to be drowning in the little monsters! My mama was a courtesan who raised me to be some gentleman's delight. Not blind myself over those French lessons and reading the same story over and over again until your brain turns to pudding, while everyone else is having wonderful times dancing and playing at whist."

"Violet, Lady Dudley promised me that she would give you a trial the instant I thought you were ready! It was no small feat to get her to give you a chance! If her husband wasn't in the direst straits from his gaming I never could have managed it.

"Think how lovely it will be," Juliet said, "tucking the children into their bed, or preparing the next day's lesson."

"Do you know what governesses *really* do, Juliet?" Violet's delicate hands twisted together. "They stand on the fringes, their faces pressed up against the stair-rail like a child excluded from Christmas. They see wonderful entertainments and beautiful gowns and intriguing men, but they are never allowed to taste any kind of pleasure themselves."

Violet tossed her curls. "They stand at a cracked mirror in their own abysmal little rooms, and watch wrinkles etch into their face, knowing that their beauty will fade away, that time is running out, but no one will ever notice."

"Why didn't you ever tell me you felt this way before?" Juliet asked brokenly.

"Because I didn't want to hurt your feelings." Violet shrugged. "I wanted to believe I could change, but I guess we're all what we were born to be."

A timid little mademoiselle who looked like she belonged in a convent school sidled up. "I want to be a seamstress, Miss Juliet," Felicity said. "Even if my fingers bleed and my eyes get sore."

Isabelle swept over, looping an arm about the girl's narrow shoulders. "It's all right to tell the truth now, *ma petite*. The game is over. And it isn't fair to put Juliet in further danger on our account, is it?" A pointed stare from the exquisite courtesan all but made the girl pull her apron up to hide her face. "We don't want Juliet to get hurt, do we?"

"N-no. Of course not. I . . ."

"The only way to get her to run back off to her safe little village in Norwich, was it? No, Northwillow—is to tell her we don't need her anymore."

The child-woman had seen enough of the streets to understand the meaning layered beneath Isabelle's words. Adam saw a tremor shake the girl. "I see you are—you are right."

"And Elise?" Isabelle turned, and Adam saw Elise, poised in the doorway, a bundle of herbs and a worn bowl and pestle clutched in her hands. "What about you? Don't you think it is time our Juliet stopped tilting with our dragons and went off and married a nice staid vicar or barrister?"

Juliet struggled up from the feathertick, stood, swaying, on bare feet, her nightgown a soft cloud around her. She curved her hands around Elise's, peering into those great dark eyes.

"Elise, you believe in Angel's Fall, don't you? Believe in what I'm doing here?"

Elise drew a tortured breath, and Adam could feel just how much the words cost her. "It's a dream, Juliet. A beautiful dream, but a dream nonetheless. M-maybe it's time we all awakened."

No one on this earth had the power to wound her as deeply as Elise did, unless it was the man who stood towering over the ruin of all she'd battled to build in Angel's Fall. Juliet's hands dropped, limp at her sides.

"No! You're wrong! All of you! I know it. I feel it, in my heart!" Tears threatened to spill over Juliet's lashes, her breast a hollow burning void of betrayal. "Get out, all of you! Leave me alone!"

Stricken expressions darted across the features of the

ladies clustered about. Answering tears shone in Millicent's eyes, Violet's hands clenching together. Juliet wanted desperately for someone to defy her. To stay.

They turned, fled. Elise paused long enough to set the herbs down on the table.

"Juliet," she breathed, and for an instant, Juliet hoped. Hoped that Elise could wash away everything that had been said, could make things the way they'd been before—before they'd dashed out the ugly truth before her eyes. Before they'd told her what a fool she'd been.

But Elise's sorrowful gaze only clung to hers for a heartbeat before she hastened out of the room.

Only Adam was left. He stood there, rigid, silent, magnificent in his severely tailored black breeches and flowing white shirt.

She wondered if the Angel of Death might be just so—indescribably beautiful, immovable as stone.

"I always knew they were teetering on the brink of returning to their old lives or deciding on the new. I thought I could help them, show them, calm their fears. It was in my hands. But once I let you come inside Angels Fall—changed the rules. Changed everything—I failed them, somehow. Are you happy now?" she demanded. "Now that they've all said what you wanted them to say? Told me that everything you said about Angel's Fall is true?"

His jaw knotted. "No. I'm not happy. But it had to be said. Juliet, isn't it time to stop this madness before someone gets hurt. You won't be able to breathe life back into them, no matter how badly you might wish it. God knows, you can't. I've tried to do it myself often enough."

Ancient wounds shimmered in his eyes, as if every sword stroke he'd ever made had scarred some secret part of him, every wound he'd ever dealt had cut his own flesh, every death he'd ever caused had deadened some part of his own soul.

What would this night's work cost him?

Juliet crossed to the window that looked out over the London night, her spine straight as her father's conscience, her eyes hot with unshed tears.

"Just—just go to bed. Leave me alone, please."

"I can only do one or the other," he said in that softly mocking voice.

"Why can't you—"

"My bed is right here."

She turned, her face drained of all warmth, and her heart cracked at the half-smile that crossed the ruggedly handsome lines of his face. He'd laughed through a thousand heartaches. She'd known that instinctively. But it wasn't a gift that she possessed.

She walked from the alcove as if she were stepping upon shattered glass, her heart bleeding from wounds far deeper than any enemy could have dealt her.

Deeper because they were dealt by those she loved.

Chapter

12

It took her hours to fall asleep. Adam marked every minute. He'd paced his tiny room, eyes accustomed to the darkness probing into her chamber where her pale features were washed in moonlight. Salty tracks of dried tears streaked her cheeks, purple-black shadows pooling like bruises beneath her eyes. But she never made a sound.

From the moment he'd first met her, she'd been heartbreakingly valiant. And attempting to break her will was the most despicable thing he'd ever done. Guilt had become his constant shadow in the years he'd lived by the sword. He'd donned it every dawn as he did his shirt and breeches, buckled it around his waist, then done his best to forget he was wearing it.

But he'd never been able to escape the chain of ugly memories—death cries and pleas for mercy on powder smoke–hazed hillsides, torturous wounds that forced men to linger on a blade-edge of agony, a far less humane fate than a swift death. And always, most potent and painful of all, the memory of Gavin, riding with Bonnie Prince Charlie across the Scottish moors, Adam's gentle, learned brother losing his soul a piece at a time in a war he'd never believed in. And why? To gain their father's approval for ̣nce in his life, and because Adam had urged him to come.

Adam closed his eyes, remembering how he'd borne Gavin to Armageddon. It was the only other time in his thirty-eight years that Adam Slade had loathed himself as completely as he did this night.

Blast, it had to be this way, he upbraided himself sternly. And Juliet's angels had been swift enough to agree with Isabelle, to show Juliet how hopeless her quest was. One glance at the older courtesan, and they'd scrambled like raw recruits behind their commander at the first blast of cannonfire. Even the timid little mouse who had dared to contradict Isabelle for a moment, grateful for the shelter Juliet had offered, had fallen in line with barely a squeak of protest. A twinge of guilt gnawed at Adam as he wondered what would happen to the child once Juliet closed the doors of Angel's Fall forever. But he shoved the question aside.

He'd find a way to deal with the girl himself, place her out of harm's way as soon as Juliet was safe. Doubtless Gavin could be prevailed upon to find a position for her somewhere on his sprawling estate in Norfolk. There was nothing the Earl of Glenlyon adored more than rescuing people from dire fates. Adam had suffered aplenty because of that particular trait in his half-brother. He might as well reap some benefit from it now.

Adam muttered a curse. What the devil was he thinking? He should be thanking Dame Fortune that Isabelle had found a way to stifle Felicity before it was too late. Truth was, the girl could have spoiled everything if the elegant courtesan hadn't interfered. But there was something suspicious in the whole situation, something that raked across his instincts like the metallic whisper of a dagger drawn from a sheath.

Isabelle.

Adam scowled and drove his fingers through the unruly mane tumbling about his shoulders. The courtesan had looked cunning as any general mounting a secret campaign, as she had moved the other women with consummate skill to chip away at Juliet's confidence.

In fact, it was as if she'd rehearsed the scene a dozen

times. Adam's brow furrowed. Why was she so anxious to go back into the streets? Of all the women at Angel's Fall, she needed Juliet's sanctuary the most. Time was the cruelest foe any courtesan had to face. Its march was inexorable as it despoiled beauty, carving lines at the corners of even the most jewellike eyes, dragging down the most perfect breasts, sucking the ripeness from the most succulent lips.

Most men desired women who made them feel young and virile and vital as a youth of twenty, and despite her queenly carriage, Isabelle would remind any suitors that time was stalking them as well, just by her very presence.

Yes, if any woman among the angels should need the haven Juliet had built, Isabelle was the one. Unless, of course, she had made other provisions.

From the time of the Trojan War, battles had been won by slipping an enemy soldier into the opposing camp to wage battle from within.

That would explain how Elise's bit of glass had gotten into the gingerbread. It would have been ever so simple for Isabelle to slip down into the kitchen and arrange things. She would have known Juliet's propensity for the sweet, could have predicted that she would eat it. . . .

Rage surged through Adam, and he embraced it, for it was so much easier to believe Isabelle was capable of such ugliness than to confront the fact that someone had slipped past his guard to aim such a potentially devastating blow at Juliet. It was all he could do to wait until Juliet slept.

But when her face was at last wreathed in slumber, he crept through her chamber on feet soundless as an assassin's, and made his way to Isabelle's bedchamber door. It stood wide open, as if the courtesan had been expecting him. Silver candelabra melted candleglow in luminous rivulets down the ducal seal of her former lover, the room furnished as lushly as the queen's own.

Curtains of the finest garnet velvet obscured the simple bed Juliet had fitted out each chamber with, mounds of lacey pillows arrayed as if waiting for a lover's head.

The armoire doors couldn't hold all of Isabelle's gowns,

ice-blue satin and primrose velvet, scarlet damask and indigo silk bursting the wooden confines, while petticoats of every color that might grace an artist's palette draped over the open doors.

Every available surface was littered with woman things; rouge to freshen the fading bloom in her cheeks, powder to whiten her curls, enough jewels to hide the fact that there was no longer such rich sparkle in her eyes, an expensive and elegant scent mantled the place like the coal-smoke that often hung over the city—completely inescapable.

There had been a time Adam had taken pleasure in such sophisticated feminine lures. But now, all he could remember was how sweet and clean Juliet's curls had smelled when he'd buried his face in their silkiness, a mesmerizing mixture of soap and rainwater and innocence.

Garbed in a buttermilk satin open-robed gown, Isabelle sat at her dressing table, smoothing some creamy concoction over her white brow. She caught a glimpse of him in her mirror and nodded her head in acknowledgment. "You managed to escape your cage at last, I see. The duke always said there wasn't a wall stout enough to hold a stallion prisoner in a stable full of pretty mares."

"That's not why I've come to your chamber and you know it."

Isabelle took one more swipe at the faint lines on her forehead, then wiped her fingers delicately upon a lace-edged handkerchief. "I don't have enough gypsy blood to read your mind, Sabrehawk. Perhaps you should tell me what this is about."

"What happened in Juliet's room a few hours ago. Why did you help me? Use your power to try to persuade her to leave this infernal place?"

Isabelle fingered the silver handle of her hairbrush. "Would you believe I've been struck with a bout of philanthropic zeal of my own?"

"Not if you wrote it in blood in St. Peter's book."

She raised the bristles to her lustrous fall of hair, brushing imaginary tangles from the shimmering skein. "We understand each other quite well, don't we, Sabrehawk? Adventurers, both of us, taking what we can from life. The only difference is that your sword is your fortune. It will serve you much longer than something as transient as a beautiful face."

"Don't try to engage my sympathy, Isabelle. Your face may not be what it once was, but I'd wager your wits are still sharp as the fangs of a snake."

"One must be prepared to use whatever weapons the fates grant us." Her lips parted in a half-smile. "Survival is, after all, the only thing that matters."

"Is it? Just exactly what is the price of your soul?"

Isabelle arched one winged brow, her eyes skating over his body from the jut of his jaw to the toes of his boots, then rising again to fix on the flap of his breeches. "I'm afraid it's higher than you could afford."

"You can keep your poisonous charms to choke the next lordling you snare, madam. I want to know how much you're being paid to sabotage Juliet from within."

"Sabotage . . ." Realization dawned across Isabelle's once-exquisite features and her laughter tinkled out like crystal prisms stirred by the wind. "You think that *I* put that glass in Juliet's gingerbread?"

"Someone inside Angel's Fall must have done so. Who else could have known Juliet's habits? Who else could have gotten inside the house?"

"Who indeed?" Isabelle pulled a face. "In case you haven't noticed, our Juliet would invite the devil himself in for tea if he looked tired and chilled."

"I've given her orders that no one be allowed—"

"And you think she'll obey you? Obviously I underestimated your powers of understanding, where women are concerned. Juliet will do what she thinks right—though the whole world calls her a fool. Even if it means she'll walk through hell itself to rescue someone who doesn't want to be rescued. You should have seen her the day she came to snatch me from the establishment the duke had set up for me. Such an earnest little mouse, she was. Her fighting bonnet anchored beneath her chin, the most abominable cloak I'd ever seen rippling about her shoulders."

Isabelle gave a careless shrug. "Believe what you will of me, Sabrehawk. My stay in this little nunnery, it's temporary at best. But I must make an advantageous match this time, and ravage my protector's purse for every sou I can, for this will be my last chance. There is no place for aged harlots but the streets. And I'm enough of a self-serving creature that I would do anything necessary to keep a roof over my head. Doubtless our Juliet would nobly starve to death in a gutter, but such an unsightly demise is hardly my style."

Isabelle withdrew the stopper of one of the glass bottles, dabbing scent between her breasts. "You should be thanking me for helping you tonight instead of treating me to a reprise of the Spanish Inquisition. You wanted to dash the stardust from our Juliet's eyes, did you not? Wanted to convince her to abandon her absurd quest?"

"Yes, damn you, but—"

"Leave it at that, Sabrehawk. Pack up Juliet's dismal collection of gowns and trinkets and carry her off to that widow person in Northwillow she's forever penning letters to. Get her out of harm's way, so that both you and I can go back to the lives we know best—midnight trysts and playing at faro. Drinking wine and pretending that we are having a magnificent time."

"There's no guarantee Juliet will agree to leave, even after the scene in her bedchamber tonight."

"No. Amazing how hard-headed good-hearted people can be. But I would advise you to find a way to convince her to leave before the unthinkable happens. There is no knowing what lengths her enemies might go to in order to remove her from their paths."

A chill trickled through Adam's veins, and his gaze probed Isabelle's feline features, searching for some hint of deception, some shadow of enough evil to slip glass into a bit of cake, to wait, silent as a cat with its prey, until Juliet took a bite. . . .

"That fate will sound like a tea with the Queen Mother if you ever do anything to endanger Juliet. If I discover you were at fault for this night's work, I vow you'll wish you'd never been born."

"You must think of some more creative threat, my sweet."

"Damn you to hell! Tell me the truth or I'll " He grabbed at that slender wrist, the lace at her cuff falling back. His fingers felt a ridge of flesh beneath them. Dark eyes flashed down, and he glimpsed the white scar slashed into her wrist. He raised his eyes to Isabelle's.

"Yes. I did it," she said coolly. "A lifetime ago. Tragedy reigned then. Odd, is it not? How desperately we can wish we were never born? Yet to take one's own life . . . in the end, that was the one thing I hadn't the courage to do."

He felt a sharp jab of something akin to compassion, wondering what had driven her to such a desperate act. But he crushed the emotion. He couldn't afford the slightest weakness with Juliet in peril. "If I find out that you have done anything to endanger Juliet, I swear by my father's grave there will be no place dark enough for you to hide."

"My heavens, what a rather enthusiastic threat. I'd not have guessed you capable of such . . . passion—outside of the bedchamber." Those wide, jewel-hard eyes flicked up to his, and he felt as if the courtesan could peel away the layers of a man's soul. Doubtless, it was an ability that had served her well.

A smile tugged at her rouge-reddened lips, her brows arching with incredulity. "You're in love with her, aren't you?"

Adam recoiled as if she'd just rammed a lance full-tilt through his chest. "Don't be absurd!"

"Mon Dieu, who would have believed that our dowdy little mother abbess could tame the Prince of Sin to her hand?"

"Blast it to hell, enough!" Adam warned. "I'd have to be mad to fall in love with a woman like Juliet!"

"Considering the tales I've heard of you—charging into battle with twenty trained assassins, leaping from cliffs into the sea below—I would say that your sanity has always been in question."

Adam glared at her, loathing everything about her—her painted face, her cynical gaze, the smile that mocked him from her lips. Love Juliet? Was it possible he'd been such a fool? God, how Gavin would laugh—Sabrehawk, losing his heart to a slip of a girl with a warrior's spirit and a quest even more hopeless than the one Gavin had launched in Scotland years ago.

"I'll be damned before I love her!" Adam ground out.

Isabelle swept to her feet with an airy laugh and glided toward the open door. "You were damned before you loved her. For a thousand years troubadours have fashioned songs of how love is the great redeemer and the most ruthless destroyer." She paused in the portal, her gaze meeting his for a long moment. "Have a care, Sabrehawk," she warned. "You may at last have met the woman with the power to destroy you."

Adam walked away, his chest feeling torn wide, black horror pulsing through him for the second time that night. Was the blasted witch right? Was he in love with Juliet?

He closed his eyes, remembering the unfamiliar hunger that she'd unleashed in him. The bursting sweetness of her mouth when he'd crushed it beneath his kiss, the primal need that tormented him to mate with her, to guard her, to fight with her and laugh with her. Not for merely a string of nights, but for all eternity.

But she was pure and good, with a spirit that burned with the luminosity of angels—the embodiment of every dream he could never have.

Adam reeled, stunned by the realization that he'd spent a lifetime trying to avoid this calamity, flinging himself across a hundred different battlefields, some part of him knowing how agonizing it would be if he ever had to face the one legacy he could hate his father for.

A bastard had nothing to offer an angel—not even an honorable name.

Chapter

13

Juliet huddled beneath her coverlets, her knees drawn up to her stomach, her arms clutched tight about her pillow, but nothing could ease the knot of despair lodged beneath her ribs. It shouldn't have hurt so much—hearing the women's scorn for Angel's Fall, hearing the truth about how they had used Juliet for the naive little fool that she was.

The laughingstock, the country church-mouse who thought she could heal the world's wounds by creating a tiny haven of peace and gentleness in the midst of the ravening streets of London.

But she'd plunged into dangerous waters—dark and deep and so swift she couldn't keep her head above the waves. Worst of all, she'd lost her courage somewhere in the tiny pantry, with her mouth bleeding and the square of ginger-bread crumbling in her hand.

"What if you hadn't been the one to eat it?" Adam had demanded, his rugged countenance fierce with emotion. *"What if one of the other women had? Or if you'd put it in the beggar's basket and some child had wolfed it down?"*

What if someone else had died because of her stubbornness in remaining here? And for what? For some wild dream that she could fashion courtesans into seamstresses and governesses and ladies' maids? That they would eagerly embrace a life of stitching until their fingers bled, banished forever into the back rooms of life where the sunlight could rarely reach?

Was that possible, after the lives they'd known? She had barely tasted such passion, and she was intoxicated with the power of it.

Juliet pressed her fingertips to her lips, remembering with sizzling heat the sensations that had swept through her at Adam Slade's kiss. Had Isabelle ever felt such soul-searing need for her duke? Millicent for her rich merchant? Jenny for the dashing young squire's son who had carried her away?

That wild pulse-pounding splendor was what Juliet was asking her ladies to surrender forever. It had seemed so simple a sacrifice when she was packing up her meager belongings in the vicarage at Northwillow, making her plans for Angel's Fall.

But that had been before Adam Slade had drawn her into his embrace, taught her the secrets of a man's kiss, infused her with the desperate need to know more, learn everything, every mystery of love—not just the chaste love that had seemed enough back in Northwillow. But a love that encompassed bodies as well as souls.

A love Adam Slade didn't want.

He'd never made any secret of his desperation to be rid of her. The women of Angel's Fall had done little to conceal their misgivings about the new life she'd promised them. But she'd been so certain that she was right. That if she merely showed them the way, they'd take pride in their independence.

Yes, she'd known the truth deep down in her soul. It shouldn't have hurt so dreadfully to have it dragged up into the light.

What was she really fighting for? Here, in this godforsaken corner of London? She was getting tired. So tired.

How odd that, in her pain, the one person in the world she wanted to run to was the man who had systematically destroyed her illusions hours before. She needed to know why he had betrayed her.

She threw back the coverlets and climbed out of bed, the floor so chilly her bare feet ached. Quietly she stole to the door of the alcove. She must have dozed sometime during that interminable night. Slade's bed was untouched, blankets tucked haphazardly beneath the pillow. But Adam was nowhere in sight.

She frowned. Lord knew, she shouldn't care that he was gone after the confrontation earlier that night, but Slade had agreed not to wander the house at night, to preserve the ladies' reputations. A heartsick laugh escaped her. Reputations that said ladies seemed not overly concerned about.

Crossing to her clothespress, she took down a long shawl and draped it about her, tucked her feet into slippers and set out in search.

She found him in the garden, silhouetted against the iron bars of the gate. Always before, he'd exuded primal animal energy, restless potency, as if every sinew in his magnificent body possessed the raw power to control any situation, triumph over any foe. But tonight, he stood still, peering through the iron bars like a pagan god imprisoned, yearning for his mistress, that silver-tressed lady sailing upon the moon.

He was stripped down to his shirtsleeves and breeches, his ebony hair tangling like midnight secrets about his broad shoulders. Shoulders that looked as if they carried the weight of every enemy he'd ever battled.

She wanted to be angry with him for his betrayal. Wanted to rage at him. Demand to know why he'd hurt her so badly hours ago. But more than anything, she wanted to close the space between them and bury her face in the solid warmth of his chest.

Was this what Jenny had faced? And Elise and Violet and Isabelle? This horrendous need that forgave a thousand sins and painted a hopelessly flawed man with the colors of fantasy until even when he hurt you, you needed him with a desperation that seared your soul?

Her eyes burned, a prickly lump of pain clotting her throat.

"Adam?" She breathed his name, and he froze for a

heartbeat, then turned to face her. She would have been prepared if he'd had his sword in hand, after the lesson he'd given her in the dangers of creeping up on a soldier, especially at night.

But nothing could have prepared her for the expression on Adam Slade's face. It was as if the moonlight's silvery blades had carved away the mask he'd worn for so long, leaving his rugged features raw and oddly new.

His shirt was open to the waist, the sheen of bronze flesh sprinkled with dark hair showing in stark contrast to the white of the fabric. And his hands were empty. It was the first time Juliet had seen him without a weapon within a heartbeat of his grasp.

One dark brow arched, and she saw him struggle to summon mockery into his fathomless black eyes. "What are you doing out here?"

"I needed to find you. Talk to you."

"What the devil can you have to say to me? That I'm a bastard—by nature as well as by birth? That you despise me? I've heard it all before, Juliet."

"No. I want to know why, Adam."

"Why I'm a son of a bitch? Years of sacking cities and storming citadels, no doubt. Gets to be a disagreeable habit."

"But if you've spent so much time warring, I'm certain you've seen scores of wounds far worse than mine. Why did my three little cuts upset you so much?"

Whatever direction Slade had expected the confrontation to take, Juliet could see her query caught him by surprise. He raked one massive paw through his dark hair. "I don't know why the devil I was so upset. I should've let you shovel down the whole mess. Would've made my life a hell of a lot easier."

The words wounded, but she would allow him no retreat. "You've seen enough wounds to gauge the severity by the amount of bloodshed. I'm certain that it took you barely a moment to figure out that mine was a minor injury. So, why were you willing to hurt me far more deeply than that bit of glass ever could?"

Adam backed away a step, his shoulders bumping the gate. The iron made a dull metallic clang as it blocked his escape. "Blast it, this is absurd! It's done. No sense hashing it over again," he groused, his craggy cheekbones a shade darker in the moonlight. "You're going to catch your death of cold running around out here in your nightgown. Bloody hell, woman, what is it with you? For a vicar's daughter, you spend the devil of a lot of time prancing about the garden in your unmentionables!"

She didn't respond to his blustering, only looked deep into those dark desperate eyes. "Adam, why did you hurt me?"

"Damnation, Juliet, leave it alone!" He started to reach for her, then stopped, his hands knotting into fists. "You don't know what you're asking."

"A simple question. I trusted you, Adam. You hurt me. But as I look at you now, I think maybe you hurt yourself even more. I deserve to know why."

"Because when I look at you, I . . . blast it, Juliet, in Scotland, my brother was headed for the gallows. I tried to take his place, but would the noble idiot let me? Hell, no! He had a lady who would live and die for him, a pack of orphans who adored him, and a worthless block-brained half-brother who'd gotten him neck-deep into a hopeless cause he'd never believed in."

A tortured laugh ripped from Adam's chest. "Gavin had everything to live for. I was nothing but a disaster, blundering from one battle into another, one more soldier in the ranks of millions destined for an early grave. I would gladly have gone to the gallows for him. Would have sacrificed anything or anyone in this world or the next to save him."

His voice roughened, softened. "But tonight, when I saw you bleeding, I knew that, agonizing as it might be, I'd have watched Gavin walk to the gallows, if by doing so, I could save you."

Juliet gazed up at him, aching, awed. "Adam . . . I . . ."

"Damn it, Juliet, what are you doing here in this hell-hole? A lost angel, searching for light where there is nothing but darkness? Why can't you see how hopeless it is? The only thing that can happen here is that you'll be destroyed?

Either swiftly, by an enemy, or more slowly, torturously, from inside yourself as you realize the truth?"

"The truth that you and Isabelle were so eager to show me tonight?"

"That truth. And others."

"Do you know what I've learned since you came charging up to Angel's Fall? You came to rescue me, but I believe that you are the one who has been wandering around, lost. Adam, you could stay with us, here, forever. Build something real instead of laying siege to places you don't care about, fighting battles that aren't your own."

Juliet laid one hand upon his chest, ever so gently, felt the throb of his heartbeat beneath the layer of sinew and satiny skin. "I need you, Adam. Here to help me. But it's more than that. I feel . . ." It took more courage than she could have believed possible to say the words. "I feel as if we were meant to find each other, that we belong together. I have feelings for you that are so—so confusing. I want—"

"Damn it, woman, are you hearing a word I'm saying? I can't stay in this blasted house much longer! Every minute I slide closer to Armageddon. Hell, this past two weeks makes the torture-fete Gavin and I suffered when we were prisoners in Scotland look like an accursed musicale! Do you have any idea what agony it is to sleep in your blasted bedchamber each night, listen to your soft sighs, see the moonlight painting your hair in silver when I can't touch you, take you?"

A shiver of lightning-hot sensation shot through Juliet, setting every inch of her skin tingling with a soul-rending need. She could almost see him, the night weaving shadowy fingers through his hair, the moonlight gilding his warrior's face as he watched her sleep. It was an image of indescribable intimacy, but it brought no stinging surge of shame.

The sweep of those ebony eyes, stormy with desperate yearning, laid siege to every belief she'd ever had. And she trembled, not in genteel horror or virginal terror at the earthy emotions rampant on Adam's face, but rather, with a raw excitement and a fierce compulsion to bury herself in his arms, to press her lips against the hair-roughened skin of his chest, to see where such a rash action might lead them.

Heat stung her cheeks as she realized what her papa would think of such behavior. But Papa wasn't here. And she was so very alone. Alone, except for this reluctant warrior, with his scarred hands and his wary eyes and rough-edged confessions.

She stood for long moments, trembling on the edge of a chasm, knowing the choice was hers. She could flee back to the house and embrace her hurt, her sense of betrayal, or she could step off the edge of this precipice of emotion, tumbling to what might be her own destruction, or the miraculous haven of Adam's powerful arms.

She'd seen the ruin a man could wreak in a woman's life, especially a man as dangerous as Adam Slade—a man who, from the moment he'd arrived, had told her he wanted nothing more than to walk away.

Once he did, she'd be left with a broken heart—the kind she'd seen reflected so many times in the faces of her angels. But until this instant she hadn't realized that there could be only one thing worse than being left behind by Adam Slade. That was never having known his passion at all.

She felt the simple fantasies of the girl she had been slip away, a woman's more complicated dreams shivering to life in their place. And she closed the space between her and Adam Slade, knowing there were no happily-ever-afters written in the stars, knowing that once she ventured forth she could never retreat back to her ivory tower of innocence. Knowing that it would leave her forever changed.

Mustering a boldness she hadn't even known she possessed, she pressed her lips to the thunderous beat of his heart, tasting the salty satin of his chest for the first time. A guttural cry tore from Adam's chest.

He manacled her wrists with his hands, trying to force her away. "Thunder in heaven, Juliet! Stop! I'm not made of stone!"

"I want to know everything you're made of, Adam. Bone and sinew, midnight eyes and a velvety mouth." Her fingertips strayed up to trace his lower lip with awe. "Who could have guessed that a man's mouth could be so tender?"

Adam jerked away. "I'll hurt you, blast it! The instant I'm

able, I'm going to walk away from this place. Walk away from you. You deserve a good man, angel. One with a clean whole heart, like my brother. Who can give you dreams instead of nightmares and heartbreak."

"I choose you, Adam. Don't you see, I finally understand. All those years, some part of me blamed Jenny for running off with the squire's son. Blamed even poor Elise for some part of her fate. I didn't know then that your heart chooses for you, and that once it does, there can be no going back, no matter what the pain."

"You don't know what you're asking, Juliet," Adam ground out, his big hands trembling.

"I'm asking you to make love to me, Adam. Please." She buried her face against his chest, her heart beating with the wildness of a caged lark's wings.

For long moments he stood, rigid. Then he pulled away. "Now I understand why I stumbled across your father on that accursed Irish road. This is God's revenge for all those years I laughed with the devil."

Juliet shook her head, confused, a little hurt. "Is it so awful that I told you what was in my heart?"

"Awful?" Adam gave a harsh laugh. "It's pure torture." Blast, he'd been so damned careful not to catch a bout of Gavin's infernal heroism, knowing that the stuff was more virulent than the accursed plague.

Who would have guessed that his scruples would make an appearance now? It was a damned inconvenient time to play the hero.

"Do you know what hell is, angel?" he asked. "It's listening to your voice, watching your lips tremble, so dewy-moist with wanting, hearing you offer everything to me, heaven after all these years. Yet knowing that I can never . . . never have you."

"But you can! Adam, you can! Even if you won't stay forever I'll accept that. But I—"

He held his hands out to her in the moonshine. "Do you have any idea the kind of horrors these hands have performed? I've killed so many men I'll never be able to wash the blood from my conscience. I've sold my sword, my skill to men I should have been helping to destroy instead of protecting. And each time I did, I sold another piece of my soul."

"No! There is goodness in you. Papa knew it. And I can sense it, too."

"Maybe there is. At least enough to know it's too late for me. I won't defile you, Juliet. Go back to your bed and your stitchery and your impossible dreams."

His gaze locked with hers, and he winced at the pain in her lovely features. He turned away. He could feel her gaze against his back, silent, sad.

"I . . . understand now," she said softly after a moment, taking a step away from him.

Hell, he knew she'd never understand in a thousand years. He sure as blazes didn't! He'd never wanted any woman the way he wanted Juliet Grafton-Moore now, naked beneath him, bathing him in innocence, resurrecting the unbroken pieces of his soul. Most miraculous of all, *she* wanted *him,* an angel offering up everything she was to a battered warrior who didn't know what the hell to do with his life now that the drums were silent.

He'd spent a lifetime taking what he wanted, devil take the consequences. Why didn't he just gather the infernal woman up in his arms and put an end to this misery? But he kept his fists knotted at his sides, his whole body shaking with the effort not to reach for her.

"I understand why you attempted to mount the gallows in your brother's place," she said in that low voice that fed a thousand fires of passion. "Why you can't stay here at Angel's Fall no matter how much you want to. It would ruin your plans if you were to love me, live the rest of your life being cared for and cherished and—"

"Cherished?" He uttered a harsh laugh. "You might as well attempt to *cherish* a tiger. You'd end up in the same condition. Torn to ribbons by the very paws you want to hold you."

"How can you be so certain? Or are you afraid, Adam? As long as you were fighting on some insane battlefield, you could ignore the truth. That it takes far more courage to live than to die a glorious death. Because if you live, you risk failing the people you love."

Adam's fists knotted, nails digging into his palms. Damn her—damn her for lancing open wounds he'd hidden forever, secrets he'd buried in the darkest corners of his soul. Damn her for knowing the truth.

But could she really comprehend all the ugliness inside him? How many people he'd failed? His mother, his sisters, Gavin. And for what? His father's approval? That pride-filled smile that meant so little in comparison to his mother's humiliation, his sisters' lost futures, Gavin's banishment? How much pain had he caused because he hadn't had the courage to confront his own father with the agonizing truth?

Adam struggled to wall up his feelings, bury them as he had so many times before. He had to get away from Juliet before she dredged the last secrets from his soul, for if she did, there would be no place left to hide.

"Under these circumstances, there is only one thing to do," he said. "I strike my colors. Surrender the field."

"You what?"

He turned toward her, just in time to see her stricken face go white as wax. "I'm leaving Angel's Fall first thing in the morning."

"But what about the threats?" she stammered. "You gave your word of honor—"

"I intend to keep it. I will hire someone to take my place. I don't know why I didn't think of that solution before, by God's blood. I've enough coin to muster a blasted army if I want to. Set a round-the-clock guard at every entrance of Angel's Fall for however long is necessary."

She drew herself up to her full height, a radiant guardian angel girding her wings for battle. "This is our home. I won't have it turned into an armed camp."

"It might as well be! You're damned well under attack!" He swore as she spun around, marching toward the house with her shawl trailing behind her.

"Blast it, Juliet!" Adam raged, storming after her. "What are you going to do? Stand your ground here, like a stubborn little idiot, until someone pulls the blasted house down on your head?"

"Yes!"

"Why, damn it to hell? Tell me the truth this time, not a pack of pretty fairy tales."

She whirled to face him, the moonlight snagging, silver in the tears that filled those passionate blue eyes. "When Papa died, I lost everything—even the house where I grew up. Everything, from Papa's favorite chair to his library of books belonged to the parish of Northwillow. I could take away nothing . . . nothing but the memory of him, the little sermons he'd preach to me, his dreams of healing . . . healing everyone—his parishioners, Mama, and my brother and sister . . . and me, when I was forever so sickly."

"Juliet, I know you're grieving."

"I'm done grieving. I'm looking for the higher meaning in all this—trying to make something good come of all the pain I caused. I spent my whole life hiding from the rough edges of life, but they found me anyway. I helped Jenny run away with the squire's son who claimed to love her. But he left her alone, penniless, swelling with his child."

Adam's jaw clenched, and he knew that his own mother might have suffered a similar fate if his father had chosen to abandon her, that he might have been vulnerable as Jenny's child, lost to the cruel winds of fortune in a world that scorned the helpless.

"Then," Juliet continued in a voice that tore at his heart, "when it was already too late, Papa went to find Jenny. We thought . . . the squire had lands in Ireland. And his son had promised Jenny that he would take her there. Papa never blamed me, only vowed he would find her . . . bring her back to Northwillow. But Jenny was in London. She died in childbirth, abandoned, alone. Both Papa and Jenny died because of me."

"Juliet, don't be absurd. They made their own choices."

"Like your brother did when he rode off to join Bonnie Prince Charlie?"

Adam recoiled as if she'd struck him. "Damn it, it's not the same thing!"

"Isn't it? I had the power to stop Jenny from running away, but I didn't. I begged Papa to find her, to mend the hideous mistake I had made. He would have sacrificed his own soul to ease my pain. In the end, he gave his life."

"He wouldn't want you to take such insane risks in an effort to appease your conscience. He wanted to shield you from danger, not put you in the center of a whirlwind."

"Why am I even trying to explain. You'd never understand my reasons for staying here. You have a family who loves you, who waits for you to visit them."

"I haven't seen them in years."

"Because you're a stubborn, blind, bull-headed idiot! If I had anyone who waited for me, who loved me, I'd run to them with all my heart. But I don't have anyone, Adam. They're dead. All dead."

Adam's throat went raw. "I'd exchange my life for your father's if I could. Give him back to you."

"Of course you would," Juliet retorted with a scornful wave of her hand. "That would be just one more grand and glorious gesture. But you can't bring him back to life. No one can. Even so, I discovered something here at Angel's Fall. There are other women like me. Maybe I don't have a father or mother, sisters or brothers to love me, but neither do Elise or Millicent or even Isabelle. They're my family now. You want to know why I won't leave Angel's Fall? Without them, I'd be alone."

The anguished words drove hilt-deep into Adam's chest. *Alone* . . . did any other soul that breathed understand the bleakness of that word so well? But he had chosen that barrenness of his own free will, while Juliet had had her father's love stolen from her on a desolate Irish road.

"Juliet." Just her name, torn from his throat on the jagged edges of a myriad of lost possibilities.

"Go, Adam. I'll still have this." She waved her hand toward the ivy-covered walls of Angel's Fall. "I absolve you of your vow to my father, free you of responsibility for me. Ride away and don't look back. After all, that's what you're best at."

Only one other person on God's earth had the power to

wound him so deeply. Adam tried to hide the gash she'd carved in his soul. He couldn't look at her . . . let her see . . .

See what? Every vulnerability that lay beneath Adam Slade's mocking laughter, harsh cynicism? That somewhere, buried in the warrior he became, was a boy who had dreamed of being like William the Conqueror, obliterating the stain of his bastardy by deeds so glorious they would blind the world to the circumstances of his birth?

She started to walk away, and Adam knew in that instant he didn't give a damn what anyone else thought now—he only cared about this woman, this angel, who knew all the ugliness inside him, yet had laid her healing hands upon his scarred soul and told him that she loved him.

Was that the last thing Lucifer had seen as he fell from heaven? The hand of an angel reaching out to him? A second chance after so many mistakes. He only had to have the courage to take it.

"Juliet," he breathed her name, and it broke upon his lips, a sound of worship, of the first faint ribbon-hues of hope. "Juliet, don't."

"Don't what, Adam?"

"Don't be alone any longer. My hands are scarred with too many sins to count. But if you want them to touch you, I swear, they will shelter you, protect you, until the heavens fall." He held out his large hand, ashamed of its roughness, fearing just the brush of his fingertips might bruise her.

She hesitated for what seemed an eternity, her eyes wide and soft in the moonlight, shadowed with the hurts life had dealt her. Then, ever so slowly, she reached out her hand, slipping her fingers into his.

Chapter
14

The contact was electrifying, terrifying in its power. Adam's heart thundered, his mind reeling with a thousand questions. How did one make love to an angel? Panic gripped him. He'd not felt shyness around women since he'd lost his virginity, but now—lord, she was so tiny, so fragile, and he was a great hulking beast of a man with no gentleness in his nature.

"Are you certain, Juliet? Certain you want this?"

"Yes, Adam." It was as if she'd just poured every star in the heavens into his outstretched hands.

He scooped her up into his arms, agonizingly aware of the precious weight of her against his chest, the warmth of her petal-soft skin shielded by the thin weave of her nightgown. Soon, the primal part of his being whispered, soon even that barrier would be stripped gently away.

"Where do you want me to take you? Inside?" Even as he said the words, he was reluctant to follow his own suggestion. The notion of sharing such intimacy with Juliet with the rest of her fallen angels so near was unsettling. And Adam was stunned that for the first time his own fierce sensual need was tempered by the desire to protect Juliet from even the possibility of whispered suspicions.

"No. Not . . . there," she said. He could sense that she

would feel it a kind of betrayal. She caught her lower lip between her teeth, a tiny crease forming between her brows in indecision.

No one knew better than Adam how great a chasm she'd had to cross to reach this pass, how desperately she must have fought against her feelings for him, and the natural culmination of them, the one that had awaited all mortal lovers since the creation of the first man and woman.

That seduction had taken place in a garden as well. But if Adam Slade could have whisked himself back to Eden at that moment, sheltered from harm and sickness and death, he would have scorned it, choosing instead Juliet's garden, Juliet's loving, all the more bittersweet in its beauty because they had only a finite amount of time to share it in. But where could they take shelter from the night?

Adam's eyes skimmed past shadowed benches and clumps of azaleas and rose cascades, statues, once resplendently nude, now modestly attired in togas fashioned of frayed sheets and pillow casings.

His gaze caught on a smear of gray in the deepest corner of the garden, the small outbuilding where Juliet kept her gardening supplies, and where she'd set up her own little hideaway where she could wrestle with her hurts and disappointments as well. "The garden house?" he suggested.

She nodded against his chest. Destination settled, he strode through the moonlit garden, to where the small building was set back against the lush vegetation. Juliet had fashioned it into a place for gentle reflection, infused it with a quiet beauty, a little sip of the serenity that wreathed her soul. Adam shoved open the door and stepped inside.

"A candle . . . I keep one on that shelf to the right," Juliet said. "Sometimes when I'm troubled at night I come here to dabble around with the plants. It makes me feel better somehow, to be nurturing something that might blossom into a thing of beauty."

So this was Juliet's own haven, the place where she came to gather up her frayed serenity. Adam didn't know what this night might bring. The only thing he was certain of was that this would alter Juliet forever, and leave its shadows, whether soft or dark, within this place she loved.

Weighed down with the enormity of what they were about to share, Adam set her down on a bench piled with soft cushions, wide enough to lie upon, then turned to fumble with candle and flint until the wick blazed. A hazy golden glow filtered through the room, illuminating rows of pots upon shelves, spades and hoes and rakes leaning tidily in a corner, a box filled with new green shoots cozied up near the bank of windows where the moon peeked in.

Everything here had the aura of being cared for tenderly by Juliet's own hands. And Adam was stunned at the depth of need he felt to have her reach out, lighten the dark places, soothe the bruised places, gentle the wild places in his spirit.

It was too deep, too raw, this sensation of vulnerability. Weakness—he'd spent his life in terror of it. Yet hadn't Gavin proved that a man could be loving and strong? Vulnerable, but brave? Yet Gavin was so many things Adam could never be.

Hell, Adam censured himself, the one thing he couldn't do was to keep standing here like a complete idiot, staring into the candle flame as if it held the answers to the mysteries of the universe. He had to turn, to face Juliet sometime.

"Adam?" His name was whispered in a breathy angel's voice. "I want you so badly, that I'm . . . afraid."

Blast, she had the courage to be honest, to say aloud the emotions clamoring inside him. Juliet, his valiant crusader, his guardian angel, his *love*. She deserved every drop of courage in his soul. He turned to her, his voice a gravelly rumble as he made an admission no torture master could ever have wrung from him before.

"I'm afraid, too. I don't want to hurt you. Don't want to sicken you when you see the scars—I've led a hard life, angel. Spent most of it on the opposite end of an enemy sword."

She reached up, touching the scar on his face. "You're beautiful to me."

The words touched him, wrung his heart. She could never

know how much. "I don't want you to awaken tomorrow and regret this," he told her. "At any time, if you have the slightest doubt about what we're doing, you have only to ask, and I'll—" The prospect bit like a savage vise about his chest. "I'll let you go, angel, without a word of reproach. Look into my eyes, Juliet. Do you promise me?"

She caught her lip between her teeth, nodded, her eyes wide and full of wonder, her cheeks stained the hue of the roses she tended with such devotion. Then she stunned Adam by not waiting for him to make the first foray with hands and mouth. She reached between them, her fingers unfastening the ties that held the front of his shirt together.

The brush of her knuckles against the fine hairs matting his chest was enough to unman him. The only thing that kept him from humiliating the devil out of himself was the knot of dread in a lump at the back of his throat. He would know in a moment if she could bear to look at the tangle of scars that twisted across his body, the legacy of the life he'd led.

Her eyelids drifted shut, like a child prolonging the delicious anticipation of opening a present as she smoothed the fabric back off of his broad shoulders. Adam's spine went rigid. He scarcely breathed. Always before women had reacted at the sight of his warrior's body—either with wild titillation at the legacy of the danger he'd sought, or with a hint of revulsion, refusing for the rest of the night to look upon the scars that marred his skin. But tonight was the first time he had felt ashamed himself.

Lord, it seemed almost sacrilege to imagine Juliet's flawless angel's hands skimming across such ugliness.

But he'd told her that he would free her from her wish to make love at the veriest whisper, and curse his tainted soul to hell, he'd never meant a vow more completely than the one he'd given her.

He gritted his teeth as his gaze snagged on those delicate fingers, smoothing in a blind quest across his skin, as if trying to memorize the texture, the heat. Then those fingertips encountered the first ridge of proud flesh, a sabre cut bisecting flesh mere inches below his nipple.

Her hand froze, those lake-blue eyes fluttering open. Adam braced himself for the worst. But the prospect of this woman drawing away in quiet horror was more than he could bear. He stepped back, breaking the contact himself in an effort to avoid the pain of even the most subtle of rejections. The absence of her touch was the most exquisite torture he'd ever known.

But she didn't draw away. She leaned down, her hair a silken cascade, brushing the sensitive skin of his stomach, spilling in the lightest, most excruciating caress across that part of him even now straining against the flap of his breeches. Then, her lips, moist, soft, and more than a little sorrowful, pressed a kiss against that scar.

"Juliet," he ground out, his head arching back, his teeth gritted against the potent sensation.

Then she was brushing his shirt away, until it drifted to the floor. The cool kiss of the air only fed the raging fires she'd lit inside him, and he dared to look at her, only because he couldn't bear to do otherwise. Soft as the shine of the single candle was, it still illuminated the puckered hole where a pike had jabbed, the indentation of a pistol-ball, the score of white lines that wove across his swarthy skin in a pattern of reckless abandon.

"Oh, Adam, Adam," she mourned. "What have you done to yourself?"

"Fought, angel. I just can't tell you what I was fighting for." It didn't seem valiant anymore, riding off on whatever quest presented itself. It seemed futile and somehow sad—and he realized how many times he'd seen that sorrow reflected in Gavin's face as he watched Adam ride away.

Adam flinched as Juliet closed the space between them, her lips drifting like the enchanted petals of a dew-kissed rose across all the raw places inside him, all the ridges of scarring, all the legacies of battles he wanted to forget.

Bloody hell, did she have any idea what her explorations were doing to him? Flavored as they were by Juliet's innocence and wonder.

"You're so—so hard," she breathed. "Every muscle and sinew. And yet." Her fingertips wisped over the dark mat of hair that spanned his chest. "So soft." The edge of her little finger brushed the gem-hard point of his nipple, and a raw oath tore from his throat.

She leapt back as if he'd snapped like a wolf at her hand. "Did I hurt you?"

"You're nigh killing me. No one has ever touched me like this."

Her delicate brows lowered in disbelief. "Adam, you don't have to pretend. I know that you've had other lovers."

"Lovers? No. I've had bedmates. Distractions from war and idleness and frustration. Never . . . this." His hand enveloped hers, pressed her palm against the thundering throb of his heart. "Hell, who would ever believe that I could feel as if—" He stopped, feeling like a bloody idiot, his cheeks afire.

"As if what, Adam? Tell me."

"No. It doesn't make any sense. Sounds ridiculous—"

"Can you trust me with it?" It was the sweetest of pleas. He yielded to it in a manner impossible before he'd first seen her face.

"As if we were both new, innocent, trying to find our way . . . " The words sounded foreign to him, as if they'd sprung from another man. The man he might have been if life and battle hadn't hardened him.

"To where, Adam? Where are we trying to find our way to?"

"I don't know. I've never been there before." Never been where? In bed with a virgin? No, there was so much more to fear than that. Making love to a woman whose soul shone bright with inner goodness? He felt so damned awkward, uncertain. God above, what a jest that was. The Prince of Sin, who had seduced legions now stood before this innocent girl without any idea what he should do next, terrified that he would frighten her, hurt her, that he would reach out to her and discover she was but a phantom conjured up from the most secret recesses of his mind.

Should he merely lay her down on the cushions and ease up her nightgown, taking her as gently as he was able? The thought filled him with fierce dissatisfaction. The one thing he did know was that a woman rarely felt pleasure in her first mating with a man. That was why he'd bloody well avoided being the son of a bitch who put her through the breaching of the maidenhead. Nothing more appalling than a weeping woman.

Yet how would Juliet react if he gave free rein to the earthy fantasies that had consumed his nights since the moment he laid eyes on her? Her body, naked except for the gilding of candlelight, his mouth seeking the sensitive hollow of her throat, the sweet swell of her breast. The peak of her nipple, fragrant and silky beneath his lips as he suckled her. The tips of his fingers questing down the soft skin of her belly to find ethereal gold curls, slick satin nestled within.

The mere image was enough to make sweat bead his brow. How the hell would he be able to go slowly if his imagination was already racing leagues ahead?

"Is something wrong, Adam?" she asked, her own cheeks blushed. "I mean, I . . . am I supposed to be doing something I don't know about? It seems so awkward, just standing here, with you staring at me like—like . . ."

"Like what?"

A nervous giggle bubbled from her lips. "Like you're a wolf contemplating the best way to gobble me up."

Her stab at humor drew a surprised laugh from him, and he cupped her cheek with his hard palm. "That's what I feel like. A wolf. Hungry to touch you, to taste you, to make love with you. But I want it to be perfect, Juliet. You deserve that. I'm just not sure I know how to give that to you."

"I know less than you do about all this. I can see in your eyes that you know what you want. If you could do anything right now, what would it be?"

"I'd get rid of that infernal nightgown so that I could see all the places I've been imagining while I couldn't sleep at night."

She stunned him by grasping the hem of her nightshift and whisking it over her head. Her hair tumbled down in a luminescent halo, the strands like rivers of gold charting the alabaster slopes of her breasts as she cast the garment aside. What had he expected? The cool distance of a marble saint, untouchable by human hands? If so, he'd been mistaken.

Every inch of Juliet was bursting with the warmth that was so much a part of her, a glow of anticipation, a heart-wrenching accessibility, though she was far more lovely than he could ever have imagined.

His throat was raw with the depth of the trust she'd given him with her selfless gesture.

"Now is it my turn? To tell you what—what I want?"

"Anything, Juliet."

"For you to kiss me. Like you did at Ranelagh."

Kiss her? What sweet torture. He threaded his hands back through the fall of her hair, drew her close enough that the points of her nipples stirred the dark hair of his chest. He felt the intimate contact sizzle to his toes. But if it was kissing she wanted, by damn, it was kissing the woman would get.

Adam tried to rein in the savage hunger clamoring inside him, the wild primal need to claim this woman as his own. Bind her to him in the most physical way possible. His lips covered hers, and he captured the breathy gasp of her satisfaction in his mouth.

Hungry, he traced the sweet bow of her upper lip with his tongue, feathered teasing strokes across her full lower lip, probed with exquisite gentleness at the crease between.

She opened for him, allowing him to sample the inner sweetness he'd been dreaming of for so many endless nights. She tasted of generosity and sunlight and new beginnings. She was warm with possibilities he'd never dared consider, and tinted with dreams he'd lost along the rugged road he'd chosen.

And for the first time in his life, Adam understood his father's obsession with the woman he'd made his mistress. For the devil himself could not have forced Adam to surrender Juliet, not for all the world.

He slipped his tongue into Juliet's mouth, felt her moist welcome close around him, the way the feminine core of her soon would, and he stroked, gently, wooing her, calming the wildfire raging in his veins. He couldn't trust himself to go further, didn't dare, when, with a moan, Juliet melted against him.

Agony, ecstasy, it speared through him as her breasts were

crushed against his chest, the hot satin of her inner arms draping around his waist, pulling him closer, tighter to her. The soft swell of her belly nestled against the bulge of his erection, taunting him with the promise of a release more powerful than any he'd ever know.

His hand swept up between them, unable to resist cupping her breast for another heartbeat. He felt the callused hardness of his palm abrading that petal-soft skin, the crown of her nipple pressing against the base of his thumb. But the sound that tore from Juliet's throat was one of pleasure, not of discomfort.

She arched her head back, her eyes sliding shut, her cheeks scarlet, breath erratic, and Adam kissed her throat, her collarbone, then sank to one knee so that his mouth could ghost a kiss across the point of that tempting nipple.

If he doubted her responsiveness to him, she obliterated his fears in that instant. "Feels like . . . fire, flowing all through me, Adam. I didn't know . . . anyone could feel this way."

"Let me show you. It can be even better." Adam swept her into his arms, laid her down amid the mound of cushions. His last vision of her was her wide wondering eyes as he rooted for her nipple, suckled it deep into his mouth.

A low cry echoed through the tiny room as he drew on her sweetness, drank of her trust. His fingers stroked the faint ridges of her ribs, skimmed the velvety column of her thighs, and a tremor rocked him to his core as he found the soft down of her feminine secrets.

She was warm and dewy with wanting, but she squeezed her legs together for an instant of maidenly hesitation before she surrendered to his touch, letting her thighs open to his questing hand.

"You're so beautiful, lady. An angel after all this time. Scares the living hell out of me to . . . have these feelings raging inside me."

"Oh, Adam." She arched up to kiss his naked chest, her tongue making a kittenish sweep along his breastbone. "It felt so—so good when you put your mouth on my breast. I want to make you feel . . . that way, too."

"I feel the same sensations of pleasure as you, angel. The

same need to be touched, kissed, not just on the mouth, but other places. If you want to." Adam threaded his hand in her fine hair and drew her mouth toward his chest.

A groan rumbled in his depths as she explored him with delicious experimentation, nuzzling and nipping, kissing and tasting, burrowing her soft cheeks against the hard sheath of muscle until he was gasping with the need to bury himself inside her.

As she worked her shy magic on him, Adam skimmed his palm over the taut curve of her buttocks. She mimicked him with delightful eagerness, but when she encountered the tight fabric of his breeches, he could hear a muffled sound of frustration emanate from her.

"Is this the way it's done?" she asked, a trifle petulant, and he could see the fiery heat in her cheeks. "I mean, the gentleman leaving his—his clothes on. I mean, some of his clothes on, while the lady—"

"It can be done this way, just loosening the flap—" Adam felt like he wanted to sink into the floorboards with embarrassment. "It's not as . . . as enjoyable. But I didn't want to alarm you by . . . " *Letting you see what a great hulking beast I am, making you afraid once you saw the size of me and realized what I was going to do to you . . .*

Blast, what was the matter with him? He'd made love to women of all shapes and sizes, some nearly as small as Juliet. Yet none of them had been virgins whose maidenhead must be breached.

"Juliet, you're so—so delicate, and I'm . . . bloody hell, look at me." Unable to bring himself to the far more carnal comparison that was giving him such qualms, Adam flattened her palm against his own large hand, the callused fingers all but engulfing hers, seeming like thick tree trunks contrasted against the fronds of a willow. "I will hurt you when first we . . . mate. And as God is my witness, I'd rather open every scar on my body than cause you any pain."

"I trust you, Adam. I want to be as close to you as I can be. When you were touching me . . . down there, it felt like liquid sunshine, bursting in every part of my body, felt like I was flying. But I wanted more. So much more. Don't be afraid to show me everything, give me every part of you."

From the first moment he'd met her, she'd surprised him. Tonight was no different. She offered him a shy smile, then her fingertips quested for the buttons straining against the flap that imprisoned him.

The exquisite pleasure Adam felt in her efforts to release his shaft were tempered with a very real fear that she would be repulsed. She was an innocent. A virgin. And he'd given seasoned courtesans momentary cause for indecision. He closed his eyes, unable to face her as he felt the last button give way. She gasped, and Adam winced, but then he felt the warmth of her hand cupping him, stroking him with a delicious sense of discovery.

He tried to fight back the surge of arousal, but it was as if her touch filled him to bursting, until it seemed the sensitive skin was drawn so tight it might split.

He stroked her hair, kissed her lips, her breasts, trying desperately to master the primal beast inside him, trying to remember to be gentle.

Gentleness—what was it? He'd been born of warrior blood, conceived by his father in outright rebellion. He'd spent a lifetime hardening his muscles with war-play, his only dalliances with women as earthy and honest in seizing their pleasures as he was.

He'd learned to take, and delighted as his partners took from him. But Juliet was different. She gave of herself with such generosity, offered the most vulnerable parts of her heart with such courage, trusted him with such a valiant spirit. Never had he wanted to be the ardent lover a woman dreamed of more than he did at this moment. But he was soldier enough to know when defeat was inevitable. He would fail Juliet, no matter how he tried to be gentle tonight.

For there was no way a man of his size could possess a virgin as delicately as she deserved, as tenderly as he wanted to. The best Adam could do for her was to make certain that she was deep in her own pleasure before he took her.

But there would be other nights with Juliet in his arms, he

promised himself. A lifetime of them if he had the courage. Nights in which she could school him in tenderness one melting caress at a time, tame the wild places inside him.

His fingers found her damp center, stroked there, teased there, until she was restless and gasping. Juliet writhed against the cushion, sobs rising in her chest, yet she yielded everything to him, entrusted him with every curve and hollow and hidden place that tempted him.

"Adam . . . oh, sweet heaven . . . " she whimpered, as sensation spiraled outward from his fingertips, tightening her womb, cinching in exquisite bliss about the nipples he had cherished with his mouth, his tongue.

She was drowning in him, wanton with need, yet it seemed not sin, but rather, redemption to immerse herself in his arms. She arched against his hand as one finger slipped inside her, his thumb still stirring the ember hidden in her secret curls. That first penetration was so strange, yet wildly sensual, wringing from her a desire to draw him deeper. As if he could read the slightest whim in her mind, Adam gratified that wish, exploring her with so much tenderness and passion that it drew wild tremors from her body.

And as the maelstrom of pleasure burst inside her, whirling her to a glittering cascade of sensation, the image of Adam's face was branded into her heart—savage ecstasy, fierce possession, and yet a vulnerability she knew instinctively no other eyes had ever seen.

A low scream tore from her throat as another crest washed over her, more intense than the last—born of his touch? Or rather, something far more devastatingly sensual—the expression on his rugged beloved face? She never knew for certain.

His hands curved beneath her knees, spreading her thighs wider, opening her completely so he could position himself between them.

His eyes, those fierce warrior's eyes, darkened to Stygian black with emotion as that part of him that made him a man first brushed the portal to her body.

"I'm going to become a part of you now," he rasped. "As if we're sword and scabbard." Just the description made her dizzy with need. Was it possible to feel this way and survive?

"Are you afraid?" he asked, gruff.

She reached up fingers that trembled. "If I had been, I never would have come to find you in the garden."

His splayed hands bracketed her hips, and she felt his powerful body flex, a pinching, stretching sensation disrupting the waves of pleasure still resonating through her body.

She tensed. "It won't . . . won't fit. I . . ."

He muffled a low curse against her breast as he hesitated, some unwelcome barrier blocking the entry to her body, and she squirmed against him, hating the discomfort, loving the feel of him, reaching for something she didn't fully understand.

"Sh, angel. It's all right," he murmured, starting to draw away. Oddly, losing his touch was far more painful.

But he'd warned her of pain, promised her pleasure, and she would have suffered far worse to give this wounded warrior, this wary vulnerable man a measure of the joy he'd offered her.

She looped her arms tight around him, pressed herself up until she felt the feverish heat of him again, telling him what she was too shy to say.

His hips thrust down, swift, sure, pain cleaving through her as the tender membrane of her innocence tore. She bit her lip until it bled, not wanting him to know how badly he'd hurt her, for despite the pain, the feel of him, so heavy, so hot, embedded in her body filled her with wonder, a sense of completion that seemed to reach into her very soul.

"Are you . . . all right?" Adam asked, kissing her cheeks, her eyelids, his voice rough with tenderness and regret.

She nodded, opened her eyes to look into his. As if he were afraid she would shatter, he moved his hips carefully, withdrawing just a little, then pressing into her again with shallow strokes that barely probed past the torn barrier.

Sweat trickled down the rigid muscles of his face, his countenance fierce with concentration, and she could sense how hard he was fighting to hold himself back, feel what it was costing him to do so—the largest measure of his own pleasure.

Much as his efforts touched her, she'd had a lifetime of being treated like a treasured bit of porcelain. She wanted Adam—all of Adam, wanted him to take all the joy he could in her woman's body.

Her fingers skimmed down to his granite-hard buttocks, and she rose up to meet his thrust, nudging him a little deeper into her sheath. His arms shook, a tortured groan grinding from his lips.

"Ah, Juliet. Have to be . . . careful . . . can't be . . . selfish son of a bitch—"

"Selfish how?"

"Want you to take . . . all of me . . . bury myself to the hilt. But refuse to . . . hurt you."

"Try, Adam. Just try. I want everything, all of you. Please."

A tremor worked through his massive frame, and Juliet wondered at her power over this man, that she could make him tremble and moan and bring such savage longing into his eyes.

His hands tightened around her hips, and he drove a little deeper, thrust a little harder, his gaze never leaving her face, as if searching for the slightest hint of more pain. Juliet arched against him, teasing him, taunting him, pleading for him.

Driven by instinct alone, she reached up to catch his flat nipple gently in her teeth. A raw cry filled the tiny chamber, a surrender, a savage sound of triumph, and Adam buried himself deep.

She had wanted to feel the full power of Adam Slade's loving, the full potency of his warrior's body. He gave it to her, yet offered her the key to more secrets in her own. He suckled and nipped, nuzzled and kissed, devoured her with the power of his passion. His hand slipped between their bodies as he thrust into her, finding the pearl of sensation, drawing it to the agonizing blade's edge of pleasure once again.

She sobbed and pleaded, took what Adam offered and gave all of herself in return, reaching greedily for a pleasure beyond even the abundance he'd given her earlier.

And as Adam drove into her fiercely once more, twice, a cataclysm of sensation ripped through her, opening a hundred fissures of pure ecstasy in every part of her, pouring all of her being into this man's keeping.

She gloried in his primal roar of triumph as he buried himself to the mouth of her womb, tremors racking him as he spilled his seed inside her.

Silence—it fell between them, broken only by the harsh rasp of their breath, the pounding of their own hearts in their ears.

With the greatest of care, Adam rolled to one side, drawing her close in arms that still trembled. Now was the time for all those witty sensual quips he'd perfected over the years. Something to make them both laugh, to tease and jest, something to fill this yawning chasm of silence that churned with emotions as swift and wild as a storm-swelled river, and three times as dangerous.

But the legendary wit Sabrehawk kept honed sharper than his blade had vanished, and he felt like a bumbling idiot, naked to the soul, vulnerable. For the first time in his life, Adam Slade didn't know what to say. It was a hell of a time to realize that, while the notorious Prince of Sin knew a hundred kinds of merry banter to follow a lusty bout of bed games, he had no idea what to say after he'd made love.

Juliet had left him so raw, so new, he felt as if he'd become a stranger to himself.

The sensation was far more terrifying than an entire rival army howling down on him in ambush. Bloody hell, it was an ambush. He'd just never expected it to come from his own wretched heart.

"Adam?" Her voice, silky warm against his bare chest. He looked up and winced at the sight of her—cheeks flushed, hair tumbled in a gold aura about her face, her eyes glistening and expectant. "Thank you. That was . . . I mean, your touching me was . . . beautiful."

Hell, he should be the one spinning out pretty words. But he lay there like a green lad, feeling as if his tongue were nailed to the roof of his mouth.

He'd tormented Gavin mercilessly for reveling in tales of

legendary loves, passions so deep they were captured in the stars forever. Adam had put aside such romantic nonsense at the same time he stopped believing there were monsters underneath his bed.

But here, now, with Juliet cradled in his arms, Adam would have traded his finest sword for a handful of the poetical phrases Gavin uttered so easily. Juliet deserved perfect words spoken by her first lover, words she could hold in her heart whenever she remembered this night that had transformed her from an innocent into a woman.

He could tell she was waiting for him to say something, hoping, her head stuffed full of fairytale dreams. Yet, he couldn't even think with her draped over him in naked splendor.

"Are you all right?" The words sounded rough even to his own tongue. "I didn't break anything, did I?" He ran one hand down the slender column of her arm. "I mean, you're so damned tiny."

She drew away, crossing her arms over breasts still blushed from his kisses. "I'm stronger than I look."

Lord, could he have bungled it any worse? He saw the glow in her eyes flicker, uncertainty stinging her cheeks. He remembered her pained confession of how sheltered she'd been at the vicarage, kept like a figurine of china lace locked up in a glass case.

"I just mean that I didn't intend to be quite so . . . uh, enthusiastic," he tried to amend.

"I suppose it's hard to be . . . enthusiastic when you're so accustomed to trysts like this." She was trying to hide her hurt, but it scalded Adam deep where no one could see.

"Hell no, I'm not accustomed to what happened here. Despite the tales you read in those blasted French novels, not all soldiers run about despoiling virgins." Perfect, Slade. Doubtless her vicar papa had kept a library of them tucked up on the shelf with his religious tracts. "What I mean is, you're my first virgin. I don't intend to make a habit of it."

He could have bitten off his own tongue when he saw the expression on her face. "Was it so terrible, then?"

"Blast, no! You were . . . " He swallowed hard. There weren't words enough to express how perfect she'd been. "What I mean is, it scared the hell out of me. Mating with a man means so much more to a woman like you that I—"

She was wilting like a new blossom too close to the sun, those huge angel-blue eyes looking up at him with no secrets, only stark emotion.

Silhouetted against the glass of the windowpanes, she was soft, vulnerable, wounded, every emotion naked as her slender body. "I told you from the first that I don't expect anything from you, Adam. Just because we—we made love."

"Love. That's the crux of the problem." But how the devil could he begin to explain. He jammed his fingers back through his hair. "Juliet, you have to listen—"

Bloody hell! All his words died as Adam gaped at the window, aghast, something fluttering past it in the darkness. A night bird? Or some creature searching for seeds or tender shoots to nibble on. God alone knew. The only thing that was certain was that Juliet was reflected back to him by the candleshine, every curve and hollow doubtless visible from the garden, and, possibly from the house itself, should anyone chance to gaze out at the night.

The knowledge that he'd carelessly left her so vulnerable cinched a vise of guilt and regret about his chest. "Here, angel, put this on." He retrieved her nightshift, thrusting it toward her.

She took it, pressing it to her breasts, and Adam wondered if he'd ever seen anything so beautiful. So beautiful that it hurt, way down deep in his chest. He grabbed up his breeches, dragging them on, then made quick work of his shirt, half hoping his actions could conceal the riotous uncertainty rending him.

He glimpsed Juliet pulling her own nightgown over her head, covering her full breasts, tiny waist, the fabric ending in a thin puddle of linen about her slender legs.

"Adam?" She peered up at him as he yanked on his boots.

"Did I do something wrong? The way you're looking at me . . ."

"Everything's wrong. I'm babbling like a candidate for Bedlam. You're looking so damned bruised." His boot heels thudded on the floor as he levered himself to his feet and sucked in a steadying breath. "Juliet, listen to me. I want you to know that I . . ."

"You didn't break anything. You didn't mean to be so enthusiastic—probably bored with the bunglings of a virgin to dispose of. And you'll never try despoiling one again, isn't that what you said?" Her gaze was fixed on her slippers as she put them on, her face half hidden by a veil of golden curls, but he could feel the hurt she was trying to hide as if it were lodged in his own chest.

"I said a damned sight too much, and none of it came out the way I meant it to," Adam ground out hopelessly. "I'm a soldier. Not some blasted poet used to laying my heart open for the world to see. All I know is—" A hundred painfully emotional declarations hovered at the tip of his tongue, trying to find voice. He grasped her hand, pressing it to his heart, as if he hoped she could sense by touch all the things he couldn't say.

He felt as if he were teetering on a sword-blade, that if he lost this moment, it would slip through his fingers forever. "Juliet . . . " Her name, so soft, so tentative it might as well be woven of angel's wings. He knew he should look into her eyes, but the feelings were too intense, terrifyingly so. He turned his gaze toward the window, color burning into his cheeks as he tried to frame the words.

Marry me, even though I don't deserve you.

Be my wife, even though I'm not worthy to touch your hand.

Bear my children and I vow I will love you for eternity.

He sucked in a steadying breath. "Juliet, I—what the hell?" His passionate declaration died on his lips as his eyes locked on the window of Angel's Fall.

The glass that had gently beckoned with a soft glow when first he'd entered the garden now shone with feverish brilliance, its subtle gold intensified into hot color.

Juliet caught at his arm, alarm replacing the hurt in her eyes, her face ice-white at his expression. "Adam, what—what is it? What's wrong?"

"The house!" Red-orange tongues of flame leapt and writhed in the window of Angel's Fall just as the dreaded words tore from his throat. "It's on fire!"

Chapter
15

The door to Angel's Fall crashed against the wall as Juliet flung it open, horror and smoke clawing in her lungs, stinging her eyes. The magic of the time in Adam's arms, the confusion and hurt that had followed, vanished as she plunged into the kitchen, struggling to see.

Fire writhed like a hell-born beast beyond the wide open doors of the drawing room, lashing out in whips of flame, coiling and striking and devouring everything it touched.

A silent scream of denial lodged in her throat, Adam's curses battering her ears, furious, hopeless as he charged after her.

Desperation mingled with terror as she raced toward the stairway to awaken the women slumbering, oblivious, above. Heat, seared her face, penetrated her thin nightgown.

Then pain suddenly exploded through her as a black-cloaked figure charged from the drawing room, slamming into her with bone-cracking force. She flew back into Adam, the two of them crashing to the ground in a tangle of arms and legs. Her eyes locked for a heartbeat on her attacker escaping through the garden door—a malevolent phantom, the embodiment of every nightmare the threatening notes had conjured up these endless months.

Rage screamed through Adam, so potent she could feel it in her own flesh, every instinct in his body urging him to give chase. Instead, he scrambled to his feet, dragging Juliet up. "Get out, I'll get the others," he rasped, but Juliet was already bolting up the stairs, shattering awareness pounding in her head.

While she'd been pleading for Adam to make love with her, someone had crept into Angel's Fall. While she'd cried out and sobbed in ecstasy one of her enemies had set the fire on purpose to . . . what? Burn everyone alive as they slept?

The knowledge was too hideous, too evil, the guilt too crushing. She couldn't grasp it, couldn't bear it.

Cries of alarm tore from her smoke-raw throat. By the time she reached the second floor, women were already spilling into the hall, mob-cap–framed faces stunned, fearful as the smoke cast its suffocating blanket across them. The women choked, coughed, mass confusion taking hold with the same fierceness as the flame.

Only Isabelle maintained her usual calm, sweeping into her chamber to fetch her jewel case, while Millicent and Violet and the others bolted down the stairs in panic.

"Forget about your fripperies, Isabelle," Adam bellowed. "Damn it to hell—"

"Where's Elise? I can't find Elise!" Angelina cried, flinging open yet another door.

Fletcher crashed into her, charging from his attic room, sword in hand, ready to fight. But nothing, no one could battle the dragon unleashed upon Angel's Fall this night.

It would devour its prey until nothing remained of the house, her dreams, her last link to her father. Was this her just punishment for what she'd done in the garden house? To lose everything she loved?

Soul-killing despair lanced through her. Lord, she had had so little from her childhood anyway—only her mother's necklace.

Her mother's necklace! It was in her desk. Suddenly it seemed as if everything she loved were captured in that delicate wreath of golden lilies.

A cry of surprise and pain jabbed her, and she wheeled to

see Elise, crumpled on the floor at the foot of the attic stairs, grasping her ankle. "Juliet, help! I fell . . ."

"Adam!" Juliet screamed for him, and somehow he was there, gathering up the fragile woman as easily as if she were a babe.

"Hurry, damn you!" Adam roared over his shoulder as he carried Elise down the stairs. "The whole place is going up!"

A sob choked Juliet, terror almost overpowering her as the fire leapt hotter, wilder, below. But to let her mother's necklace burn was unthinkable!

She wheeled around, running deeper into the house, weaving through the winding corridor in an effort to reach her bedroom. She stumbled, fell, her lungs screaming for breath. Embers filled the air like fireflies, singeing her hair, burning her skin.

She was almost to the room, when a giant seemed to grab a handful of her nightgown, yanking her off her feet. She crashed to the floor, scrambled around half expecting to see some monster woven of glowing flame. But it was Adam, rising out of the smoke like a pagan God of fire, an inferno more powerful than the one destroying Angel's Fall flaring in his eyes—rage, white-hot, terrifying.

"Have you lost your mind?"

"Let me go! I have to get—"

"Whatever the hell it is, it's not worth your life!" Adam scooped her up in his sinewy arms and turned, running down the hall. Juliet fought against him, certain in a heartbeat she would have had the necklace in her hand, loathing him and herself and the treacherous feelings they'd unleashed in each other.

But when they reached the top of the stairs, she gaped down in horror. Flames were weaving around the banister, climbing up the bottom step.

"A-Adam!" she croaked. "Can't get out that way!"

"It's our only chance." He charged into Isabelle's room, dumping Juliet on the bed.

"What on earth are you doing?" she choked out, but he was already swathing her in suffocating folds of coverlet. Her air-starved lungs protested, her head swam, as Adam hauled her back into his arms.

"Hold on, Angel." She heard his assurances, muffled through the cloth. "I'll get you out."

But Juliet knew he'd wasted precious time protecting her. When he charged through those flames, God alone knew what price he'd pay for it.

Juliet heard his curses, oaths or half-formed prayers? Felt herself plunging downward. The fire roared, blotting out all sound, until she only felt the sharp gasp of pain that rocked Adam's chest. Intense heat seared the last wisp of air from her lungs.

Red dots whirled before her eyes, unconsciousness sucking her down, down, only the jarring of Adam's desperate stride keeping her from total darkness.

Then he staggered, fell, and she tumbled from his grasp. She expected to be plunged into flame, but instead of the hard wood of the floor, she landed on something far softer.

She clawed her way out of the coverlet, felt other hands helping her. She emerged, a wave of fresh air slamming into her with the force of a blow as she sucked in a tortured breath.

The garden—she was back in the garden, crushing a bed of heart's ease, while Adam knelt on all fours, his face soot-blackened, choked coughs all but shattering his ribs.

"A-Adam . . . Juliet, are you all right?" One of the women asked.

"I'm fine, blast it," Adam choked out. "A little singed around . . . the edges. But I'll live. No thanks . . . to her." He cast Juliet a fulminating glare. "What the . . . blazes were you . . . doing?"

Anger sliced through her, fueled by poisonous guilt. "Why didn't you leave me alone? I could have . . . could have gotten it out!"

"Gotten what out?"

"My mother's necklace." The words were a raw wound inside her.

"You mean you could've roasted like a blasted Christmas goose!" Adam raged. "Look at that fire! Most people prefer to . . . wait until actually *in* hell before . . . drowning in flames. Or did you think you could walk right through them? St. Juliet at the stake?"

Cruel—the words were cruel—or were they born out of sheer terror, furious helplessness?

"Damn it, Juliet, *look* at it!"

He grasped her by the shoulders, forcing her to see the fire leaping at the window panes, thrusting red-gold fingers out beneath the sashes. Even the roof was being consumed.

Grief ground down on her, as she saw flames reflected in the window that had been her bedchamber's. And she knew with stark certainty that her mother's treasured chain of lilies was nothing but a pool of molten gold.

"It was all I had left," she choked out, tears pouring down her cheeks. But the necklace was gone.

Gone. Just like everything she had loved, her father, Jenny, this house. Absurd to feel as if the house had been a kind of friend, to be missed and mourned, but from the instant she'd painted the angels above the front door, she'd felt as if she'd finally found somewhere to belong.

Juliet flinched as someone touched her arm, looked up to find Elise, her eyes huge and haunted and glistening with tears.

"J-Juliet? How—how did the fire start? Do you think it was my fault? I'd washed some things for Fletcher, hung them to dry near the hearth . . ."

"No. It wasn't your fault, Elise." The enormity of the atrocity jolted through Juliet. "When Adam and I ran in from the garden house, there was . . . was someone in Angel's Fall . . ."

"But the new locks—" Violet said, bewildered. "Fletcher claimed Cuchullain himself couldn't break them."

"I left the door unlocked myself." The words seared Juliet's conscience. "When I . . ."

When she trailed Adam into the garden, hoping to seduce him.

"You left the door open, and someone sneaked in?" Isabelle demanded. "Didn't you see them? At least catch a glimpse so we could go to the authorities?"

"No," Juliet said, her cheeks hot with shame and desolation. "I didn't—I couldn't—wasn't aware until it was too late. They had already carried out their plan."

"Plan? You mean to say someone did this on purpose?"

Felicity gasped, bewildered. "Who could have done such a vile thing?"

A tremor rocked Juliet. "Someone who hates me." *Enough to burn it,* her mind finished, *burn it down.* And she had given them the perfect chance.

But who could have set the fire?

As if in answer to her question, a roar started in the street beyond the garden walls, a cacophony of voices, people pouring in through the open gate.

Juliet stared into the sea of faces, the knowledge someone had despised her enough to do this awful thing paralyzing her, sickening her.

Who? Who had set the fire? Destroyed every dream?

It could be any one of these people who loathed her with such deadly venom.

"Oh, Papa," she whispered inside. "Papa . . . " Was she praying for a miracle from the one angel she knew heard her every prayer? Or was she begging for the forgiveness he'd always offered her so readily.

What had she been thinking, casting aside her responsibilities, her every belief, wandering out in her nightgown to lie with Adam in the garden house? A man who didn't love her. She had failed again, failed completely.

Was this fire her punishment?

If so, it was a horrifyingly harsh one. She wouldn't be the only one to suffer. Every woman who had been under her care would be hurt by this. And she could do nothing to help them. She had nothing left to give.

"The roof is going to go!" Came a voice with a thick Cockney accent.

Juliet turned to see it cave in, crushing everything below. She watched, numb as the spectators flung themselves at the fire, dousing it with bucketfuls of water, the fire brigade joining in the battle.

They didn't know there was nothing left to fight for.

Angel's Fall was gone.

Ever since he'd charged up to Angel's Fall, Adam had been doing his damnedest to blast Juliet out of the place. Even as he'd held Juliet in his arms, making love to her with tender fury, he'd been planning to sweep her away from here, to take her somewhere safe. But he couldn't have outflanked her more brilliantly than this fire had if he'd spent a year plotting strategy.

Angel's Fall lay in ashes. She'd have no choice but to leave it now, leave London. Yet as Adam trudged out of the smoking ruin, the others who'd fought the fire plodding in his wake, it was damned hard to feel anything like triumph, or even a dull satisfaction. Especially when his smoke-stung eyes found Juliet.

She might as well have been stranded on a solitary island of grief. The women she'd tended so lovingly had withdrawn into the shadows. Even loyal Elise stood apart, as if some invisible wall had barred her from offering comfort. In a way, Adam supposed that it had. Never, in all the time Juliet had been at the helm of the haven for courtesans, had she ever revealed her own vulnerability, her own pain. Or the heart-rending fragility she kept hidden beneath the resolute jut of her chin and the fierce determination in her angel-blue eyes.

This Juliet was a stranger to the women she'd loved so long.

She was curled up on a stone bench, one of those ridiculous statues silhouetted against the dawn behind her, the makeshift toga concealing its naked marble glory soot-blackened and askew. The cloth of her nightgown was singed, her hair a tangle of wild golden curls. But it was her eyes that slayed Adam—wide blue pools of despair in a face that had always been alight with hope.

Bloody hell, what was it about dreamers like Juliet? Like Gavin? When they were flitting about all sunshine and star-drunk you wanted more than anything to dash the dreams from their eyes, force them to face the bleak reality everyone else had to confront. But when the same dreamer was forced to gaze into the heart of the storm, their beautiful illusions torn away, it was like watching the last star in the heavens flicker and fade to darkness.

Exhaustion and stinging burns, smoke-seared lungs and soot-gritty eyes should have consumed Adam at the moment, but they were nothing in comparison to the empty aching hole the sight of this shattered angel carved into his soldier's heart. But he had the right to go to her now, hold her, comfort her, offer his love, unworthy as he was, in place of her broken dreams.

His imagination swelled with images of his dark-haired babes nursing at her breast, clambering about her skirts and pressing sticky kisses to her cheeks, making her forget the ugliness of this fire, those who hated her. He would love her until he banished the last wisps of this disaster from her memory, and would fill her heart with the laughter and love she deserved.

"Juliet?" Her name cracked in his raw throat, and she looked up like one awakened from a nightmare, only to find reality even more horrible. He reached out to her, but she evaded his touch, forcing herself to her feet. She was trembling, so fragile he was afraid the brush of the wind would make her crumble to dust. He tried to catch her eye, but she was staring past him, at the other men who had battled the fire, a bedraggled army tramping behind him from the fray.

Juliet raised a shaking hand to her cheek, brushing away a stray tendril that clung to the last of her tears. And Adam felt as if a blade twisted in his heart as she approached Mr. Smythe, the man who had led her neighbors in battling back the inferno.

Adam sensed the effort it took to draw the tattered remnants of her dignity about her. God in heaven, how could she look so infernally beautiful, ethereal, despite this hell? A fairy queen whose magic kingdom had been set upon by dragons of the most virulent kind.

"My papa always said to look for some hint of goodness even in the most terrible of misfortunes," she said in a soft voice. "That way we could hold God's comforting hand in our worst trouble."

Adam started forward, wanting to scoop her into his arms, away from this place, these people who could hurt her. "Come on, Angel, we have to—"

"No, Adam. I have to—to tell Mr. Smythe . . . " She turned back to the scrawny merchant, her features vulnerable as the first flower of spring in a winter wind. "I want to thank you for . . . for proving that Papa was right. I know you've not been pleased to be our neighbor, but when the house was afire, you came to help . . . to try to put it out."

"Of course we did," Smythe said.

Her lips struggled to form a brave smile. "It's just as Papa says. Love does triumph over hate in the end. I'll never forget your kindness."

"Kindness?" Smythe's eyes all but popped from his head. "Bah! You think I all but roasted myself to a cinder out of some blasted notion of Christian charity? It's my own house I was trying to save. If the fire had gotten out of control, it could have devoured everything I own!"

"Aye," Cyrus Morton snarled, "we waited long as we dared before we pitched in, made sure that this den o' harlots would be burned to rubble."

A sword-thrust would have been more merciful. Adam could see the words cut right to Juliet's heart. What little color had stained her cheeks faded away, her lovely angel's face bleak, her celestial eyes barren, broken. "You . . . you mean you . . ."

"Said it in plain English," Smythe sneered. "Not that you'd understand. I only regret that you and your sin-spawned women weren't inside it when the roof fell! 'Course there's always time for whoever did this to finish the job."

"That's enough, you bloody fool!" Adam snarled, one hand shooting out to collar the merchant by the throat. A black haze of terror jolted through him at the possibility that even greater danger might await Juliet in the shadows, the evil that had consumed Angel's Fall not yet sated. Slade wished like hell for the days when he could have snapped the idiot's neck and rid himself of the black surge of fury swirling in his veins.

"Adam, no." Juliet's hand closed on his wrist, such a small hand to battle the lions of injustice. "It doesn't matter what they say." Her voice broke, and he could feel the disillusionment flowing through her like poison.

"Damn it, they're pompous imbeciles! Just get the hell out of here, all of you bloody vultures, or I swear to God, I'll—" The threat died on Adam's lips. The dread warrior

Sabrehawk had spent a lifetime flinging himself into battle over such incidents. But suddenly it seemed so blasted futile. What could he do to mend the disaster that had befallen Juliet tonight?

Cracking the heads of these sons of bitches might make him feel a hell of a lot better, but it wouldn't raise the walls of her house again. Beating them to a pulp wouldn't erase their words from her memory. But knowing that didn't calm the violence storming in the dark places inside him.

He shoved the scrawny idiot away from him, still half afraid he'd slam his fist into the man's face. But Smythe ran like a rabbit, the other neighbors darting away, eyes wide with fear. Hell, they should be afraid. Adam was starting to scare the bejesus out of himself.

There had been only one other time he felt this raging sense of futility, this killing helplessness, this depth of fury. The day Gavin had strode into the lair of his most cruel enemy intending to trade his life for Adam's own.

Sucking in a steadying breath, Adam turned back to Juliet, every fiber of his soul wanting to cradle her in his arms as he had hours before, comfort her as best he could with his rough warrior's hands.

But he stopped reaching out to her midmotion, his hands still empty the instant he saw the expression on her face. Frigid, brittle, her eyes glittered at him with something akin to loathing. Adam felt it pierce to his very core.

"Don't touch me!" she cried.

"Juliet, I know how—how you must feel," he said, wishing to God he had Gavin's gift for knowing the perfect thing to say to salve a wounded heart. "And I'm damned sorry, lady—"

"Sorry?" she demanded, incredulous.

"That this happened." He waved an awkward paw ineffectually at the rubble. "I'm sorry that those blasted curs said what they did."

"At least Mr. Smythe and Mr. Morton were honest. Why don't you have the decency to tell the truth as well? Follow the two of them to the nearest pub to celebrate. Find Mother Cavendish—I'm certain she's cracked open a keg of gin in honor of the fire, and I doubt she'd mind sharing."

"Juliet, I'm not rejoicing."

"You should be. Isn't this exactly what you wanted all along? Angel's Fall closed down, me packed off to God knows where, out of the way?"

There was enough truth in the words to sting. But they struck him like a blow after the closeness they'd shared a few hours ago. Adam's cheeks heated. Hell, she was right. He'd wished Angel's Fall to perdition on numerous occasions. So why the devil did he feel as if his heart had been torn out of his chest? Because he still felt the press of kisses on his skin, the delicious yielding of bodies and souls. "It's no secret that I wanted you out of here, away from London, somewhere safe. But I didn't want the house to burn. Surely you have to believe that."

"Do I? Ever since you arrived here I've heard tales of your ruthlessness. The brave Sabrehawk resorting to all sorts of unspeakable things."

"The heartless Sabrehawk. Hell, who knows, maybe I even started the fire." He struck out with the black humor that had ever been his shield; his own dreams, so fragile, so precious, conceived in the magic of the garden house were crumbling to ash.

"I was a fool to believe—believe that love would triumph over hate." A wild broken laugh tore from her lips. "To think, I actually thanked those men for . . . for putting out the fire when they really wished us all dead. What a blathering fool I was."

"Juliet, stop this." Adam grasped her arms, unable to bear it. "They're sanctimonious pigs who don't matter a damn."

"And what are you?" Tears welled up in her eyes, her chin jutting up. "Don't you dare pretend that you regret this! If I hadn't been chasing after you in the garden house, I could have stopped the fire." A world of guilt contorted her face.

"Don't be ridiculous! You can't believe that!"

"It's the truth! I'll never forgive myself for what happened tonight. There's nothing left. Nothing."

"Angel, I know this seems like the end of the world. But people are damned resilient. Believe me. I know. A year from now, you'll be settled in a new life. You'll barely remember this place, what happened here." He'd see to it, damn his soul. Fill every minute with loving.

"I hope you're right. I hope I can forget what an empty-headed fool I was." Her eyes were cold when they met his, the love that had shone in them while they'd made love extinguished like the blaze of the fire, almost as if their loving were some sort of cruel dream that had never been real at all. "But most of all I hope I can forget you."

Adam drew back as if she'd struck him. "You don't mean that," he rasped. "After tonight in the garden house—"

"It was a mistake. A horrible mistake. One I'll pay for for the rest of my life. I'll never forgive myself—or you!"

She was destroying him, shattering him as no cannonfire ever had, abandoning him in a wasteland of pain. She blamed him for what had happened. But even more chilling, she blamed herself. The change wrought in her face was the most horrible thing Adam had ever seen.

It was as if her words had drained the final embers of life out of her, extinguished the sparks of fury in her eyes, leaving them empty of all but desolation as she looked about the ruined garden.

Flowers lay scorched, blackened, the herbs she'd tended so carefully trampled beneath careless feet. The iron gate swung open on its hinges, creaking out a keening lament. There was nothing left to guard inside the stone garden walls except for broken dreams.

Adam's gaze swept the bench that had held the basket of food for the beggar children every night since he'd arrived at Angel's Fall, and he wondered how the waifs would keep their stomachs full and their fingers warm without the bundle of hot rolls and meat pies Juliet had provided.

"Juliet, where are we going to go? What are we going to do?" Millicent asked, looking forlorn and strangely child-like.

The query did what even Smythe's cruelty could not. Hot spots of color stained Juliet's cheeks, her voice harsh, fists white-knuckled and shaking. "I don't know! Why are you looking at me as if I had all the answers? Can't you see what a fool I was?" Her self-condemnation tore at Adam's heart like the fangs of a wolf.

"No!" Felicity cried. "That's not true."

"The proof is all around you!" Juliet swept her hand toward the smoking ruin. "You could have all burned to death because of my stubbornness and carelessness and . . . and for what? So you could pretend to learn how to sew even though you hate it?"

"Juliet, listen—" Elise rushed forward, but Isabelle grasped her by the arm.

"Stop, Elise. Reflect," the Frenchwoman interrupted. "Look at this ruin. It is hardly fair to expect Juliet to play savior to us after all she has lost. We cannot play these games any longer."

Elise swallowed hard, drew back, but Adam could sense the pain in this, Juliet's most fragile angel, and the resignation.

"You're right. Of course," Elise agreed, but Adam heard the slightest tremor in her voice. Where the devil would she go now? Where would any of them go? Hell, it wasn't his responsibility, was it? Any more than it had been Juliet's.

"'Twill be lovely to be independent again, don't you think?" Isabelle asked. There was something in her face that raked across Adam's battle instincts, a brittle brightness. His gaze flicked to the jewel chest still clutched to Isabelle's bosom.

"Easy enough for you to say!" Millicent cried. "You're the only one who managed to carry anything away from the fire!"

Isabelle's lips curled in what was almost a smile. "It comes of long practice, my dear."

Practice? Adam wondered darkly. What an odd thing to say. Or had the fading courtesan known all along what was going to happen here tonight? He recalled the strange conversation they'd had, Isabelle, always hinting at things, hiding things, concealing motives that no one could discern. It was possible life had taught her to be thus, just as Adam had learned to gird himself in an armor of recklessness, carelessness when it came to his bastardy. Or perhaps there were more sinister reasons hidden behind Isabelle's brittle mask.

Whatever the truth, did it matter now? With Juliet all but

ready to collapse with heartache and exhaustion? There would be time to cut to the heart of this later. And by damn, he would do so after—after what? After he found somewhere to stash the rest of these women until he could get them decently clothed. An inn would be perfect, except that if he marched them through the common room garbed in their nightshifts it would incite a riot. Besides, Juliet didn't look as if she could make it to the end of the street without fainting dead away.

Adam scowled, gnawed at the inside of his cheek. "I know a place we can use temporarily," he was stunned to hear himself say. "My brother's townhouse."

"The—the earl's house?" Fletcher choked out. "You're going to take them to the earl's house?"

"You have a better damn suggestion? Just get my blasted horse before I change my mind."

The boy raced off, and Adam stalked to the well. Scooping up one of the buckets abandoned on the turf, he drew enough water to wash his face, anything to keep from watching Juliet standing there so alone.

He splashed the handfuls of water over his cheeks and jaw and gritty eyes, letting the moisture cool the burns where embers had struck his skin, washing away the soot. When he straightened to wipe away the water with the tail of his shirt, his nape prickled with wariness as someone laid one perfectly manicured hand upon his shoulder. He wheeled around to see Isabelle, almost untouched by the ordeal.

"You must think of this unpleasantness as dealing with a battle wound, *mon ami,*" she said. "The swifter you tear the blade from Juliet's flesh and cauterize the wound, the sooner the end of pain."

"What the devil do you know about it?"

"Just that the sooner Juliet is settled elsewhere, the sooner she will forget."

The words were similar to those he'd spoken himself, but he jerked away from Isabelle, loathing the woman in that instant. It was so damn easy for her, wasn't it? Gazing at the destruction all around her with her shuttered eyes and lips that kept a thousand secrets. She had saved the only thing that mattered to her, her treasure box snatched out of the very flames. But then, from the first he'd known Isabelle had that feline ability to land on her feet, no matter what precipice she was tossed off of. It was an ability Adam had long admired, had cultivated in himself. Why did it suddenly seem so chilling, sinister?

"One thing you may be certain of," Adam growled. "Once Juliet is settled, I'll damn well find whoever was responsible for that blaze."

"But of course you will, you stubborn fool. You didn't get all those scars by leaving well enough alone." She gave a wry smile. "This is what you wanted, *non?* An end to this insanity? Why not embrace it as good fortune? Carry Juliet to safety? I have eyes. I see the way you look at her. 'Tis your chance to sweep her onto your charger like a knight errant and play the hero."

"I'm no bloody hero, and you know it." But Adam was dismayed by the sudden knowledge that at this instant he wanted to be one for his Juliet.

His retort was cut off by the sound of hoofbeats, Fletcher running up, leading Adam's mount. And Adam wanted nothing more than to scoop Juliet into his arms, ride as far away from the world as possible, carry her off into some kingdom of dreams where he could love away her pain, wash away the memories of Angel's Fall and the fire and the heartbreak that had so altered her eyes.

But to carry a woman to such a place, you had to believe in fairy kingdoms yourself, like Gavin did.

Adam strode to Juliet. "I'm taking you to Glenlyon House."

"No!" Juliet protested. "I won't take your charity—"

"You'd rather freeze out here than accept my help? What the blazes are you going to do? Run all over London in your nightgown singing for your supper?" He dared not give her any quarter. "Or would you prefer that I take you to the inn, Juliet? Stroll through the common room with all your enemies drinking toasts to the destruction of Angel's Fall, gloating over their triumph?"

Agony slashed in jagged streaks across her face, and for a moment, just a moment, he hoped his harsh words would lash up the magnificence inside her; Juliet Grafton-Moore, the woman he'd first laughed at, grown to respect and then, God help him, come to love. Jesus, God, he'd never known that emotion could hurt far worse than any battle wound.

If he couldn't bestir her to fight for herself, maybe there was another way. He could get her to fight for her fallen angels.

Guilt was a damned underhanded tactic, one that didn't sit well in his stomach. But he had no choice. Adam forced his mouth into a mocking sneer. "Perhaps you're ready to embrace martyrdom, but are you willing to condemn Elise to it? Millicent and Felicity and all the others?"

"The house is gone. I've nothing left to give."

"Well, that's too damned bad, because they're all looking to you, Juliet. You owe them better than this."

She raised her eyes, and Adam watched her stare at the cluster of women who had drawn back into the shadows. "You're right. They'll need someplace to stay while they make other arrangements. I don't have any choice but to make use of the place you offer. But won't your brother object to former courtesans invading his family home?"

"It's not as if we were moving in permanently. And Gavin rarely comes to the city anyway—not since that unfortunate ruckus his oldest son kicked up while touring the Tower of London. I think the guards have orders to shoot Drake on sight." It was a feeble attempt at humor, one that fell dismally flat.

She gave another sick laugh. "I suppose an earl's house is as good a place as any to arrange for the new protectors the ladies have been searching for all this time. Perhaps the earl can provide a list of suitable candidates."

She started to turn away, all but fell. Adam's hand shot out to steady her. "Damn it, Juliet, you're ready to drop. Fletcher!" he bellowed to the boy who was hanging back, the reins of the gelding in his hand. The lad jumped in surprise.

"Make yourself useful, for pity's sake. We'll need a coach—two of them if you can manage it. Otherwise, we'll have to make two trips."

"Aye, Sabrehawk. I'll be back in a trice." Fletcher handed over the gelding's reins and sprung into action.

"I'm going to ride ahead, prepare the earl's servants for the invasion," Adam barked after him. "I'm taking Juliet with me."

"No!" Juliet protested. "I'm not going with you. I'll wait for the coach."

He didn't bother to argue with her. Mounting the gelding, he leaned down from his saddle and scooped Juliet into his arms. He wanted her to struggle, to rage at his dictatorial ways. Wanted to goad her into defying him as she had from the first moment he'd looked into her eyes. But she only stiffened for a heartbeat, before surrendering the battle.

Adam's heart sank as her eyelids fluttered closed. She lay agonizingly still against his chest, as if a part of her had died.

Chapter

16

Glenlyon House had the aura of a giant cat drowsing in the warmth of the new-fledged sun. Elegant, exquisite, every stone was witness to the exorbitant tastes that had driven the family to the brink of ruin until Adam's father had wed a wealthy merchant's daughter to recoup the Glenlyon fortunes.

Gazing up at the edifice, Adam wondered if that salvation had been worth the anguish it had caused. A whole generation lost in misery.

His father, denied his dream of becoming a soldier, saddled with a wife he held in contempt when he was already in love with another woman—a woman pregnant with his bastard.

Adam's mother, the beautiful laughing Lydia Slade, who forsook her family, her good name, traded her future to live a charade. And Gavin's mother, that poor simple girl who had her heart broken by the knowledge that her reluctant husband had done his best to forget she existed, lavished his time and adoration on another family, slept in another woman's bed a day's ride away from her.

And Gavin—the heir born of this cursed marriage—he had paid the highest price of all—despised by his father until he'd been driven to attempt to win his love on a battlefield for a cause he never believed in, with a sword he'd never wanted to wield.

Only one good thing had sprung from that morass of pain—the bond between half-brothers, merely three months apart in age, worlds different in personality, had been forged in rage and resentment and mistrust, tempered by time into a fierce love, though they understood each other not at all.

But even that close bond had fallen victim to the wild years of Adam's adventuring. Guilt constricted about his throat like a too-tight neckcloth. He'd ignored Gavin's letters, brushed aside pleas that he return home to see a new niece or nephew, a new man-killer of a horse Gavin had managed to gentle, or to visit with Mama Fee, the old Scottish woman who had kept house for the fugitive brothers in a wild cave in the highlands.

Hellfire, the way he loved Gavin, it should have been easy to ride up to his manorhouse, stomp into the entryway in the big boots the children loved. Those few times he had, he'd been welcomed with such delight it had been damned near embarrassing.

Showered with kisses from Gavin's wife Rachel and the bevy of children, embraced by Gavin, and carried off as if he were Odysseus returned from his voyage.

After all the pain Gavin had endured, it was heaven to see him happier than any mortal had a right to be. It was what Adam had wished for his brother for so long. So why did it open up such a raw place in his chest when he saw Gavin and his lady love? He'd never guessed the truth until now, as he rode through his brother's gates with Juliet Grafton-Moore in his arms.

Envy—that bitter poison that had almost destroyed any chance the half-brothers had at closeness as boys had popped open again like Pandora's box.

And no matter how much Adam loved Gavin, no matter how happy he was for his brother's joy, he couldn't help resenting the fact that he could never reach out to a woman like Juliet, offer her his hand in marriage, his body to shield her from any harm the fates might hurl at her, his hand to clutch in travail as she brought his child into the world. Hell, he couldn't even offer her an honorable name, only one tinged with scandal and stained by bastardy.

Maybe for the brightest and most brief of moments he'd dreamed it was possible. But it hadn't taken long for bleak reality to crush such fantasies.

How had he gotten into this accursed predicament? He'd been so blasted careful not to let anyone near his heart. He'd learned from his love for Gavin what incredible pain could result.

Yet Juliet hadn't stolen his heart. Sabrehawk hadn't possessed a heart for her to steal. Juliet *was* his heart. Everything good and decent that remained in Adam was caught in the cup of her hand. Not that it mattered. She was as far beyond his touch as Gavin's fabled moon-lady who plaited her silver tresses with ribbons of night. And she hated him now. The agony of it wrenched inside him.

Hell, from the time he'd been an unruly boy, Adam had been clumsy as a dragon in a crystal chamber, smashing whatever delicate things came within reach. But he'd never regretted anything so much as he did the ruin he surveyed now, every time his gaze dropped to Juliet's face.

She hadn't said a word the whole endless ride from Angel's Fall. Had barely opened her eyes. Even her breathing was shallow, as if it took too much effort, crushed as she was underneath disillusionment.

And Adam wanted to shake her until her teeth rattled, until she flung defiance at him. He wanted to kiss her until her lips softened, and her eyes grew warm and alive again. But he'd lost the right to do anything but make this period of transition as painless as possible for her.

He had to dissolve the last bonds created in Angel's Fall, help the courtesans get on with their lives, then tuck Juliet back where she belonged. In an ivory tower filled with fairy dreams far away from the world of fires and angry mobs and worthless scoundrels like Adam Slade.

Adam guided his mount up the drive, drew rein beneath a marble cornice carved with the Glenlyon crest. None of the lamps in the front of the house were lit. Adam thanked the fates again for his brother's dislike of London's "elegant herd."

Had he lost his mind bringing these women here? Adam wondered. Allowing the Glenlyon family home to be invaded by a harem of fallen women might be beyond even Gavin's famed generosity.

Still, under the circumstances, it would be better to ask Gavin's pardon than risk refusal, Adam reasoned. Where the blazes else would he be able to hide a flock of women of ill repute until he could get them decently clothed?

No, the best he could hope for was to bribe the servants with a keg of brandy so Gavin would never suspect the full extent of this disaster.

Adam winced inwardly, damned uncomfortable at the notion of being dishonest with his brother. Yet the happenings of the past month were far too tender a subject to be probed even by Gavin's wise and gentle hands. Juliet would forever be the sweetest ache in Adam's scarred soul.

Bracing Juliet with one brawny arm, Adam dismounted, the jarring of boot soles striking the cobblestones shooting spikes of exhaustion through his legs. But he shoved it away, reaching up to lift her into his arms. It was as if even the meager weight of her soot-stained nightgown was too great for her to carry.

"I can walk," she started to protest, pushing at him with a hand that trembled.

"Of course you can," Adam grumbled, taking the stairs two at a time. "You're shaking like a blasted leaf. Our entrance is going to cause enough of a sensation among my brother's servants. But if you want to increase the effect by crawling over the threshold on your hands and knees, angel, far be it from me to stop you."

Most times, he could've bounced a little thing like Juliet over his head on one hand while he knocked on the door with the other, but the fire and countless sleepless nights had robbed him of a measure of his legendary strength.

He set her on her feet, wishing like hell he'd grabbed a frockcoat or cloak or something to cover her with, conceal her nightgown-clad frame from prying eyes. But the only shelter he could offer was his own broad shoulders. He stepped in front of her and vented his frustration by booting the door until it rattled on its hinges.

He was just about to kick it again when it flew open. Adam's heart plunged to the toes of his boots. Doubtless the earl of Glenlyon was the only nobleman in Christendom who answered his own door. Gavin stood on the threshold garbed in a dark gold waistcoat, breeches and a white shirt with inkblots on one sleeve, his golden mane tousled, his spectacles sliding down his nose.

Perfect, Adam thought grimly. At least his luck was consistent. At the moment, he would have preferred facing a firing squad than his half-brother's incredulous gray gaze. "Adam?" Gavin hurled himself at Adam, all but knocking the wind out of him as he wrestled him into a playful embrace.

"Bloody hell, where the blazes is the footman?" Adam groused, a hundred strained muscles in his body screaming in protest at such rough treatment. "Don't tell me. He's sick with a cold and you didn't want to get him out of bed."

"Don't be ridiculous." Gavin's sensitive mouth pulled into a devilish grin. "He made a trip to the tooth drawer and his jaw swelled up three times its size. Damn, it's good to see you, brother!" Gavin laughed, tugging the soot-smeared remnants of Adam's shirt. "I know it's been a long time since your last visit, Adam, but you didn't have to dress in such elegant style just to impress me. You look like the very devil."

"I feel like the devil. Tell me Rachel and the brats aren't here," Adam pleaded with faint hope, wondering how the devil he'd explain the coming invasion to his redoubtable sister-in-law.

"Unfortunately they're back in Norfolk. Drake had a close encounter with my latest Satan-spawned horse and broke his arm."

"Is it serious?"

"No. But Drake takes after you, a nightmare of a patient. Rachel is attempting to make certain he doesn't drive the servants to suicide or murder his little brothers in his frustration. She'll be horribly disappointed to have missed you."

"I'm sure she will be, especially once she finds out why I'm here. Never known Rachel to miss an opportunity to give me a royal scolding." Adam grimaced.

Gavin's brow furrowed with concern. "What have you done now? Are you in trouble?"

"In a manner of speaking. I, uh, brought someone with me."

Adam stepped aside, color burning into his cheeks. Gavin's eyes snagged on Juliet for the first time, his jaw dropped in surprise. But after an astonished pause, he smiled, his manners as polished as if he received young ladies in their nightgowns every day.

"My brother shows a distinct lack of chivalry letting you stand out on the landing, milady. I'm Gavin Carstares, Earl of Glenlyon, your servant." He gave a courtly bow. "And who, may I ask, are you? My brother doesn't even offer a proper introduction, and after all my efforts to civilize him!" He shook his head with such sorrowful resignation it was all Adam could do not to punch him.

"This is Juliet," Adam snapped.

"A lovely name. *'Soft, what light through yonder window breaks? It is the sun and Juliet is*—'"

"Blast it, no infernal poetry or I swear I'll break *your* arm!"

Juliet stepped forward, looking heartbreakingly young and vulnerable garbed only in her nightgown. "There's something else Adam's not told you. Something a good deal more important. There will be more ladies arriving momentarily."

"More ladies?" Gavin arched his brows. "How many more?"

"A coach full," Juliet said. "Maybe two."

"By damn, I always suspected Adam would collect himself a harem chasing all over the globe. Rachel said it would only take one woman to bring this proud soldier to his knees. Blast if I wasn't right for once in my life! I should have placed a wager on it, by Zeus."

"Your lordship," Juliet continued. "It's best to get this all out in the open. You might have heard of a place called Angel's Fall?"

"Angel's Fall?" Gavin's eyes lit up. "The refuge for fallen women?"

Of course his brother had heard of the place, Adam thought fatalistically. Hell, the miracle was that he hadn't trundled himself over there to pitch in teaching the women how to stitch a fine seam.

"So you're the young woman who has stirred up such a tempest," Gavin said. "You're quite notorious."

Adam saw Juliet's knuckles whiten as if she were bracing for another blow. "Obviously the women are not of the reputation most nobles would welcome into their family homes, your lordship. I certainly understand if you refuse to take us in."

"You always said I was to use the house as my own, Gav," Adam interrupted. "Bring half the blasted army if I wanted to. That's what you said. So I did—just the half that were camp followers instead of the half that were soldiers."

"Miss Grafton-Moore, I am honored to meet you at last. I'm perishing to know how you ever ran afoul of my ox-brained brother. I can't wait to write a letter to Rachel about this."

Adam paled at the thought. "She doesn't need to know, does she? The women will only be here a little while—long enough to fit them out in new wardrobes. They've not a stitch among the lot of 'em."

Adam gritted his teeth at the expression on Gavin's face. "Blast, don't look at me that way! I didn't undress them! They were in their nightgowns. The house burned in the middle of the night. Just summon up a batch of seamstresses willing to work night and day. I'll pay whatever it takes."

"I'll see to it at once." Gavin crossed his arms over his chest, enjoying Adam's discomfiture entirely too much. "After all, we can't have the ladies prancing about Rachel's front lawn in nothing but their unmentionables."

"You mean you're going to let us stay?" Juliet stared at Gavin, incredulous.

"You're most welcome here." Gavin winked at her. "I'm thrilled to finally meet one of Adam's women after all these years. You must be the most patient of ladies to tolerate my brother's antics. If I ever rounded up a pack of females the way he has, Rachel would have my head on a platter."

"I'm not one of Adam's women . . . I mean, I . . ." Red stained her cheeks. Adam ached for her, as her eyes flooded with pain and self-condemnation, and the stark realization that no matter what the future brought, she *was* one of his women forevermore because of what had occurred in the garden house.

He was crushed by guilt at the knowledge that he was the man who had made this most precious of angels fall. And furious with his brother, with those eyes that probed too deeply, that heart that sensed pain in others far too readily.

Gavin's features softened with compassion. He reached out, enfolding Juliet's hand in his long sensitive fingers. Adam hated him for the gentle comfort he conveyed so easily. "This is your home for as long as you need it, my dear," Gavin said.

Tears welled over Juliet's lashes, her lower lip trembling despite the efforts Adam could see her make to quell it. Envy burned in Adam's gut like acid that it was Gavin who had managed to touch her pain, soothe it, instead of himself.

"Let's get you upstairs, summon up the maid," Gavin suggested. "A hot bath and a nice long sleep will hearten you after all you've been through."

Gavin took her arm with ineffable tenderness, guiding her toward the stairs, and Adam ground his teeth. Juliet leaned on his brother with the utter confidence everyone showed Gavin, trust that he would not let them down, instinctive certainty of his goodness, his kindness. A fiery ball of regret lodged in Adam's throat as he trailed after them.

Hadn't this always been the way of it? From the time the two boys had chased after their little sisters, Gavin had always been the one they ran to with their little hurts. When a beloved kitten died, Gavin made it a tiny coffin and held a solemn funeral for the bereaved, complete with a supper of ice and bonbons. Adam had fled at the first sign of tears, only daring to return when the worst of the storm was over to gruffly thrust a new kitten into his sister's arms.

He almost protested when Gavin stopped to usher Juliet into the nearest bedchamber. Adam's jaw clenched at the memory of when he'd last been in this room—the old earl had sent Gavin there to retrieve his grandfather's sword to carry off to war. A part of his brother had died the instant he took the weapon in his hand.

A part of Adam had as well—the Glenlyon townhouse, part of his father's legacy a bastard was never allowed to touch—a tangible reminder that there were other facets of his father he could never claim—like an honorable name.

Yet it seemed as if Gavin's presence in the past eight years had warmed away those chill memories, the former pristine elegance of the chamber made homey by several well-worn books abandoned on a table, the writing desk holding a bit of Celtic interlacing that Gavin had painted with infinite patience. A tent made out of silk coverlets was draped over chairs while three toy knights on wooden horses and a hand-carved dragon peeked from inside the makeshift structure.

"Forgive the mess," Gavin said. "The last time my children were here they made this their castle, but hadn't much time to play in it. I promised them a blood oath I'd leave it undisturbed until their return. I hope you don't mind?"

"No." She reached out her fingertips, touching one of the toys. And hot envy welled up in Adam, a fierce wish that his own sons had wrestled with the coverlets and sent the knights charging, children born of his love for Juliet. Children who would never be. Unless, a tiny voice whispered inside him, a life had been conceived in the garden house, during their loving.

Adam felt a savage wave of hope. Then she would have to wed him, to share his life, his bed . . . No. It was vile to even think of forcing her hand that way. It was better to let her go.

"Wait here while I summon up the maid. Until she comes, Adam will take care of you."

Adam gritted his teeth as his brother strode out. God, how he wanted to take care of Juliet. Such a simple wish—

one as old as the first man who had loved a woman. But the best way he could take care of Juliet was to get as far away from her as possible as soon as possible, so she could forget him.

Yet the thought of life without Juliet left him with the kind of barrenness in his soul that drove men to fling themselves to certain death upon the battlefield, welcoming the dark abyss that was the only force that could extinguish such soul-deep pain.

He turned to see her sink down on the bed, looking forlorn, a tattered angel far from heaven. She stared down at her filthy hands as if they held the broken pieces of her spirit, and she knew the instant she opened her fingers, they'd drift away like fairy-dust or moonbeams and leave her in darkness.

He wanted to cross to where she sat and kneel down, cupping her hands in his own battered ones. He wanted to mend what was broken inside her. But Sabrehawk's hands were made to wield a sword, to fight in battle, to slam into tables or walls in fits of temper. They weren't hands that could soothe away fear and failure. In that instant, he would gladly have severed his rough sword-toughened hands if he could have exchanged them for his brother's gentle ones.

"Your brother is a remarkable man," she said quietly.

Adam ground his teeth, but couldn't deny it. "Gavin is everything I can never be." The admission was exquisitely painful. "Juliet, I—"

"I'm grateful for all you've done—finding us a place to stay. Offering clothes."

I'd put the moon into your hands if it were mine to give, a voice inside Adam whispered. "I failed to protect you. It's the least I could do."

She angled her face away from him, fragile golden curls trailing across one pale cheek. "I'm very tired, Adam."

"Hell, yes, you must be exhausted. What can I do for you?"

"I just . . . need to be alone." Her lips trembled. "It's time I got used to it."

Adam winced. She'd not only witnessed the destruction of her dreams, but of the makeshift family she'd fought so hard to build with her own hands, gathering the lonely, the abandoned into her generous heart.

He wanted to say something wise. He wanted to reach out to her. He turned and walked away. For the first time in his life, the dread warrior Sabrehawk knew what it felt like to be a coward.

Adam had suffered through month-long sieges that had been less exhausting, but at last the invasion of Glenlyon House was finally complete. Every chamber was bursting with ladies of the night. Enough bath water had been hauled up and down the stairs to drain the river Thames. The few garments Rachel had left behind had nearly incited a melee among the women as they fought over elegant ball gowns and exquisite *robes d'anglaise*. The losers in the fray had been reduced to wearing what clothes the women servants could spare—a situation that had Gavin's maids nearly quivering with indignation.

It had caused quite a sensation among the earl's servants. The footmen kept crashing into walls, their eyes on the house's newest guests. The maids—not of his lordship's philanthropic bent—were torn between curiosity and righteous indignation.

Juliet's angels weren't making the transition any easier. Isabelle sashayed about as if she were lady of the manor; the simpler girls, awed by the grandeur, blustered like banty hens to hide their unease. Yet no amount of bravado could conceal the truth from Adam's eyes.

Juliet's angels were as confused and rudderless as a troop of soldiers whose general had fallen. She hadn't emerged from her room since Adam had left her there.

There hadn't been time to think, let alone chase after her while settling the women into their new lodgings. But now, with the house so quiet, everyone from the bootboy to Isabelle asleep, there was nothing to drive away the images he knew would haunt him forever—not the fire, nor even the hatred that had shone in Juliet's eyes. Rather, the sight of Juliet's hands idle for the first time since he'd seen her. No seam to stitch or buns to bake, no ink-smudges on her fingers as she taught little Felicity how to shape her letters.

Those images had driven Adam to Gavin's library to get roaring drunk, but for the first time in his misbegotten life, he doubted he had the stomach for it. He was sickened by the memory of Juliet's soot-smudged face, her star-fire eyes lifeless and empty.

The last thing he needed was an altercation with a young Irish hothead, whose features were suddenly hard and older, hero-worship driven from the raw-boned planes of his face. But Fletcher had tracked him down with the single-mindedness of his infernal race, burning with outrage.

Adam took a gulp of his brother's finest brandy, wondering why everything tasted like ashes.

"Well, boy, you're damned well perishing to say something. Might as well spit it out before you explode."

"Late last night, before the fire, Elise came up to my chamber in the attic. She told me what you did—how all of you banded together and mocked Miss Juliet, made her feel foolish and naive, as if Angel's Fall was nothing but a brainless child's game."

Adam swallowed hard. He'd hurt Juliet on purpose then, hoping to save her even greater pain, hoping to shelter her from the evil that had stalked her for so long. He hadn't known then that even greater pain was to come.

"I respected you, Sabrehawk. But now, I know the truth. Any decent man would fight for Miss Juliet, shed his last drop of blood before he'd abandon her."

"I never said I was a *decent man.*" The boy's scorn shouldn't hurt so much. Damnation, Adam hadn't asked for the hero-worship that had shone in Fletcher's gaze. He'd tried time and again to force the lad to see him as he really was—hopelessly flawed, fighting his way through life with his sword because he didn't know anything but battles and blood, championing other men's quests for hard coin because he had no dreams of his own.

"I did what I had to do," Adam ground out. It was a miserable excuse. One that knotted in Adam's gut.

Fletcher snorted in disgust. "Those are the words of a coward. I understand everything now. You never gave a damn about me. Only endured my bumblings for pay. You betrayed the women in Angel's Fall. Were willing to turn them all out onto the street because it wasn't *convenient* for you to stand by Juliet and fight for what you know is right."

"Damn it, the women went along with the scheme to drive Juliet away from here."

"It was the only thing they *could* do to keep her safe. But you—you're strong enough, skilled enough to defend her. Defend them all from anyone who would try to hurt them."

"Blast it, boy—"

"But you turned your back on them. God forbid you bestir yourself to guard them. It might have taken some effort. It might have taken some *heart*. Something you don't have."

Bloody hell, if he didn't have a heart why was his chest burning like fire? "Fletcher—"

"Don't! You sicken me! I know you think me a reckless fool, but I'll tell you something, Sabrehawk. I'd rather die in a good cause before I turn twenty than to become what you are." It was the voice of a boy suddenly tempered into the steel of a man.

Adam's hand clenched on the snifter of brandy. "You're already a hundred times the man I could ever be, Fletcher. My brother—I'll speak to him. I'm certain he can see to your future as I never could."

Fletcher turned, started to stalk away. Adam waited for the silence. Instead, the youth paused at the door, his voice suddenly low, rough. "I never knew my father. But when I was a boy, I tried a hundred times to imagine what he'd been like. When I met you, I hoped . . . I wanted to believe my father had been like you. Now—I'm ashamed to have ridden at your side."

Adam stood, silent, still, alone. For over a year, Fletcher had been his cross to bear. Adam had been dogged by the young Irish fool, the clomp of Fletcher's eager footsteps trailing behind him as common as the sound of his own breathing.

He'd imagined the blissful quiet once Fletcher was disposed of. Anticipated riding the countryside alone, as he had for so long. All that time, Adam couldn't wait to be rid of his troublesome young charge. But now . . .

Adam drove his fingers back through the tangled waves of

his ebony mane. Blast and damn. This was a hell of a time to realize just how much he'd miss the lad when he was gone.

Candle in hand, Adam wandered the hallway of the townhouse where he'd never belonged, stalked by ghosts of the boy he had been and the man he had been destined to become before he took his first breath, his first step.

A man without even an honorable name. A man not worthy to kiss the sole of Juliet's slipper.

He flattened his palm on the door of his father's study, and entered the room he'd avoided for so many years. It was filled with books about wars other men had fought, lined with weapons the old earl had wielded only in practice for battles he'd never fight, littered with pictures of heroic charges other men had led.

It had always felt like a tomb to Adam, only one image within it not a testament to the old earl's unrealized dreams. The portrait that hung above the mantel visible from the desk where the earl had spent so many hours.

Adam held up the taper until its glow spilled on the gold-framed image. Adam's mother perched on a swing, a gown of sky-blue satin billowing about her, her flame-hued hair woven with lush Stuart roses. Barely sixteen, her eyes brimmed with girlish hopes, her lips curved in a smile of indescribable beauty, as if she held the sweetest of secrets in her heart.

Years ago, she had told Adam that the portrait had been started on the day the earl's son had first said he loved her. A glorious betrothal ring, a magnificent wedding, and a passion like those whispered in legends were forever possible in that frozen moment in time. Before greed and weakness had stripped it away and left Lydia Slade only a terrible choice. A life of shame, or one without the man she loved.

From the time Adam had been old enough to understand the heartbreak that blossom-cheeked girl would face, the sight of the portrait had closed like a fist about his heart.

What on earth had induced him to come here now?

"It's easy to see why he loved her." The voice from the corridor should have startled him, but it didn't. Gavin had always had a positive genius for tracking anything wounded to its lair, intending to heal it. Adam cast a glare over his shoulder, saw his half-brother standing there, peering up at Lydia Slade's face with affection and understanding. "There was such a vibrancy about her, so much laughter. I remember as a boy I couldn't take my eyes off of her whenever she entered the room. Father said it was always that way. The first time she swept into a ballroom—"

"Did father tell you what she looked like the *last* time she swept into a ballroom?" Adam said bitterly. "The last time she was welcomed into polite society? Or how about the last time her mother spoke to her before pretending that she was dead."

"She loved father. Was willing to sacrifice—"

"And what was he willing to sacrifice for her, Gavin? He didn't have the courage to defy his father, nor the decency to let her go, perhaps find another man who would give her his name. And then, after your mother was finally out of the way—" Adam swore, sickened by himself. "Damn, I didn't mean it that way, Gav. Forgive me."

"I know," Gavin said, no censure in his eyes, only the shadow of an old pain.

"It's just that, when she died, I thought . . . I was certain . . . I know she had to be as well . . ." Bloody hell, how could it hurt so much even now, years later? Hurt so much he couldn't even form it into words.

"Certain of what?" Gavin prodded.

"That father would wed her. Make her his wife. He loved her. She'd borne seven children for him. With your mother dead, there was no impediment in his way."

"I wondered about that myself. Maybe by that time they didn't need any vows to bind their love. They'd already said them in their hearts."

"Blast it, still spouting your romantic rubbish." Adam grimaced. "Do you know why he didn't marry her? Because of what he'd made her when he took her to his bed. A courtesan. A mistress. From that moment she could never be a fit bride for an earl. God forbid that he dishonor the Carstareses' name. Of course, my mother—she'd sacrificed her honor, her life, everything out of love for him."

"That was her choice, Adam. It's not for us to judge."

"How can I judge him when I was the most reprehensible of all?" Adam's chest felt torn open, wide.

"What could you possibly have done that was so terrible? You were father's pride. He loved you above all the rest of us."

"And that love was so damned important to me that I dared not risk losing it. No, I couldn't confront the selfish son of a bitch, demand that he marry my mother, that he stop tormenting you."

"Adam, don't blame—"

"I didn't blame him. No, that would have been honest. Brave. I rode off to play soldier, to fulfill his dream for me, his wish. That's what I told myself. Do you want to know the truth, Gav, after all this time?"

"If you want to tell me."

"I ran away from Strawberry Grove so I wouldn't have to look at my mother's face, see the hurt she tried to hide. I fled so I wouldn't have to see my sisters grow up."

"They're beautiful. All of them," Gavin said, pain and pride mingling bittersweet in his voice. "You should go home, Adam, see them—"

"I can't." Adam squeezed the words past the lump in his throat. "When I left, they had the same look in their eyes as mother did when the portrait was done—as if a thousand glorious possibilities danced just within their grasp. They'd been raised like princesses, their tiniest wish fulfilled from the time they were laid in the cradle. But it was all a lie, a cruel charade. There were no ballrooms for them to conquer, no admirers who would flock to the door with betrothal rings tucked in their sweaty palms."

He glanced at Gavin, saw the sorrow shading his features, knew that his brother felt the same helplessness to aid the sisters they both adored. "In time, they'll find a man worthy of their love. Someone who won't care about the circumstances of their birth."

"You're still dreaming, Gav. The ugly fact is that I

betrayed them. Christianne and Maria and the others. I had to keep father's love at any cost. Be his favorite. That exalted position mattered so much to me that I didn't defend them, force him to see what he'd condemned them to. Hell, they couldn't even take up a sword—"

"And ride off to die a glorious death in battle?"

"Yes, damn it! I always assumed I'd die on the battlefield. Hell, with the chances I took it's a miracle I didn't."

"Maybe it was Juliet's love that kept the musketballs from piercing you, the swords from driving home. Maybe your shield was a love yet to be born."

The possibility was too painfully sweet. It couldn't be real. "No, Gavin—"

"Why not? You love her. She's in love with you."

The words lanced through him, spilling devastating yearning in their wake. *"Was* in love with me," Adam confessed, his voice raw. He hated himself for that weakness. "She came to me, Gavin, there in the garden. She'd wandered into the night to ask me to make love to her."

"I see."

"Damn it, it was wrong for me to take her! Maybe for a moment I thought there was a chance for us—but it was a dream, Gavin. Look at me! Look at her!"

"You look miserable as a bear with its paw in a trap. Love feels that way sometimes."

"If she did love me, she doesn't any longer. She blames me for the fire. She blames herself. She thinks that if she hadn't come to me that night she could have prevented it."

"She's had a terrible shock."

"No. She's come to her senses and so have I. Damn you, one more word about Juliet, and I swear, I'll walk away and never come back. I can't endure your damn prying."

"All right. All right." Gavin held up his hands. But Adam knew his brother too well to be fooled. The dread Glenlyon might have surrendered this skirmish, but the war wasn't over yet.

Gavin turned, thrusting his hands in the pockets of the frockcoat he'd dragged on sometime during this interminable day. He paced to a shelf, laden with their father's cherished collection, miniature soldiers cast of lead. Adam was surprised he hadn't swept every reminder of the old earl's obsession with battle out of this room, this house, after what it had almost cost him.

"I always wondered what is was you were seeking as you traveled the world over, restless and wandering and full of anger and fight," Gavin said after a long moment. "You were fighting Father, just like I was."

"Only you defeated him. You always stood up to him with such quiet courage. From the time you were a boy."

"It was easy for me. I had nothing to lose. From the start he had a kind of quiet contempt for me. I could only remind him of the forced marriage that had ruined his life. But in the end I did the same as you. I picked up a sword and fought in his name. Traded all my high principles for a chance to see pride in his eyes just one time before he died. Ironic that the last word he received was that I'd been branded a coward at Prestonpans."

"You proved your courage a hundred times over since that battle. Fought like a thousand demons to save life, not take it. And I thank God every day that the fates rewarded you with the love of a woman like Rachel."

"That love is the most precious thing in my life, Adam. Waking up with her in my arms every morning, I'm still awed by the miracle, the wonder that came after so much darkness and blood and death. Sometimes, I still have nightmares—wake up drenched in cold sweat, believing that I sent her away from me in Scotland, to protect her from the fate I'd chosen. She risked exile with me, the possibility of never seeing England again. When she walked into my prison cell to break me free—God, I was so terrified."

"Juliet tried to go back into the fire, wanted to find what was left of a necklace that had belonged to her mother." Why the hell was he telling Gavin this? It hurt far too much. "When I realized she was still inside, I nearly lost my mind I was so damned afraid—"

"*'He that hath wife and children hath given hostages to fortune . . .'*" Gavin quoted gently. "Bacon said that so many years ago. If I were to write it, I'd say that any man who loves gives hostages to fortune. The need to protect, to defend is so fierce. The only thing worth killing for."

Adam's face set, grim. "I'll find whoever set that fire, Gav. Stake my life on it. And they'll pay for what they've done to Juliet."

"Ah, you'll deal out vengeance, exact retribution. I think your lady will find them cold comfort once you've left her alone."

"Damn it, Gav—"

"I saw your Juliet's eyes, Adam. They're as deep and knowing as a highland loch, and as steadfast. A woman such as your Juliet loves but once, with all her heart, or not at all."

The truth of that resonated in Adam's very core and he buried his face in one hand. "What do I know about the ways of a woman's heart? I'm a soldier. A warrior. All I understand is how to fight. Hell, I never planned to marry, let alone . . ."

"Fall in love? You want to know the secret of loving? The secret is that loving shouldn't weaken you or chain you or hurt you. Loving makes you stronger than any sword ever forged by human hands.

"Adam, love isn't about valiant charges against impossible odds. It's not about revenge. Love is about healing. Redemption, even when we don't believe we deserve it."

Gavin reached out, grasping Adam's shoulder with fierce affection, an understanding so complete it was painful. Then, without a word, he turned and walked away, leaving Adam alone.

Chapter
17

It was hours later when Adam knocked on Fletcher's bedchamber door. After a moment, the sleep-tousled youth, swimming in one of Gavin's nightshirts, glared at Adam with hard disillusioned eyes. "What do you want?"

Adam straightened, knowing what he had to do. Knowing how damned hard it would be. "What happened at Angel's Fall was so ugly, so evil, I wanted to believe that it was over. The fire had consumed everything. But I have this feeling in my gut that whoever is responsible for this is still out there. That Juliet's enemy might . . . " Adam swore, grinding his fist against the throbbing in his brow. "Damn it, can such sick hatred be satisfied by the destruction of a house? Mere brick and wood and stone? Or does it need something more tender to sate its appetite upon?"

"I don't know. I hope not. I pray not."

"The women are safe here, for the time being. A man would have to be mad to strike at the Earl of Glenlyon's townhouse. My brother may look half dazed most of the time, lost in a fog of books and poetry, but ask any English soldier who was in Scotland after Culloden Moor, and they will tell you that under that sleepy-lion appearance, Gavin Carstares can be dangerous as hell."

The boy only stared at Adam, stubborn as everyone who

inhabited that misbegotten scrap of land across the Irish Sea. He wasn't going to make Adam's task any easier.

"What are you trying to do, Sabrehawk?" Fletcher scoffed. "Ease your conscience? Juliet and her ladies aren't your responsibility. You said that before. Remember? You don't give a damn what anyone thinks?"

The boy had claimed Adam was a coward. Now they'd both discover if it were true.

Adam paced over to the window, his gaze locking on the moon, awash in a sea of mist. "I've spent hours turning what you said over and over in my mind," Adam said, "and I've come to tell you that you were right, boy. About me. About everything. I didn't want to care about anything or anyone. When you fight as many battles as I have, you learn how fragile life is. The man you've been drinking with, laughing with, can be dead in the space of a heartbeat, and all you can do is watch him bleed."

Adam closed his eyes for a moment, remembering countless faces. Remembering how he'd deadened his own heart just so he could survive the endless string of destruction. But Juliet had brought that heart back to life, whether he'd willed it or not. And there could be no turning back.

"Fletcher, sometime between the night I nailed you into a barrel and tonight, when you flung the truth in my face, I realized that—" Adam drew a deep breath. "I didn't give a damn about your uncle's money anymore. I . . . cared about *you.*"

Something sparked in Fletcher's gaze, as if the boy almost wanted to hope, but was afraid—afraid his hero would fail him again. Was it worth that risk?

"I just pray I haven't discovered the truth too late. For God knows how long, you've wanted to watch my back in battle. Now I'm asking you for something far more important. Will you help me build life instead of deal out death? I'm not even certain I know how to begin. You see, I haven't given a damn about anything for a very long time."

Adam held out his hand to the boy. Saw Fletcher's gaze flick down to that sword-scarred, battle-toughened hand. Then the boy grasped Adam's fingers, fiercely. Fletcher smiled, his eyes lighting as if he'd follow Sabrehawk to the halls of hell.

Neither of them saw the cloaked figure in the shadowy street beyond, watching, watching, hatred burning in the night. *Fools*. They thought it was over, but they were wrong. They would pay for their interference. And Juliet . . . her fate was as it had always been . . . in her own hands.

Evening cast shadows in lacy patterns through the window, life beyond the glass panes continuing with callous disregard of Juliet's breaking heart.

Five days she'd spent in self-imposed exile in the chamber Adam's brother had given her. She had heard the ruckus of the other women's arrivals, the rushing about of maids, the babble of quarrels, but she'd allowed the army of Glenlyon servants to contend with the confusion. She hadn't had the strength.

The most she could manage was to drag herself down to meals at the insistence of the earl himself. She didn't dare offend him in the view of the kindness he'd shown.

But she barely spoke, barely ate, achingly aware of the empty chair where Adam should have sat. Adam, who had avoided her at all costs from the moment he'd left her in the chamber alone.

The instant she'd finished pushing her food around the plate, and everyone was excused from table, she'd returned to her chamber, where she'd wrestled with an uncertain future.

What should she do with the rest of her life? There was no family to turn to, and she could hardly rely on the earl's generosity forever.

Besides, the notion of taking anything that might be traced back to Adam Slade was insufferable. No, she had to find a way to be independent. Find a position . . . there was only one that might still be open to her. One that had been offered by the querulous Widow Widdlemarch an eternity ago on the front step of the vicarage. A place as a paid companion.

For the fifth time, Juliet crossed to the desk in the corner of the room, borrowed pen and ink, and tried to compose a letter to the crotchety old woman. But she couldn't even think of Sadie Widdlemarch's dull blue eyes without wincing in remembrance.

The memory of the girl Juliet had been there, on the vicarage stairs, perched on the edge of her great adventure. She'd been stuffed to the brim with dreams and determination, armed with the certainty and faith that she could truly make a difference in the world, accomplish all she'd set out to do.

She was sadder now. And wiser. Her eyes opened wide to reality.

And there was no use putting off the inevitable a moment longer. She sank down into the chair yet again and took up the pen, dipping it into the well of ink.

How did one write that they had been a miserable failure? Everything had turned out as disastrously as the old woman had predicted. The fire had left Juliet with nothing. Every shilling of the modest legacy her father had left her was gone. Even her mother's necklace.

There was nothing left for her to do but accept the widow's offer, *if* it were still open to her.

She closed her eyes, picturing the rolling hills of Northwillow, trying to capture the restfulness of the sleepy little village where nothing ever changed; there were no ugly mobs, no troubling handsome warriors appearing as if transported from another age, where mighty knights fought dragons to save their ladies fair.

Where the worst fate that awaited her was a gentle scolding about what a fool she'd been.

Northwillow, everything the same, quiet, serene.

Heaven would think she'd embrace the familiarity after all this time, that she'd be ready to bury herself in tea cakes and idle gossip, sketching landscapes by the lake and reading by the grate at night.

Any number of women would give anything to secure such a position—companion to an old woman in a lovely house. Food and shelter, a way to make one's self useful.

It was the kind of fate she'd wanted for her angels. Independent. Safe. Yet how bleak it seemed after the passion she'd tasted in Adam's arms—years without hearing a man's deep rumble of laughter, without seeing black eyes flash in temper and emotions far more tender. The rest of her life without the touch of a man's hand, without trembling in awe or tasting desire on lips melting into your own.

Juliet brushed away a wayward tear in self-disgust. What on earth was she doing? Mourning the loss of Adam after what such earthy desires had cost her? Yet even through all the pain that had come after, her dreams were filled with the taste of him, the feel of him, the gentleness in his big hands, the desperate love that had shone in his gaze, and the fear that had wrenched at her heart.

But what they'd shared had been an illusion, as much an illusion as Angel's Fall itself. It was over. Time and again from her vantage point in the window, she'd seen Adam riding off somewhere. Leaving at first light, returning after everyone was asleep. Why? To escape having to see her? To avoid looking into her face, confronting the terrible mistake they'd both made?

Now she understood the clinging sadness in her ladies' eyes those times when they thought no one was watching. The sorrow for what could never be. Perhaps it was best to turn away from the arms that had held, the hands that had caressed, but the pain . . . she'd never felt so alone.

A knot of tears clotted in her throat, aching as she forced herself to scrawl a few lines.

I am returning to Northwillow if you will still employ me. Please send money for the stage and take it from my first month's wages.

There was far too much left unsaid. She had no delusions that the widow would allow her to keep such silence on the subject once she arrived back in Norfolk. Yet Juliet couldn't write more.

She signed it, sanded it, then sealed it with wax and scrawled the widow's direction on the front. She would take it downstairs, ask one of the footmen to post it.

Pressing the letter to her bosom, she crept out into the corridor, down the stairs. She'd almost reached the table in the entryway where his lordship's correspondence awaited posting, when she heard voices through a half-closed door.

"No, Millicent, you've stitched it on upside down. Let me show you."

"But Juliet said—"

"Juliet's not here," Violet said. "We'll just have to get along as best as we can without her. Now, let me help you rip the stitches out and we can begin again."

Puzzled, Juliet crossed to the door, peering through the crack, astonished by the scene unfolding before her eyes. The chamber buzzed with industry. The pianoforte stood in the corner, draped in half-stitched petticoats. The rug was all but obliterated by a length of amber cloth, Felicity on her hands and knees, snipping out a pattern with borrowed shears.

Millicent and Violet were clustered with the younger women, bent over their sewing with a fierce concentration. Gowns in various stages of construction littered the room. Mouths were pursed in frustration and determination, brows furrowed, fingers busy with needle and thread.

There was a valiant defiance in the little scene. One that knotted emotion in Juliet's throat, made her flatten her hand against the door and push it wider still. Not even the flighty Violet glanced up from her labor.

It was Angelina who glimpsed Juliet first—and then only because she was forced to retrieve her thimble.

"Juliet?" She all but shoved the bit of silver behind her back, like a child caught with a forbidden bonbon. Countless gazes leapt from the work to Juliet's face, and she was stunned to see the women peer at her with a curious mixture of defiance and reproach.

"What are you doing?" Juliet asked, one hand still on the door latch.

"Stitching on a sleeve," Millicent said with a toss of her head. "I got it upside down last time. But don't worry, this time I'll set it right."

"But you hate sewing."

"Discovered I hate sitting on my skirts, all helpless, even more."

Felicity rose to her feet, the shears clasped in her chapped hands. "His lordship was going to hire seamstresses to make gowns for us. But Millicent said if we made our own and—and do well enough, his lordship might give us a little of his lady's sewing now and again."

Juliet stared, astonished. Millicent, who had spent every sewing lesson grumbling as if she'd been ordered to spin straw into gold, rallying the others to stitch?

Millicent heaved a long-suffering sigh. "Me and my brilliant ideas. Probably the only chance I'll ever get to have a gown made by a fancy lady's seamstress, and I cast it away!"

"But—but why? This makes no sense. I thought you didn't want . . . I mean, you made it clear that you couldn't wait to escape Angel's Fall."

"I told Harry Tupper he was the handsomest man alive, too, and he looks like a rat with his cheeks stuffed," Violet said. "Don't worry, Juliet. You don't have to concern yourself with us. We've got it all talked out, the lot of us. You don't have to be saddled with us any longer."

"What she means is, we understand," Elise amended hastily. "You want to leave London, after all the ugliness and trouble you've suffered. But, you see, we . . . we have to stay here. We were thinking, if we all work together, we might just have a chance to make a better life."

Shame burned in Juliet's belly, rushed up into her cheeks. It was what she had worked for, dreamed of, this sudden bond linking the women together. It was something she'd despaired would ever happen. The knowledge that they had done so now, when everything was lost, was both bitter and indescribably sweet.

"I know what you're thinking with that look on your face." Millicent brandished the bodice she was working on like a sabre. "You're thinking we've lost our minds. Well, you're not the first. Isabelle thought so, too. The instant we told her our plan, she swept out of the house to find herself a protector. And today she packed up her treasure box and took herself off for good."

"Good riddance, I say!" Violet tossed her head. "We

didn't let her slow us so much as a single stitch. Nor will you when you trundle yourself back to Northwillow."

"Don't trouble yourself about us, Juliet," Elise said far more gently. "We'll be just fine. You taught us well enough. From now on, we'll help each other."

"But where will you go? Where will you stay?" Juliet asked, the countless difficulties involved in such a venture racing through her mind.

"Mr. Adam—he's seeing to it now," Felicity piped up. "He just told us this morning that—"

"Hush!" Angelina blustered. "We're not supposed to tell!"

Juliet turned to Elise, who picked nervously at a seam. And she knew the best tactic for getting to the bottom of this mystery would be to get her away from the others, wangle an explanation. "Elise, could you help me with something in the hallway?"

Elise put her work aside and hastened to do her bidding. Yet the girl who followed Juliet into the corridor seemed a stranger. For the first time since she'd known Elise, the young woman was blooming.

"Elise, what's this all about?"

Elise raised glowing eyes to Juliet, her thin fingers trailing to a miniature suspended around her neck by a faded ribbon. A tiny chipped image Juliet had never seen before. "Mr. Slade is going to find us a place to live."

"He's searching for a home for you?"

"He's been searching ever since we came here but hadn't confided in anyone but the earl. This morning, Adam told us what he was doing."

Juliet blinked, her memory filled with images of Adam trudging into Glenlyon House at such odd hours. Not in an effort to avoid her, as she'd believed, but rather because he was championing the cause of her scattered angels. Was he mad? She'd finally admitted he was right—that she'd been naive and idealistic and foolhardy.

"But it's dangerous!" Juliet objected. "Whoever set that fire is still out there, lurking somewhere in the city. If they were bold enough to strike once, they will do it again."

Elise's chin bumped up a notch. "We know there are dangers. But some things are worth the risk. He said . . . oh, Juliet!" Elise's eyes filled with grateful tears and she clasped the miniature in her hand. "Our children . . . they can come to us."

"Children?" Juliet glanced down to see the miniature Elise displayed—a tiny chubby-faced babe grinning toothlessly up from the porcelain. So this was the explanation for so much of the sorrow in Elise's face. The indescribable sense of loss that had haunted her eyes.

Juliet was sick with regret and self-blame. Why had she never pressed her friend? Prodded her to tell what was bothering her? "Elise, I didn't know you had a babe. Why didn't you ever tell me?"

"About my little Will? There was nothing you could do. Nothing anyone could. It hurt too much to even speak his name."

"But how . . . how did it happen? How did you get with child?" Juliet grimaced. "I'm sorry. That was a ridiculous question. Of course, if you were entertaining men, it was bound to happen sooner or later."

"I wasn't a—one of those women then. Only after when I had no choice."

"Then how—?"

"When I was fifteen I went into service as a maid at the Darlington estate. Lord Darlington had just come into his inheritance. He was . . . quite glutted on power, I fear. He forced his attentions upon me."

"That's abominable!" Rage at the injustice seared through Juliet.

"I don't know why he fancied me, shy and solemn as I was. But it was a game he played, catching me tidying up the bedchambers or changing the linens. He'd lie in wait and . . ." Elise shuddered.

"You should've put a kitchen knife in your apron pocket."

"And stabbed the master?"

"But someone should have stopped him."

"Who would have believed me if I'd told? His mother? She would have condemned me for inviting him, luring him. I would have been turned out into the streets. My little brother was all the family I had left, and he was ill. What coin I earned paid for his keep. After a few months, Alexander died. But by then, I was already with child."

"But it was his lordship's child! He was responsible!"

The pain of that time, the helplessness, was still etched in Elise's face. "When I couldn't conceal my pregnancy any longer, his lordship's mother turned me away without a character. No decent household would hire me after that."

"And Lord Darlington just let you go?" As vicar's daughter she'd heard enough to know the horror, the suffering of the poor and weak. "You might have starved! And your baby! When I think of it . . ."

Elise shrugged. "I suppose I was lucky in a way. At least Lord Darlington promised to see to the baby's upbringing, see he wasn't hungry or cold and was taught some useful trade. But there was one condition. I wasn't ever to see Will again."

"That's inhuman to separate a mother from her child! So cruel! You should have told him to go to blazes!"

"And strip away the only chance my child had of a full belly and warm hands and toes? How could I risk exposing my child to the kind of life I was forced to lead after I left the Darlington estate? There are people in the brothels, evil people who would take a child's innocence and delight in it." Elise trembled.

"I sold my mama's wedding ring for the money to pay for this portrait." She brushed with reverent fingers the chipped miniature. "The day my babe was weaned from my breast, one of his lordship's servants came and took Will off to a place his lordship had found. Simple people, they were, who cared for him until he went off to school. Sometimes, I'd stand outside the gate and watch him. He looked so sad, so alone. I always feared he was wondering why his mama didn't want him."

Juliet forgot her own pain, reached out to clasp Elise's thin hand.

"That's when I started sending him things. Little toys and sweetmeats. It sickened me, the way I had to earn the coin, letting other men touch me. And Will could never even know that his mother had sent the gifts. At least not until he was grown. But it was the one thing that gave me pleasure, picking out little trinkets for my boy. A few weeks ago Lord Darlington found out about the gifts. He guessed the truth. That was why he accosted me on the street that day."

"The vile despicable monster!"

"I wasn't whoring anymore, Juliet. I swear it. I just . . . just had a few coins tucked away—"

"Hush. It doesn't matter."

"Lord Darlington pushed me against the wall, lifting my skirts as if he were tormenting me *that* way. But in reality he only wanted to conceal from his friends the fact that he was warning me. He whispered in my ear that if I ever sent anything to my boy again, he would fling Will out into the streets."

"Oh, Elise . . ." Juliet felt the fiercest regret. Elise had wrestled with this terror, this pain, alone.

"Will was his child, Juliet. How could a boy's own father be so cruel?" Elise swiped the tears from her cheeks. "Last night, I couldn't sleep. The earl, dear man that he is, has the place fairly riddled with his children's toys. I was looking at a Noah's Ark, thinking how Will would be amazed by all the little animals, when Mr. Slade, he came trudging in, all tired. But he stopped, so kind, though he tried to hide it with gruffness. It's just his way."

"I know." Juliet could remember countless sips of tenderness she'd tasted in her days with Adam Slade. The tiniest spark in those ebony eyes, twist to his lips. The bashfulness, the compassion hidden behind blustering and fierce denial. A tenderness all the more precious because he took such pains to hide it.

"He saw the miniature, asked me about it," Elise continued. "I've not taken it off a single day since it was painted, but I always kept it tucked under my clothes, where no one could see. I couldn't bear anyone asking about Will, for fear I'd cry. And once I started weeping, I'd never stop. But that night, Mr. Adam looked so sad and forlorn, I thought maybe my tale would distract him from his own troubles. I never expected . . ."

A shiver of pure joy worked through Elise. "When I told

him the story, he sent Fletcher off straightaway to get Will. Promised me that he'd bring him home."

"Adam did that?"

"He said he'd go himself, but there was some business he had to see to first. Something important. He thought he might be closing in on the person responsible for the fire. But he thanked me, and said that if we were going to build Angel's Fall again, we'd need a nursery. With a pack of women like we would gather, Will wouldn't be the only babe to come along."

The enormity of the girl's confession staggered Juliet. Her knees went weak, and she grasped the back of a gilt chair for support. "You said Adam was going to find you a house. Someplace to live. That's not the same as—as a haven like Angel's Fall. Surely he can't mean—he thought I was insane! He told me so a hundred times!"

"Well, he must've lost his mind as well, because I never saw a man work harder, or be more determined, than he is."

Juliet reeled. Adam promised there would be another Angel's Fall? A home for Elise and the others to make their own? And a nursery—she hadn't even thought of including a nursery. But Adam had. He knew all too well the children who resulted from such liaisons. He might have suffered like Will, been alone, friendless, had his father tired of his mother.

She'd never thought what bastardy meant. A castoff child. A child most sanctimonious fools would say should never have been. A child whose unforgivable sin was just daring to be born.

Adam had seemed so scornful of everything Juliet had tried to build, just like Millicent and Violet and the others. But somehow, in the crucible of the fire, something extraordinary had been forged. Something far more precious than walls and tables and cloaks and even necklaces wrought in golden lilies.

Wonder and hope beat painfully to life in her breast, bursting with something even more agonizing and beautiful.

Love.

Juliet flung her arms around Elise. "Thank you for telling me this. I have to—have to find Adam—talk to him. I've been so awful, blaming him for what happened. I said the most horrible things to him."

She was appalled by the remembrance of her cruel words, haunted by the memory of his eyes. The silent pain as he let her batter at him with her words, hurting him in a way no one else could have, striking past his armor into a heart all the more vulnerable and tender because he fought to keep it so well hidden.

"But you're not supposed to know any of this! He made us swear."

"Where is he? Elise, do you know?"

"He went out just after Isabelle left for good. You should have seen the magnificent carriage she left in. He'd said he had some things to check on at the old Angel's Fall."

Juliet turned and ran, bursting into the study where the Earl of Glenlyon sat working. His compassionate gray gaze leapt up from the letter he was writing.

"Juliet," he said, rising to his feet with a sleepy-lion smile and coming to stand before her. "It's good to see you out of your room. I'm just expecting a visit from a friend of mine who leaves for the colonies in two weeks. Adam insists that Fletcher—or should I say *Kieran*—needs a fresh start. Seems the boy has a genius for getting into trouble, leaping into fights that aren't his own. Reminds me of Adam when he was that age."

Gavin chuckled. "Of course, I'd imagine taming a new continent will be enough of an adventure even for Fletcher, although I'd wager Adam is going to miss the lad more than he'll ever admit." The earl grimaced. "Listen to me rattling on. Is there anything I can do for you?"

"Could I borrow a horse? A very gentle one? I . . . I need to go someplace."

"You're not thinking of leaving us?" Concern shadowed that expressive face, the face of a dreamer, so different from Adam's. "Adam would never forgive me if I were to lose you."

"It's Adam I have to find. To tell him . . ." Impulsively, she scooped up not the hands of a peer of the realm, but the hands of Adam's brother, the man Adam loved and trusted.

"I know about what he's doing—trying to restore Angel's Fall. The ladies slipped and told me." Her throat ached with emotion. "I hurt him so terribly the night of the fire. That's the most abominable thing about loving someone. You know right where to strike when you want to hurt them."

Gavin Carstares's hands tightened on hers. "You love him, then?"

"With all my soul. But he's never spoken of . . . I mean, he's made it clear he's never wanted a wife. He's a wanderer, used to a life of adventure. I'd not want to tie him down. I couldn't bear if he were unhappy."

"Ah, Juliet, Juliet." Gavin stroked her hair back from her face. "No wonder my brother has been behaving like a wounded bear. I always knew he'd surrender his heart as reluctantly as he would surrender his sword. But once he encountered a lady brave enough to take it, it would be a treasure worth the fighting for. I would go with you, but—"

"No! It's kind of you to offer, but wait for your friend." Her cheeks stained red. "Fletcher's safety is most important.

"Ah." Gavin raised his brow in realization. "Not to mention the fact that wooing beneath the eyes of a spectator can be most awkward, can't it? And I've never been able to resist teasing my brother unmercifully. Tell Larch in the stable to saddle Stardust for you. She's my daughter's horse, and gentle as a lamb."

"Thank you. So very much."

"No, my dear. Thank you. My brother has spent forever fighting ghosts he couldn't see, trying to cast himself to death because of his birth, his mother's pain, and my father, God rest his soul. Give him a reason to live, Juliet."

Juliet pressed a grateful kiss to the earl's hand. "Bless you for loving him, your lordship."

"He hasn't made it easy at times." Gavin grinned. "When I was wooing my Rachel, he was insufferable. She shot me and I . . ."

"Your wife shot you?"

"Of course, she insists the pistol went off by accident when I tried to wrestle it away from her. She was most put out that I'd ruined her grand escape by bleeding all over the place. After all, one can't drag a wounded hostage all the way to Edinburgh. Far too inconvenient."

Gavin chuckled. "Never mind. I'm certain Rachel will adore telling you the tale of our courtship, especially if Adam is there to embellish it."

"Good luck with Adam, my dear." A solemn light shone in his eyes. "I've been praying that he would find you for a very long time."

Joy filled Juliet as she ran down the corridor. It brimmed over as she dashed through the earl's gardens to the stables. When at last she guided her mount out of the townhouse's gate, she shivered with delight.

All the color that had bled from the world the night of the fire spilled back onto the palette of the city, the hues bursting with life, with possibilities.

She'd lost possessions—a house, a necklace. But she'd won so much more.

She turned the mare toward Angel's Fall, her heart dancing.

Chapter

18

Betrayal. Adam had seen all of its hideous faces often enough in the years he'd earned his fortune with his sword. He'd grown inured to it, toughened his soul to it so he could bear confronting it again and again.

He'd lifted the most gorgeous masks and discovered what poison lurked beneath. Officers thirsting for glory, willing to buy it by scaling the dead corpses of the men they led. Greedy men willing to steal anything from another man's gold to the virtue of his wife.

Yet as he watched the elegant establishment Isabelle had swept into an hour ago, he felt sick to his very soul.

He'd waited long enough for her to get neck-deep in skulduggery before he intruded. It was the patient hunter who captured its quarry.

His hands tightened into fists on the reins. It was time to put an end to the madness, to cut to the root of the evil that had destroyed Angel's Fall and his lady's dreams. And Isabelle was his only possible link.

There were secrets in the Frenchwoman's face, locked beneath the slightest tightening of her lips, the nervous jump of her gaze, the furrow of concentration that carved between her delicate brows.

Hell, he was grasping at straws. He knew it. Maybe

chasing after phantoms. But the person who had dared attack Angel's Fall had to have been familiar with the routine of those inside. Had to know any weaknesses that could be exploited.

Isabelle had been in her chamber that night, true. Yet she'd not been caught unawares the way the rest of them had. Her treasure box had been in her arms, an almost eerie calm gracing those feline features as she swept out into the garden.

He had to discover exactly what she knew. Had to discover the villain who had destroyed Angel's Fall so that such a disaster could not repeat itself.

His jaw set, grim. Familiar hunger for the kill surged through him. From the time he first stepped on a battlefield, he'd been notoriously ruthless. But that soldier had not believed in anything or anyone. He was the image of mercy when compared to Adam now. A man who loved. Who cared too damn much. Who would take any risk, fight any battle, ferret out any enemy to see his lady safe.

A delivery boy balancing a large parcel started to wobble past him, and Adam dismounted, reaching out to stop the lad. "Do you know who lives here?"

"Why, a lady, sir. French she is, and demned high in the instep, if you get my meaning. She's just moving in."

"Is she now?"

"Aye, sir. You never saw such a stir. Been deliverin' pure mountains of furniture an' gowns an' such. An' a coach and team for the stables. As fine a set of mares as I ever saw. She must be passing wealthy to afford such a set-out."

"Indeed." Adam scowled. "It must have been raining gold coins and she stood beneath the shower."

"Mebbe she came into an inheritance. Do you think so? A rich uncle or some such dyin' real convenient like?" The boy flashed a cheeky grin. "Wish I could find me a rich uncle. What d'ye think my chances are?"

"Obviously miracles do happen," Adam said. "Allow me to assist you, boy. I'll deliver the package to the lady."

The boy hung back, dubious. "I don't think I should surrender it, sir."

Adam flipped the boy a coin worth three times his due. "The lady and I are acquainted, and my visit is something in the way of a surprise."

"Ah, well then," the boy conceded. "I was to take it around to the servant's door."

Adam sketched the lad a bow and took the parcel. Within a matter of minutes, an apple-cheeked housekeeper had been taken into the conspiracy to surprise her new mistress. She showed him through a well-appointed kitchen, down the corridor, and into a small withdrawing room to await her lady.

Adam set the parcel down on a gilt table and withdrew to the shadowy corner to wait. A quarter of an hour had passed before Isabelle swept in. Garbed in exquisite poppy-hued satin with a silver-gauze bodice, she looked every inch the courtesan. Emeralds dripped down the powdered curve of breasts displayed to the greatest advantage by the low-cut neckline. Her hair was twined with ropes of pearls. Lace frothed at her wrists, and a smile that should have been dazzling curved her sensual lips.

"My darling, I had no idea you would be here so soon!" she protested. "But I had the bedchamber made up first, just in case—"

"Forgive me if I don't take you up on your *generous* offer," Adam sneered, stepping into the light and turning to face her. Isabelle froze as if he'd leveled a pistol at her heart.

"Sabrehawk!" Her cheeks flooded with crimson, one hand fluttering up in an attempt to cover the emeralds, but the necklace was far too lush, the stones far too plentiful to cover with one feminine hand. "What—what are you doing here?"

"Delivering a parcel. Shall we see what it is?" He stepped to the table. Isabelle darted to block his path.

"No. I've not the least curiosity. Now, I fear I am very busy so you'll have to leave."

"You've been busy, I'd wager, Isabelle," Adam said bitterly. "From the look of it you've worked a blasted miracle. One day dependent on Juliet's charity, then stripped by the fire to one nightgown and a box of trinkets.

261

The next week, a veritable army delivering every known luxury to your own establishment."

Isabelle's chin jutted out with belligerence. "It is lovely, is it not? My new lodgings. I'm particularly fond of the bracelet." She brushed back the lace at her wrists to display an exquisite ring of green fire that must have been worth a fortune.

Adam's gut was seared with fury as he remembered Juliet's anguish over the loss of her own mother's necklace, how she'd all but run back into the fire in an attempt to save it. But she had already broken away two of the golden lilies, pawned them in an effort to keep Angel's Fall running.

His hand flashed out, catching Isabelle's in a viselike grip. "Everything has a price, Isabelle. It's obvious yours was high."

"If one must be a whore," she said brutally, "it is wisest to be a high-priced one."

"And I suppose if one must be a traitor, it is better to be the vilest kind imaginable."

"Traitor?" Her brows arched in surprise.

"No more games, Isabelle! How did you come by this wealth? There is only one possible way. You betrayed Juliet for a blood price. You are responsible for the fire."

"I was upstairs in my bedchamber! You saw me come out of my room when you and Juliet came to warn us of the blaze!"

"And you conveniently had all your treasures tidily boxed and ready to scoop up before you fled. Hell, you probably smuggled half your gowns out before as well. Maybe I should go upstairs and check in your clothespress."

"Have you run mad? I've always kept my treasures together, ready to scoop up at a moment's notice. One never knows when a protector will tire of you and decide to turn you into the streets. It only makes sense to be prepared."

"Someone unlocked that back gate, Isabelle. Someone let an accomplice know when to creep in, to set the fire. It had to be someone inside Angel's Fall."

"It wasn't me. I have an aversion to bathing in fire. It's bad for the complexion, don't you know."

"Damn you, Isabelle! I'll shake the truth out of you if I have to. Now tell me—"

"Madam?"

Adam bit off a curse at the housekeeper's voice.

"A thousand pardons, madam, but the gentleman is willing to give two hundred pounds for the silver service."

Isabelle wheeled about, looking flustered. "Mrs. Brooke, tell him to wait."

"But he's hungering after the gilt vase on the mantel. I told him that you'd likely sell it—"

"Mrs. Brooke, enough! I have a guest!"

"What the devil is going on here? You're selling the silver? Hell, you must've just bought the stuff!"

"Just delivered yesterday, sir." Mrs. Brooke shook her head dolefully. "Lovely it is, too. 'Tis a shame never to use it."

"Get out, now, or I'll tell the man he can buy you as well!" Isabelle snapped. The servant scurried out with a wounded expression.

Isabelle made a great show of smoothing the lace at her cuff. "As you can see, I'm quite busy at the moment. If you'll excuse me—"

Adam stepped in front of the door, blocking her escape. "You're not going anywhere until you give me an explanation, Isabelle."

"Mon Dieu, why are you tormenting me? Go back to your swordfights and your adventuring. You're free to leave now. What happens here in London is no longer your concern."

"Juliet is my concern."

"Take her with you, then! Or trundle her back to that provincial little village she came from. I know what I'm doing."

"And exactly what is that?"

She sighed. "You'll not leave me in peace until you know, will you, Sabrehawk? If you must know, there has been a man eager to become my new protector for months now. A merchant. I've accepted his offer. True, he stinks of the shipyards, but he is fabulously rich. Enough to give me all the things I deserve as his mistress."

"Like silver?"

"Silver and gold and emeralds. I come at a high price."

"But you're selling the silver. Why? It makes no sense!"

"I will earn every bracelet, every bit of silver or gold a hundred times over in the time to come! He said that if I would allow him to come to my bed, he would surround me with treasures fit for a queen. Isabelle, Queen of the Barges!"

She gave a mocking laugh. "How far I've fallen from his grace, the duke. However, I took my merchant at his word. He'll receive the appropriate bills for my purchases as expected, and will never need to know that instead of twenty place settings of silver there are only two sets in the drawer. As for the other accoutrements for decorating the household—men see nothing beyond the end of their own nose when they are amorous. He'll never notice how many things he paid for that never appear."

"But that still doesn't explain anything. Why not keep the things if this merchant is supporting you?"

"Because I need money."

"Then ask him for it—"

"He's not a fool, generous as he is. He'd ask what it was for. And I hardly think he would agree to supporting a haven for fallen women just to amuse me."

"A—what?"

She tossed her head in defiance. "I'm using whatever I can scrape together to finance a house to replace Angel's Fall."

Adam staggered back a step, stunned. "You mean that you—that all this—"

"You don't need to gloat over what a fool I am. No one is cursing this as idiocy more thoroughly than I am."

"But why? Why would you do such a thing?"

A faraway light came into the courtesan's eyes, and she fingered the emeralds as if they held some secret too painful to bear any longer.

"I was barely fifteen the night my mama squeezed and powdered and pinched me into a plaything for *le Comte de Rouette*. I wished most devoutly to die."

Adam fought a sharp jab of sympathy, rage.

"If there had been any place I could have run away to, any place I could have found haven, I would have done so. But there was not. My fall from virtue was as unavoidable as it was brutal. *Le comte* was not a gentle man."

Adam didn't want to feel that sense of kinship with this woman, not when Juliet might be in danger. But he was all too aware how narrowly his own sisters had missed such a fate—missed it by the depth of their father's purse, and the generous spirit of the legitimate half-brother who had embraced them when he had every reason to ignore their very existence.

"I left *le comte* with a token to remember our affair by, however. My maid's sewing shears embedded in his flesh."

"You killed him?"

"No. Only stabbed him in the thigh. I only wish I'd had better aim, so I could have saved other girls from my fate. I was frightened out of my wits. You see, he'd tired of beating me and decided to go after my mother."

"He was a sick son of a bitch! Tell me where he is and I'll kill him for you."

She shrugged one elegant shoulder. "Such heroics are hardly necessary. He's been dead these many years. And my mama might as well have been. She's never spoken a word to me since that day. I had ruined everything by not becoming *le comte's* mistress, you see."

She met Adam's gaze, sharing with him a moment of complete understanding. Two people battered by the fates, two fighters who had clung to life tenaciously if not honorably. Two who questioned whether the victory had been worth the price they'd paid. Yet both of them had been changed forever by the compassion of a naive angel who had made them believe in goodness, in beginning again.

"Isabelle, I . . ." Adam's voice roughened. "Forgive me for judging you. Hell, it's like fighting with shadows, never knowing who is responsible for trying to attack Juliet. I have to ask you. Do you want to be this merchant's mistress?"

"It's what I am, *ma doucette*. At least this way, the others will not have to suffer going back to such a life."

"Neither do you. I've already enlisted my brother's help. We've found the perfect place away from the city, far from the mobs and the poverty and the dirt. It's a huge rambling house, with fields and gardens. Gavin is drumming up enough sewing through his philanthropic friends to keep the lot of you busy until the millennium. He's finding teachers in the arts and all manner of enjoyable things as well, so it will not be all drudgery. All that's needed is a headmistress to keep the unruly chits in line. Someone older, wiser."

"Insufferable man! It's evil of you to mention a lady's age." But her relief gave Adam a glimpse of the girl she must have been, spirited and lovely and brave. "I fear my merchant is destined to be quite brokenhearted."

Isabelle chuckled, shaking her head. "Look at us. Two confirmed cynics racing off to tilt with dragons with no weapon to wield against them but Juliet's dreams. It's abominable. I wonder which of us feels like the biggest fool?"

"I do. Somewhere between wanting to throttle Juliet and haul her back to Northwillow nailed in a barrel, I fell in love with the woman." Adam drove his fingers back through his ebony mane, scowling.

"Mon ami, it cannot be that bad! Your face is like a man confronting some grave calamity."

"It just occurred to me that if you are not the one responsible for that fire, someone else is. And I don't have the damnedest idea where to find them."

"Surely they must be satisfied now? The house is in ashes."

"Is that kind of venom satisfied with consuming bricks and wood? Or once it's had a taste of victory does it need to strike deeper?"

Isabelle shivered. "We will keep her safe among us, Sabrehawk. No one would dare strike at Juliet while she is in the earl's house. You'll hunt down whoever dared to harm her. And when you do . . ." A hard smile lifted Isabelle's lips. "You will show her enemy the peril to be found at the point of Sabrehawk's blade."

Chapter
19

Twilight dipped the scorched rose petals in purple dye, softening the desolation left in the fire's wake. Juliet wandered through the forlorn garden, the flowerbeds she'd tended so lovingly trampled beneath the heedless feet of those who had battled the flames. Yet here and there amid the crushed plants brave new shoots poked their fragile green heads, a testimony to the fact that there was new life preparing to blossom beneath what seemed utter ruin.

She knelt next to her patch of foxglove, the tall stalks of flowers bent and broken. But she tucked fresh dirt around the half-exposed roots and used the ribbon from her hair to bind the stalks upright.

Who knew? They might just heal, heal the way her heart had been healing in the hours since she'd ridden away from Glenlyon House.

She tingled with anticipation, her gaze straying again to the gate beating a soft tattoo against the garden wall as the breeze swayed it to and fro.

Where was Adam? It seemed as if she'd been waiting for him an eternity, planning out what she would say to him, reveling in imagining what it would be like to have him draw her into his powerful arms, take her mouth fiercely with his own.

If he could forgive her for the ugly things she'd said, was there some chance that he would ask her to marry him? Or was it cruel even to think of tethering a wild bird of prey like Sabrehawk to one hand? Would she be condemning herself to the hell of watching him grow restless and unhappy, his eyes filled, not with love for her, but rather an unslakable thirst for far-off places and mad adventures that sent raw sensation searing through every nerve?

True, he was rebuilding Angel's Fall. And his brother believed that Adam loved her. Yet how could she be certain until she looked into her weary warrior's eyes? Until she could gently strip away the last veils that hid his heart, to see the truth within?

She sank down, the ground cool beneath her, the grass soft. Maybe Adam had been detained at whatever business he had gone to tend. It was possible that he wasn't coming here at all. The shadows were beginning to lengthen, and it couldn't be wise to remain here with darkness coming. She hated the whisperings in her ear of all the threats she'd received, the vileness of them, the cruelty.

Whoever had burned the house had surely achieved their goal, and could no longer have any interest in hurting her, could they? Yet there were other dangers in the street that her experiences at Angel's Fall had made all too clear.

She stood up. No, it was better to retrieve the mare and return to the earl's establishment. There, she could wait for Adam all night if need be.

The sudden snap of a twig behind her made her heart catch in her throat. Heat flooded her cheeks and her pulses tripped in anticipation as she whirled around expecting to see Slade's towering frame, that rugged face struck with surprise.

"Adam! I've been waiting . . ." She stopped, pressing her fingertips to her lips in dismay as she saw not Sabrehawk's mocking dark eyes, but rather, the ghostly smear of Barnabas Rutledge's angular features, his black frockcoat fluttering in the breeze.

"Mr. Rutledge," Juliet said, fighting back her disappointment and trying to summon up a smile. Tension eased out of her, for Rutledge had ever been the most solicitous of neighbors, so concerned for her, always hovering with that worried expression in his sunken eyes. Now he looked exhausted, a little ill, a bandage wrapped about his left hand.

"Miss Grafton-Moore." He sketched her an awkward bow. "Forgive my intrusion, but I saw you from the window of my shop. Allow me to tell you how sorry I am for your misfortune. I know this house meant a great deal to you."

Juliet cast a glance toward the burned hulk. "I did love this house. But I discovered there are other things far more important." She glanced down at his hand. "You injured yourself, my dear friend. Let me look at it."

"No! No, thank you." He thrust his hand behind his back as if to hide it. "I—I already came over and—and gathered some herbs for a poultice, the way you insisted I should whenever I wished. It's a trifling wound. Nothing to concern yourself with considering your own great trouble."

Juliet patted his arm. "You have never been any trouble. My only friend in this neighborhood for so long."

"There were so few people I could speak theology to. Your company was the greatest of gifts." Rutledge cleared his throat. "I just wanted to tell you that you will be sorely missed. And I wanted to return these to you." He rummaged in his pocket with his uninjured hand and drew out a handkerchief-wrapped bundle.

She took it, unfolding the fine white cloth. A gasp burst from her lips as two golden lilies spilled into her hand, their diamond centers winking up at her.

"The links I pawned from my mother's necklace!"

Rutledge shuffled his feet, ill at ease. "I remembered your face when you surrendered them to me, the pain, the loss. The least I can do is to return them to you. Consider them a gift."

She closed her fingers over the bright petals, pressing her fist to her heart. "You're so very kind." She stood up on tiptoe and brushed that parchment-dry cheek with a kiss.

Rutledge's face suffused with color, his voice trembling. "No, you are the one who is kind, Miss Juliet. One of God's rare innocents, far too good for this world. I would do anything in my power to protect you."

She'd never heard such passion in the pawnbroker's voice, and she ached a little, remembering his stilted marriage proposal. She'd thought his heart was not engaged, but perhaps she had hurt him worse than she'd believed?

As if aware how much emotion he'd exposed, Rutledge turned away from her, clearing his throat. "When do you leave the city?"

Juliet smiled. "I won't be leaving at all."

Rutledge wheeled around, his long face drawn in lines of confusion. "But the house—it is ruined. And I know that you have no money, or you would never have pawned the bits of your mother's necklace."

"True. But Adam—" She blushed. "Mr. Slade is helping me to recover."

Rutledge's eyes widened, his complexion taking on an even more sickly cast. "Slade? That vile libertine? You cannot mean to accept anything from such a man!"

Juliet felt a wave of protectiveness squeeze her heart. "Mr. Slade is not at all what he seems. He is generous and kind and—"

"He is no such thing!" Rutledge cried in alarm, his fingers fluttering in agitation.

"He has offered to rebuild Angel's Fall for me."

"Rebuild it? Is he mad? No, he doesn't want to lose his nursery of depravity, a veritable banquet of women to sample! It grieves me to have to tell you the truth about him, but there can be no help for it. It is my duty to warn you."

The pawnbroker straightened as if expecting a blast from a firing squad. "Miss Grafton-Moore, I have seen this man engaged in—in acts of the utmost depravity with my own eyes."

"Mr. Rutledge—"

"It's true. I swear it upon my soul! I witnessed Slade cavorting with some sinful woman in the garden house the

night of the fire. The two of them were naked and writhing."
Hot spots of color stained Rutledge's gaunt cheeks. "There
can be no mistaking him, though I cannot say for certain
who his wanton partner was. I regret to offend your modesty
this way, but—"

Juliet's face burned. How on earth had the pawnbroker
seen? Through his window? A shudder worked through her
at the thought of the gaunt man watching the garden at
Angel's Fall, prying with those strange intense eyes.

She was sick that anyone had glimpsed the searing
intimacy she and Adam had shared. But the joining of their
bodies had been a thing of beauty, not some sordid spectacle. She lifted her chin. "Mr. Rutledge, *I* was the woman in
Adam Slade's arms."

The pawnbroker stumbled back as if she'd cudgeled him,
his eyes hot with disbelief and horror. "No! It cannot be!
You—you are an angel! You would never debase yourself."

"I have never experienced anything more beautiful. Sa-
cred. I came to the garden tonight to wait for Adam. But it
seems he has been detained."

Rutledge clutched his throat in his bandaged hand. "This
is my fault. This horrible thing! God forgive me for not
having the courage to save you before . . . but I loved you! I
was loath to take such drastic steps. . . ."

There was something wild and a little frightening behind
the pawnbroker's eyes, like the flickering of a tiny black
flame. "I'm sorry for your pain," Juliet said softly. "You
have been a good friend. But all has worked out for the
best."

"The best? Slade has turned you into one of those filthy
creatures of the flesh who have infested this house. They've
tainted you with their poison just as I always feared they
would! I should have killed him the first night I saw him at
the inn!"

Juliet's spine stiffened. "It was my choice to make love
with Adam. And I pray I'll have a lifetime in his arms. I love
him."

"Love him?" The cry wrenched from Rutledge's throat.
Juliet's fingers tightened on the golden lilies, her gaze

flicking to the mare cropping grass in the farthest corner of the garden. "Now, if you'll excuse me, I need to get back to Glenlyon House." Juliet started toward the horse, suddenly eager to get away from the garden and the condemnation in Rutledge's eyes.

She'd barely taken a step when a hand flashed out, grasping her arm with surprising strength.

"Mr. Rutledge, release me at once. I've nothing more to say."

"You think I will just stand back and let you plunge yourself into Satan's arms? No! I failed once. I will not be so faint of heart again!"

Juliet stared into Rutledge's face, and it was as if she were staring into the eyes of a stranger. Dark things, ugly things, frightening things lurked within those sunken depths, things she had never glimpsed there before.

An image burned into her mind—her fingers pressing a key to the garden gate into the pawnbroker's hand, telling him to gather whatever herbs he wished from the garden.

"The fire!" she gasped. "It was you. How else—" She choked off the words, something akin to panic lodging at the back of her throat. *How else could Rutledge have seen her with Adam in the garden house?*

"I—I mean, your hand—" She fought to cover her blunder desperately, "you must've burned it when you were helping the others fight the fire." But she could see in the curl of his lips that he knew she was lying. She knew the truth.

"Come now, Juliet. You know I never came here to help the night of the fire." Terrifyingly gentle, his words rasped against Juliet's nerves, leaving cold horror in their wake.

"No. I—I'm certain—"

"I was too busy tending the burn on my hand. When you ran into me—"

"You're mistaken! I—"

"You left me no choice!" Rutledge mourned. "Refused to heed my warnings. I had to take drastic measures to wrench you from the influence of those harlots. Save your innocence."

She was in danger, terrible danger. Juliet could see the hot coals of fanaticism in his gaze, the terrible belief that God's vengeance was his to mete out. She had to get away, find some way to distract him so she could escape.

"You seemed a saint to me," Rutledge's voice cracked. "How was I to know what Slade had already made you? A vile creature of the flesh! A whore like my own mother was!"

"Your mother?" Juliet edged toward the gate. If she could break free, reach the street, she might have a chance. But who would help her? The neighbors who had delighted in the destruction of Angel's Fall?

"I was to be a vicar," Rutledge said. "Rain, fire, and brimstone down upon sinners from the pulpit, terrify them into saving their worthless souls! I read myself blind, clawed and struggled until I was offered the vicarage at Millberry. But my rival discovered the truth about my past. My mother had been a whore. My father any one of a hundred men. I wasn't fit to take my place in the pulpit."

Juliet shuddered, hearing in Rutledge's voice the hatred, the intolerance that her father had always grieved over, man indulging in his own petty loathing and cruelty and attributing it to God.

Dots of foam flecked the corners of Rutledge's mouth, his eyes sunken pits touched with madness. "But Slade shan't have you! I'll not be thwarted again by such filth! I'll find a way to defeat him." He hesitated, a smile creeping across his lips. "There is only one thing to do. Yes. I know how to save you."

"Let me go! Mr. Rutledge—"

"Oh, I'll let you go. You needn't fear, lovely Juliet. But before I do, I'll see to it that Adam Slade will never be able to look upon your face again with anything but horror."

God in heaven, what was he threatening to do? Juliet fought to tear away from him, but he held her as if each of his thin muscles were strips of iron. "Let me go! Stop this before—"

"Don't be afraid, my sweet," Rutledge said with fiendish tenderness. "I will save you from him. And from yourself."

She started to scream, to fight, willing Adam to ride

through the gates. Adam . . . oh, God, he was her only chance. But if Rutledge dragged her away from here, how could Adam ever find her?

She struck at Rutledge's face with her fist, the petals of the golden lilies cutting into her palm until she felt the warmth of her own blood.

The lilies . . .

Something hard collided with the back of her head. Lights exploded behind her eyelids and she crumpled to the ground. She forced her fingers to open, saw the golden lilies tumble to the earth.

Such a tiny clue, such a faint hope. Adam would never find her before it was too late.

"Adam . . ." Juliet squeezed his name through her parched throat as Rutledge scooped her into his arms.

The last sight she saw was Barnabas's eyes glowing down at her like portals to some private hell, as the world drowned in darkness.

A demon was pounding her skull with a spiked mallet, cracking it into the back of her head again and again until she feared she would retch.

Thick webs of blackness suffocated her, yet they couldn't completely conceal the diamond-hard lump of terror lodged in her breast.

Adam . . . she clung to that name as if it were a sword, knowing she had to fight, had to remember where she was, what had happened. Yet each time she tried to open her eyes, her head seemed ready to split.

Slowly, she attempted it again, lifting eyelids that seemed weighted by lead. A small room swung dizzily about her as she fought to pull it into focus. Rusted muskets, pots and pans, tarnished silver, an elegant music box, and a mounted set of antlers wove into a macabre pattern, creating a world that made no sense, nightmarish, unreal.

"You're waking up, are you?"

That voice, so solicitous, should have soothed her. Why did it strike raw terror in her heart. It was familiar . . . familiar . . .

A figure materialized before her, wavering like a phantom. Barnabas Rutledge . . .

"Help me," she croaked, but her throat was hoarse, her hands bound, helpless, behind her.

"I will help you, my dear," Rutledge said in soothing accents that chilled her blood. "I've done my best to watch over you ever since you came to this sinful place. Even kept vigil outside the earl's townhouse night after night, praying for your soul. I'll take care of you now. You needn't worry any longer."

With all her will, Juliet forced back the veil of unconsciousness, tried to grasp fragments of what had happened. She'd been in the garden, waiting for Adam, and Rutledge had come to give her the golden lilies. . . .

In her mind's eye she saw the bits of gold tumbling from her bruised fingers, felt the terror, the hopelessness. The horrifying truth cascaded into her consciousness, the realization she was in danger, Rutledge's dark threats, her helplessness against him.

She tried to stand up, stagger toward the door, but ropes bit into her flesh, binding her hands and feet, lashing her to what looked to be a chair.

"You mustn't struggle so, my dear," Rutledge said, a harsh rhythmic scraping sound raking at her nerves. "You'll bruise your wrists. Just rest. It will be complete soon."

"Complete? What will be complete?"

"Your salvation. The knife is almost sharp enough."

Juliet felt as if he'd slipped the blade beneath her skin, cold and relentless. Merciful heaven, what was he going to do to her?

"This must be done delicately. Delicately. We don't want you to suffer any unnecessary pain. I just have to heat it over the coals until it's nice and hot."

"What—what are you talking about? Please, what are you going to do?"

Rutledge went to scoop out a shovelful of hot coals from the fire. Juliet winced as he jabbed the blade into the glowing orange center. "I am going to alter your face, my dear, so it will no longer be such a carnal temptation to men like Slade. Nor any man. If the blade is hot, it will cauterize the slash at the same time I cut you. You see, I can be merciful."

Merciful? Juliet reeled, bile rising in her throat. "You can't mean to do this."

"Of course, I would rather turn away from this deed. But it is necessary. *'If your eye offends thee, pluck it out.'*"

"But the Lord also said blessed are the merciful. There was no violence, no cruelty in Him, only love and understanding."

"But I do this out of love for Him, Juliet, and for you. If your papa, the vicar, were alive today, he would applaud my efforts to save you."

"My papa was a man of peace and love, a man who sought to heal, not destroy."

"And I shall heal you. You needn't fear for your future, my dear. I am not a man bound by beauty of the flesh. I will take care of you, help you repent your sin in the years to come. You will always have a home here with me."

"I'd sooner die in the streets!"

The man actually looked hurt. "You think you'll go back to Slade? That a man like him can love your soul enough to be blind to your ruined face? He'll despise you, be repulsed by you when your face is as flawed as your virtue."

"Adam will kill you for this! He's an expert swordsman. You could never defeat him!"

"It was never my intention to fight him. Although, if he should come here, I'll put a pistol-ball in his chest. I've given the matter great consideration, trying to think of a just price for his interference. It came to me as I carried you from the garden. His punishment will be the image he'll carry of you once this ugly business is finished. Slashed and scarred, branded like some vile harpy. He'll dream of you and wake up screaming."

Horror sluiced through Juliet. Horror at the image of Adam finding her, witnessing Rutledge's fiendish marring of her face. No physical wound Rutledge could inflict on Adam would be deeper, more devastating than seeing her thus.

Adam was a man who already had too many dark

nightmares, too many chains of guilt and regret hidden beneath his laughter.

The blade was growing brighter, and Rutledge scooped it from the coals, holding it up into the light. It glowed, the metal hot, the blade hungry.

"It is time." Rutledge paced toward her, the blade glowing. He poised it so near her cheek she could feel the heat on her skin, anticipate the bite of the blade as it found flesh. "The question is where to begin."

Chapter
20

Fury and frustration pulsed through Adam's veins, battle instincts scratching claws of dread against his nerves. He leaned low over the neck of his horse, driving it to faster speeds, his heart hammering.

Blast, had Gavin been out of his mind, allowing Juliet to return to Angel's Fall alone? Yet Gavin had believed Adam was confronting Juliet's enemy. He'd believed she was safe. Otherwise Adam knew his brother would never have let her ride off.

Adam had believed she was safe, too, as he'd tightened the noose about Isabelle. But he'd been wrong. Dangerously wrong. And now Juliet could be in peril.

Bloody hell, he felt so damned helpless. He did not have a clue where to begin searching again for the monster who had hurt Juliet. But he would turn the earth inside out if he had to—to flush out whatever beast had been stalking her.

With every bit of his will, Adam fought to calm himself. He would find her in the garden, safe, mourning her foxglove and her heart's ease, or sitting in the garden house, trying to piece together the broken bits of her dream.

There was no more reason for anyone to attack her now, was there? They'd burned her out, and no one except Gavin and Juliet's angels knew that the haven would rise from the ashes.

He guided his horse around the corner, his gaze falling on the blackened hulk that had been Juliet's home. It still made his breath clutch in his throat, the thought of how easily she might have died that night, the knowledge that someone was twisted enough to unleash that kind of vengeance upon her.

He'd spend the rest of his life keeping her safe.

Adam reined his mount into the garden, glimpsed the mare Juliet had ridden cropping sprigs of grass in the corner of the garden. Relief jolted through him. She was here somewhere.

Adam flung himself from his horse, bellowing her name, his eyes sweeping the trampled garden. Nothing.

He glimpsed the garden house, charged toward it, images playing through his mind. The alabaster curve of her breast as he'd kissed it, the catch of her breath as he suckled her. The wide wonder in her eyes as he pierced her maidenhead, aware he'd just been given the most precious gift imaginable.

Love. The love of a woman he didn't deserve. A woman of quiet courage, of fierce conviction, a woman who believed in justice and the triumph of good over evil. And was willing to fight as valiantly as any soldier ever born for people she barely knew.

Adam charged up to the garden house, flung open the door. He could feel the points of his temper jabbing the way they always did when he was afraid. Knew that once he found Juliet, he was going to kiss her until her knees melted, then bellow at her until her eardrums crumbled.

"Juliet?" he called. "Blast it, Juliet, answer me." But there was no sound but echoing silence.

The mounds of pillows that had made their bed were still tumbled, his discarded neckcloth lying on the floor. Soft lace shadows were pooling in the deepening twilight. But Juliet was nowhere to be seen.

His muscles knotted, his nerves on a blade-edge of awareness. She'd come to Angel's Fall, just as Elise told him she had. The mare was still here. Where could she have gone?

Adam stalked out of the garden house, his gaze sweeping the grounds. What the devil had she been doing here? Poking about?

Suddenly his gaze snagged on a ribbon fluttering in the breeze. What had she called the plants last time? *Foxglove?* No, *fairyfingers.* Hell, only Juliet would try to tie the blasted things upright after they were half scorched and ground into the turf.

Adam stalked over to them, to take the end of the ribbon between his fingers. Damn, something was wrong. He could feel it with the same certainty he'd sensed an assassin's blade inches from his back. He could hear the danger deep in his own vitals.

He clenched his fist, sickened as he saw footprints, a man's, a woman's . . . Juliet's. There had been a struggle. The certainty weighed in his gut like a cold lump of stone, images of Juliet battling some mysterious assailant, terrified, that phantom enemy who had run from Angel's Fall the night of the fire.

Soon it would be dark. How the blazes could he track Juliet if she'd been dragged away from the garden? It would be fiendishly easy to disappear into the bowels of the city with one lone woman.

"Damnation, where could she be?" Adam knelt down, examining the area, praying for something, anything that might give him a clue where she'd gone.

He was just about to stand, to search somewhere else when he saw it. A handkerchief tangled in the branches of a rhododendron, something glimmering, half crushed into the ground beside it. He dug the object out. Cradling it in his palm, he held it in the fading light.

What the devil? It was a golden lily, petals bent, the diamond center dulled with dirt. A link from Juliet's mother's necklace. The one she'd tried to run back into the fire to save. How in the name of the saints had any of it survived? No, Adam reasoned. No one had ever reached Juliet's room while fighting the fire. It had collapsed when the roof fell.

Then how was it possible?

There had to be some explanation. Something he had to remember. He closed his eyes, then opened them again, his gaze locking on the fairyfingers Juliet had attempted to resurrect. That was it! The day he and Rutledge had argued in the garden, Juliet had said she'd pawned two links from the necklace to keep the shelter running. The only way the golden lily could have gotten here was if the pawnbroker had brought it.

Rutledge? Adam should have felt relief. But instead his nape prickled with wariness. If the pawnbroker had returned the lilies to Juliet she would never have left them to be trampled, forgotten. Something was wrong. Terribly wrong.

His gaze scanned the area, noting crushed plants, smeared footprints, Juliet's and a man's larger ones. The signs of a struggle? Or just more ruin from the night of the fire?

He bent over to touch a crack in the stem of the foxglove. It was still sticky, fresh as a new wound.

Was it possible that Rutledge could be involved in all that had happened? Intense sunken eyes blazed in Adam's memory, eyes filled with hatred, loathing, and an almost fanatical aura of worship when they looked at Juliet.

It was one heartbeat from such emotions to madness. Adam had seen it in the officers he'd served, tasted it on the slaughtering fields of the battle of Culloden Moor.

Adam's jaw hardened. He turned and ran toward the dismal shop that loomed over the blackened garden wall.

Once when he'd lost at gaming, Adam had pawned the ring his father had given him. He'd never quite rid himself of the bitter taste of the experience.

Adam drew his sword and stealthily entered Rutledge's shop. The place was an accursed rat's warren, stuffed with debris, a motley collection fashioned of human misery and suffering. A gold-framed portrait of someone's child dangled haphazardly on a wall. What had caused the owner to pawn it? That same child sobbing with hunger? Or the need of the parent to guzzle gin?

Men like Rutledge were the worst kind of vultures, preying on desperation, picking the bones of people's dignity. Yet now Adam was afraid the man had chosen another quarry.

Juliet. Bloody hell, where was she? She was nowhere to be seen; there was only the sound of voices from deeper inside the building. By the dim light filtering through the window, Adam wove toward the noise, his heart thundering, every muscle in his body tight with desperation, forgotten prayers upon his lips.

But never, in a thousand nightmare scenes of battle, had any sight struck horror into Adam's soul like the scene that greeted him as he reached the back room of the pawnshop. A glowing blade poised a mere hairsbreadth away from Juliet's soft cheek, her eyes wide with horror.

"Rutledge, stop!" Adam commanded.

"Adam!" Juliet choked out his name, the pawnbroker wheeling about, white-faced.

"How—how did you find us?" Rutledge choked out, the blade trembling in his hand. "Come another step and I'll slash her face," he warned.

The slightest flick of his wrist would scar Juliet forever. The thought of her carrying the mark of this madman was unspeakable.

Adam froze. "Hurt her, and I swear I'll kill you."

"You think I care? I'll sacrifice my life, if need be, to protect Juliet from herself!"

"Protect her? You've got a blasted knife at her face!"

"And I'm going to use it, Slade. Scar her so that no man will ever look at her with lust again. I have to do it because of you."

"Because of me?"

"You fornicated with her in the garden house! I saw the two of you together!"

Adam's gut lurched at the knowledge that this man had watched something so searingly private, so unbearably precious. "What the devil business is it of yours?"

"I was her guardian long before you were! A proper guardian, watching through the windows at night. I thought she was an angel, so good. I was afraid for her, afraid she would be tainted by the wantonness of those women. I did my best to frighten her away from this accursed place before it was too late. But the whores infected her with their vile plague, and you—you poisoned her."

"I was the one who defiled her," Adam snarled. "If you want vengeance, strike at me."

"Your soul is already lost to the devil. There is still time to save Juliet's! Now throw down your sword or I swear I'll cut her throat!" Rutledge's knife flashed down to that slender column.

"No!" Juliet cried out. "Adam, don't!"

But Adam glanced from the knife to his own sword, that sword that had protected him in countless altercations. But it had been easy to charge a foe when he wasn't in love with the prisoner. Now the battle instinct honed by countless engagements was dulled, all but frozen, his head filled, not with discovering his foe's weaknesses and capitalizing on them, but rather with a hundred nightmarish possibilities that left Juliet bleeding, dead.

Adam's hand tightened on the hilt of his sword a moment more, then he flung it away from him. It clattered to the floor. "The sword's down," Adam snarled between gritted teeth. "It's down."

Juliet cried out a protest, tears welling from her eyes.

What kind of a twisted madman was Rutledge? And how the devil could he disarm the man before he scarred Juliet forever? Adam groped desperately for some way, any way, to goad Rutledge into making some mistake, giving Adam an opening. "What *sin* did Juliet commit, except being within reach when I needed a woman to bed? It was my favorite game to play to while away the time I was stuck in that infernal house."

"You could have had any of the other women!"

"I did," Adam lied. "More than half of them. But you can imagine it was small challenge. What entertainment would that be? No, to get Juliet into my bed—that was a far more difficult quest." Adam gave a harsh laugh. "It's not every man who can tempt an angel to fall! You certainly didn't."

"Damn you to hell, don't you dare—"

"Are you telling me you didn't dream of Juliet? Of kissing

her, touching her?" The thought made Adam want to retch, but he had to jab at Rutledge's vulnerabilities, set him off balance.

Dark red stained the pawnbroker's cheeks, and he trembled so hard Adam feared a line of blood would well where the knife blade lay. "I fought against such carnal thoughts!"

"I bet you had to fight damned hard at night, alone in your bed." Adam's lip curled in mockery. "But you didn't have the courage I had to take her, despite all her pretty protests. Perhaps you are used to being rejected by a woman you desire." Adam let his eyes harden. "But I am not."

"Stop it, Slade!" Flecks of foam dotted Rutledge's thin lips. "She was an angel! A woman of virtue!"

"Do you think I cared? I lured her into the garden house late at night, by begging for some sort of poultice for one of my old wounds. Claimed it was aching so fiercely I could get no rest. And once she was so far from the house no one could hear her scream, I forced her."

"Adam! No! Can't you see how—how angry—" Juliet pleaded. "It's not true!"

"I like my women that way, Rutledge," Adam sneered, edging toward the pawnbroker. "All those years as Sabrehawk I learned to take what I want. And I wanted Juliet." The man was teetering on the brink of madness, wild rage writhing in his white-ringed eyes.

"Adam, stop!" Juliet cried. "Are you mad?"

Rutledge was quaking, shaking. "No. I saw you together—heard her . . . she was crying out in passion."

Adam shot him a tigerish smile full of mockery, scorn. "That's what you dreamed of, wasn't it Rutledge? Juliet crying out for you? You should have flung her down in the garden house. I would have willingly shared her once I was done."

With an animal roar, Rutledge drew back the knife to slash at Adam, murder in his eyes. But at that instant, Juliet shoved hard with one foot. The chair toppled over, hurling Rutledge off balance as it splintered with a deafening crash, throwing her out of Rutledge's reach.

Adam dove for the man, crashing into him body-long.

The knife slashed Adam's arm, as he fought to subdue Rutledge. It should have been easy enough, but the smaller man fought with the power of a zealot—and that most dangerous of qualities Adam recognized too well, the savageness of a man who did not care if he lived or died.

Adam glimpsed Juliet tearing at her bindings, trying to get free, that single glance fraught with danger. Rutledge slashed at Adam again. Fire spilled in a hot line of blood down his chest. Rutledge broke free, scrambling behind a tower of wooden chests that nearly reached the ceiling. Adam struggled to his feet, diving after Rutledge, but it was too late. The pawnbroker drove his shoulder into the wooden sides of the mounded chests, sending them crashing down onto Adam.

Juliet screamed, a hundred cudgels seeming to slam into Adam, driving him to the floor. Breath was crushed from his lungs, his head swam, his stomach roiling as the falling chests battered him.

He fought not to lose consciousness, fought to get out from beneath the chests, but they had the weight and power to do what Rutledge could not. Imprison him just long enough for the man to escape him.

The room whirled, pitched. Adam glimpsed the pawnbroker scrabbling away from him, knife in hand, those eyes fixed on Juliet, so helpless, struggling against the bindings that still tied her to the chair. Adam knew in that horrifying second that Rutledge wasn't fighting to kill Adam. He didn't give a damn if Adam killed him. Rutledge's one object was to get his knife blade to Juliet's face.

With a guttural roar, Adam tore free of the weight that pinned him. He launched himself at the man, not caring if the knife embedded itself in his own flesh, just as long as he could keep it from harming his love.

He heard Juliet's cry just as the knife flashed at her cheek. Adam dove, plunging his right hand between her skin and the blade at the last instant. He clenched his fist around the blade, pain screaming through him as the knife bit deep, battling with his other hand to wrench the blood-slickened weapon away from Rutledge.

"Adam!" Juliet was sobbing. "Adam—"

In that instant, she tore free of her bindings. Adam never saw her strike, only heard the cracking of wood as she bashed the chair into Rutledge's head. Rutledge shrieked, fell, letting go of the knife as he plunged toward Adam.

It was over in a heartbeat. The pawnbroker fell back, his eyes staring, sightless, at the ceiling, the knife imbedded in his chest.

Dead. The monster was dead. Why the hell was Adam still so bloody scared?

"Adam!" Juliet flung herself against him. "Oh, God, you're hurt."

He tried to crush his fingers tight over the gaping wound in his palm to stem the bleeding. A black oath tore from his lips as she ripped at her petticoat, then forced his fingers to unfold, revealing what lay beneath. A sob tore from her as she saw the brutal gash.

Tears streaked her face as she tried to bind the wound with the cloth. "Your hand . . . there's so much blood!"

Adam gazed up into her face, the tiniest cut on her cheekbone wrenching his raw emotions with images of the destruction that might have been. "It doesn't matter, Juliet."

"How can you say that? The hand that wields your sword—it's cut so badly. Oh, Adam, what if—if you can never . . ."

She didn't put it into words. She didn't have to. *What if you can never grasp a sword again?*

Sabrehawk—he'd spent a lifetime earning that sobriquet, carving out that legend. His gaze flashed to the sword lying on the floor, a gleam of silver, one more legacy from his father.

"This is my fault," Juliet cried. "When I think of what I cost you—"

"You're safe. That's all that matters." Darkness was claiming him, pain rippling through his body in suffocating waves. His ribs ached, his head . . . hell, his hand felt as if he'd dipped it in flame.

Adam sagged down to the floor, trying to focus on Juliet's

eyes—eyes filled with love and forgiveness and the shadings of self-blame it would take a lifetime to love away.

Adam bit back a groan, using the last of his strength to lift his bandaged hand. "This is not . . . so great a sacrifice," he whispered as darkness claimed him. "Ah, Angel . . . don't you know . . . I'd cut out my heart to save you pain?"

Chapter
21

Adam's ordeal was almost over. The nightmarish trip to Glenlyon House was but a hazy nightmare. The surgeon had made short work of the cuts on his arms, stitching them while Adam cast out jests from between white lips. Yet as the medical man worked over Adam's hand, the jests had faded, died, the silence pressing down on Juliet's chest until she could barely breathe.

The earl, who had kept up lively banter to distract his brother from the pain, now prowled the chamber like a caged animal, his face grim, his gray eyes filled with sorrow. Fletcher, having delivered little Will to his mother's arms, huddled in the corner, face tear-streaked as a child, forced for the first time to acknowledge that even the greatest heroes were mortal. Juliet sat on the bed at Adam's side, holding his uninjured hand in both her own.

He feigned a carelessness, as if his whole identity did not hang in the balance. Sabrehawk—the sobriquet that had masked the hated label of bastard for so long.

Yet when the doctor spoke, Adam's fingers tightened around Juliet's.

"I'm so very sorry, sir," the gnomelike medical man said with a shake of his head. "There is little I can do. The tendons are badly damaged. Perhaps some day we'll have the knowledge to repair them, but now . . ."

Juliet's heart plunged, a thick knot of tears in her throat. Dear God, what she had cost him in that moment he'd plunged his hand between her face and Rutledge's blade. Had he known the sacrifice he was making even then?

A choked sob broke from Fletcher's throat, and she saw Gavin cross to his brother, one hand squeezing Adam's shoulder. There were tears in the nobleman's eyes.

"In time, you might be able to curl your fingers," the doctor said. "But as for anything as strenuous as wielding a sword—you'll never be able to exert that much force again."

Juliet's breast filled with unbearable grief, as if something had died, *someone* had died. She had cost Jenny so much, had sent her father out to die alone on an Irish road. Now she had cost Adam his sword.

She released his hand, stood up, and paced to the window to hide the tears streaming down her cheeks.

"Gav." Adam's voice sounded just a little tight. "You'll have to break out your finest bottle of brandy and send it to a Major David Weatherly with my compliments."

The earl turned to him, surprised, yet Juliet knew Gavin Carstares would send the man his last drop of blood if his brother asked for it. "Weatherly? Who is he?"

"The best swordsman I ever fought. Came damned near to beating me on more than one occasion. It's only fair to let the man know what he's just been condemned to."

"And what is that?" Gavin asked.

"A scourge more irritating than the Seven Plagues of Egypt. From now on I'll be sending all these brainless young fledglings eager to match swords with a legend to fight him."

"I'll see to it." The earl's voice broke over the words. "Adam, I . . ."

"I know." Pain, understanding, and gratitude were rough in those simple words. They pierced Juliet to the core.

She listened as the doctor left, the earl following in his wake. Fletcher drew near, anguish in the lad's voice. "You'll always be a hero in my eyes. After all you've done—"

"No, boy. All I want is to be your friend. That means more to me than any hero laurel ever could."

"You are more than that. The father I never had. I . . . love you. Is it weak of me to say it?"

"Loving doesn't make you weak, boy. It only makes you stronger. Juliet taught me that. I watched so many lads like you die. If only one could be spared, I thank God you were the one. Fletcher—*Kieran*—my sword is over on that table. I won't be needing it anymore. I would be honored if you would take it. After all, I won't be with you in the colonies to watch your back."

Fletcher crossed to the table, picked up the blade. And Juliet knew it was Adam's way of sending a piece of his heart with the boy he'd come to love as his own. A legacy of hope, of trust, of faith. Not the burden Adam's father had cast onto his two sons. "Now, get the devil out of here, boy, and give an old soldier some peace."

Fletcher peered down at Adam a long moment, a glance that understood all, forgave all. Then he walked from the room, leaving Juliet and Adam alone at last.

"Juliet?"

"I'm here Adam." She dashed her tears away with her knuckles and came to the side of his bed.

"Don't cry, angel."

"I can't help it. Your hand—"

Tears fell free, a hot ball of anguish in her chest. He smiled, but there was so much tenderness in it she couldn't bear it.

"I should never have gone back to the garden. It was just that when Elise told me what you were doing—that you were resurrecting Angel's Fall—I could hardly believe it. I wanted to find you, tell you how much I . . . oh, Adam, why? Why are you doing this for me?"

"I discovered I believe in you, lady. Too damned bad I didn't figure it out until after the fire, when everything was gone. The night we came here to Glenlyon House, I went to look at a portrait in Gavin's study. My mother, when she was sixteen—young and beautiful, full of hope."

"She was on a swing," Juliet said softly. "Laughing. I saw it when I asked his lordship for a horse."

"She loved my father to desperation, and I suppose the fact that she'd lay with him was inevitable. But I kept thinking that afterward, after my father had bent to his family's will and married Gavin's mother, after my mother's family had disowned her . . . that maybe, if she'd had somewhere like Angel's Fall, where she could go to think, to be safe, she could have found the precious gift you've given me. A second chance."

"Oh, Adam—"

"Maybe she would still have chosen the same path. Maybe my father's love was worth all the scorn and pain from the rest of the world. But I would have liked her to have that choice. And I realized that she did not. Once my father had taken her to his bed, she was completely in his power. And even with the greatest love, that is a terrifying thing."

Juliet touched his face. "I'm just so sorry. I—"

"No. No more tears, no more regrets. Don't you see? I might never wield a sword, but I can still touch you, feel you." Adam looked away. "Of course, if you have to mourn something, you might just think what you've done to my reputation."

"I—I know, I—"

"Oh, not the Sabrehawk nonsense. My reputation as a hell-raising rogue. It's in tatters. No self-respecting scoundrel will ever speak to me again. I've betrayed them most dreadfully."

"Did you?"

"Falling in love is unconscionable. I fear there's no help for it. You'll have to marry me."

Joy leapt in Juliet's heart, then her brow creased, troubled. "Adam, you don't have to. Marry me, I mean."

"It's the only way I can think of to keep you out of trouble. Not enough room for both of us in a barrel, and as often as I plan to make love to you, I prefer to do it in the comfort of a bed."

She wanted so much to kiss him, to bind him to her forever, her most fervent wish come true. But she couldn't bear the thought of doing so if it would somehow imprison the spirit of this wild reckless wanderer. "But you've spent a lifetime adventuring, traveling the world. I couldn't bear it if you were unhappy, tied to one place, and . . ." He could never know how much the next words cost her. "And to one woman. You might get bored, weary."

"Bored with you running amok?" Adam's chuckle choked off in a gasp of pain, and he clutched his healing ribs. "My love, I've been on battlefields that seemed downright serene in comparison to the last few weeks under your roof."

The words stung just a little. Heat flooded her cheeks, and she looked away.

"Juliet." He rasped her name with infinite tenderness, catching up her hand in his uninjured one. "I'm a soldier. Gruff and hard-mannered. I've spent a lifetime hiding my feelings behind a jest. But that doesn't mean the feelings aren't there, beneath. I love you, angel. Want to be your husband. I want to make love to you every night and fill you with my babes. Babes I'd never even dreamed might exist until I saw them smiling at me from your eyes."

"Oh, Adam! But are you certain? I mean, just because of your hand . . . do you . . . I mean, are you—"

"So that's what you're afraid of. Juliet, I'd decided to lay down my sword before I faced Rutledge. In the new place I've bought for Angel's Fall, there are two houses and I'm having a sheltered corridor built between. One for the ladies, and the other . . . I'd hoped, dreamed that if you could ever forgive me—" He swallowed hard, his voice rough with emotion. "I want to build a home there. I want to lay down all my anger and bitterness and build something real and lasting."

His good hand cradled her cheek, ever so gently.

"I ran away to war, wanting to forget. Who I was, what I'd cost my mother, even the resentment I felt toward the brother I loved more than anyone else in the world. But every time I swung my sword, it was still there. The enemy wasn't at the opposite end of my sword, it was inside me. There was no escaping it."

His eyes burned with love, stripped bare, all the more precious because she knew what it cost him to reveal it to her. "For the first time you've given me something I want to remember. You loved me. You, an angel so far above my touch it seemed almost sacrilege to dare to love you, let alone seek a future with you."

"I'm not an angel, Adam. I'm a woman, one who loves you so much."

He tangled his fingers through her hair, drawing her mouth to his, taking her in a fierce hungry kiss that told her a thousand things he could never say. "Marry me."

"I'll marry you this minute if you want me."

"And deprive your angels of fitting you out as a bride? I may be notorious for my courage, but even Sabrehawk isn't *that* brave. Still, it's a relief that you love me, my angel." He grinned, pulling her down into his arms. Twin devils danced in his eyes. "After all, a man can't spend his whole life living in sin."

POCKET BOOKS
PROUDLY PRESENTS

NIGHT SONG

KIMBERLY CATES

Available from
Pocket Books

The following is a preview of
Night Song. . . .

Hannah wished the child would cry, add his thin wails to the keening lament of the wind lashing against them. There was something terrible in his silence. Something frightening in the stillness of the tiny hand she held in her own as he trudged along beside her.

Pip had to be exhausted. Her own feet dragged through the sucking mud as if the soles of her shoes were millstones, the sodden layers of her skirts and meager cloak bowed her shoulders and weighted her chest, holding the chill against her skin. The portmanteau she carried in one hand felt like it was stuffed with iron bars, instead of what few clothes she'd managed to fling together for Pip and herself.

But at least the rain had finally stopped.

Night bruised the edge of the horizon, devouring what little light managed to pierce the last wisps of storm clouds.

It seemed as if she and Pip had been wandering forever, braving the Irish sea in a dilapidated fishing boat, battering themselves in countless jolting mail coaches carrying them to no destination in particular, only farther and farther away, deeper into the English countryside.

Worse still, they'd been on foot for two weeks now, ever

since the store of coins she'd carried away from the pawn-broker's shop in far-off Ireland had dwindled away.

But this was a journey that would never be finished, not until Pip was grown into a man. A man who could fight back, rather than a little boy at the mercy of someone who could batter with fists and with words.

Her one hope was that she'd managed to buy them enough precious time to vanish into the mist—but at what price? She'd betrayed those who trusted her, failed those who had depended on her, lied and deceived them in quiet desperation until they would never forgive her.

Her stomach growled, and she pressed her hand against it, fighting back waves of sickening hunger. It was three days since she had eaten, a handful of green apples that had left her retching in a ditch.

She'd fed the little boy the last crushed bit of pie that she'd snatched from a wooden bowl of chicken feed set out on the doorstep of a cottage a village ago. But his stomach must be devouring itself by now, torn by the talons of hunger.

He hadn't murmured a word of complaint, but she knew he couldn't go on much longer. The cough that had plagued him these past weeks was growing worse, hammering at his narrow chest. A raw knot of despair lodged in her throat. Had they traveled so far only to die on some unfamiliar road? Starving? Cold? Alone?

No, she'd promised she would take care of him. She'd guard him with her very life. But she was tired. So tired. And grief pressed like a boulder against her battered heart.

"Just a little farther, Pip," she encouraged, more for herself than the boy.

He turned his face up to hers, huge gray-green eyes screaming out words he'd never say: *I'm frightened. I'm hungry. Please don't let him hurt me.*

Helplessness and desperation gnawed at Hannah's courage. God in heaven, they needed somewhere to rest, just for a little while. Long enough to get a decent night's sleep. Long enough to untangle the aches from their knotted muscles and to dry their clothes beside a heavenly warm fire.

Long enough to mourn . . .

No, she couldn't think about that now. Didn't dare. She had to find some way to go on. She sought strength the way she had throughout their trek.

Though her own arms were throbbing, Hannah shifted the handle of the bag into her left hand, then bent down and scooped Pip up, pressing his small body so close she could feel the beat of his heart. After a moment, the boy melted against her, burrowing his face into the hollow of her neck. It was a gesture of trust, all the more precious because it was so hard-won.

It was dangerous to love anyone so much. That was a lesson Hannah had learned with brutal clarity over the past few years. Her heart, ever wary, seldom risked, was in danger of being broken yet again. But she couldn't help it, couldn't stop it. For each time she looked at him, she saw another gentle face with eyes the gray-green of a mist-shrouded glen.

Don't let him suffer as I have done, the plea would haunt her for eternity.

A cough racked Pip's small frame. He stifled it against her shoulder, then glanced up at her with guilt-ridden eyes. How many times in years past had he been made to feel ashamed, thinking he'd committed some dire transgression by succumbing to that cough?

She battled back rage, and pressed a fierce kiss to his damp temple. "There, now, my little man. It's all right," she soothed. "Just cough it out."

But a splinter of alarm twisted deeper into Hannah's frayed nerves. A hale, hearty child's strength would be challenged by the brutal trek the two of them had made these past two months. Pip's lungs were already weakened.

She had to find some kind of shelter before it was too late. Find a temporary job where she could earn enough coin to fill Pip's stomach, and to rent the small cottage she'd promised him, hidden like a fairytale bower so deep in the Yorkshire moors that no one could ever find them.

But when she'd stopped in the tiny hamlet of Nodding Cross that morning, pleading for some employment, the cluster of villagers lounging near the smithy's had admitted that there was only one place she might have hope of finding a situation.

Her gaze swept up to the crest of a hill. There, out of a wreath of mist, rose a shadowy structure, smears of candle-light setting windows aglow.

It didn't look like the house of an ogre, but the villagers had painted it in tales dark as legend, wrapped in some evil enchantress's spell. Within its confines supposedly dwelt a most capricious dragon.

One so vain he'd swept aside his tenant's cottages so his view of a nearby lake would be unobstructed. A taskmaster so ruthless he'd gobbled up a dozen assistants in the past eight months and spat them out, broken and babbling.

The men had stumbled into the village after they'd escaped, with tales so grim they chilled the bone. Tales of their master rousing them in the middle of the night, keeping them at their desk for days at a time, forcing them to choke down whatever food they could manage as they labored.

You'd be better off to let the wee lad perish in the hedgerow in peace, a stingy goodwife had advised, busily tucking a clean cloth over a basket of bread.

Slivers of ice flowed through Hannah's veins, but she glanced down at the wet guinea-gold curls plastered against Pip's head, her jaw tightening with determination. She'd bargain with the devil himself to get the boy into shelter tonight.

"Is that the by-count's house?" Pip quavered.

"Yes, sweeting."

His little arms clasped tighter about her neck. "The lady with the bread said the by-count is mad."

Hannah understood all too well the vibrating terror in Pip's faint voice.

"I hope he *is* in one of his notorious temper fits," she said, tossing a stray strand of auburn hair from steady gray eyes. "If we're very lucky he'll be angry enough to have thrown out a few more of his servants. If he needs someone to light his fires or clean his clothes, he might just let us inside."

Pip burrowed closer. "Don't want to go inside."

"Hush now. It will only be for a little while. I won't let

anyone hurt you." It was a rash promise. One she knew all too well she might not be able to keep.

Worse still, hadn't she been hurting Pip herself? Dragging him from pillar to post, without food, without shelter, without anyplace to call home? A child needed a home. No one knew that better than Hannah did.

A wide carriage sweep wound in a silver ribbon to the grand entrance of the mansion. Braces of lanterns blazed on either side of the massive twin doors, spreading puddles of gilt across the Palladian portico with its graceful white pillars. Hannah searched for a path that would lead her to the servant's entrance. But as they trudged toward the far side of the house, the front door suddenly flew open, spewing out a spindly ink-stained man with wild eyes, a half-open portmanteau tucked under one arm. A trail of clothes spilled out in his wake.

"Get back here before I break your neck, you bloody fool!" A deep voice roared from the cavernous interior of the house. "I haven't even paid you yet!"

Not even the inducement of coin could give the little man pause. He jumped as if a firebrand had just been thrust down the back of his breeches, and he all but bowled Hannah over in his haste to flee.

Pip scrabbled down to the ground in raw terror and shrank back to hide behind a stone pillar, but Hannah couldn't take her eyes from the man charging out the door in pursuit. She knew in a heartbeat that it was the Viscount of Ravenscar.

Eyes like blue flame glittered in the lanternlight, something hard and dangerous in those heartstoppingly handsome features.

He towered over the height of most men, emanating such fierce intensity it seemed as if charges of lightning flowed through his veins instead of mere blood, barely controlled energy pulsing from every inch of his frame, making one wonder—or fear?—what might happen if he ever fully unleashed it.

Patrician cheekbones slashed down to a blade-straight nose. Hair was tossed in wild black waves across a noble brow, and a cleft marked a chin of granitelike stubbornness.

"What the devil—" The viscount slammed to a halt a mere instant before he would have crashed into Hannah. "Get the blazes out of my way so I can drag the incompetent fool back by his infernal collar! I've the devil of a lot of work to do tonight!"

Hannah stood her ground, fighting back the alarm clamoring in her chest. "I suppose you *could* shackle him to a wall, providing you have some chains stashed in a stray dungeon somewhere," she managed to say without so much as a betraying tremor in her voice.

He shot her such a searing glance that she was stunned that the moisture soaking her clothes didn't turn into steam. "I'd do it, by damn, if I thought it would do any good! But the authorities get infernally touchy about a little reasonable torture nowadays, no matter how much the blackguard deserves it." A mouth full and sensual, curled with the ruthlessness of one unused to being thwarted. "Oh, what the hell, the little weasel is probably halfway to Nodding Cross by now."

At a glance, she could tell that this nobleman was everything she loathed in a man—and feared. Perhaps she was the one not in her right mind, bringing Pip to such a place, putting him in the power of such a man again. Yet this was only a temporary measure. She and Pip wouldn't be important enough to stir up the viscount's formidable wrath.

Muttering an oath, Ravenscar wheeled back to the house and started up the stairs. Hannah couldn't let him slam the door. She grabbed his arm, stunned at her own rashness.

"Wait, my lord! Please!"

He turned to glare at her hand clutching his sleeve. "I prefer to get back under a roof. The dampness in the air is playing havoc with the starch in my cravat."

But when her fingers only tightened, his scowl carved deeper. His eyes glittered, his voice suddenly terrifyingly soft. "Before you wreak any more destruction on my sleeve, perhaps you might enlighten me on one point. Who the devil are you, and what the blazes are you doing on my doorstep?"

She would have been less alarmed if he'd bellowed at her.

Hannah bolstered her courage and forced herself to meet his smoldering gaze. "I've come to save you the inconvenience of—of digging the manacles out of your family dungeon, your lordship."

"You what?" he demanded in deadly quiet.

"I heard about your difficulties while passing through Nodding Cross."

"Is that so?" His lip curled in a sneer. "And just which difficulties are those? As you see, I haven't sprouted three heads and I don't spit fire—at least unless I'm severely provoked. However, if I ever *were* going to roast somebody, now would be the time."

Hannah fought the urge to take a step backward. "I heard that there are few stout-hearted enough to be in your service long. And since I never could resist a challenge, I was searching for the servant's entrance to ask for employment."

"Of course you were." He gave a bark of harsh laughter. "After all, I always make it a practice to hire vagrant women wandering past my door, then show them the key to the silver closet."

Outrage and shame seared Hannah's cheeks at his contemptuous dismissal. One would think in the past months she'd have grown used to people regarding her the way they did the dirt beneath their feet—bothersome and vaguely unpleasant—something to be brushed away as hastily as possible so as not to dull their own luster.

But her greatest blessing and most hazardous curse had always been a core of inner pride, one that hadn't allowed her to crumble when the family fortunes had been swept away.

She wanted to tell him to go to the devil, but the muffled sound of a cough from behind the pillar made her bite her tongue. Steel poured into her spine, defiance bumping her chin up a notch. "Your lordship—"

Ravenscar's eyes narrowed. "I know I'm reputed to be a few steps shy of a waltz, madam, but even I'm not crazy enough to usher someone of your ilk into my house. Besides, I've got an entire staff of servants who, believe it or not, are able to tolerate my moods well enough. It's just these damned weak-spined assistants who aren't man enough to endure a little bellowing."

"Then maybe you need a woman."

"A woman?"

She'd thought her humiliation couldn't get worse, but the insufferable man eyed her with a new, even more cutting disdain, and Hannah was appalled to realize he thought she was propositioning him in a most improper way. Doubtless the arrogant oaf couldn't conceive what else he could possibly need a woman for. Only the stifled sound of another of Pip's coughs kept her from slapping his lordship square in his obnoxious face.

"A tempting offer, but I fear I must decline," he mocked. "My tastes tend to be a trifle more fastidious."

"I was offering nothing of the kind!" she blustered, hating him. "I only meant to say that maybe you need a woman to do whatever tasks the weak-spined men can't."

"You mean be my assistant? Don't be ridiculous," he scoffed. "You couldn't possibly take over Willoughby's tasks."

"How can you be so certain unless you tell me what they are?" At this point she wouldn't have been shocked to learn that Willoughby's job was feeding virgins to the monster under the stairs and starching neckcloths in a brew made of babies' teeth.

"Tell me, whatever—your—name is—"

"Miss Hannah Gray—Graystone," she lied hastily.

"What are your particular talents, Miss Graystone? I mean, besides running about the countryside looking like a drowned cat? I don't suppose your accomplishments include the ability to transcribe music?"

"M-music?" she echoed dully, gaping at him. Music seemed as incongruous to a man like his lordship as a fetching rose-pink bonnet would be tied beneath that intimidatingly masculine chin.

As for her knowledge of the stuff, it ended at singing the Celtic folk songs she'd once heard about her father's estate.

"That's right. *Music,*" he repeated. "Melodies, harmonies, often played upon instruments like the pianoforte—usually so badly it assaults your ears."

"I—I adore music." It was true. She adored it the way she adored the art of Michelangelo, with a good deal of awe and absolutely no aptitude. The statues might as well have sprung from Zeus's head, for all she understood the process of their creation.

"But why—I mean, if you're a composer, why not write it yourself?" What was she trying to do? Convince the man *not* to hire her? Blast her blunt tongue—she never could leave well enough alone.

"Why don't I write the music down myself?" he echoed, his mouth curving with bitter humor. He extended beautifully shaped hands, long-fingered and strong and dauntingly masculine, a signet ring glittering in the light spilling from the door. "I'd get ink stains on my fingers. There's nothing so appallingly vulgar."

"I—I can do that."

"Do what? Be appallingly vulgar?" In that instant, Hannah was leveled by the devastating power of his smile—one full of irony.

"I can write music." It was a blatant lie, but the possibility of pleading with this man, asking him for a safe haven out of the generosity of his heart would be as futile and humiliating as begging the moon for a cup of sunshine.

He stared at her, obviously stunned. "I'd have to be mad to take you into my house—a total stranger. I doubt you have recommendations from your former employers stashed beneath your shawl."

"What do you have to lose? If I fail to suit, you can fling me out in the morning. But there is a chance I might just answer your need."

He frowned. "There is something puzzling about you. You wander the countryside like the veriest beggar woman—yet the cut of your clothes is genteel enough."

"I'm so relieved that your lordship approves of my seamstress," Hannah couldn't help snapping.

"Even more intriguing, you speak with the culture of a lady in any drawing room I might name. To be sure, you're muddled up a bit with that Irish accent, but I'd wager you weren't spawned in some thatched hovel despite your appearance."

"Of all the insufferable—my birth may not be as exalted as yours, but it's respectable enough, I assure you. A name without stain—with some honor—" Hannah ground her teeth to stop the words.

"No, you're most certainly not a servant. I'd advise you to be careful where you get a job. I've known plenty of masters who beat your kind of impertinence out of servants with a cane. The question is, what are you doing, shaming this illustrious name, wandering about at night in the middle of nowhere begging for some menial job?"

She dared not give anyone a hint of where she'd come from, lest the hunter tracking her and Pip should somehow catch word of it. "That is my affair. Whether or not you choose to hire me is yours."

Desperation clawed at Hannah, pride choked her. She'd never begged in her life. But she was excruciatingly aware of the tiny boy even now cowering behind the cold stone pillar. "Please, my lord, I . . . I beg you." She forced the words from her throat. "I've traveled so far to find work. You're my last hope."

She half expected the ruthless viscount to brush her out of his way, to stalk into his house and slam the door. But he said nothing, only grinding his fingertips against his left temple.

"Do you have family, my lord?" she asked.

His gaze flashed to her, eyes piercing, broad shoulders suddenly rigid. "The villagers may claim I hatched from beneath a rock, but believe it or not, I do have family—far away from here." He grimaced, irritation marking his features. "What damnable impertinence! Father would say it's no more than I deserve, I suppose. After all, I've been brainless enough to stand out in the carriage sweep babbling to you."

He was going inside, she saw the intent in every harsh line of his face. She had to take a risk, see if this arrogant nobleman had a heart.

"I'm not begging a job for myself alone," Hannah began, but a rash of coughing erupted from behind the pillar.

"What in damnation is that infernal racket?" the viscount blazed.

"Pip."

One brow arched with caustic humor. "Pip? Don't tell me. It's some sort of new plague brought back from the West Indies."

"No. Pip is a little boy. Pip, come here," Hannah called. She prayed that if they could get inside, Pip would at least be fed, get a little warm. Surely, once in the house, she could manage to stall this man long enough to do the child some good.

Ever so warily, Pip stole out from behind his hiding place, edging toward her as if he were a mouse crossing the gaze of a ravenous hawk. But once he stepped into the light spilling from the door, he stood, stiff as a lead soldier, braced for the viscount's inspection. Hannah was certain the child wanted nothing more than to bury his face in her sodden skirts. His courage broke her heart.

"What the—God's wounds!" The viscount swore as a horrible cough racked Pip's delicate frame.

Eyes of lightning-storm blue flashed to hers. "Are you out of your senses, dragging a child about in this—you could've waited until the storm passed!"

He was glaring at her as if she were an idiot. No other attitude could have scraped more ruthlessly across Hannah's ragged nerves. She would have liked nothing better than to fling an epithet into his arrogant teeth and storm away, but she didn't dare for Pip's sake.

"It's too bad you weren't there to consult before we set out!" she said with a preciseness that bespoke her inner fury. "But we're here now."

"Where the devil did you get the child?"

"Your lordship doesn't know where children come from?" She was evading, desperately. Expected him to rage. Instead, a spark of hard amusement lit his eyes.

"I own to having some idea, ma'am. Is he yours?"

"Yes."

She saw his gaze flick down to her left hand, bare of a wedding ring. Let the man think whatever he wanted of her. She didn't care. If he concocted some explanation in his own mind—however sordid—he'd be less likely to be prying about searching for real answers.

"You came out chasing that poor man, raving that you had work to finish tonight. Take us in, and I'll go straight to the task, start right away and stay up all night if you'll just let Pip curl up by the fire." It was a risky gamble. She only hoped she could hide her own abysmal ineptitude until the boy was warm.

The viscount shot her a glare, his eyes dark with what must be impatience. "Absolutely not."

Hannah's heart fell like cold stone. She fought the urge to just crumple down onto the gravel carriage sweep and never get up.

"Wet as you are, you'd ruin the upholstery. Besides"—he pulled a sour face—"you smell like a wet dog. It can wait until morning when you're less likely to offend my sensibilities."

"Pardon us for being wet and cold," Hannah snapped, about to add that she and Pip would attempt to starve to death quietly on his lordship's front step. Then she stopped, the meaning of his words suddenly striking her with such force she all but dropped to her knees with relief. "M-morning? You mean . . ." She hardly dared give voice to it, she'd known so many crushing disappointments the past months.

"I might as well give the folk of Nodding Cross one more example of my insanity so some poor fool doesn't have to strain his brain thinking something up. Simmons!" the viscount bellowed. A strapping footman all but dove from the door, a healthy respect for his master's ill temper showing in his simple face.

"Aye, my lord. You wish me to sweep 'em off the property?" Simmons asked, casting a glance at the two disreputable forms the storm had blown in.

"I want you to put them in Willoughby's room."

"Willoughby's?" The servant couldn't have appeared

more stunned if the viscount had commanded him to set fire to his coattails.

"Yes, Simmons. The craven cur has gone the way of all the others. Miss Graystone will be taking his place."

"Will she, my lord?" the servant said, but Hannah could tell it translated to *Have you lost your mind?* "You want me to—to install the lady and young gentleman in the chamber across the hall from your own." It was a statement, but Simmons was obviously trying to make certain his master was aware of what he'd ordered.

"How the devil else am I going to wake her up in the middle of the night if genius burns?"

"Yes, my lord, but—perhaps your lordship would like me to lock them in?"

"Afraid they might murder us all in our sleep, eh, Simmons? Well, if she has a butcher's cleaver stashed in that bundle, I'd just as soon they kill me first. That way I won't have to listen to the maids wailing."

"Aye, sir."

"And Simmons," he cast out. "That meat pie Cook served tonight was definitely inferior to her usual standards. You might as well feed it to them."

Hannah's mouth was already watering, but it pinched her pride dreadfully to take 'his high and mighty lordship's' castoffs. She should be grateful, but he was making it difficult with his mockery, his arrogance, his negligent casting out of favors that meant so much to both her and Pip.

Yet what had she expected? That the viscount would usher them into his own library, draw off her half-boots and stockings and chafe her numb feet until they were warmed by his own exalted hands?

"Miss Graystone."

She jumped at the rough-satin of his voice, and guilt stung her cheeks, as if he could peer past her lowered lashes with those fire-blue eyes and read her very mind.

"I'll be in the music room at dawn. Be late at your own peril. You've heard tales of my temper. I'd advise you not to court it." With that, he turned on the heel of his glossy

Hessian and stalked into a chamber three doors down. After a moment, a ripple of notes drifted out, oddly discordant, igniting the restlessness, the uncertainty, the fears clamoring in Hannah's own breast.

Look for

Night Song

**Wherever Paperback Books
Are Sold
Coming Soon from Pocket Books**